I0818280

Also by Michael E. Petrie

You're The Only One I Can Trust

This Guy's the Limit

All original songs featured in this story,
as well as videos of the author's sailing adventures
can be found at

Michael E. Petrie's YouTube channel

SAME ROAD, DIFFERENT PATHS

A Novel

Michael E. Petrie

SAME ROAD, DIFFERENT PATHS

Copyright © 2025 Michael E. Petrie

All rights reserved.

No part of this publication in print or in electronic format may be reproduced, stored in a retrieval system, or transmitted in any form or by any means, electronic, mechanical, photocopying, recording, or otherwise without the prior written permission of the author.

This is a work of fiction. Names, characters, organizations, places, events and incidents are either the products of the author's imagination or are used fictitiously. Any resemblance to actual persons, living or dead, or actual events is purely coincidental.

Published by Dorus Mor Books

FIRST EDITION

ISBN: 978-1-647048-47-1

To my Dad. I love you.
I just wish we could have met sooner.

All photographs featured on the front and back covers of this book are either of, or taken by, the author.

Front Cover Photograph Legend (from left to right):

Top Left:	Drop City Commune
Top Right:	Championship Rodeo - Bull riding
Middle Left:	Whale Bones - Point Barrow, Alaska
Middle Center:	Sailing Past Diamond Head - Oahu, Hawaii
Middle Right:	Author & friend at Tongan Luau
Bottom Left:	Sailing across Pacific Ocean
Bottom Right:	Author with Smoky

Back Cover Photograph Legend (from left to right):

Diving from Boat anchored off Lahaina, Maui
Eiffel Tower-Paris
Finish Line Honolulu Marathon
Tongan Dream Home Raffle
Navigating with Sextant
Pago Pago, Samoa
Rodeo - Bareback Bronc Riding
Water Tower- Downers Grove, Illinois
Capitol Records Bldg-Hollywood, California
First Surfboard-Zuma Beach, California
Sign at Andrews, Texas

Life is like surfing. God sends us waves. It is up to each individual to decide which waves we are capable of riding and which ones we should let pass us by. Sometimes it's a nice easy ride, sometimes we find ourselves in over our head; some waves naturally move us to the left, some to the right; sometimes we wipe out, other times we get the most amazing experience of our life. But those who merely sit on the sand without paddling out at all miss it entirely.

Michael E. Petrie

I can live in the present and think about the past. It's really nice to look back and see the arc of your life and how it's all connected, how you got from there to here. You can see the line. It really has been an adventure.

T.S. Garp

You really don't understand your life until you tell the story.

Umberto Eco – author, The Name of the Rose

PREFACE

SAME ROAD, DIFFERENT PATHS is an autobiographical novel. At age fifteen I began keeping a journal. This story is based upon that journal. Most is true, some is how I wanted it to be, portions I tamed down a bit, and a tad is totally made up, but everything in this story did happen in some fashion. Many of the journal entries in this story are verbatim; however, characters have been altered, combined, changed, and should not be construed to resemble any single living person; and events have been modified, enhanced, and arranged for greater story cohesion. A very wise literary agent once told me that facts without proper arrangement and a few coats of varnished embellishment do not make for a good story. What follows, then, is fiction … but factual fiction.

PART ONE

1

POOR LITTLE FOOL

His parents sometimes danced in the living room. Records playing on the phonograph, small black vinyl discs, each with a large hole in the center, 45 RPMs, stacked in multiples on the spindle, each seemingly waiting their turn to drop down onto the turntable and fill the room with music. Early rock-n-roll: Buddy Holly, Richie Valens, Everly Brothers.

Right now it was a song by Thurston Harris that began with nothing more than a frolicking drumbeat and a lot of humming: Mmm-mmm-mmm. Then the singing started: *Little bitty pretty one … come sit on my knee … I'll tell you a story, happened long time ago, little bitty pretty one, I've been watching you grow.* A song one might interpret about a parent and a child, but no one was paying any attention to the lyrics. Not Mary or Joe Perry, who were jitterbugging, and certainly not their little son Michael, who was too young to decipher the words; he just liked the humming.

His dad spun his mom around and around. They were young and full of energy, dancing and laughing. His dad waving hands in the air, his mom's dress swirling as she twirled around. Both unaware of their son sitting at the top of the stairs in his Roy Rogers pajamas, an aerial view down into the room below with its lipstick-red colored walls.

The boy watched for a long while, he liked seeing his parents interact this way. It made him feel safe, secure, a living product of love. The next record slid down onto the turntable with a plastic plop. The Teddy Bears' slow, soulful, mournful singing: *To know, know, know him is to love, love,*

love him. Joe pulling his wife close, the two of them swaying in unison, a slow box-step. As the song ended, they were cheek-to-cheek, a tighter embrace, kissing.

Four-year-old Michael Perry stirred on the top step, making the slightest creaking noise in the momentary silence before the next 45 dropped. They heard the sound, their embrace interrupted.

"What are you doing up?" his mother demanded with mock sternness.

From his father, "Get back in bed! Now!" Nothing mock about that. Scampering back to his bed, his father's words bellowing after him, "And don't get up again!"

"I'll go up and lay with him awhile, Joe," Mary Perry spoke quietly to her husband. "Just till he falls asleep. Then I'll come back down."

Joe sat heavily onto the gold-colored sofa, facing the large picture window with a view out to the gravel road that ran past their house. He tapped a cigarette out from a pack laying on the end table, placed it between his lips and lit it. The mood was broken, even if his wife did come back down soon. Mary had never been the spitfire Joe had imagined when they'd first met. She was a sexy, raven-haired, hot-blooded Chicago Italian in her tight pencil skirt. Then there was one steamy lust-filled evening on their honeymoon and Bam! She got pregnant. He was barely a husband and already on his way to fatherhood. She would not allow any sexual advances during pregnancy, saying it just seemed unnatural. But her lack of desire only seemed to increase after the birth of their son. Sure, Mary liked to dance and laugh and socialize with friends, but their sex life was minimal at best. So, romantic moments like tonight being rare, it was with a real sense of loss that the mood was broken.

Another record spun on the Victrola, Ricky Nelson crooning about being somebody's poor little fool. Sometimes that's how Joe felt: a fool. A fool for enduring such infrequent amatory indulgence. A fool for being in love with a woman who deprived him of his husbandly rights. But admittedly, he felt it less and less as time marched on, replacing what he did not get at home with other successes.

When his son was first born, Joe was pumping gas down at Chappy's Shell Station to support his family. A damn gas pump jockey. He worried how they'd ever get by. But he had his own business now. Building houses. Indeed, he'd built with his own two hands the very house they now called home. He'd managed to save a few bucks before the kid was born, when Mary still worked, and purchased a small piece of land. Bought it on the cheap because it was in the middle of a field, landlocked and practically worthless with no access road. A well-seasoned local real estate lawyer named Godwin Gruber helped him get a legal easement to cut through the land owned by others that surrounded the parcel, and Joe created the road where his house is now located. Plowed through the dirt and weeds of an open prairie and brought in the gravel. It was the building of this first house that spawned the business of building homes for others.

The post-war American economy was booming, people were moving to the suburbs, buying houses, and starting families. A friendship was forged with Mr. Gruber. The elderly lawyer saw a hard-working determination in young Joe and an opportunity for himself. The lawyer began buying foreclosure properties at heavily discounted prices, much of it vacant land lost in bankruptcy by small-time farm families, and contracted with Joe to build houses on them. They became a team. The little village of Downers Grove, Illinois was growing by leaps and bounds. Joe speculated that one day the little country town in which he'd grown up just might converge with big-city Chicago, roughly thirty miles distant, in a non-ending stream of civilization. "Wouldn't that be something?" he actually whispered aloud, only slightly louder than the cows he heard lowing in the distance. Joe felt real pride at being a facilitator of such progress.

Of course, to say his wife was completely without any sort of passion would be incorrect. She displayed total passion for their son, Michael. Motherly passion. Too much, in Joe's opinion. Far too much. She doted on his every need, fussing over the child incessantly, calling him her little Baby Jesus. That would make us Jesus, Mary, and Joseph, he thought to himself, a caustic smile crossing his lips at such absurdity. The boy took most of Mary's attention. No time left for Joe, it seemed. Much like the Biblical Joseph who was so prominently featured in the story of Christ's birth, right up until the Christ-child was born. Then hardly a word about Joseph appears in the Bible afterward. Relegated into obscurity after he'd served his purpose. That's how it sometimes felt to this modern-day Joseph as well.

In all fairness, the child did have a few minor health issues that caused his mother to spend more time caring for her son than she otherwise might have. Since he was two years old Michael suffered from chronic ear and throat infections, causing him a great deal of pain. He would often cry all night long, interrupting Joe's sleep, even as Mary got out of bed to coddle her child. Joe felt sorry for the little guy, but the seemingly nonstop wailing was more than he could sometimes bear. It was a relief to leave all that behind as he'd head off to work each morning.

Joe took a deep draw from the cigarette, sighing the smoke outward before extinguishing the butt into an ashtray on the side table. Though he often felt unsatisfied at home, Joe felt important and satiated at work. His crew looked up to him and the smell of increasing monetary success was intoxicating. Also, was it his imagination or was Godwin Gruber's secretary coming on to him each time he visited Godwin's office? A few years older than Joe, she was a curvy brunette who wore dangling earrings and low-cut dresses. Joe found reasons to visit the office more and more frequently. She always greeted Joe with a smile that seemed more than just a smile. But one could never be sure, women were hard to read. So, one afternoon Joe answered her smile with a wink. She winked back.

2

SILENCE IS GOLDEN

Six-year-old Michael Perry sat on the floor of his room playing with his Fort Apache play set. Little rubber figures of soldiers, horses, and Indians engaged in battle, attacking and defending a plastic U.S. Cavalry fort of the same name. He could hear his parents arguing in the kitchen.

"You have to take Michael to work with you, there's no other choice," his mother was saying to his dad.

"I can't have some kid around all day. I won't get any work done," his father replied with raised voice.

"He's not *some* kid, he is *your* kid. Your son. And keep your voice down, he'll hear you," she admonished.

"I don't give a shit! This is my house. I built this house. I'll talk any goddamned way I want to!"

Godwin Gruber and Joe had gone their separate ways a few months ago. So, to help make ends meet during the subsequent lawyer-less business dry spell, Mary had been working as a secretarial temp at the insurance company downtown. Michael usually spent the day at his Nana's when she worked.

It had been a somewhat less than completely amicable split between the business partners that took place one evening when Mr. Gruber summoned Joe to his office after Joe had already worked a full day. They sometimes met in the evenings to talk about future lots coming up for sale and other business matters, though Joe preferred being there during normal working hours when Alma, Gruber's sexy secretary, was present. This time, when Joe arrived, Godwin seemed disgruntled.

"What's the matter?" Joe asked him.

The venerable lawyer sat at his large, laminated desk, elbows on the desktop, fingers of his hands tented, his head crowned with a sparse constellation of birthmarks visible through thinning gray hair, his mouth chomping on a well-abused stogie. The overhead fluorescent light illuminating the geography of his aging face, exaggerating the sagging eyelids, cords of throat wattle, all of which became abruptly animated as he angrily bellowed, "I'll tell you what's the matter, Joe!" Then, exhibiting great effort, stopping himself, pausing, as if collecting his thoughts, rethinking what words he intended. "Look, I like you, Joe," Gruber continued more calmly with avuncular intonation, stolidly focused now, "but, the way I see it, you are heading toward a heap of trouble."

"What trouble? I'm not heading toward any tr..." Joe began to object, but Gruber spoke right over his objection.

"Listen, I've been around since Christ was a corporal. I know how the world works. To be blunt, the real problem here is I truly believe that you, my friend, are headed toward divorce court."

Joe was stunned. What the hell was Godwin talking about?

"Look, I know you've been doing the pickle-tickle with my secretary. I let that slide. Men do that. Alma's a big girl, she can take care of herself. I figured you were shrewd enough to keep that one under the radar. No harm, no foul." With his right hand he removed the cigar from his puckered lips and leaned forward across the desk, getting closer to Joe. "But now I'm hearing rumblings that she's not the only skirted orifice you've been dipping your wick into. You have a beautiful wife at home, so why you are out tomcatting around is beyond me. But that wife of yours is not stupid. If she doesn't already smell a rat, she will eventually. This is a small town, hard to keep secrets. That's what worries me. I cannot risk some pushy divorce lawyer tying up my closings with claims that your wife is suddenly entitled to a marital share of our business … *my* business. I've got too much at stake and just don't need the aggravation."

Extinguishing the cigar into an ashtray on the desktop, Gruber then leaned back in his leather chair, creating more distance, locking his fingers behind his head. Joe noticed the man's armpits were damp, the fabric of his white shirt darkened with perspiration. They sat across from each other for several silent moments. Finally, the lawyer's phlegmatic closing statement. "Sorry Joe, but all good things must eventually come to an end. I don't think we can continue working together any longer."

And that was that. The lawyer/builder quasi-partnership that had launched Joe's construction business was ended, kaput. This was shattering to Joe, who felt as if he and Godwin had become far more than business partners; he considered Godwin a close friend. Almost a father figure, maybe even a wise grandfatherly one.

Driving past Frenchy's Tavern on his way home that evening, Joe found himself needing a drink. Sitting at the bar, staring into his emptied glass, he wondered what the hell he was going to do now to support a family. Afterward, Mary offered to get a job to help out, but it was an option he disliked immensely.

"My mother cannot take him today," Michael heard his mom say.

"Well, figure something out. He's not coming with me."

"He's your son. You two never spend time together. He idolizes you. Yet, you never do anything with him. Take him to work with you. He'll enjoy being with his dad for a whole day."

She was correct. Michael was excited to be going off to work with his dad that day. He even tried to dress in clothes matching his dad's: Khaki slacks and white shirt, open at the collar, with the sleeves rolled up two turns over the forearms. As far as the boy was concerned, the tattoo prominently displayed on his father's forearm was the only thing setting them apart.

First stop was at the adjacent town of Westmont where his dad sauntered into Leo's Donut Shop, Michael similarly sauntering right behind.

They took a seat in a booth toward the back, Joe's usual spot to meet with cronies and discuss business matters. Two of his crew were already seated. A waitress immediately appeared and poured coffee.

"Who ya got with ya there?" the woman cheerfully inquired. "Looks like Big Joe and Little Joe."

"Yeah, I'm stuck with the kid today," the father replied with an audible sigh. The waitress disappeared and Joe slapped some dollar bills down on the table, "Mike, go on up to the counter and buy us some donuts."

"What kind?" Michael asked.

"Any kind you want," replied his father. "Take your time. Do a good job picking them out."

"Okay," the boy nodded, happily trotting off.

"It's good you takin' the boy out to work with ya. Never too early for the young'uns to start earning their keep," one of the men seated at the table remarked.

"Kids today," said a second man, shaking his head, "most of 'em a bunch of spoiled, lazy brats sitting around watching TV all day."

"Your boy looks like a good enough kid," the first one added, watching the boy eagerly fetching the donuts. "A real chip off the old block, huh Joe?"

"Chip? Sure, I suppose," Joe answered dubiously. "Though, sometimes I'd swear he must be the damn milkman's kid." Everyone at the table laughed.

One of the men rolled a set of blueprints out flat across the table and they began discussing details of the construction project it depicted. Moments later, Michael returned with a tray of donuts, some with sprinkles, some without. He sat down next to his dad and proceeded to eat the pink one with chocolate sprinkles. Some crumbs landed on the plans. Joe brushed them away onto the floor. "Go get us some coffee refills, will ya?" Joe told his son, sounding slightly agitated. "But be careful, coffee is hot."

Michael grabbed three empty cups off the table and, once again, trotted over to the counter where he asked the waitress to please refill them. She did, offering to carry the cups back to the men. "No, I'll do it," Michael told her, proud to manage balancing three cups filled with piping hot coffee.

Walking slowly and carefully, coffee sloshing within the cups in his little hands, he managed to reach the table without spilling a drop. While attempting to place the cups onto the table, however, one of them tipped, spilling hot coffee all over the blueprints.

"Jesus Christ!" his father hollered, startled by the spill and trying to keep the hot liquid from rolling off the table onto his lap. "Damn it! Look what you did. I told you to be careful."

Michael's lip began to involuntarily quiver.

"Oh Christ, now you're gonna cry? Go on outside, get in the truck and do your crying. Wait there for me."

"When will you come out?" Michael asked, his voice warbling, feeling humiliated by his father scolding him in front of everyone.

"I'll be out when I'm done here. Now go, or I'll give ya something to really cry about!"

They drove out to the construction site where Joe was framing a house. "You wanted to come to work with me? Okay, I'm gonna put you to work." At birth, his son had been the biggest newborn in the entire hospital. More than nine pounds. He and Mary had originally agreed to name their baby Arthur, in homage to her Italian father Arturo who died when Mary was a teenager. But one look at his new son and Joe declared: "Too big to be named Arthur. He looks like a Mike to me. *Big Mike* his friends will call him. Probably grow up to be a star football player." Joe had never been a fan of football, had never played the game himself, and only watched a game or two during his limited time in high school; this was merely the bromidic visual he mentally conjured.

But, at this stage in his development, Michael was a pale, scrawny kid. A skinny stick figure of a boy, anemic looking, almost like one of those starving children from impoverished third-world countries one sees on the news. So, Joe wasn't sure just how much work the boy might be up to handling. "I want you to grab that metal trash can over there and walk all around the outside perimeter of this job picking up any trash you see. I want it all cleaned up out there. Got it?"

"Got it, Dad," Michael replied with more enthusiasm than was due.

"Do a good job for me and maybe I'll let ya come with me again sometime. But be careful, there's nails and sharp objects everywhere," Joe warned.

Michael spent the next hour dragging the increasingly heavy metal trash can around the property, picking up every piece of scrap and trash he could find. He wanted his dad to be proud.

"I'm done, Dad," he finally announced, re-entering the framed structure and pointing to the filled trash can a few feet away

"You sure?" the father asked, looking down at the boy from atop an eight-foot ladder.

Michael nodded.

"I better not find one shred of trash out there," Joe warned, stepping down from the ladder, a flat carpenter's pencil slid between the top of his ear and his temple, worn like some piece of fashionable blue-collar attire.

"You won't," Michael affirmed with confidence.

"Okay, good enough," handing his son a push broom, "now sweep up the inside and pick up any scraps as you go."

As he swept, Michael carried on a one-way conversation with his dad. It wasn't often he had his dad all to himself to talk with, so he was making the most of it. Joe could hear the kid rambling on and on but paid little attention to whatever the hell he was talking about. His shrill child voice grated on Joe, causing the father to wonder when the hell the kid's voice would ever change? At what age would he stop sounding like one of Alvin and the Chipmunks?

The boy's prattling continued, nonsensical gibberish that Joe couldn't care less about. Like Disneyland. The kid really wanted to go to Disneyland, going on and on about how great Disneyland was, describing all the rides and attractions to be found there. Christ, Disneyland was two thousand miles away in California. Joe had been there once, years ago, long before there was a Disneyland. A beautiful enough place, but to trek all that way just to see Mickey Mouse made no sense.

And ponies. The high-pitched little-boy voice droned on and on about wanting a pony. Downers Grove was still a rural town, several of his friends lived on farms and had ponies. If he had a pony, he excitedly proclaimed, he could become a cowboy; seamlessly shifting into how great being a cowboy would be, going on and on with such childish zest for life that it simply wore Joe out. What planet was this kid living on? Cowboys? Did cowboys even still exist in this day and age? Certainly not in Chicago? Too much television had warped the kid's brain.

Atop the ladder again, Joe looked down toward his son. Michael was leaning on the motionless broom handle, still jabbering away. I swear, kids shouldn't grow tongues till they are of an age where they have something intelligent to say, he thought to himself. "Hey, how about a little less yacking and a lot more pushing that broom?"

3

ASSASSINATION

Mary stood staring out the kitchen window into the backyard where her young son was playing catch with a friend. She watched the baseball being tossed back and forth like a ping pong game. It was mesmerizing. But tears were in her eyes. Her mind was trying to comprehend the horrific news she had seen earlier on the television. A tragedy only eclipsed by the unexpected death of her own father when she was just a young girl. She had been her daddy's little princess and losing him was the greatest hurt of her lifetime. This cut almost as deep. President Kennedy had been shot and killed in Dallas, Texas. By a lone gunman, it was reported. Why would anyone want to kill such a wonderful, handsome, charismatic leader? A good Catholic man, the nation's first Catholic president.

She looked over at three-year old Jaimie sitting in a toddler chair watching cartoons on the same TV that had delivered the awful announcement just hours ago, clapping her hands and laughing with joy. Their family had grown. God had blessed Mary with two beautiful children, first a son and now a daughter. But she found herself wondering in what sort of a world was she raising her children? It seemed to be a world of increasingly senseless violence.

Days later, Joe was driving his pickup truck along Lemont Road, past the duck pond, with his son riding on the passenger side. The boy sat listlessly, looking out the window at dozens of ducks floating upon the water, when a voice on the radio talking about the recent deaths of both the president and his assassin prompted him to ask, "Dad, why did the president have to die?"

Joe had his mind on other things, work projects, materials to order, scheduling crews. The question jarred him, interrupting such ruminations. "What?" he asked, somewhat impatiently.

"Why did someone kill the president?" Michael repeated.

"I dunno. A lot of sick people in the world. But people die when it's their time, I suppose."

"So, it was President Kennedy's time to die?"

"I suppose so," Joe answered, absently.

"Dad?" Michael asked.

"Yes, yes, what?" Joe hastily responded, annoyed by the questions preventing him from more important thoughts.

"What do you think happens to a person when he dies?"

Joe took his eyes off the road for a moment and gave his son a look.

"I mean," Michael continued, "the nuns at school taught us that death brings us closer to God. That if we lead a good life and avoid sin, we will get to meet God in the afterlife. In heaven. Seems to me that dying should make people happy, but everybody's sad."

"Yeah, I know. The nuns taught me the same stuff when I was your age."

"So, is that what *you* believe?"

"You really wanna know?"

"Sure."

"Okay. I guess you're old enough for a more grown-up explanation. I think that when you die they put you in the ground and worms eat you. The end."

"No heaven or hell?"

"Probably not. I think that's a fantasy for weak people to believe because they need a promise of reward or threat of punishment to keep them in line."

"So, you don't think the man who shot the president will go to hell?"

"I think they will put him in the ground and when the worms get done with the president they will start on the shooter."

"Seriously?"

Joe sighed. "Mike, nobody knows the answers to what happens after you die. Anyone who claims to know the answer is lying. You asked me what I think. I don't know any more than anybody else. Hell, the nuns could be absolutely right for all I know."

They drove on in silence, Michael pondering the words of his father and Joe calculating in his head how many cubic yards of concrete to order for the foundation of a new project.

4

NO COMPLAINTS

Joe got out of the car to pump gas into his wife's brand-new Chevy Impala while she waited in the passenger seat. The kids were in the back. A station attendant had approached but Joe waved him away, preferring to fill the tank on the shiny new vehicle himself. Mary had really wanted a Cadillac, but Joe thought such cars were too flashy.

"Come on, Joe, we can easily afford one," she pleaded. "You've got one of the most successful businesses in town now. Your wife should be driving a Caddy."

"Listen," he admonished, "I don't need my wife showing off, driving around in some fancy car. And I don't wanna drive one, either. Customers see me driving around in a goddam Cadillac, they'll think I'm gouging them. My workers might get a bug up their ass, too. A nice new Chevy every couple of years says to the world I'm successful. A Cadillac says I'm an asshole."

As the gas was pumping, Joe strolled around the station, whistling, looking into the service bay, nodding at the mechanic. Joe was thinking how fortunate he was to have escaped the life of a gas jockey. He'd come a long way, indeed. A major home builder now. A whole new chapter in his life. His first foray into business years ago with Godwin Gruber had taught him a lot. Since then, he and a couple other builders had joined together to develop their own subdivision. What had not long ago been an empty dried up soybean field way out south of town was now a modern neighborhood of new homes they named Green Knolls Estates. Joe had discovered the secret to success was not building one or two houses at a time, it was building a dozen or more at a time. A big gamble, but one from which he'd profited nicely. He was approaching the threshold of becoming what many might consider wealthy.

And just in time, too. They had a second kid now, born almost nine years after the first one, a daughter named Jaimie. Another mouth to feed. To be brutally honest, Joe had never wanted to have a kid in the first place, much less this second one. Two kids, Joe mockingly thought to himself – living proof that he had been able to enjoy engaging in sex at least twice with his less than libidinous wife.

Though he shunned fancy cars, there was little else he denied his wife and children. They lived in one of the biggest, most modern houses in all of Downers Grove, a house built by Joe's company as a showpiece. His son attended an expensive Catholic school, St. Mary's of Gosten. Little Jaimie was still too young for school but would likely follow her older brother's pricey academic path. His wife had all the clothes, shoes, purses any woman could want, and a maid came in once a week to clean the house. It was his *duty* to provide for his family. There was very little he asked for in return. Mostly just some peace and quiet when he got home from work and a good dinner on the table.

It was 6:30 Friday evening when Joe walked in the house after a particularly grueling day dealing with subcontractors and the city planning department. As soon as he cleared the door, his nostrils were assaulted by a terrible stench. Mary was cooking fish for dinner. Those damn Catholics and their no meat on Friday rule. Joe had been raised Catholic himself, but long ago cast off all predilections of the faith. And he hated fish. Hated the way fish tasted and hated the way they smelled. Walking directly into the kitchen, he pushed his wife roughly aside, angrily grabbing the pan containing the offending fish from the stove and heaved it out the kitchen door into the backyard.

"I told you, don't ever make fish for dinner!" he shouted, opening the windows and switching on a floor fan, trying to get rid of the smell. "You know I can't stand that shit!"

"What am I supposed to cook on Fridays, Joe?" Mary responded, frustrated.

"I've had a hard day and I don't appreciate walking into a house that stinks. You can make any damn thing you want, just so it's not that damn smelly fish."

"Macaroni and cheese?" Mary suggested. "Again?"

"Whatever you want … but make me a steak. A goddam steak! The kind of day I've had, a man deserves to eat meat."

He got like this sometimes. His temper would erupt without notice. He wasn't a violent man, Mary had long ago decided, he just needed to yell sometimes. Blow off steam. It wasn't a big deal really, though she hated the kids witnessing it. He was a good husband otherwise. A good provider. She had no complaints. So, Mary cooked him a steak, while she and the children ate mac and cheese.

5

I LEARNED IT FROM MY HORSE

It was summer, no school, plenty of time on his hands, and fifteen-year-old Michael Perry found himself rather bored. His dad, who had little tolerance for wasting time, told him to take that boredom and turn it into something productive, but what?

Ever since he was a little kid, he enjoyed writing. Michael had a toy typewriter back then and used to type out stories on it, pretending to be some great novelist or a reporter for some large metropolitan newspaper like *The Daily Planet*. So, to resolve his boredom it only made sense to do what he'd always enjoyed. I should write a story, he decided.

With that decision made, he sat down and thought about what to write. It should be something about which I have some expertise, he further decided. Except, I'm only a teenager and don't really have any expertise. Finally, he settled on simply writing about the real-life experiences of a fifteen-year-old boy. Things that actually happened. Things that *are* happening. A journal, a transcription of contemporaneous musings that may become an ongoing chronicle of his life and times. But how to start the first chapter?

Staring at the blank page before him, Michael finally put pen to paper: *Everything I know about girls I learned from my horse.* He chuckled at this opening line, began to cross it out, decided to leave it alone, and continued on.

JOURNAL

A guy gets interested in a girl for any number of reasons, I suppose. With Penny Jardine, it was because we shared a love for horses. You see, for my 13th birthday my parents bought me a horse, the very best gift of my entire life. I'd wanted one as far back as I can remember and, after years of begging and pleading, now I finally had a horse of my very own: a chocolate brown gelding standing fifteen hands, part Morgan/part Welsh pony. I've always enjoyed reading stories about the West and cowboys, so I named him Smoky, from the Will James novel *Smoky the Cow Horse*.

I really loved Smoky, and Smoky, I'm convinced, loved me. We spent every day together. I loved riding Smoky, feeding him, grooming him, cleaning his stall. Anything and everything involving Smoky was fun. I sometimes even slept in the barn just to be close to him. We were absolute best friends.

Anyway, Penny Jardine was just a year older than me, lived only a couple miles away, and owned a beautiful tan and white pinto horse named Sundance. She and I would gallop on our horses through the open fields, wind screaming in our faces – it felt like we must be riding a hundred miles an hour! Riding was exciting and Penny was fun to be with.

There was one day, though, I especially remember. It was a year or so ago. Sundance had thrown a shoe and couldn't be ridden, so Penny and I were riding double on Smoky. No saddle, just bareback. That's when I discovered (perhaps we both discovered) male and female bodies *scooped* together in the sway of a horse's back and bouncing in unison to its gait can be a very arousing experience!

Then it started to rain – I mean it abruptly began dumping buckets from the sky – so we galloped back to Penny's house in the downpour. That's where things began to take a turn, going from just riding buddies to something more.

Arriving at Penny's place, we put Smoky inside the barn, a stall right next to Sundance, and sat around in the hay loft talking and drying off. Penny found a pack of Winstons she'd hidden in the loft and we began smoking cigarettes like fiends. Though, in hindsight, a foolish thing to do with all that dry hay around.

Anyway, there we were in the hay loft, lying on our backs, staring up at the spiderwebs in the rafters, passing the cigarette back and forth when, after a while, things started getting pretty, shall I say, *intimate*. Penny snuggled up real close and began whispering things in my ear. Sexy things. I never really thought of Penny in a *girlfriend* sort of way, so had no clue how to handle this turn of events. I wasn't sure just how involved I wanted to get with her, but her wet clothes were now somewhat transparent and clinging to her body in a way that seemed to encourage at least some sort of involvement.

I had my arm around her and all that rot and started thinking about maybe kissing her. Okay, let me admit, right here and now, that I'd never kissed a girl before. After a few minutes of silent inaction on my part, Penny whispered, "Chicken?" Seriously? Me? Okay, I admit, maybe I was feeling a little bit chicken. I had never been in a situation like this before and was beginning to get nervous as hell. Then she did something that shocked the hell out of me. She leaned over and sort of let her breast fall into my hand. Or did I reach up for it? I'm not sure. I'd never actually felt that part of the female anatomy before, although I'd often thought about it.

By this time I was feeling pretty darned sexy, so I kissed her real hard on the lips. She responded by rolling over onto her back and pulling me on top of her. We were rolling around in the hay (literally) and making out like crazy. Now don't get me wrong, I think about sex as much as the next guy, but I never did anything like this before. I mean, by this point some of her clothes were off and strewn atop the bales of hay. I guess I sort of knew what was going on and where this was all heading, but suddenly all those years of Catholic school teachings began to compete with what I was now feeling. It became a mental tug-of-war between guilt and lust. But even as my brain was sorting through this conflict, my hands continued groping and my lips continued kissing! I kind of wanted to stop but couldn't.

Then, all of a sudden, a loud blast of thunder rocked the entire barn, causing a pile of loose hay to come crashing down on us. Perhaps it was Divine Intervention taking over my lack of voluntary control, I cannot say. It scared Penny and she screamed! Startled, I shot to my feet. I looked down to see Penny half-naked curled up in a fetal position, green hay in her brown hair. The golden opportunity to lose my virginity (Is it even called that for a guy?) had passed. With a real sense of self-consciousness, I tucked my shirt back into my jeans and Penny pulled her clothes back on – making me look away while she did.

We both felt pretty ill at ease with each other after that day. It became difficult to remain just pals after what had happened between us, but we were not really boyfriend/girlfriend either. Eventually we just sort of stopped hanging out together. Sometimes I find myself missing her friendship, just riding horses together and stuff. We used to have fun times together. What I learned from that day riding double in the rain on Smoky is that friendships with girls can change inexplicably and suddenly.

I've since learned other lessons from my horse, as well. Perhaps most importantly: What the parents giveth, the parents can taketh away. Spending so much time with Smoky, I found myself neglecting my academic responsibilities and was on the verge of failing several classes. I tried to pay attention in class, but it was hard to focus, my mind would wander. I just wanted to be outside riding my horse. It got so bad that the school guidance counselor suggested I abandon any aspirations toward college, just take shop classes and concentrate on simply trying not to flunk out entirely. My parents, to put it mildly, were not at all happy. My father warned that if I did not bring my grades up, Smoky would have to go.

I studied harder, but to little avail. My grade point average improved only slightly. Never in my wildest dreams did I think my dad would *really* sell my beloved Smoky right out from under me. But he did. Mom pleaded with him on my behalf to give me one more chance, suggesting they just *ground* me from my horse for a while instead of getting rid of him. But Dad was like an immovable object.

On the day Smoky's new owner was scheduled to pick him up and take him away, I decided to run away from home – or more accurately, to *ride* away from home. I took Smoky out of his stall, tacked him up, threw on a saddle, mounted up, and took off for the high country. Okay, so there is no "high country" in Illinois. It's just an expression I heard in some old cowboy movie. I figured we would ride off, disappearing into the wilderness, eventually making our way out to Colorado or some such place out West, like in the Will James stories. I could ride my old pal Smoky as we worked cattle on some enormous ranch.

The futility of this idea did not take long to sink in, and soon I returned home to relinquish Smoky to his new owner, whom I had kept waiting for several hours. It was a sad, sad event, watching my horse being loaded into a trailer and driven away. I was crying. Mom was crying. Dad helped load Smoky into the trailer.

But that is not the end of the story by a long shot. Sometime later, I learned that Smoky had died. I gasped at the news and burst out sobbing when I learned the cause of his demise. He had escaped from his corral and was hit by a large truck as he trotted down the highway ... in the direction of *our* house. Upon hearing this gut-wrenching news, I felt certain that, like those other noble beasts Rin-Tin-Tin and Lassie, Smoky was trying to return to me, the boy who loved him. Grief and guilt consumed me. It was all my fault. If I would have just studied harder Smoky would still be alive. The looks my father cast my way confirmed this. I cried my eyes out. My mother cried her eyes out. My father just shook his head. If there is a horse heaven, I can only imagine that Smoky is prancing around that celestial pasture waiting for his boy to join him one far off day.

Now if that is not the saddest story you've ever heard, you have no heart. But it's all true. I swear. To this day, I still really miss old Smoky.

6

THE DEAL

Thursday, the day of the traditional November Thanksgiving feast. The Perry family assembled pre-prandial around the formal dining room table that got used perhaps twice a year, but was Mary's most cherished furniture, adorned with settings of her good china and silverware. Joe took his place at the head of the table, Mary at the opposite end, Michael along the side, Nana seated next to him, with Jaimie seated on the opposite side. The turkey had been carved and presented on an ornate platter in the center of the table, alongside green beans, mashed potatoes, cranberry gelatin still in the exact shape of the can from which it emerged, ambrosia, sweet potatoes, and a gravy boat. They began passing the food around the table.

"Would someone like to say grace?" Nana asked, when everyone had food on their plates. The family did not customarily say grace before meals, except at Thanksgiving and Christmas and always at Nana's request.

"I'll do it!" Jaimie volunteered.

"Thank you, Jaimie," Nana said.

"Bless this food and us who eat it," she recited, giggling. Everyone at the table chuckled, which encouraged the children to go back and forth saying more silly things and laughing ever more loudly.

"All right. That's enough," Joe admonished to settle the kids down.

"Let's all go around the table and say what it is we are most thankful for," Mary suggested. "I'll go first. I am very thankful for my wonderful family sitting down together to celebrate this lovely Thanksgiving holiday."

"I'm thankful we have an extra two days off from school," Jaimie said.

"Me too," Michael concurred, "but Jaimie, you're just in elementary school. Wait till you're in high school. Then you'll *really* be thankful for extra days off from school."

"Well," Nana said, "any day I am still above ground is a good day. So, I am thankful for that." Nana was Mary's mother and the only living grandparent the children had from their maternal side.

"Me too," little Jaimie agreed. "I'm thankful to be sitting here at Thanksgiving with my Nana."

It was Joe's turn. He looked around the table, his eyes landing on his son. He wasn't a bad kid, as teenagers go, but since reaching adolescence it seemed to Joe that the boy had grown increasingly cocky and disrespectful. His mother tolerated it better than Joe. For Joe, it was a constant battle of wits between father and son. An unmistakable endeavor of balance in which no child should be allowed to prevail.

The boy's hair hung long over his ears and forehead, sweeping down to cover half of his face, a follicular veil throwing the boy's face out of symmetry and completely covering his right eye. How the kid could see anything from under that hair, Joe wasn't sure. "I'm thankful Michael is going to get a haircut tomorrow on his day off from school," Joe contributed.

"Sure," Michael muttered acerbically, barely audible for his father to hear, "when pigs fly."

"What was that?" the father demanded.

"Nothing," came the son's stroppy answer.

"You will get a haircut tomorrow. Is that clear?" He was tired of his son's attitude and disgusted with him looking like a bum.

"Precisely how many hairs do you want me to cut?" A truculent riposte.

In an abrupt magmatic eruption, his father's fist pounded the table, making all the dishes and glasses rattle. Grabbing one of Mary's fine china plates from the table that Michael had piled with food, and tossing it onto the floor, he shouted, "If you're gonna look like a damn animal you can eat your dinner on the floor like an animal!"

Michael was horrified, as was everyone else seated at the table.

"Only two kinds of men look like that," Joe angrily continued shouting, "communists and queers!"

Michael smirked at his father's lack of cultural literacy, taunting him. "So, which one would you prefer I be?"

His father gave him a menacing look. It was all he could do to keep from wiping that smirk off his son's face with a fist.

"Happy Thanksgiving everyone!" the boy snapped with hostility. He stood up and left the room as Jaimie began to cry.

Michael retreated downstairs to the basement to sulk. The basement was a nicely finished area with linoleum flooring, pool table, television, Hi-Fidelity record player, and was one of Michael's favorite places to go. An isolated oasis offering some degree of privacy from peering parental eyes. He liked to just sit down here alone sometimes in the semi-darkness, listening to music and pondering life in typical teenage wondering; at times, wandering toward something bleakly spiritual, a morbid meditation of gloom and festering angst. It was the only room in the house where he could crank up the volume with some degree of impunity, listening to Beatles, Yardbirds, Cryan' Shames, Shadows of Knight, and Rolling Stones records. According to his dad, however, none of those bands will still be around in five years and nobody will even remember the Rolling Stones or Beatles. "None of them can hold a candle to Dino Martin or Frank Sinatra," his father would proclaim. "This generation of long-haired freaks play in *groups* because they don't have the talent to make it as solo performers."

Before too long, Nana came down to join Michael. She always seemed so much cooler than his parents and had long been his most trusted confidant.

"What was all that about?" she asked innocently.

"I have no idea what set him off, all I was doing was sitting at the dinner table minding my own business."

"Really?" She wasn't buying that explanation.

"Okay. My dad has been on me to get a haircut ever since forever," he conceded. "A couple months ago I joined a band. We call ourselves The Droffs. I'm the drummer."

"I see," said his grandmother, not really understanding the correlation between playing in a band and haircuts.

"Nana, to play in a rock band nowadays a guy's gotta have long hair. It's especially important for a *drummer* to shake a hairy head while keeping the beat. People just expect it. But growing my hair long has created major problems with my dad. This is the reason for the fight we just had upstairs. He says it makes him sick for his son to 'look like a girl.' He is so behind the times. Things are different these days. Lots of boys wear their hair long now, and I'm sure no one will mistake me for a girl."

"No, I am certain no one will do that," she agreed.

"Hey, I may regret saying this someday, but I think adults are amazingly stupid! Oh, not you, Nana. Most adults, though. Maybe stupid isn't even the correct word. More like closed-minded. My father especially. Maybe this is what is called the generation gap? I don't know. I just hope I don't become like him when I'm an adult."

"Well, I guess we will just have to wait and see, won't we?" she replied in a soothing voice. "So, when your band plays, do you get paid money?"

"Of course," he answered without hesitation, but rethinking the honesty of that answer, clarified. "Well, maybe not so far. Mostly we've played for free at a few places just to get known. But, for sure, our next gig will be for money. I just know it."

"Let me talk to your father, see what I can do," she offered. "If nothing else, your father is, first and foremost, a businessman. A true capitalist who appreciates making deals. If, as you say, having long hair earns you money, he just might give you a chance to prove it."

A deal was, indeed, made. Michael's share of the proceeds from The Droffs' first paying job was ten dollars. When Joe looked in the mirror to shave one morning, the check for $10 was Scotch-taped to his mirror at eye level. At first, he was miffed by the audacity of the kid for so smugly taping it where Joe could not possibly avoid seeing it. Then, shrugging his shoulders as he deftly removed the check from his view, muttered, "If this crazy world wants to reward my son for looking like a bum, so be it."

7

JOURNAL

Our bass player's dad owns a plumbing store in Westmont and our band usually rehearses at his shop in the early evenings after business hours. Today, being a pleasant Saturday afternoon, we rehearsed at my house. I had to coax my dad to let us set up in the garage. Somewhat reluctantly, he agreed.

With the overhead two-car garage door wide open, there was plenty of room for all of us with our amps, drums, mics, and two huge speakers mounted on poles raised six feet above the floor.

Once we began playing songs, there quickly appeared a small group of kids from around the neighborhood in our driveway listening to us play. We had not planned on an audience, but it was kind of nice. The audience grew and soon there were twenty or more kids assembled, listening, dancing, and just generally hanging out. Everyone having fun.

That is, until a neighbor came by and told us to stop playing because the *noise* was too loud. We did not stop right away, so he entered the garage and rudely unplugged the speakers. All the kids in the driveway gave a collective moan. From out of nowhere, Dad appeared. He and the neighbor exchanged words, and Dad told him to leave. Then Dad – who usually hates our loud music – said, "Turn the volume up as loud as it goes. I want to be able to hear it ten blocks away!"

We spent the rest of the afternoon playing our music at full volume, dozens of kids clapping and dancing in the driveway. Soon several adults from the neighborhood arrived: Not to complain, but to join in the revelry. Mom came out with snacks, and it was like a huge neighborhood party. Most fun band practice EVER! And Dad was the hero of the day.

8

THE DUET

The first time he saw her, she was standing in the hallway looking at a poster hanging on the wall near the high school auditorium. Mousy brown hair, held back atop her head with a pink scarf, curving down to flip just above her shoulders. Wearing a pleated skirt, flowery blouse, and white canvas PFs with lacy ankle socks. Cute, but rather ordinary looking. Not necessarily the kind of girl hormonally rabid teenaged boys usually notice, but there was something compelling about her nonetheless.

Stepping up to get a closer view, of her not the poster, Michael offered a cheery, "Hey!"

With total nonchalance, not even looking at him, came her indifferent response, "Hello."

He gave an audible cough, hoping for her to look his way, but she continued focusing her attention at the poster on the wall.

"What's this?" he asked, referring to the poster.

"Can't you read?" she replied with a trace of sarcasm.

"It says auditions," he read aloud. "Auditions for what?"

"For the operetta, silly," she answered, still curtly.

"What's an operetta?"

She turned to look at him for the first time, and that's when he saw it. The smile. She smiled and it was like bringing the sun indoors, turning everything brilliant.

"It's a musical," she informed, politely.

He stood there dumbly, unable to respond with words, still absorbing her smile.

She tried again. "A play? On stage? A play on stage where the actors sing and dance?"

"Oh," he finally managed. Then, trying to regain some element of composure, "Are you going to be in it?"

"If I get a part, I will. I am definitely auditioning."

"You are? Uh, yeah, me too," he stammered. "I'm going to audition, too."

"Well, I will see you there then." She smiled again and walked off. He stood alone, watching the swaying pleats of her skirt oscillate and the flip of her hair bounce girlishly as she moved down the hall. Michael did not even know her name, but all at once she'd become the central object of his devoted awe.

Her name was Kimberly. Michael watched her audition, competing against a dozen or more other hopefuls for a part. In Michael's opinion, Kimberly was clearly the best. When she sang it was with the voice of an angel. No, he thought, more like a choir of angels all coming from one set of pipes. Surely, she would land the female lead. And she did.

The show was called *The Blue, Blue Sea*. The story of star-crossed lovers: a young sailor named Johnny Dee and his one true love, Dorie Davis. But alas, Johnny and Dorie's love affair was never to be. Poor Johnny becomes lost at sea and, thinking Johnny had perished, Dorie marries another man. In the end, Johnny *does* return, only to discover Dorie is now a married woman with children. Kind of sappy, Michael thought to himself, but Miss Barnes, the director, insisted it was a very sad and moving story.

Michael had never before auditioned for any school plays, had neither sung nor listened to operetta music, nor acted on stage. So, he found it nothing short of miraculous that he was cast as Johnny Dee, opposite Kimberly's Dorie Davis. He could not believe his fantastic good fortune.

On stage, the Johnny and Dorie characters pine away for each other, lost in a love that will never be. Off stage, Michael clearly had fallen head over heels for his leading lady. Rehearsing a scene, he would often be required to put his arms around Kim. Oh, this was heaven! Taking her in his arms and singing the title song to her: *Oh yes my heart is yours, my love, as you suppose it be. And cry no fear you'll have me near beyond the Blue, Blue Sea.* The director thought Michael was doing an excellent job playing the part, but in truth there was no acting involved at all. He sang to Kimberly and meant each word. His heart was, indeed, hers. Often Miss Barnes would shout, "CUT!" and Michael would still be embracing Kim, not wanting to let her go. He loved every minute of every rehearsal with her.

Though Michael had fallen for Kimberly, he couldn't be certain if the feeling was mutual. So, he asked her out on a date. They took the train to Chicago to see the movie *The Bible*. Kimberly chose the movie. Afterwards, they walked along the lake shore.

"What a wonderful movie," Kim said. "It won an Academy Award, you know. I think it is the best movie I have ever seen."

As they continued strolling, Kimberly asked Michael to sing to her. At first, he wouldn't, feeling self-conscious. They were in public, though there were not many other people in the immediate vicinity. She offered to compromise by singing a duet. It was their duet from the operetta, and they sang it with all the flair they would be expected to bring to their on-stage performance, dancing and swirling to musical accompaniment playing inside their heads that only they could hear.

The song concluded with them gazing romantically into each other's eyes. Silence followed, surrounding them, the only sound being lakefront waves lapping upon the shore, feeling as if they were the only two people on earth and this was their own personal sandy playground. It was there on that beach, under the stars, that he kissed her for the very first time. She kissed back, eagerly.

"Is that for real, or just practicing for our big stage kiss?" she asked.

"Oh, it was for real," he answered. "At least, for me."

"I was so hoping you would say that," she replied. "It was the most *real* kiss I have ever experienced."

They kissed again.

"I wish every day could be like today," Kim said.

From that moment on, they were a couple. Both on stage and off.

The operetta was a success, though Michael would scarcely have noticed if it had flopped. He was over the moon just being with this girl, his head in the clouds and oblivious to what anyone may have thought about the production.

Months passed. It had been snowing so long that all records for Chicago area snowfall had been broken, yet Michael and Kimberly's high school romance grew ever warmer. They spent nearly every waking minute together, even attending church services together on Sundays, Kimberly advancing her way to the communion rail with Michael right behind. Her parents, devout Catholics, were pleased their daughter had fallen for a nice Catholic boy. Though, a bit shorter haircut might be nice.

Michael's parents, however, were not quite as enthusiastic about the relationship as were Kimberly's parents. Kim in her final year of high school, a senior; Michael, a year behind her in school, made her an *older woman* in their eyes. "She will go off to college or into the working world after graduation. She will be an adult and you will be just a little high school boy. She's gonna outgrow you, son," Joe warned. His mother often adding, "You should be dating lots of girls, girls your own age, and enjoying your high school years."

But Michael paid little heed to such parental advice. He had found the girl for him and felt no need to date others. His parents just had no clue, no understanding of how much in love and how serious he and Kimberly had become: Kim making clear she would like to get engaged, saying couples who don't become engaged just drift apart after graduation from high school.

"That will never happen to us," Michael assured her. "Never!"

They talked about marriage. They talked about love. Though, they really knew nothing of either. High school sweethearts fated to be together forever, they thought.

9

JOURNAL

My home life is filled with such hostility. My dad and I have really been getting into it. Nothing I do pleases him, and he rides me relentlessly about everything, calling me "a lazy good-for-nothing!"

Kimberly is the only thing in my life that is truly good, and the only time I am truly happy is when I'm with her.

Last night she and I parked at a favorite spot to talk and stuff. *Happy Together* by The Turtles came on the radio. Kim looked at me with her special smile. "That should be our song," she said. When she smiles like that, I become absolute putty in her hands.

The pink lipstick she wears, and the sweet fragrance of Heaven Sent, *her* scent, really gets to me. So seductive. We started making out, but it quickly escalated well beyond that. Every time we are alone together, it is like my hands have a mind of their own and just cannot stay away from Kimberly's vital body parts. Oh, we still have not gone all the way or anything (yet), but nearly. I'd sure like to! There have been so many times when she has really, really wanted to as well.

We are both tired of being chaste and hungry for sin but, crazy as it sounds, whenever we get close, I am the one who says *no*. Why is it me who ultimately says no, you ask? I'll tell you why. Kimberly is extremely religious and struggles with the constant tug-of-war between what she *wants* to do and what she knows we *shouldn't* do. And Kim is convinced that if we *go all the way* before we are married God will punish her by making her pregnant with a deformed baby! Seriously, she is certain the baby would be born with two heads or something. She actually told me that. So, no way I want to be part of bringing down God's wrath on her.

It's tough being a guy sometimes. It really takes a lot of willpower to control myself. I pray every night for help in staying strong. We talk about the day we will marry, when there won't be anything holding back our arousals. We talk about how our life together will be, living right here in Downers Grove, raising a family, growing old together, and all that kinda good stuff. Our blissful future together. God, I love her so much!

10

THE NIGHT THEY CALLED IT A DAY

Kimberly had been away at college in Missouri for what seemed like an eternity but was only a semester. She and Michael wrote dozens of letters to each other and there were frequent phone calls. It seemed to Michael that his father had been completely wrong, absence had only made their hearts grow fonder.

But when Kimberly came home for Christmas break, something was different between them. They began having arguments. Some quite heated. They had seldom argued before, so this seemed entirely foreign to them both.

She returned to college after the holidays, and her letters abruptly stopped. A barrage of correspondence from Michael went unanswered. When he felt he just could not take it any longer, he placed a telephone call to her dormitory. Calling from a pay phone to assure privacy, night snow falling outside the phone booth while Michael shivered inside, uncertain whether calling her was the right move, but desperately needing to know how things stood between them.

What he discovered was a crushing blow. In a voice devoid of emotion, Kimberly stated that their relationship was *over*! He heard her words, but his mind had difficulty processing their meaning. It just seemed so impossible for it to truly be over. Across the miles he whispered into the phone that he still loved her.

"I really wish you wouldn't have said that," she replied, this time allowing emotion to creep in. From the quiver in her voice, Michael could tell she was now crying.

"Why?" he asked. "I don't get it. We planned to get married. How did it go from that to this so quickly? You don't love me anymore?"

"I do. Sadly, I do. I think I will probably always love you. But this is where I am now, and this is *who* I am now." The phone that hung on the wall in the open hallway of her dormitory where Kimberly took the call offered little privacy. She wished she could say more, explain better. "Michael, you're seventeen years old. Don't you want to get out and see some of the world first? Sow some wild oats?" He did not reply. "Even if *you* don't, *I* do." There was a long pause, then, "I don't want you to call me here again." She waited for some response from him. When none was forthcoming, she added, "Okay?"

"Okay," he mumbled into the phone, unable to prevent tears from forming as he placed the phone back into its cradle. The sunlight and beauty that Kimberly had brought to his life had now been sucked away; the world, suddenly seeming stark and without song, gone from color to black and white.

Walking home along the frozen tree-lined street, eyebrows rimed with frosty ice particles, tears frozen on his cheeks, somnambulant in grim certainty that he would never again find such love. If it had been possible to awaken some glimmer of perception that her words, rather than calamitous, could somehow be a fortuitous shove in the trajectory of his life, it might not have seemed so intractable. But that was well beyond his imagining.

A solitary car passed, clanging snow chains on tires sounding like dissonant sleigh bells, the sheen of headlights on wet pavement giving a polished waxen glow. This was the night they called it a day.

PART TWO

11

CALIFORNIA SON

The summer that Joe had spent as a young teen living with his Uncle Al in Riverside, California had always remained at the forefront of his memory as the best summer of his life. He had felt glad to escape, however briefly, from small-town Midwestern life and a father with whom he did not get along particularly well. He preferred to think of Uncle Al as his other father, a better father, a man he looked up to, admired, emulated; and to think of himself as Al's California son. Given a choice that long-ago summer, Joe would have easily chosen to remain in California with his uncle, instead of returning to the frigid winters with an icy father in No-Where-Ville, Illinois.

Perhaps, Joe often pondered, if he had been allowed to live with Uncle Al, his entire life might have turned out different. Maybe he would not have joined the army to escape a life of mundane drudgery. He had no regrets about serving in the military, but maybe it all would have been somehow different. Perhaps, just maybe, that German boy he killed would still be alive today. Killing someone was a memory he'd been unable to shake, even after all these years.

It was eighteen days into the second semester of his third year at Downers Grove High School that Joe dropped out and enlisted in the army. December 4, 1945, the very day of his seventeenth birthday, found Joseph Perry in Fort Sheridan, Illinois with induction papers in hand.

After basics, he was shipped overseas. The long, hellish boat ride across the Atlantic was something Joe never wanted to repeat. Endless sky, endless ocean, endless motion … seemingly endlessly. Every soldier on board was sick, sea-sick, gut-wrenchingly sick. The kind of sick from which there is no hope of cure other than to jump overboard and end it all with a splash, an option many on the ship had likely considered more than once. Joe would be happy to spend the rest of his days on this earth without ever seeing the cold gray ocean ever again. And if he ever found himself on any sort of boat again, it would be too soon.

World War II had ended. Stationed in Germany, part of the post-war cleanup, one day the officer in charge asked the enlisted men if any of them knew how to ride a motorcycle. Joe immediately answered in the affirmative. A total lie, Joe had never even sat on a motorcycle but, he figured, how hard can it be? In the army they say you should never volunteer, but Joe volunteered and soon found himself part of an elite motorcycle corps to police the town and surrounding German territory. Under the command of General Ernest Harmon, it was a brand-new unit called The Constabulary, a separate unit from the military police created to enforce laws and train the Germans in the American Zone. The part of military life Joe liked least was taking orders. As part of The Constabulary, now it would be *he* who gave the orders. The assignment fit him like a glove. Made him feel like a somebody for the first time in his life.

In the immediate aftermath of the war the people of Germany had no leadership, no law or order. The country was a mess. The mission of Joe's unit, essentially, was to straighten out this war-ravaged country that had come to ruin under Hitler. Among their other duties, The Constabulary provided general military and civil security, patrolled the borders, seized contraband, and controlled displaced persons. There were twenty-five motorbikes in The Constabulary mechanized calvary unit. Joe and his fellow *Blitz-Polizei*, as the Germans called them, lived in a motor pool separate from the rest of the army. Joe regarded himself as having procured a very plum assignment. Of course, that was before he knew just how dangerous a mission it could be.

He quickly learned the art of motorcycle riding and became highly adept at it. Skilled. Necessary skills. The war may have been over, but there remained tell-tale signs that not all German people were happy about it. Booby-traps were everywhere. Invisible wires strung between two trees, intended to decapitate the military motorcycle riders as they patrolled the streets. Such things were almost commonplace. Hitler Youth, brainwashed by *Der Fuhrer*, especially resented Americans coming into their country and trying to tell them what to do, many viewing these uniformed motorcycle-mounted *Blitz-Polizei* as akin to the recently defunct, black-uniformed Nazi SS. But these were Americans. In nearby Sonthofen and Stuttgart, there had been whole universities of a sort that taught young boys, and girls too, Joe supposed, to embrace pogroms, hate the Americans, hate the French, and hate anyone else who stood in opposition to Hitler's vision of German greatness.

On patrol one evening, cruising a serene tree-lined street, Joe heard a noise: *ping, ping, ping, ping*. "What the hell?" he muttered to himself, slowing down as his partner continued on ahead. No idea what the pinging sounds were, until something went burning through his boot, sending pain into the calf of his right leg, causing him to fall, the motorcycle toppling over on him. Lying on that German street, beneath the weight of the heavy bike, the fusillade continued, *ping, ping*. The motorcycle his shield, Joe noticed movement in the bushes several feet away. There looked to be a rifle barrel pointing from the bushes. Releasing his gun from the holster, Joe fired several rounds in the direction of that movement.

Moments of silence that seemed like a lifetime passed before Joe wriggled out from under the cycle, creeping cautiously toward the bushes. When he got close enough, what he saw made him recoil. Lying dead in a heap, still clutching a small caliber rifle, was a young boy. Very young. Not more than thirteen or so, a remnant of the Hitler Youth.

He was dead for certain, Joe could tell. Hell, anybody would be able to tell. Near-white-blond hair now soaked a purplish red. Blue eyes, still open, a gelid death stare hard as a carapace, devoid of life, staring up at nothing, yet seemingly retaining the last vestiges of a hate that refused to pass. What might have been a youthful, handsome face mere moments ago now had the entire jaw blown right off from the rest of his skull. It was a gory, grizzly sight. Joe wanted to puke. No words could describe the emotions pulsing through him. Complete disgust for having killed a mere child.

His partner, having heard the shots fired by Joe, or perhaps merely discovering that Joe had lagged behind, roared back on his motorcycle, throwing the bike down and rushing to where Joe stood staring down at the blood-soaked corpse of the German boy. There they both stood, breathing heavily, trembling, staring. It was the first dead person that Joe had ever seen in his entire life, and he had caused it. "Sweet Jesus, I killed him. I didn't know," Joe muttered. "I didn't know it was just a kid. Son of a bitch!"

They stood staring at the body for a long while, neither uttering another word. "Not your fault," his partner spoke suddenly, breaking the catatonic silence, "You's just defendin' yourself." True enough, but it didn't help. Not much anyway. "Forget he's just a kid. He was tryin' to kill you. Goddam Hitler youth! Wish it'd been me what killed him," Joe's partner shouted, kicking the dead boy in the ribs right where he lay. It was like kicking a bag filled with sand. "Lousy kraut got exactly what he deserved. Shit! Shooting at an American *Polizei*. What the hell? You should be glad you shot him. Better him than you."

Joe looked up from the prone, lifeless body and into his partner's face. He saw rage in the features of his fellow American, his brother in arms. Drool was sliding out the corners of his mouth. His eyes looked wild. It was as if he were so angry at this dead German boy that he wanted to kill him all over again. But it was Joe who had done the deed.

His partner remained with the body as Joe remounted his bike, returning to base to report the killing to the officer in charge. Though the vision of the boy who Joe had reduced to a bloody heap would remain clear in his mind's eye evermore, Joe never saw the dead boy again. Had no idea what was done with the body. No idea what the boy's name might be or who his family might be.

Ancient history now, but killing that German boy changed Joe. His very life changed and, he was pretty sure, not for the better. Not long after this incident, Joe had a tattoo inked onto his forearm. His flesh permanently stained in memory of the boy's death, as his mind and soul already were. It was a heart with a bullet piercing through it, blood dripping, and the German words, *Der Tod wird euch befreien*: Death will set you free.

Joe looked down at the tat still on his arm, then rolled his sleeve down over it. He should never have left California.

Joe's business had been extremely prosperous. He'd worked hard, put up with nasty cold winters, shoveling snow, freezing his ass off at construction sites, only to come home to a frigid spouse and screaming kids. Now he was nearing forty years old. It was time he did something for himself, something big. He could finally afford to fulfill his long-held dream.

"I wanna move to California," he announced one evening at dinner.

It wasn't easy convincing Mary to make the move. "Our home is here," she told him. "Your business is here. You are asking me to uproot everything we have spent a lifetime building. Our friends are here. I don't know a soul in California." And finally, the trump card: "My mother is here." She refused to leave her mother who had lived close by all these many years and been an integral part of their family.

"She can come too," Joe told her. "I always liked the old broad. She's good people. I'll build a little mother-in-law spot for her in the backyard of our new home in California."

But Nana, as the kids had always called her, also had no desire to uproot her life with a move to some foreign place by the ocean. She loved the tiny suburban village of Downers Grove, pointing out that it was a wonderfully wholesome place to raise a family. California she wasn't so sure about.

Joe stuck to his guns, though. The Perry family moved to Southern California, Joe figuring he would build houses all over the sprawling San Fernando Valley, picking up right where he left off. Only this time, doing it all in the shade of swaying palm trees.

12

BEACH MONKEYS

It was the summer after high school and Michael, because he'd once been a volunteer lifeguard at the Downers Grove Community Pool, landed a job working for the Los Angeles County Department of Beaches at Zuma Beach in Malibu. He felt like he'd been thrust into one of those beach party movies he had enjoyed as a kid.

"It's a really fun job!" he excitedly told his parents. "I get to be outside in the sun at the beach every day ... and they even pay me for this! Not to mention, the job keeps me in great shape because we must run two miles on the sand and swim one mile in the ocean at 6:30 each morning. What better job could there possibly be?"

His father couldn't hold back a smile. The kid seemed to be really enjoying his first California summer, just as Joe had done so long ago. "Well, just remember, it's only for the summer," he admonished his son. "Then you'll need to think about getting a real job. Or go to college."

In his off hours, Michael enjoyed surfing. New to the sport, he picked up on it quickly, feeling an instant affinity with the ocean. There was nothing quite like being propelled along the crest of a breaking wave, popping up to his feet, taking the drop, and burying the rail into a swift bottom turn.

He had just finished such a ride and was coming out of the water toting his board – a nine-foot Velzy purchased for thirty dollars – when he saw Maggie for the very first time. She was sitting, full lotus style, on a beach towel all by herself. Pretty, with summer colored skin, blond hair, bangs swept across her forehead, and wearing a very skimpy bikini.

"Hello," she said, squinting up at him into the sun as he approached.

"Hey," he replied lazily, trying to sound cool. "Howzit goin'?"

"It goes good. Really good. I watched you surf."

"And? How'd I do?"

"Not too bad."

"You a surfer girl?" he asked.

"Nope. I just like to sit on the sand and watch people surf."

She smelled like sunshine and coconut oil. "Mind if I sit on the sand with you?"

"Not a bit."

He laid his board down parallel to her towel and sat on it. "No way I could sit like you with my legs twisted into a pretzel. Geez, is that even comfortable?"

"You've never heard of yoga?" she asked, perplexed.

"I'm discovering there are lots of things I have never heard of. But, you know, I'm pretty sure that if I looked up the phrase Perfect California Girl in a dictionary there would be a picture of you."

She flashed a crooked little smile that Michael found instantly charming, giving her face a cute comical look, reminding him of Goldie Hawn from the TV show *Laugh-In*.

"I am pretty sure you won't find that phrase in any dictionary but thank you. You *did* mean that to be complimentary, right?"

He smiled back, nodding.

"How about you, the perfectly tanned California surfer boy?"

"Looks can be deceiving," he warned.

"How so?" she asked.

"Just moved here a month ago."

"Really? From where?"

"The Midwest," he told her.

"Hmm, the Midwest, you say? Sounds exotic," she mocked. "Well, I'd say you have adapted well," adding with a snicker, "looks like a case of Cal-euphoria to me."

Maggie showed up at the beach each day after that. Michael's shift ended at 2:30 and they spent the afternoons together, often escaping to Maggie's house. She lived close by in an impressive home on a hill with swimming pool and tennis court. They'd jump in Michael's Chevy convertible – actually his mom's car, but it was his for the summer – cruising along Pacific Coast Highway with the top down, their hair blowing wildly in the wind, The Who blasting from the eight-track, *Magic Bus*; Michael singing along to Maggie, one hand on the steering wheel, the other exploring her thigh, *I waaant it, I waaant it.* And Maggie shaking her finger at him, singing in mock reprimand, *Well, you caaaaan't have it!* The two of them giggling and laughing the whole way.

At Maggie's they had the house all to themselves, since her parents were divorced and her mom worked long hours as a professor at a nearby university. They would swim in the pool, ride skateboards on the tennis court, Maggie would make them lunch, and they would make out like crazy on the sofa until it was time for her mother to return home from work.

Some evenings he would stay and have dinner with Maggie and her mom, who Michael found to be an amazingly cultured and intelligent woman. He enjoyed discussing politics and art with her around the dining room table. Even though knowing little of either subject, just conversing with Maggie's mom was a stimulating learning experience. When it came to politics, her mom was extremely liberal. Completely the opposite of his own parents. In fact, she was downright radical, expressing admiration for the outspoken communist UCLA professor Angela Davis, a woman Maggie's mom called friend.

But for all her worldliness and *artsy-fartsyness* – artsy-fartsy being the term Maggie liked to use when describing artists and art lovers – her mom did not seem to have a clue when it came to current music. She once asked him if Creedence Clearwater Revival was a band that played *religious* music. A die-hard atheist, she would not approve of her daughter listening to any sort of "church music." Michael laughed and assured her that CCR was definitely *not* a religious band.

"So, how was your day at work, Mr. Lifeguard?" Maggie asked one afternoon as she met Michael at their usual spot near the Zuma Beach number six food stand.

"Pretty interesting, I'd say. A damn near life altering event happened. It involved getting totally stoned."

"You mean you smoked pot?" Maggie said, feigning astonishment.

"And it might be my last time, too," he offered.

"Say it ain't so," Maggie teased. "Pray tell, what calamitous event could have spawned such a decision?"

"Well, you know, at the far end of Zuma there is that private road that goes up a steep cliff and ends at the Big Rock portion of Point Dume?"

"Yes, but it's chained off. Nobody can drive up there," she said.

"Right, the chained gate bars all vehicles from entering the road, except for county vehicles. A special *D key* unlocks all such gates at all L.A. County beaches, and lifeguards possess such a key."

"I see," she said.

"So, since almost no one ever ventures past the gate to drive up that road, some of the lifeguards like to sit on the edge of the cliff where they can smoke dope without discovery. From that lofty perch they can see anyone who might be down on the beach, but it's unlikely anyone down there might look up and see them."

Maggie nodded, indicating she was listening to his story.

"So, this morning four of us drove to that secluded little spot, sat on the cliff and proceeded to get stoned. Gee, ya think the public would find it comforting to know guys entrusted with saving lives at the county beaches are high on illegal substances?"

"Utterly shocking," Maggie quipped.

"Anyway, sitting there, high above the beach, we looked down and noticed a large congregation moving about on the sand."

"Nothing surprising about that," Maggie remarked.

"Sure, except that, at some point, one of the guys pointed in that direction, saying, 'Hey man, is it just me or, like, do all those people look like … monkeys?'"

"Monkeys?" Maggie asked, incredulously.

"Yep, monkeys," Michael replied. "So, our entire group all leaned over the edge of the cliff and looked a little closer."

"And?"

"And one of the guys says, 'Yeow, you are totally right man, they *do* look like monkeys!' Then another guy says, 'This must be some really good shit, man. We gotta be hallucinatin' because everybody knows they don't let no monkeys on the beach.'"

"How astute," Maggie commented dryly.

"Well, there's monkeys on the beach today, man," I told them. "Ain't no doubt about it, those are definitely monkeys down there."

Maggie gave him a quizzical look.

"So, trying to make some sense of it, somebody then surmised, 'Maybe it's some kinda special monkey day. Maybe the zoo made a deal where monkeys could be on the beach today.'"

Maggie sniggered. "Oh lord, you guys must've been so ripped."

"We all just sat there trying to absorb the absurdity of there being a special *monkey day*. Finally, I told the guy, man you are dumb as a post. That is the stupidest thing I've ever heard!"

"What did he say to that?" Maggie wanted to know.

"He just said, 'Yeah? Well, if it isn't monkey day, then explain to me why the hell we are *all* seeing a bunch of monkeys down on the beach. And tell me why they are all wearing human-type clothes!' So, we all looked again, even more intently this time. No doubt about it, below us was a beach full of monkeys walking around wearing clothing."

"You're serious?" Maggie accused.

"For sure! At this point, someone in our little group of highly trained lifeguards recommended that we quit smoking so much dope, to which the rest of us immediately concurred."

"So, what happened then?" Maggie wanted to know.

"We all got in the county lifeguard vehicle and headed back to our workstations. I spent the next several hours seriously worried about the monkey hallucination and contemplating never smoking marijuana ever again."

Maggie's jaw fell open with exaggerated astonishment.

"Of course," Michael concluded, "we were all greatly relieved later in the day to learn a film crew had been down on the beach filming a Planet of the Apes movie."

"Oh! You creep!" Maggie shouted, kicking sand at him.

"Got'cha!" Michael laughed, dodging the sand blast aimed at him. And off they went, jumping into the car and heading for Maggie's house. Crosby, Stills, Nash & Young blasting from the radio, *Teach your children well.*

As summer's end approached, so did the job at Zuma Beach. Without the lifeguard job, there was little incentive to make the long drive out to the beach each day and the couple's time together became less frequent. There also had developed a falling out between Maggie's mother and Michael, so he felt less welcome to stick around for evening dinners as he had done much of the summer. Oddly enough, it had to do with God and intelligence.

It began one Sunday when Michael took Maggie to church with him. Her upbringing completely devoid of religion, Maggie had never in her life been to Sunday services of any sort. She wanted to see firsthand what church was all about. When Maggie's mother found out that her daughter had been to church, she flew into a rage – ranting about exposing Maggie to spiritual fairytale nonsense! "Believing in all that mumbo-jumbo is no different than belief in gnomes or pixie dust," she shouted.

"Geez, I'm not trying to *convert* Maggie or anything," Michael tried to explain. "In fact, I rarely even go to church these days. She was just curious and asked if I would take her." Maggie's mother, Michael discovered, liked to think of herself as liberal and open-minded but, apparently, atheists are no more tolerant of ideas outside their zone of influence than are religious zealots.

Her mother, with pretentious appropriateness in accordance with her position as a college professor, touted herself as an intellectual – a card-carrying member of a brainiac society called Mensa, comprised of people who, when tested, proved to have a high-level IQ.

The culmination of their falling out came one afternoon when she administered the Mensa test to Maggie and her lifeguard boyfriend. Hopeful her daughter had the intellect; she was certain the boyfriend did not. Her apparent disappointment when Maggie fell short of the required score was underscored only by increased disdain for the church-going surfer who *did* meet the required score. From that point on, Michael felt unwelcome and fun afternoons at Maggie's house dwindled.

It became obvious that what they had enjoyed was just a fun summer fling, and they both seemed fine with that.

"So, what are you gonna do now that summer's over and you don't have your job any longer?" Maggie asked.

"I guess go off to college. Someplace far away so I won't have to live at home. Kinda leaning toward Colorado. I've applied to a few schools and, believe it or not, there's a couple who are willing to accept a clod like me."

Maggie chuckled.

"Problem is, I don't know what my major should be, because I have no idea what I want to be when I grow up."

Maggie nodded knowingly.

"Fact is, my dad is such a successful businessman, it's kinda intimidating. I doubt I could ever be as successful as him, no matter what career I decide on."

"So, don't sweat it. Just study whatever interests you," Maggie suggested.

"Yeah, sure. Maybe music. What about you? What are your plans?" Michael asked.

"My dad is an exec at a big studio in Burbank. He can get me a really good job. I was not really planning to do that, but maybe I will. Take a year before heading off to UCLA to study art."

"Burbank. That's in the Valley, right? That's where my family lives. So, maybe we will see each other around."

"That would be cool," she agreed. But they never did.

13

NOT OUR KIND

The college dorm room was far from luxurious, with cement block walls, a flickering neon light attached to the ceiling, a tiny cot for sleeping, and a small metal desk. The feature Michael liked best was the corner window with a dead-on view of the Colorado mountains. Otherwise, the room more resembled a prison cell than a dorm room.

He shared the meager space with fellow freshman Jarrod Berg, a cocky charismatic Jewish fellow whose family had recently relocated from New York City to Denver, causing Jarrod to lament the loss of his first great love, Harriet Schwartz, whom he had no choice but to leave behind in the Big Apple. Michael commiserated, recalling the heartbreak he felt when he and Kimberly broke up, a hurt not yet totally healed. The two became fast friends.

In high school Michael had enjoyed acting in school plays, so an audition for the college production of *Barefoot in the Park* was first on the extracurricular activities list. He was, once again, utterly amazed to land the lead male role. But this time he thought to himself: Wow, a college production – the big time!

Cast as female lead was a sophomore from New Jersey majoring in pre-law named Ebony Yoder. She was talented and attractive, so much so that Michael found himself feeling woefully inadequate and self-conscious in her presence. The director, Mrs. Kilpatrick, who may have now had misgivings about casting an immature freshman boy for such an important role, suggested the two spend time together offstage and get more comfortable with each other. Michael and Ebony then began going out.

"So, freshman, what do you like best about college life?" she asked on their first date, opening with small talk.

"So far I like just about everything," he answered.

"Come now, be more specific," she coaxed.

"I like being on my own for the very first time. And I'm enjoying meeting different types of people from all over the country. My roommate is a Jewish guy from New York. In fact, I've met kids here from all over the world; Thailand and countries I've never even heard of."

She smiled, nodding agreement.

He continued. "I'm enjoying the diversity. It's really interesting. The town where I grew up felt completely *white bread*."

"Explain," still coaxing.

"It was like this All-American small town out of some turn-of-the-century novel. In fact, it isn't even called a town. It's called a village. The Village of Downers Grove. Our claim to fame? It is one of the only places in the nation to have a cemetery right in the heart of town, right on Main Street, across from the grocery market."

"Kinda weird, no?"

"Never really thought about it. Lots of old-time military heroes buried there, going all the way back to men who fought in the War of 1812. Civil War soldiers, too. But not *just* military, also abolitionists who used their Downers Grove homes as stopovers in the underground railroad."

"Interesting. *Downers* Grove, now there's a curious name for a place," she remarked.

"Oh, we learned about this in elementary school. Named after a man named Pierce Downer. He was the first white settler in the area. Laid claim to a grove of trees or something like that. Hence the name."

"Makes sense, I guess," she nodded. "That's in California?"

"No, my family only moved to California last year. It's the town where I grew up in Illinois. We had no minorities. At least none I ever saw. No Black people. No Mexicans. Not even a Mexican restaurant. There was exactly one Asian family. Chinese. The girl was in my class, Lily Choy – I remember I had a crush on her in third grade. They owned Choy's Laundry on Main Street."

She laughed. "Oh, come on. You're making all this up. That is so cliché. Sounds like a made-up fantasy town … excuse me, village."

Some weeks later, Michael called home. His mother was pleased to hear her son was adjusting to college life and had found a girl he found interesting. Pleased he was moving on from the heartbreak she knew he felt after the breakup of his high school relationship with Kim.

"Ebony's really great," he told his mother. "She's so talented and smart and pretty."

"I'm happy for you, Michael," his mother replied.

"I've never met anyone like her before. We've become close friends, but I can't deny feeling some romantic inclinations as well."

"You said her name is Ebony?"

"Yes. It's pretty, don't you think? She's different from any girl I've ever known. First Black girl I've ever dated, too."

Silence on the other end of the line.

"Mom, you there?" he asked.

Continuing awkward silence. Then, "Just a minute. I think your father wants to speak with you."

A few more moments passed, he could hear his parents' muffled voices discussing something, then his dad came on the line. "What's this? You're dating some negro girl?"

"She's from New Jersey. A really terrific girl," he told his father.

"Listen, son. I did not send you all the way out to some damn school in Colorado to date Black girls."

"But Dad …" Michael began.

"I'm serious. This is gonna end right now. Do I make myself clear?"

"I don't understand it," he told Ebony. "I have never heard either of my parents make a racist remark in my entire life. I had no idea they are prejudiced. I am completely shocked."

"Guess it's easy to never say a racist word when there are no minorities to develop a prejudice against in that white-bread fantasy town you described," she surmised. "When the race issue actually intrudes upon their white world the repressed prejudice emerges."

"It's crazy," he told her. "Makes no sense. They never even met you."

"Doesn't matter," she sagaciously explained. "You are like a blank slate, growing up like you did. I did not grow up in that sort of homogenous world. So, I am not at all surprised. See, I already know not to tell my family that I'm dating a white guy. I know they would not approve any more than your folks did. It's just how that generation was raised. It is up to our generation to change things. For now, though, maybe it's best we just remain friends."

It was Friday afternoon and Michael was sitting alone in the dorm room listening to music on KIMN radio when Jarrod entered and asked, "Hey bro, what'cha doin' this weekend?"

"Not much. Just some catching up on my studies."

"Nope. Wrong answer. That is definitely *not* what you are doing. You are coming with me to my parents' house in Denver for the weekend."

Michael was hesitant. He was behind in some of his studies and could use the time to catch up.

"Come on. It'll be fun," Jarrod insisted.

"Okay. Sure, why not?"

That's where Michael met Erica, Jarrod's sister. Erica, a seventeen-year-old senior at Wheat Ridge High School, was a cute redhead with a heavy New York accent and clever comedic timing that kept Michael laughing the entire weekend. There was mutual infatuation, a "connection" as Erica put it.

The two began seeing one another, spending the next several weekends together, Erica making the drive to Michael's school, explaining to her parents she was going to visit her brother but spending her whole time with Michael. During the week, when they were apart, letters from Erica would arrive daily, filled with humorous prose that Michael so enjoyed. One of the letters included Erica's senior school photograph. On the back she had written *I know I look extraordinarily precious & adorable. Don't you think the photographer did a good job touching up this photo? He did a total Streisand on me, uncrossing my eyes, straightening my teeth, & erasing my acne. We gave him an extra hundred dollars for doing such a great job! So, you can spend all your time away from me just looking at my picture. Love, Erica*

Then, one weekend, Erica failed to show up. Michael called several times, but there was no answer.

"Hey, what's going on with your sister?" Michael finally confronted Jarrod.

"What do you mean?" he responded. But Jarrod knew exactly what Michael meant.

"I have not seen or heard from her. Is she okay?"

"Not to worry. She's fine."

"Then what's going on?"

"What's going on? Okay, I'll tell you what's going on. It's over between you and my sister," Jarrod said, completely devoid of his usual amiability. "Consider yourself dumped, my friend."

At first Michael thought Jarrod was joking, playing some sort of prank. But the look on Jarrod's face was not one Michael had ever seen before. It was almost hostile.

"Dumped? But why? We were getting along great."

"Too great. My mother decided she did not want Erica seeing you any longer."

"What? Why? I thought I was getting on fine with your mom."

"You were. She liked you. She still likes you. That's not the reason."

Michael looked blankly at his friend. It was then that Jarrod told him the most preposterous thing he had ever heard in his life. "It's not your fault, so don't go taking it personally. It's just that you're *goyim*."

Michael had never heard such a word before, but Jarrod spat it out in a tone generally used for obscenities. Surely there was some misunderstanding here. He tried to clear up the entire matter with assurances that he was most certainly not any sort of *goyim*.

Jarrod's response was mocking. "Oh, but you are. You're *goyim*."

Michael still looked perplexed.

"*Goyim* is a non-Jew. That's you. Erica was getting too attached, and my mother put a stop to it."

"You can't be serious. A non-Jew? Are you kidding me? What is this, the dark ages?" Michael had a hard time comprehending. This was some sort of religious/ethnic thing? Non-Jew? Surely nobody really harbored such old-world biases in this day and age.

"Look Mike, you're my friend, I like you. I'm just telling it like it is. It's nothing personal. Being Jewish is a serious thing. You're a nice enough guy, but ..."

"But not nice enough for your sister to be involved with," Michael finished for him.

Jarrod shrugged his shoulders. "You are not a Jew. If you were, you would understand. And don't bother trying to see her or call her or write to her. It's over, plain and simple."

Nothing personal? How could Jarrod, his roommate and supposed friend, someone from his own modern and arguably enlightened generation, be so bigoted? Surely there was no way Erica subscribed to all this nonsense. Though, several days passed and no one answered the phone when he called Erica's number.

Michael Perry sat alone at the cold metal desk in the cement walled room looking out the tiny window, watching the setting sun casting a glow on the mountains. Janis Ian's song, *Society's Child*, began playing on KIMN. A mournful, haunting tune about racial discrimination. The teenaged songstress, who also wrote the song, singing about how her Jewish mother would not let her date a Black guy, the mother explaining: *he's not our kind.*

Apparently, it is not just being Black. It's *anyone* who is different. Anyone who is not Jewish is not your kind as well, Michael was thinking.

Several hours away, Erica Berg lay on her bed crying. She could hear her parents arguing in the other room. "We never should have left New York!" her mother was shouting. "Our daughter is growing up in a goddammed cultural wasteland out here in the West. We should send her back, she could stay with my mother, be with legitimate people, graduate with her own kind."

14

FEELIN' GROOVY

At the on-campus theater, poet Rod McKuen, appearing upon a slightly elevated stage and seated on a backless stool, read aloud to a packed house. Michael watched a group of students in the front row wearing beads and Indian headbands, eyes closed, internally absorbing each and every word of prose from the famous poet, nodding their heads in unison to some unheard beat. Flower-sniffing, cloud-hopping hippie-dippies his father would likely call them.

Among them was a girl with the most flawless alabaster skin and once-in-a-century face framed by long auburn hair resting in final curls upon an embroidered full-length dress that left her softly dappled shoulders exposed. Feathers were braided into her hair giving her a wild, yet docile, appearance. Michael thought her to be the most beautiful girl he'd ever seen. More than beautiful, she was like living, breathing art. He simply could not take his eyes off her.

He worked his way closer. She gave him a brief, dismissive glance.

When the reading stopped, and applause ended, she turned, facing him with a steady, opaque look. "You grok?" she inquired.

Michael wasn't sure if he heard her correctly. Perhaps she was foreign. "Grok?"

There emerged an inscrutable look on her exquisitely featured face. "Mmhmm, grok," she confirmed with a sympathetic cluck. "Michael Valentine Smith? Stranger in a Strange Land?"

Michael had absolutely no idea what she was talking about, but he truly liked watching her lips move and hearing her velvety voice. A look of bemusement was all he was initially able to offer.

"*My* name is Michael. And yes, of course I grok," he finally replied with no understanding of what that meant.

A smile emerged. She looked amused. "Hello Michael who groks. I'm Joni."

The rest of the evening Joni and Michael were quite the carefree flower children, skipping and frolicking merrily through campus and out onto the streets of the town, wearing daisies purchased from a street vendor in their hair. Joni began singing Simon & Garfunkel songs and soon they were crooning duets and dancing along the sidewalk like some hippie version of an old Gene Kelly movie. "Feelin' groooovy," she sang, while Michael harmonized. Just watching her move was like poetry in motion and when they finally kissed – *she* kissed *him* actually, taking him completely by surprise with her assertiveness – it was like an incredible hit of oxygen that left him gasping for more.

That night found the two of them at a run-down old house where one of her friends from the event lived. They sat, camped out on the floor sipping wine, sharing skinny hand-rolled joints, listening to Buffalo Springfield and Leonard Cohen on the stereo.

"So, are you a student here? I've not seen you around. And, believe me, I would definitely remember if I had," Michael asked, passing the joint to Joni and realizing he knew almost nothing about this girl.

"I *was* a student," she replied, inhaling and passing it back. "I dropped out, decided to just shine it on. I needed to find my *thing* and didn't think I was going to find it sitting around listening to a bunch of *old* people teaching us useless stuff that no longer even applies to this modern new world."

"Old people. The professors, you mean?"

Absently combing fingers through her hair, revealing downy ginger follicles at her hairline, she nodded.

"Makes sense, I suppose," Michael said, nodding too.

"Our lives are of our own making, and I am anxious to be out on my own living it."

Perhaps a couple years older than he, there was a wildness and self-assuredness about her, a certain worldliness that he found himself envying. "I'm anxious, too," he agreed, extending the bogie in her direction. "I sorta view college as more of a steppingstone, though. A cautious first step before going out completely on my own."

"No, I get it," she said. "In a way, it is easier for me, I suppose. I'm female. I think a lot of boys stay in school nowadays just to avoid being drafted. But if I were a guy and the government tried to draft me, I would simply refuse induction. I'd flee to a more free-thinking country, like Canada."

She passed the J back to Michael.

"I think it's all a bit more complicated than that," he demurred, reaching out and taking it.

"I sometimes wonder what the world will be like when we are older and running things," she offered with a conciliatory shrug. "Perhaps someday there will be a president who smokes big fat doobies and gets high, just like we are. It's inevitable, don't you think? I mean, practically our entire generation gets high. Odds are, one day one of us will be in charge of things. A president who is a *head*. What a concept. Maybe it will even be someone who dodged the whole draft thing. Someone who is against war. Maybe someday there will be a president who will finally put an *end* to wars." She sat, nodding her head, contemplating the possibilities. Then, as an afterthought, "Maybe even make drugs legal. Wouldn't that be just grand?"

"You really think we can change the world to be like that?" he asked.

"Only if the world doesn't change us first," she replied.

He took a long drag from the waning roach in his hand, holding the smoke deep into his lungs till it caused him to choke and cough.

His coughing caused her to crack up. "You're precious," she said. Then she sat silent for a long while, looking intently at his face, examining every line and pore, his eyes, his hair, as if etching and defining the details of his features, trying to press her memory indelibly with the image of someone she very well may never see again.

It made him feel self-conscious. "What are you staring at?" he asked.

"Someday when we are old and nasty looking," Joni spoke prophetically, "and we think back upon our long-spent youth, it will be the memory of nights like this that will make us smile."

God, she was beautiful. The way the reddishness of her hair contrasted with the milky porcelain of her face gave her an almost doll-like appearance. "You will never be nasty looking," Michael assured her.

With an incandescent smile, she stood and pulled him to his feet by the hand. Leading him like a pet on a leash to the backyard, they collapsed upon the grass and made love under a sky full of stars in a way that was both wanton and tender. With no admission of this being his first, Michael only hoped his lack of experience did not betray him.

Afterwards, still wrapped in each other's arms and lying in the grass as they gazed up at the heavens, Joni told him she loved him.

It took him by surprise. "I'm still licking wounds from the last time I allowed myself to fall in love," he told her. The fragments of emotional shrapnel still surrounding the hole in his heart from Kimberly apparently not completely healed, recently ruptured yet again by the aborted romance with Erica Berg. But this was more than he cared to reveal.

Joni gave him a look, as if he had misunderstood. "That's cool," she said. "But I can still love you. Even if I were never to see you again, just know that on this particular night, at this particular spot in the universe ... I loved you."

15

DROP CITY

Spring Break. Though she had vanished from his life even more rapidly than she had entered, the words of Joni, the girl from the poetry reading, that life is of your own making, were firmly planted in his brain as Michael, with his belongings crammed into a duffel bag, put out his thumb and proceeded to hitchhike southward down Interstate 25 through Colorado and beyond, intent on seeing what life on the open road might be like.

Not far outside the city of Pueblo, just a day before Easter Sunday, he got caught in a tremendous hailstorm. Drenched and being pelted by golf balls falling from the sky, he walked along the middle of the highway with thumbs pointing in both directions semaphoring in solicitation of a ride. He didn't care what direction the ride might take him, so long as he got inside a nice warm car.

Before long, he was picked up by three guys around his own age with long hair, dirty jeans, and love beads: hippies. Two were Boulder University students on their way to Santa Fe for Spring Break. The third was a draft dodger on the run who claimed his name was Siddhartha.

"You're kidding, right?" Michael asked, upon learning the name.

"I kid you not," he responded. "But you can call me Sid." He looked a few years older than the others, with shoulder length brown hair and full beard. Michael startled at something that moved hidden in all that hair. It was a snake wrapped around his neck. The snake, Sid announced, went by the name Flower. "She's a female, of the boa constrictor genus, and measures about four feet in length," he said. "When she's not coiled around my throat like a reptilian necktie, she lives in this small metal file box." He pointed to a tin container on the floor at his feet, painted entirely in a psychedelic paisley, with air holes punched into the lid and a handle with which to carry it.

The students dropped Sid and Michael off in Las Vegas, New Mexico and proceeded on their way. Sid said he knew some people there at New Mexico Highlands University where they could crash for the night. "They're real groovy people. You will like them," he said.

Among them was a young woman whom everyone called Crazy Diane. It was easy to see why Crazy Diane had earned such a moniker, she seemed to occupy some cosmic plane that no one else could quite follow. Diane told them about a commune where she had lived, a place called Drop City, located near the town of Trinidad, Colorado – roughly one hundred thirty miles back in the direction from which they had come. That's where they should go, she recommended, if Siddhartha needed help escaping the country. Sid was anxious to head straight there the next morning.

Drop City seemed in the middle of nowhere, surrounded by Southern Colorado desert. The commune consisted of a number of dwellings, small geodesic domes that looked to be constructed from scrap metal and arranged in a circle around a larger dome in the center, called the Big Dome. Siddhartha entered the Big Dome and announced he'd been sent by Diane.

"You mean, Crazy Diane?" one of the residents asked with a cheerful grin.

Sid nodded.

"Welcome friend," another said. It seemed everyone knew *Crazy Diane.*

A slender woman wearing a flowing robe welcomed them with a hug, claiming to be a very close friend of Diane. A curtain of hair covered much of her face, but her smile was kind. Her name was Ilona. A toddler clinging to Ilona's robe followed in her wake. She introduced the child as her son, David. He was barefoot, clad only in an oversized T-shirt and walked around banging a toy guitar.

That night, Michael slept in the kitchen of the Big Dome, along with Siddhartha, Ilona, and little David. It was difficult sleeping as there was ongoing activity with people coming and going throughout the night, the Big Dome being a sort of gathering place.

At one point during the early pre-dawn hours, there appeared to be some type of impromptu meeting going on. It involved some young men with buzz-cut hair supposedly on their way to Canada, military inductees gone AWOL, seeking advice on how to escape the country. One of the commune elders, a hippie in his forties at least, confabbing with these military men, suggesting clandestine routes across the U.S. and ways to avoid detection entering Canada. The short-hairs were difficult to hear. They spoke in hushed tones and kept looking around the dome to see who might be listening. Michael remained huddled beneath a blanket on the floor, finding the conversation fascinating but eventually fell asleep.

It seemed that no sooner had he dropped off to sleep than he was reawakened by a new group of individuals making noise preparing breakfast. As the sun rose, filling the dome with natural light, more and more people meandered in until nearly the entire community was assembled. Michael was still sleepy, but ravenous. Everyone in the commune ate the same breakfast at the same time in the Big Dome, food everyone called pancakes but was more like bread with melted cheese and honey on it. Michael found it surprisingly good tasting.

With a full belly, he walked outside into the brisk early morning air. The sun was shining, birds chirping, and various critters scampering about. Savoring the tranquility that only early morning hours seem to provide, he was suddenly startled by a loud Tarzan-like yell directly to his left, pivoting quickly, looking up to ascertain the source of this auditory intrusion. Emerging from another dome about twenty feet away on the side of a hill was a naked man with long dark hair and flowing beard: the Tarzan yeller. A large hirsute fellow, he urinated in a hands-free manner while scratching his hairy chest, then – breathing a sigh of relief – stepped back into the dome, slamming the door behind him.

Nudity was commonplace, but one fellow with long red beard and brilliant orange hair that bounced just above his milk-white shoulders, seemed to never wear clothes. How he avoided sunburn out in the desert sun was a mystery. Much to Michael's disappointment, however, only a very few of the females at the commune seemed to follow this *au naturel* example. Still, he enjoyed watching the gentle to-and-fro swaying of unfettered breasts beneath the simple peasant blouses worn by most of the women.

Days came and days went. At some point Siddhartha vanished from the commune and was never seen again. Michael figured Sid dodged his way to Canada or Mexico – leaving Flower in Michael's care, since he awoke one morning to find the snake's tin box had been placed on the floor right next to where he had been sleeping.

To Michael, Drop City was like a pretend fort one might build as a child out in the backyard, made from sticks and blankets and rocks; a secret, cozy place, primitive but pure at heart, satisfying an atavistic urge to sleep upon the ground, smell the dirt.

He was learning a great deal about this so-called counterculture.

"Establishment folks may think of us as just a bunch of misanthropic *hippies*," one of the commune elders explained with high moral dudgeon, "but Drop City exists to forge a new concept in living. Mankind, by its very nature, is a selfish species. To obtain advantage for the *self*, the strong always will prey upon the weak. Rules and laws necessarily must be created and implemented to suppress this selfish aspect of our nature. But laws and rules must remain minimal and diligently monitored. None of the rules here are designed to curtail freedom of thought or expression.

"This is the path the new generation is discovering. *Your* generation, Michael. Most older people do not understand it, but this is the very real contribution that your generation is making to society. For a generation to merely accept society as it finds it, without trying to effect improvement, would not only display a lack of progress but clearly be regression. We are on the cusp of a whole new age. The older generation has had their turn at bat, very soon the tide will turn with an entirely new approach to solving the world's problems.

"It is an awesome responsibility to carry, but change will come. By observing the older generation, younger people will learn that the derision and destructive results realized from prejudice, racism, and capitalism can be corrected by a generation more in touch with the common good. We are helping to bring about a new order in the world! The change is already underway." Such disquisitions were frequent.

Michael was beginning to get restless. He felt it was time to move on. He had become friends with a fellow former Chicagoan named Vic, a large fellow, taller than six feet with the body of a linebacker, and a crazy nimbus of wiry hair that stuck out in all directions looking like a cross between Albert Einstein and Bride of Frankenstein. Vic had already been at the commune several months and was ready to head further west. "I really dig the *Drop* but it's time to blow this pop stand. Let's hit the road together." Michael needed no further convincing.

Vic and Michael hiked out into the desert, away from Drop City, in the direction of a highway they knew was located somewhere over the horizon. Shortly after leaving, the weather changed from sunny and warm to cloudy, cold and storm threatening. Not the best conditions to begin a journey, but they stuck out their thumbs and hoped for the best.

The first day's progress was rather discouraging, having hitchhiked little more than twenty miles from their point of origin. They slept on the side of the road, in a ditch a dozen feet from speeding cars and trucks rolling down the highway, under the vast desert sky; a sleeping bag would have been a luxury.

With the crack of dawn on a new day, they found themselves back on the highway just outside of Raton, New Mexico. It was a large expensive-looking car that slowed down and stopped a few feet from where they were standing on the side of the road, thumbs out. In their mutual experiences, most often the cars in which rides were offered were older, some beaters, or VW vans and bugs – standard hippie-mobiles. So, an expensive vehicle like this was unusual. Also unusual was the color: bright red. The passenger side window silently powered down, the driver leaning over, shouted, "You boys need a ride?"

Vic approached, leaning with his elbows resting in the opening the lowered window provided, and peered inside. The driver was a middle-aged man, bald, bespectacled, wearing an orange Banlon shirt with vertical red and black stripes that hugged a protruding belly. The interior was black, the seats pleated leather. "Nice car," Vic told the man.

"Lincoln Continental," the driver replied. "Plenty a'room for you fellas and a nice smooth ride to get comfy in."

Vic opened the car door and slid into the front seat. The driver gave him a look, as if appraising the size of this big vagabond he just picked up. Michael got in the back, holding his duffel bag on his lap.

"So, where you longhaired groovy fellas headed?" the driver asked, attempting to sound hip but failing miserably, while accelerating back onto the highway.

"L.A.," Michael answered from the back seat.

The driver turned his head for a better view of his other passenger, then slapped his hands on the steering wheel and declared, "Well ain't that cool? Very cool! I'd be happy to take you boys all the way … so long as we all get along and things work out."

"Don't see any reason why they wouldn't," Michael agreed.

"Well, that's just hunky dory," the driver said gleefully, reaching toward the passenger seated next to him and enthusiastically slapping Vic's knee.

The Lincoln driver was wearing tight shorts and penny loafers with no socks. It wasn't necessarily the clothing, but Vic thought there was something fucking odd about this guy. And it was annoying the way the driver kept touching Vic's leg as he carried on a one-sided conversation about young people traveling the open road, being way out here in the desert, and how hitchhiking might not be the safest thing for young people to do.

After a half hour of such nattering, Vic announced, "Hey, I gotta pee."

"I'm sure there's a service station not too far up ahead," the Lincoln driver offered.

"Gotta pee right now," Vic insisted. "Need to pull over."

The driver exhaled with annoyance, blubbering his lips like he had just caught a chill, and the car began to slow. When they came to a stop, Vic climbed out of the big red car, quickly opened the rear door, and said to Michael, "You gotta pee too. Get out here!"

Michael exited the car, dragging his duffel, and Vic slammed both doors shut. The Lincoln driver sat for a long minute before realizing that neither boy was in need of urinating, then shrugged his shoulders and sped away.

Michael looked toward his friend. "What's all that about? He was gonna take us all the way."

"Yeah, sure. All the way," Vic retorted with sarcasm. "Might be wrong, but I got a really bad vibe from that guy." He put his thumb out as another car approached.

They were able to catch a series of rides, taking them incrementally closer to the California border. Then, at a desolate desert location near Kingman, they were offered a ride from fellow hippies in a VW bus and entered the Golden State together on a real high that lasted almost all the way to L.A.

Somewhere on the outskirts of Los Angeles, they were picked up by a middle-aged husband and wife driving a Mercedes Benz.

"Another fancy car?" Michael warned.

"At least it's not fucking red," Vic responded as he got in.

They learned the driver's name was Terry and he was some sort of musical composer/director working in the TV and movie business. His wife said her husband wrote songs for Walt Disney's Wonderful World of Color television show and for Disney's *Jungle Book,* a movie for which he was nominated for an Academy Award.

"Outta sight! Man, you're doin' some really far out stuff," Vic remarked with more than a tinge of awe in his voice. But the couple seemed far more interested in learning about the vagabond hippie life of their newfound passengers, about hitchhiking across the Great American Southwest and tales of Drop City. So, Vic and Michael, but mostly Vic, regaled them with stories of hippiedom as they drove.

The couple dropped their passengers off near Glendale, California and, as they drove away, Michael noticed an old, faded bumper sticker attached to the Mercedes that read *LSD not LBJ.* Very cool, he decided. Perhaps it was possible to be a middle-aged Mercedes owner and still be hip, but probably only in California.

One more short ride took them to Griffith Park where a massive love-in was going on. There must have been thousands of kids, and some young-at-heart adults, congregated in the park. In the air was a spirit of joy and frivolity mixed with feelings of peace and love that only being stoned *en masse* can create. Vic and Michael sat high on a hill, both literally and figuratively, overlooking the merry-go-round, the pungent aroma of their generation permeating the air, illegal substances being passed around with an aura of total impunity.

"I'm not just stoned, I'm goddamn Flint-stoned!" Vic declared.

"Yabba dabba doobie!" Michael agreed, both of them erupting in mindless laughter.

Music was everywhere. All around people were dancing, some gyrating wildly while others moved slowly like some form of ancient Tai Chi. A girl with pupils dilated to the size of black saucers danced over and told Vic she loved him while ceremoniously bestowing around his neck some love beads which, she said, she had strung herself especially for him. Vic offered her the two-fingered peace sign in return.

Perhaps as an afterthought, with no other beads to give, she reached into a fringed leather bag hanging on her shoulder and extracted a pair of dark sunglasses. Bending down to his seated level on the grass, she placed the frames upon Michael's face. "There," she offered, "looks groovy on you," before prancing off, waving her hands toward the sky, continuing her dance.

"No wonder the older generation fears us," Vic proclaimed as he toked on a fat joint. "We are changing the world from the uptight place *they* created to one where freedom of expression is the order of the day. And all this freedom frightens the hell out of them!"

Next morning, Vic and Michael found themselves standing at the on-ramp to the 101 Freeway with thumbs extended, trying to hitch a ride out of Los Angeles. "We gotta go to San Francisco, man. That's where it's really at," Vic declared. "You think that love-in was outta sight? Ya ain't seen nothin' yet. Haight-Ashbury is like the far out, free love, freaky capital of the world!"

But when they reached the central coast town of San Luis Obispo, for some reason Vic decided he'd gone far enough. "I've got a cousin here, second cousin actually. He goes to school here. I'm gonna just hang in with him for a while. You go ahead. You're gonna fuckin' love Frisco."

So, Michael continued on alone, easily catching rides up the coast, arriving at the *City by the Bay* just as the sun was setting, figuring he would have no trouble finding a place to crash since his experience thus far had been that generous groovy people can always be found if you know where and how to find them. But in *The Haight*, he discovered, he was merely one among many embracing the freak life, a face lost in the crowd.

Sitting down on a busy sidewalk, he extracted from his duffel bag the small paisley painted metal box and removed his pet snake, Flower, from her dark home, exposing out into the light of the waning sun what he hoped would be his secret weapon for meeting like-minded people. But sitting there silently on the sidewalk with a large snake wrapped around his neck garnered little attention from the local flower children.

Finally, a young woman wearing an Indian blanket poncho approached him. At her side, connected by a short rope leash, was a German Shepherd dog wearing a red bandana around its neck. She stood staring down at this boy on the concrete walkway with a snake.

"They arrested my old man," she said, offhandedly. "He was arrested for the crime of not having anywhere to go. How is that a crime when he was right here all along?" she asked, bewildered. "They put him in their little fuzz car and took him away. They'll be coming for me too. I just now it."

She wasn't making sense. Probably too stoned to make sense, Michael thought.

"You share a oneness with the reptile. So, here, take my dog," she said abruptly, dropping the frayed rope-leash down next to Michael. "His name is Pax. I don't want no piggies hauling him off too." With that, she wandered off, leaving the dog behind. It laid down upon the sidewalk and put its head on Michael's lap.

Perhaps he would have better luck finding shelter elsewhere, away from the heavily hippie-populated Haight-Ashbury district, but he'd exhausted himself hitchhiking up the coast and into the city and had little energy to move on. Further down the block several people loitered at a bus stop. Michael got an idea. Fishing from his pack the sunglasses he'd been given by the girl at the love-in, Michael stood up and began walking in their direction.

A bus arrived. It was now quite dark as Michael, wearing shades and with a snake tucked around his neck, boarded the vehicle with Pax, the German Shepherd, and took a seat directly behind the driver, who assumed them to be a sight-impaired person and seeing eye dog. The City of San Francisco offered free transport for people with handicaps, but something seemed out of kilter to the driver who continued keeping a close eye on them in the oversized rear-view mirror.

They'd traveled only a few blocks when the driver noticed something odd about what was draped around this blind passenger's neck. He thought he saw it move. The driver looked closer, taking his eyes off the road for a long moment. "Oh Lord Jesus!" he exclaimed. "A snake! A snake!" Frantic, the bus driver swerved to the side of the busy street and screeched to a stop at the curb. The bus door folded open. "Off! Get that thing off my bus! Right now!"

That first night in the city was spent curled up with Pax in a darkened alley near an overflowing trash bin, sleeping on pavement smelling of urine and oil. Dense San Francisco fog rolling in, chilling him down to the bone, the wayfaring life of a free spirit looking rather grim from this vantage point. He felt depressed and alone in a cold, cold city. A sad homeless waif, longing for the relative comfort of his dorm room at school … but Spring Break had ended long ago.

16

PRODIGAL SON

Joe Perry was having mixed feelings about moving to the Golden State. It had been his long-held dream to move to the West Coast, but it wasn't such an easy transition to make. His wife missed her mother terribly. Jaimie missed her grandmother and seemed to be having difficulty making new friends. Jaimie was a sweet kid, perhaps a bit too sensitive, wore her heart on her sleeve, but sooner or later, Joe felt, she would surely have friends.

Joe missed a few of his cronies back home, as well. But mostly he missed all the money he used to make in Illinois. He knew how to work the system back there. Here it wasn't so easy. Everything was government regulated; the People's Republic of California he'd heard many people joke.

Joe was studying to get his contractor license, because it was illegal to build houses in California without a state issued license. No license was required back in Illinois. Joe had never been much good at written exams, but figured how hard could it be? He'd been building houses and commercial buildings for years. Probably knew way more about construction than the people who made up the exam questions. He'd get the coveted license and then it would be off to the races! He was ready to release the parking brake on his California construction career and stomp his foot all the way to the floor, pedal to the metal. And it better happen soon because everything in California was so damned expensive. They had arrived with what Joe thought was a lot of money but were whipping through it at a rapid pace.

One thing he knew with absolute certainty, though. He had dropped his last dollar on any sort of education for his son. No more. Not another red cent. The kid dropped out of college to go hitchhiking around the damn country, lamely explaining he took off over Spring Break and just *sort of forgot to return to school.* Forgot? What the hell was this dumb-ass kid thinking?

This was a whole new level of stupid. You would hope he would at least have the sense to realize it's either keep your ass in school or you'll find yourself getting an all-expenses paid trip to Vietnam. Hell, maybe getting drafted might kick some sense into the boy. Knock the stupid right out of him, make him a man. Though Joe wasn't at all certain his son could survive a stint in the military. The boy had a certain wide-eyed fragility of spirit that would be lost permanently, crushed beyond repair. Joe still carried the scars of his own experience. Looking down at the tattoo on his forearm, the memory of the dead German boy remained fresh. He didn't really wish that upon his own flesh and blood.

But when his son showed up at Joe's door looking like some goddam hippie hobo, stinking to high heaven with a flea-infested dog and a goddam snake, it was the last straw. If sonny-boy thought he would be welcomed to the warm bosom of his loving family, he had made a serious miscalculation. The prodigal son had been met with justifiable contempt, his father mandating proper grooming and removal of the animals, especially the snake, before he would even consider allowing his son to spend a single night under Joe's roof.

"As for college," Joe informed his son in no uncertain terms, "you're on your own, bucko. You can forget about returning to that expensive out-of-state university you left. I understand local community college is not terribly expensive. I suggest getting a job to pay for tuition. Of course, if you prefer, there is always the military."

PART THREE

17

REESE

Registration day for the Fall semester at Los Angeles Pierce College, located in the West San Fernando Valley, was when he met him, standing out amongst the hordes of longhaired students and preppie-types scurrying from table to table to sign up for classes. Black cowboy hat casually tipped back atop his head exposing a thick shock of short jet-black hair, a lanky six feet tall with dark Native American copper complexion, Jay Yazzie looked more like he belonged on the set of a Western movie, though ambiguous whether as cowboy or Indian. His registration card indicated an agriculture/animal husbandry major, commonly known on campus as aggies. And he competed on the school's rodeo team. A conversation between the two began and a friendship was born.

On the far side of campus, removed from the warren of classrooms, administration buildings and the like, was the aggie section complete with barns, farm animals, pastures, and a rodeo arena where the team practiced riding bucking horses and bulls. Michael's childhood love for horses was rekindled and he soon found himself spending time there, absorbing the argot and assimilating into the cowboy lifestyle.

Within the little crowd of college cowpokes, new faces drifted across the landscape like tumbling tumbleweed. One of those, the sweet face of Reese Walker. Flirting with Michael in a discreet, quiet, shy kind of way ... coquettish: "Hi, I'm Reese. You know, like the peanut butter cup candy?"

Just eighteen, with shoulder-length honey-blond tresses and a curvaceous body packed ever so tightly into her Wrangler jeans – standard regalia of the rodeo crowd – the clothing brand's two matching Ws stitched on rear pockets moving up and down deliciously as she moved. At her slender waist, a buck-stitched belt with big trophy buckle she had won barrel racing her horse. But it was her come-hither smile that had Michael coming hither from the moment they met.

As attracted to her as he was, Michael found himself feeling a weird sense of insecurity, fretting she was a bit too much cowgirl for a Chicago wanna-be cowboy. It was obvious from the flirtatious looks she floated toward the bull riders on the team that it was going to take more than just wearing a big hat and pointy-toed boots to make the grade with her. The National Sports Council identified bull riding as the single most dangerous sporting activity in America, and Michael had no desire to climb aboard one of those vicious, long-horned behemoths. But one afternoon, as the team was practicing, he was given the opportunity to try his hand at it, to go from onlooker to participant.

Straddling the bucking chute, looking down at the bull just inches below him, he began to get cold feet. Then he looked out at the bleachers on the periphery of the arena and saw Reese with several of her girlfriends watching. Sitting his backside down onto the bull, a couple of the experienced riders began giving him pointers, helping him place his gloved hand properly into the bull rope. His heart beating faster, his face must have betrayed trepidation.

"You know, riding bulls is the toughest, most audacious athletic task there is. You don't have to do this if you're not ready," his friend Jay advised, rather solemnly. But he shook off Jay's words; Reese was out there watching, and this was his big chance.

Feigning courage he did not truly possess, nodding for the chute gate to open … bull and rider exploded into the arena! Lost in a trance of intensity beyond the physical thrill and craziness, the incredible force and energy of a wild bull twisting, turning, and bucking, he quickly discovered, must surely be the closest to raw exciting danger any man could hope to conquer. And conquer he did, staying aboard the bucking bovine for the required eight seconds and making his dismount without incident. The seasoned cowboys were all cheering, likely surprised that he survived. Reese and her friends were on their feet in the stands cheering, too. Jay clapped him on the back, "Way to go, buddy!"

Walking out of the arena, feeling ten feet tall, bolstered by admiring looks from Reese, it felt like more than a singular act to impress her. It was the intoxicating exhilaration of danger, such as he had never before experienced, and he wanted more of it. An instant adrenaline junkie, he was *hooked* on riding bulls.

At dinner with his parents, several months and a dozen bull rides later, Michael was telling them about his cowboy exploits and how exciting it all was. Producing an 8x10 black and white glossy photo of himself riding a bull, Michael presented it to his mother. "Here, I brought you both something. I want you to have this. There are always a few professional photographers at the rodeos snapping pictures. This is one they took of me."

"Ohh, I can't look at that," his mother groaned. "It's too dangerous. I don't like to think of you doing things like that." Giving only a cursory glance at the photo in her hand and shaking her head added, "I've always prayed every night to your namesake Saint Michael the Archangel, for him to watch over you. But I will pray even more now."

Handing it off to her husband, Joe stared at the photo for several long moments. Michael was pretty sure his dad would appreciate the photo; bull riding being such a manly, all-American, rugged endeavor. Not something a long-haired commie hippie would ever do.

"Why are you riding a cow?" his father asked with a distinctively sarcastic tone.

Michael assumed his dad was joking with him, but handing the photo back to his son, the deadpan look on his father's face made it clear he was not.

"No, Dad. The picture is for you guys," he said, pushing it back along the tabletop toward them. "That's me riding a really rank bull in a rodeo. I thought you'd like it."

"Hmph, looks like a cow to me. Rodeo? Rodeo people are just a bunch of rummies, like carnies and gypsies. Jesus, a cowboy? When are you gonna grow up and act like a man, for God's sake?"

By mid-winter Reese and Michael had moved in together, taking a small one-bedroom apartment near school. In cowboy parlance Jay Yazzie queried, "You just gonna *winter-up* with her, or is this somethin' more serious?" But it was obvious, their relationship had become quite serious. This was a couple in love.

"All I wanna to do is make you happy for the rest of our lives," Reese said to Michael on the first night in their new apartment together.

"I feel exactly the same way," Michael agreed.

And they were happy. Reese would cook them dinner, then they would do the dishes together, snuggling afterward on the old couch they'd bought at a garage sale and watch TV: Sonny & Cher Comedy Hour, Mary Tyler Moore, All in the Family. Sometimes, instead of television, Michael would play guitar and sing to her. He only knew a few chords, but Reese would sit mesmerized. She never had a boyfriend sing to her before.

Michael heard Reese in the kitchen one evening doing her own singing, crooning along to a song on the radio ... *I'm the happiest girl in the whole USA*. He stood in the doorway watching as she danced and sang, holding a spatula as if it were a microphone. Noticing him observing her, stopping self-consciously, she smiled and told him the Donna Fargo song was *her* song because it described exactly how she felt. He swept her up in his arms and kissed her, swaying back and forth together for the rest of the song.

In addition to being students, both Michael and Reese had jobs: Reese a part-time teller at Security Pacific National Bank and Michael at Calabasas Saddlery, loading hay onto trucks and delivering feed to local horse ranches, many owned by Hollywood celebrities. The Saddlery itself was owned by the host of TV's The Newlywed Game, Bob Eubanks, who nearly a decade earlier was a Los Angeles radio disc jockey and a driving force in bringing the Beatles to Los Angeles for their 1964 North American tour. The British band gave their first major press conference at the Cinnamon Cinder Club in North Hollywood, a club owned by Eubanks. But, even before all that, Bob Eubanks was a student at Pierce College and developed a zeal for horses and rodeo. He still enjoyed roping calves and steers and was partial to hiring from the current crop of college cowboys at his alma mater.

Getting ready to start their day of school and work, Michael shaving his face, Reese brushing her teeth, both listening to John Denver on the radio singing *Country Roads*. "You know," Reese remarked, removing the toothbrush from her mouth, soapy bubbles clinging to her teeth, "every time I hear that song it reminds me so much of you. Your voice sounds so much like John Denver, it's amazing."

"Well, thank you, honey," Michael replied, sluicing, then patting his clean-shaven face with a towel.

"I'm serious. You could have a future in music someday. I really think so."

"That's nice of you to say, but right now I'm late for class and then off to deliver hay."

"You should bring your guitar with you. Never know. You might get a chance to sing for Kenny Rogers or one of those guys you deliver to and get discovered."

He kissed her. "You're sweet. Gotta go. Bye."

Springtime, with newly emerging buds on the trees outside their window and warm California breezes, it seemed as if they had only just begun to dip into their ration of euphoric romantic temperament. But with summer, it all took a detour.

Rob Mattis, an old friend from Michael's high school years, popped in unannounced for a visit, arriving, astonishingly enough, via private jet. "It's my boss's plane. I'm just a glorified errand boy. Believe me, I don't get to jaunt around like this every day. But when he wanted me to zip over here to the Coast for him, I jumped at the opportunity. Who wouldn't, right? And what a great opportunity to look you up and see each other again, old buddy."

Embracing with manly hugs and claps on the back, then standing back at arm's length, sizing each other up: Mattis looking preppie in khakis, penny loafers, and V-neck sweater; Michael in cowboy boots, jeans and western buckle.

"So, um, what's up with the cowboy outfit?" Mattis wanted to know.

Michael summarized his foray into rodeo, Mattis silently taking it all in, nodding his head. "Hmmm, so what you're telling me is that you're doing this whole cowboy bit for a chick."

"No, no, it's not like that," Michael tried to explain, but for naught. The whole attraction of rodeo life was lost on his friend, the conversation then quickly shifting more toward the commonality of reminiscing all the fun times they shared back in their school days.

They sat up late talking, as old friends who have not seen one another for a long time do. It was around 2:00 a.m. when Mattis said, "Hey, wanna free ride back to Chicago? I'm the only passenger on the plane, plenty of room if you wanna hop aboard."

"I can't," Michael answered. "I've got stuff going on here. Besides, I can't just up and leave Reese."

"Oh, come on! Don't be a chump. Return to the old stomping grounds, cowboy. It'll be a blast, just like old times."

"I, uh, I don't know …."

"What part of 'golden opportunity' do you not understand?" Mattis asked, cocking his head like a puppy not understanding a command.

"It's summer. I'm offering you a free flight back to Chicago on a private jet ... and the chance to do fun stuff together again back in the homeland. The flight is just one way though, I'm afraid. You'll have to somehow get yourself back here to California ... that is, if you ever decide to return after all the partying we're going to do."

Errand boy or not, Michael was very impressed by the seeming success of his old school chum and, never having flown on a private jet before, it was too good an offer to pass up. He ran it past Reese and was pleasantly surprised that she offered little resistance. After waking her up and explaining the whole thing to her at three o'clock in the morning, she sleepily asked, "When are you leaving?"

"In a few hours."

"Seriously? How long will you be gone?"

"Couple weeks, I'd imagine. Just see a few old friends, visit my Nana, hang out with Mattis. Stuff like that. Probably get bored after just a few days. Can you call the Saddlery and tell them I got called out of town?"

"Of course. Oh God, I love you. I really do. I don't want to be away from you, sweetie. But wow, flying on a private jet. This really does sound like something you'll regret if you don't do it. I'll miss you every moment you're away. I really will."

Making love somehow seemed to consummate the decision. Afterwards, lying close together like two spoons in a drawer, just before drifting off to sleep, he whispered, thinking she was asleep and could not really hear, "I don't deserve you."

"I know," she whispered back.

18

LEAVING ON A JET PLANE

The plane, a French Falcon, was plush and fast, passing commercial jetliners off in the distant sky like the proverbial tortoise and hare. "What does something like this even cost," Michael asked, breathlessly taking in the plane's cabin, not even trying to contain his obvious sense of awe.

"You know the old saying, right? If you have to ask what something costs, you obviously cannot afford it," Mattis laughed. "But I will tell you this, maintenance alone on this aircraft exceeds a million dollars per year."

Michael let out a whistle, shaking his head, "Wow, so this is how the *other half* lives!"

Stopping in Pueblo, Colorado for refueling, the two friends wandered out onto the tarmac, standing alongside the plane as a ground crew pumped fuel into it. People inside the terminal were looking out at them through glass windows, apparently intrigued by two such young men with their private jet.

"Those people staring at us probably think we are movie stars or something," Michael commented.

"Or rich playboys," Mattis added, laughing.

Soon, back in the sky, the Rocky Mountains below were giving way to a vast expanse of flat land extending all the way to the Windy City.

"Won't be long now till we're back in good old Chi-town," Mattis said, looking out the plane's window. "Gonna get laid tonight. I told you I'm dating Dulcie Ryder, right?"

"Yep. Lucky you. She was really cute in high school."

"Remember her friend, Kendra? Kendra Paul?"

"Of course. I still remember sophomore year making out with her at a party. I have a vivid memory of us listening to the Beach Boys' Pet Sounds album. We started kissing to *Wouldn't It Be Nice* and by the time it got to *God Only Knows* I was heading to first base. But then she started going steady with what's-his-name, that basketball player?"

"Well, she doesn't have a boyfriend right now. Maybe the four of us can double date."

Within hours of landing at Midway Airport it was all arranged. The boys would meet the girls at some restaurant downtown at the Loop. It turned out to be a steak place, decorated in kitsch Western motif: branding irons and spurs adorning the walls and waitresses donning short, fringed Annie Oakley skirts and pink cowboy boots. "This place should make you feel right at home, cowboy," Mattis joked as they entered. Then, spotting the girls sitting at the bar, he made a beeline in their direction, giving Dulcie a pretty serious kiss.

Kendra swiveled on her bar stool to face Michael, a gracious smile prompting a hug from him and a kiss on the cheek. She looked amazing. Both girls did. But, Michael thought, Kendra especially so. No longer simply the cute teenage girl he had known in school, looking extremely grown-up now in black dress, high heels, hair and make-up fashionably perfect.

Kendra spoke first. "You haven't changed a bit," she said. "You look exactly the same as the last time I saw you."

"Is that good or bad?" he replied. "Because you have changed a lot, you've gone from wow to WOW!" It was a good line, without his meaning it to be a line, and from that moment on conversation was free and easy between them, between all four of them, as if no time at all had elapsed since high school. Laughing, reminiscing, and enjoying each other's company, they progressed from the bar – where, not quite yet of drinking age, they had merely been occupying space – to the dinner table. The filet mignon the waiter brought to the table so tender and delicious it was all Michael could do to restrain himself to eat in a civilized fashion rather than wolfing it down.

After a splendid dinner, a Checker Cab deposited the four of them near the walkway along the lakefront. With waves lapping at the shoreline and a full moon overhead, they strolled. Kendra, walking with the perfect posture of a ballet dancer or high-fashion model, began telling them about her first two years completed at Bryn Mawr College, a fancy all-girls school apparently of some renown back east in Pennsylvania that Michael had never heard of. She'd returned to Chicago for the summer, staying at her father's downtown apartment. Her parents were divorced, and her father was in Europe for the summer. Kendra had the place all to herself.

"Let's go there," Mattis volunteered. "Back to your place."

And so, they did. A taxi dropped them off in front of a building with sky-scraping stature, located directly across from the circular Marina Towers buildings. An elevator ride to one of the uppermost floors, then doors opening and Kendra leading the way into the apartment. It was truly magnificent, like something right out of a James Bond movie. Kendra opened sliding glass doors leading to a balcony that offered amazing views of both the city skyline and the lake beyond. Michael was rendered speechless. Never had he experienced such opulence.

"God, Kendra. This is the most beautiful apartment I have ever seen. What does your dad do to afford all this?"

"I know. It's nice, isn't it?" she replied without a hint of bragging. "He's a lawyer. Corporate work, travels all over the country on business, sometimes to Europe too. That's where he is right now. I've lived in this apartment, off and on, since I was little. Guess I've grown somewhat immune to just how impressive this place is."

"I thought you grew up in Downers Grove, like me," Michael said.

"I pretty much did. My parents split up years ago. I lived in Downers Grove with my mom, but some weekends and most summers I'd come here to stay with my dad. He's a great guy, really. We are very close. I know he feels bad that he can't be here with me right now. But he left me plenty of spending money, the keys to his car, and told me to try and have a fun time without him. All to assuage his parental guilt, I'm guessing." She chuckled, self-consciously. Then, changing the subject, "Hey, how about some music?"

Making her way to a large cabinet containing a TV screen and stereo equipment, pausing several moments, selecting the right music, the room filled with the opening bars of *Wouldn't It Be Nice*.

"The Beach Boys? All right, very funny. Who told you?" Michael asked, blushing.

They all laughed. "I cannot tell a lie," Dulcie replied, feigning a look of guilt. "Mattis told me the story and I thought it was so cute, I had to tell Kendra."

"Yes," Kendra added, "and now I finally understand why all these years I always think of you, Michael, every time I hear *God Only Knows*."

Everyone laughed again. Then, three tracks into the Pet Sounds album, Mattis and Dulcie disappeared into one of the bedrooms, not to be seen again until morning.

Kendra and Michael reclined on the sofa, watching the city lights twinkling outside in the night, listening to the sound of traffic on the streets far below, and the music of the Beach Boys. The moment felt intimate, Michael leaning close to kiss her lips, Kendra letting him. Feelings of arousal beginning to emerge. Then, interrupting further kissing, she said, "Picking up right where we left off, are we?"

"It almost feels as if no time has passed at all," he answered.

"Ah, but time has indeed passed," she told him, breaking their embrace and shifting her position on the sofa to put a few inches between them. "Tell me about your life in California."

The mood simmered from burgeoning heatedness to old friends just talking, feeling quite comfortable in each other's presence. Although there was a brief reluctance on his part when she finally asked about his rodeo adventures, figuring she could not possibly have real interest in any aspect of the cowboy life ... not this classy Bryn Mawr girl with the fancy penthouse apartment. But she was insistent, so he complied.

"In this so-called *Age of Aquarius* where our generation talks so much about freedom," Michael began, making little air quotes with his fingers at Age of Aquarius, "rodeo really is the ultimate freedom. Traveling from rodeo to rodeo, going wherever the open road takes you, free as a bird. I have a bunch of cowboy friends and we all just hang out together, party together, and rodeo together. Both college rodeos and professional."

"Colleges have rodeos?"

"Sure. Lots of schools out west have rodeo teams, just like football or any other sport. Some schools even offer rodeo scholarships."

"Gee, who knew?"

"Anyway, my one buddy, Jay, is an American Indian ..."

"Wait!" she interrupted with a laugh. "Your friend is an Indian cowboy? Isn't that an oxymoron?"

Not sure what oxymoron meant, he continued, somewhat bemused. "If Jay were here, he'd tell ya the *best* cowboys are Indians. Anyway, we both ride bulls. For me, there is absolutely nothing quite like the thrill of exploding into a crowded arena aboard two thousand pounds of wild Brahma bull! I am thoroughly addicted to that rush."

"Brahma bull riding? Bet there's not too many Hindu cowboys," she laughingly teased.

"None that I've met," he answered with a resigned shrug.

She chuckled. "You actually ride Brahma bulls?"

"Mostly bulls. Every once in a while I might also get on a saddle bronc or ride some bares," he replied.

"You're kidding, right? How does someone ride a bear?"

Now it was his turn to laugh. "Not bear, like grizzly bear. I mean bares, as in bareback broncs." She still looked puzzled. "Bucking horses. There's two kinds: saddle broncs and bares ... one is ridden with a saddle, the other ridden bareback."

"I see," she said, nodding her head. "And this is fun to you. It all sounds incredibly dangerous to me."

"It's a life I never knew growing up. One I'm discovering completely on my own, independent of everything I've been raised to know. Sure, it's dangerous, but everything in life is dangerous. It's all just a matter of degree."

He paused momentarily to determine if he might be boring her.

"Tell me more," she quickly reassured him. "This is all just so amazing."

"Oh, hell. Maybe I just watched too many cowboy movies growing up, I don't know. And it's sorta funny, I was a hippie in Colorado cowboy country where I started college and became a cowboy in hippy-dippy California. But I sorta feel like I have finally found the real me, the me I was always meant to be. Not just some kid from the suburbs."

He continued talking for some time. Unlike Mattis, who had displayed no interest when his friend tried to explain rodeo, Kendra sat transfixed, finding his description of rodeo life strangely alluring.

"Are there rodeos around here?" she wanted to know.

"Um, I suppose so," he answered haltingly. Though, if there were, he was pretty sure they would be nothing like the ones in the West.

"Take me to a rodeo," she said. "I really want to see you ride." Then, stretching her arms in the air with a yawn, signifying she was calling it a night, added, "It's a long drive back to the burbs ... and I think you've lost your ride." She gestured to the closed bedroom door beyond which Mattis had disappeared with Dulcie. "I think you should spend the night right here."

Any look of hopeful anticipation on Michael's face was quickly shut down. "Don't get the wrong idea. I mean, spend the night *right here*," she said, pushing her finger into the sofa cushion, "on this nice comfy couch."

That single night turned into an unanticipated lengthy stay at Kendra's apartment. Each day exploring the sights of the Windy City together, going to shows, eating in nice restaurants, walks along the lakefront; sometimes with Dulcie and Mattis joining them, sometimes not. Arriving in Chicago via private jet, hanging his hat in a downtown penthouse apartment, and cruising the finer establishments of the city with a beautiful, sophisticated woman on his arm, the redolence of romance and affluence was totally enticing. And, in an era of budding female independence, Kendra *insisted* on paying for many of their excursions – with money left for her by her absent father. To Michael, it all felt like visiting an upscale parallel universe from the one where Reese and rodeos existed. By the third night, he was invited to share her bedroom.

19

THE L WORD

It was Kendra who found it. Stashed away on a partially hidden shelf at the back of one of those corner magazine stands that sell what seems to be every publication known to the civilized world. A thinly folded newspaper with a black and white photo of a bronc riding cowboy on the front page: *Rodeo Sports News*, the official publication of the Rodeo Cowboys Association. Paying for the paper, Michael began scanning the list of sanctioned rodeos listed on the pages, discovering that there existed a whole Midwestern rodeo circuit he never knew about.

"There's a rodeo in Sikeston, Missouri this weekend," he muttered absently.

"Oh, let's go to it!" Kendra shouted, looking over his shoulder at the listing and tugging at his elbow excitedly. "Missouri is not that far. We can take my daddy's car."

"Entry fee is thirty dollars."

"You ride, I'll pay!"

"You're going to pay my entry fee? I can't let you do that," he protested.

"Sure! I have total confidence in you. It'll be like betting on a horse race, only I'm betting on a cowboy – you!"

Parking Kendra's shiny Mercedes Benz at the rodeo fairgrounds amid a sea of mud-splattered pickup trucks and horse trailers, every vehicle displaying the official blue oval-shaped decal of the Rodeo Cowboys

Association, Michael found it utterly amazing there could be so many cowboys within shouting distance of Chicago. The two made their way over to the rodeo arena, turning a few heads in the process, the Midwestern cowboys checking out the newcomers; Kendra's mini-skirt and sexy thigh-high suede boots drawing the most attention. As for this stranger with the pretty lady, the locals remained standoffish, curious if he had any talent at riding.

Soon enough the time of reckoning arrived, Kendra laying a zealous kiss on her cowboy before taking a seat in the spectator stands to watch Michael ride. Several cowboys were waiting for him at the chutes to help pull his rope. In bull riding, no saddle comes between bull and rider. The rider sits directly onto the animal and tightly fastens one hand to a long flat braided rope called, appropriately enough, a *bull rope*. A handle is braided into a portion of the rope, the other end of the rope goes around under the bull, through a loop, and back up so that the tail of the rope can then be wound around the rider's hand. Generally, a second cowboy helps to pull the rope tight around the bull while it's in the chute. This is all that keeps a rider connected to a bull for the required eight seconds, a relatively brief period that many have called *the most dangerous eight seconds in sports*.

Michael, straddling the chute containing a blondish palomino-colored bull, could hear the announcer's mic blasting: "Our next rider has come all the way from California to compete here today." If there was a built-in wariness against non-locals, far-away California was as non-local as it gets. The cowboy helping with Michael's rope offered a sardonic grin, chiding, "Well, well, a blond bull for a blond California prunie. I hope yer ready, Mr. Californee, 'cuz this here bull is one hell'uv'a buckin' son-of-a-bitch."

Taking his seat atop the bull, pulling his cowboy hat down so tight it caused the tops of his ears to bend, wrapping the rope tightly around his right hand and sliding up close, inhaling a deep breath, then nodding for the chute gate to open … the bull leaping out into the arena with rocket-like G-force, bucking and spinning. At some point an air horn goes off, signifying eight seconds have elapsed. The California rider releases his hand and goes flying off the bull, somehow managing to land on his feet in the arena dust. A clown lures the bull away. The ride is over. Kendra, up in the stands, is beside herself, applauding and screaming. The local cowboys are clapping the California bull rider on the back, laughing and joking with him. He has proven himself. But then the score is announced: 65. A low score. An initiation fee – welcome to the Midwest circuit. Michael understood: Keep riding like that and future scores will get better.

For Kendra, it was all terribly exciting. She completely understood why Michael was so enamored with the rodeo scene. Basically, it was the exact opposite of how either of them had been raised. She was living in a time when so many of her generation seemed obsessed with counter-cultural defiance of the older generation's norms. But this was turning anti-establishment rebellion on its head, not only rebelling against the older generation, but also their own generation. No drugs or peacenik hippie stuff here. This was a cowboy rebellion perpetrated by a suburban Chicago kid, plunging himself into a very different culture than either of them had ever known, one fraught with danger, travel, and excitement. Michael had morphed from the simple schoolboy she used to know and now achieved a sort of folk hero status in her eyes.

The next several weekends they traveled together to rodeos, often in small towns far away from the Chicago metro area, putting miles on the Mercedes and experiences on their life resumes. The Midwest rodeos were every bit as Wild West, these were real cowboys competing with the same fierce determination as any rodeo anywhere, and Michael was relishing being the young California bull rider with the fancy car and attractive *little honey* who always fawned over him as they walked about the fairgrounds, cheering him on whenever he rode. Kendra was immensely enjoying the flirtatious attention from the cowboys, but it was clear to all she was only interested in one buckaroo. And no matter how he did in the bull riding, back at the motel room Kendra made Michael feel nothing less than a champion!

"I feel like I've got my own personal groupie," he told her one evening, driving the Mercedes back to the city.

"You do, silly," she twittered.

It was the first weekend in August, driving the fifty-some miles back to the city from a rodeo in Kankakee, down a dark and lonely two-lane country road, Judy Collins' folksy-country hit *Someday Soon* playing on the radio, crooning about a girl in love with a rodeo cowboy and vowing to follow him wherever he roams. Kendra reached to turn it up, singing along, flashing smiles Michael's way.

"It's true," she gushed when the song finished, restating the lyrics: "I *do* know a young man who rides in the rodeo, and I'm quite happy to follow him down the roughest road I know." Then, leaning close, she whispered into his ear, "I love you." Those were the words Michael heard. What Kendra actually whispered was, "What would you do if I said I love you?" But Michael's brain did not process it as a question, rather a statement: *I love you*.

He drove on without reply. Kendra's use of the L word was like a bucket of ice water being thrust into his face. Very sobering. The couple weeks he told Reese he would be gone had already expanded to more than a month. A lot had happened in that time. Things he should not have let happen. The whole illicit, torrid thing with Kendra. This sojourn to the Midwest had been an exciting diversion, but it was time to get back.

"I'm gonna be heading home to California," he announced to Kendra as they approached the city, traffic beginning to slow on the expressway.

She appeared stunned by this. "Why?" she asked.

"It's just time. That's all."

"So, this is that part in the movie where the cowboy just rides away?" her voice carrying a tone of disdain.

He let it slide, driving without a reply.

"Take me with you," she offered, suddenly.

"What? That is crazy. You'll be going back to that fancy college in a few weeks. And what about your dad? Won't he want to see you before you head back off to school?"

"I'm just not ready for this to end," she said. "You and me. This whole cowboy thingy. This whole summer. I am just not ready for it all to end!"

"Kendra, I feel the same way. It's been great these past weeks with you. The best time I can ever remember. Really. But it's time. You know what they say, all good things must eventually end."

Leaning across the car's center console, using both her hands to unbuckle his belt, open the zipper of his jeans, moving her hand inside, and speaking in her most seductive voice, "Say you'll take me with you."

Using all the will power a young man in that position could muster, he pushed her away. "I can't! In fact, I hardly have enough money to buy a plane ticket. We've been spending more than I've been winning. No way I can afford two tickets."

In a heartbeat came her rebuttal. "I still have over two thousand dollars left of my dad's money. I'll take all the money out of the bank and, if you'll just take me with you, I'll pay *both* our air fares to California!"

Two thousand dollars was an absolute fortune, and reflecting upon all the fun times, not to mention great sex, they had all summer, it was tempting. But what about Reese? No, no, this was crazy. Truly insane. Kendra again moved her hand inside the front of his jeans, while Michael did his best to keep the car on the road without swerving.

The very next day he flew back to California … with Kendra.

20

WELCOME TO L.A.

Before the plane even landed at LAX he knew that this had been a colossal mistake. Being with Kendra in Chicago had been fun, exciting … and wrong. Still, if he had just left it there, returned to the West Coast alone, no one would ever know. But now, back on his home turf in California the two worlds were on a direct collision course, and he had no idea what to do about it.

The next couple days they stayed at a Marriott near the airport. "It'll be like a little vacation," he told Kendra. "Just the two of us hanging out here by the pool, relaxing and drinking margaritas." The undisclosed real reason, of course – he was hiding out from Reese until he had developed some sort of plan.

After two days of doing little more than working on their tans, she pressed, "This is fun, but when do I get to meet your friends? All these cowboys you've been telling me about. Especially the Indian one. I've never met an American Indian before."

Oh, what the hell. They couldn't stay holed up in a hotel forever. Time to venture out, take the metaphorical bull by the horns and see what happens. "You wanna meet cowboys?" he resolved as they chowed down dinner at the hotel coffee shop. "Fine. Let's go."

Renting a car, driving north on the 405 freeway, then Highway 101 through the San Fernando Valley toward Thousand Oaks, off at Kanan

Road, left on the frontage road; a little more than an hour total travel time before finally stopping at a small roadside bar in what seemed to Kendra to be the middle of nowhere. In the gravel lot filled mostly with pickup trucks, he parked the rental under the canopy of a small copse. Kendra, exiting the car, took in the establishment, a single-story stucco building festooned with wagon wheels and a sign on the roof: QUARTER HORSE INN – DANCING – COUNTRY WESTERN MUSIC.

Inside, the place was swimming with voices and faces, a fortissimo of loud staccato fiddle music with Charlie Pride crooning *Is Anybody Goin' To San Antone* emanating from the juke box, the aroma of stale beer and cigarettes, people wearing cowboy hats lined up against a long wooden bar, some seated on stools, others just leaning and standing. A few couples were dancing – gliding along the dancefloor like synchronized figure skaters – while several men were shooting pool over in the far corner. Kendra, standing there near the entrance door taking it all in, not sure just what to think, turned and looked at the cowboy who brought her. "Wow!" was all she could manage.

"Wanna dance?" Michael asked as soon as they entered.

"I wouldn't even know *how* to dance to this kind of music," Kendra replied, flummoxed.

Pulling her by the hand onto the dance floor, "Come on, I'll show ya. Let's cut a rug."

He began spinning her around, old-fashioned jitterbug-style, reminding Kendra of the dancers on American Bandstand she had watched as a kid. It was fun. The song ended and another began, a whiny steel guitar and some guy's mournful warbling about how his gal isn't looking for true love, she's just *Window Shopping*. Kendra had never heard the song before, but Michael somehow knew all the words and began singing along into her ear as they danced, managing between verses to inform her, "Great old song. Hank Williams. A classic!"

Twin fiddles and a mandolin began the third song, but she held up her hand in a gesture indicating stop, enough. Tendrils of hair lay damp against Kendra's forehead, her upper lip dewy, face glistening with perspiration. Fanning herself sprightly with her open hand, "I need a break," she ceded with exhaustion.

"Let's grab a beer," Michael suggested, leading her by the hand toward the bar.

Several of the men at the bar nodded hello, some clapping Michael on the back, welcoming him by name. All of them decked out in big hats, cowboy boots, big buckles.

"So, who is this little lady?" says one of them, his hat worn at a rakish tilt, giving Kendra the once over.

"Guys, this is Kendra. Kendra, these are the guys. Kendra's sort of, um, visiting ... from Chicago. She wanted to meet some real cowboys."

"Well, howdy Ma'am," one of them says, tipping his hat.

"Okay, let's not overdo it," Michael cut in, laughing. "Kendra, this is Teddy Bridges. His family owns a couple hundred acres over in Simi Valley. Be careful of him, he likes to fancy himself as a smooth operator with the ladies."

Kendra giggled, giving Bridges a big smile.

"And that big guy next to him, with his back to you, is Jay Yazzie."

Hearing his name, Jay, pivoting to face in their direction, exclaims, "Hey, pard! Where ya been? Haven't seen ya around fer awhile." Without waiting for a response, adds, "And who is this sweet mama?"

"You're Michael's Indian friend!" Kendra blurts without thinking, quickly regretting her inartful words.

"Little lady, I'm probably his *only* friend," Jay responds, causing some laughter among the ranks.

"No really, he's told me stories about you," Kendra says reprovingly, shaking her finger at him, adding to the levity.

"All of 'em absolutely true, I'm sure," Jay says.

"See, the reason there's so many stories about Yazzie here," Bridges chimes in, putting his arm around Jay in a comradely manner, "is cuz he's always gettin' in trouble cuz he's such a big, dumb, fuckin' moron ... excuse my language. But no, I'm serious. I remember one time, not long ago, right here in this very bar, some humongous asshole, bigger than old Jay here, shoves Jay, trying to get him to fight. Jay just stands there like some damn cigar store wooden Indian, like Kaw-Liga, not moving a muscle, staring the guy down. As soon as the guy turns his back, Jay, brandishing a beer bottle like it's some kinda warclub, shatters the bottle over the big guy's head. But that fella just shook the glass out of his hair, turned around and stood there with the most menacing grin on his face. You should'a seen the look of absolute terror on our old buddy here."

"Oh my God, what happened next?" Kendra asked anxiously, though wondering what a Kaw-Liga was.

"Well, watching all this unfold, a couple of us tried to tackle this Goliath who seemed to have a skull of Novocain. Soon a bunch more cowboys jumped into the fray, swinging fists and smashing furniture. At that point, the bartender, in true Wild West fashion, put an end to the altercation by pulling a shotgun out from behind the bar and threatening to blow everybody to kingdom come!" Pausing for effect before finishing the story, then, "But you know what the best part is?"

Kendra shook her head.

"Once the fight broke up, fearless Jay here was nowhere to be found. Disappeared. Flew the coop. Everybody had cuts and bruises from the fight 'cept old Jay. When he finally shows back up, not a scratch on him."

Jay took a slug of beer, set the glass down on the bar, and turned to Kendra with conspiratorial closeness. "Yeah, that's not quite the way I remember that story. But I'll spare ya the real details, you bein' a lady and all."

An hour or more passed, telling stories, drink after drink, the jukebox playing on and on, when Bridges drunkenly asks, "So, what happened to yer main squeeze? I saw Reese just a week or so ago and she was all, 'Oh boo hoo, I miss Michael so much ... can't wait till he gets back ... I love him sooo much.'"

Kendra bristled, staring down at the Coors in her hand, using her finger to chase condensation down to the bottom of the bottle before looking up at Michael, fixing him with a look that burned of silence, all at once questioning and accusing. It was a look that stopped all of them in their tracks, no one speaking another word.

Finally, a guttural utterance from Yazzie, "Uh oh."

Bridges, catching on that something was up, began shaking a finger at Michael, doing his best Ricky Ricardo voice: "Ohhh, Lucy, I think you got some 'splaining to do."

Yazzie, putting Teddy in a headlock, dragging him away a few feet farther down along the bar, saying, "Bridges, I think you might just need to shut the fuck up now."

"Kendra, I guess we should talk," Michael said, sheepishly.

"Hmm, ya think so?" Kendra answered, as if he had just stated the obvious.

"Let's go sit out in the car."

She took a long pull of her beer, slamming the bottle down on the bar. "Okay ... let's!" Kendra answered snappishly, heading for the exit, Michael trailing behind her.

Passing Bridges and Yazzie at their new location along the bar, Teddy, now released from the headlock, began waving his hand at the escaping couple, trying to gain their attention, shouting departing advice over the din of bar noise, "Hey man! Wet birds don't fly at night ... remember that, man!"

"What the hell does that mean?" Kendra asks, turning her head to look back at Michael.

Ushering her toward the door with ever quickening pace, "Who the hell knows?"

They sat inside the car in total silence for what seemed a very long time. The windows fogging over from their breathing, blocking the world out. Tiny rivulets rolling down the glass offering only distorted visibility to the outside.

"Okaay," she says, very slowly, drawing out the vowels. "Are we going to talk, or just sit here all night?"

Clutching the steering wheel tightly with both hands, Michael stared out through the windshield at the blurry darkness beyond, his mind struggling for purchase on his thoughts, trying to find the right words with which to begin, then finally turning his head to face her, but without utterance.

"So, who is this Reese?" she asks acerbically, letting the final S of Reese sibilate on her lips. "Some damn little cowgirl you were having a fling with?"

He began explaining, slow and cautiously at first, then words began erupting rapidly, probably offering more detail than was necessary. It became a blurting confessional moment that somehow took on a life of its own, until eventually collapsing upon itself.

Then he waited. Waited for some sort of response, expecting the worst.

But her demeanor remained calm, as if, perhaps, mentally processing all she had just heard. "You *live* with her," Kendra stated, repeating one aspect of Michael's confession. "So then, that's why we are staying at a hotel by the airport?"

Michael nodding, added, "You said you didn't want it to end."

"Neither did you … but now you need to get this sorted out. Decide how you want this to go," she demanded without emotion.

He was astonished by her pragmatic calmness.

"Take me back to the hotel now."

Leaning close to kiss her, she pulled away, saying, "You just go and take care of what you need to do."

After being away from her for so long, Reese looked even more radiant than he remembered. He wasn't able to take his eyes off her and told her so.

"I lightened my hair. You like it?" she asked.

"Me like it!" he grunted, like some horny cave man, pulling her close and kissing her hard on the mouth.

She gave a fluttered laugh, gently pushing him away. "I see you missed me."

The laugh, the careless push, all at once perceived by him as somehow infused with an ethereal sense of her knowing. A feeling of really *bad karma* quickly creeping in, beads of perspiration emerged on his brow. His fingers twitched nervously. Oh crap! Somehow, she knows.

But Reese did not know. Although, she quickly sensed something was not quite right, his body language oddly suspicious. Reaching up to brush back a lock of hair from his dampening forehead, she wondered what it could be.

"I have to tell you something," he offered as prologue.

She stood waiting, her expression concerned yet serene, and he could only wonder at a face capable of conveying both at once. Then, dispensing entirely with any semblance of subterfuge, another full confessional rapidly flowed from his lips, again containing more detail than was truly necessary.

Reese was completely taken aback, finding his words all at once too hurtful to be believed, her eyes becoming liquid, turning away to hide emotion, then shifting back to glower at him suspiciously. There was no way to measure the depth of dung in which he was now standing, but he sensed an immediate palpable change of barometric pressure in her presence.

"Do you love her?" Her tone decidedly frosty.

"No, not really," he parried, before realizing that was clearly the wrong answer. "I mean, no. Absolutely no! I don't know what the hell I was thinking." Taking her hand in his, continuing, "Reese, I love you. Only you."

Disconsolate, removing her hand from his, more emotional evolution, all the way from frosty to white-out arctic. Frustration and anger competing, pushing hurt to the side, culminating with a splenetic outburst. "Get out! Get out! And get rid of her!"

Leaving the apartment, the slamming of the door still echoing in his ears. Oh God, what had he done? He loved Reese. He hated himself for hurting her.

But he also felt sorry for Kendra. He had hurt her as well. She had flown all the way to California for naught, and spent the remainder of the money her father had left her in the process. Chastising himself for taking such unfair advantage of a girl who, obviously, had been carrying a torch for him since high school, he truly hated breaking her heart so brutally.

It was not at all the ending Kendra had anticipated when embarking upon this furtive romp with Michael. For her, merely a final whimsical adventure before settling down and marrying the man she truly loved: Her boyfriend at school this past year. John – a senior at Haverford College, whose proximity to Bryn Mawr had, some might say, fatefully brought them together – wanted to be her fiancé. His proposal, on bended knee, offering up a diamond in a velvet box did not go quite as well for him as he might have hoped. Kendra, having grown up watching her mother and father fall out of love and ultimately divorce, wasn't certain that marriage, especially so young, was the prudent life course. Fortunately, John was the patient type and when she turned down the velvet box, truthfully confiding she just wasn't one hundred percent sure, he suggested she go home to Chicago for the summer and think things through. He promised he would be waiting when she was ready.

And then, this other guy whom she had known in high school, tangentially for the most part except for one brief solicitous teenage kissing session at some party that she honestly could not completely recall, trumpeted into her summer. He was nice enough, and maybe even sort of cute, but certainly not anyone who could interrupt her feelings for John, her thoughts of the future, and all that entailed.

That is, until the whole cowboy thing. That intrigued her. Suddenly finding herself wanting something different, something more, before crossing over the Rubicon toward a life of marriage, family, and sameness that she could only hope might be better than what she'd observed in her parents. The concept of some Wild West rodeo lifestyle was about as *different* as anything she could have conjured, something so foreign that she pronounced it ro-day-oh before Michael corrected her with ro-dee-oh: Him painting a picture of rugged derring-do so vividly feral it made her moist in areas that need no mention. All at once, in her eyes, he went from being just some boy she once knew in school to being a blazing symbol of chimerical rebellion and adventure.

Oddly now, just as quickly, he had lost all such stature. But she harbored no regrets for, what some might call, her transgression of exploring this divergent path. It put things in perspective. The final page of a steamy, but mostly plot-less, paperback romance novella she would soon forget. A preferred ending scenario, she briefly lamented, might have involved Kendra bidding *adieu* to her summer cowboy, perhaps even breaking his heart – indeed, shattering it – on her way back to a place less foreign, and to the man she would marry who was waiting patiently for her return … but no matter.

21

JOURNAL

I'm crashing at Jay's place, writing this in the dark while he's asleep, holding a flashlight in my left hand while putting pen to paper with my right. A sleepless night for me, so much going on in my head. Reese kicked me out of our apartment because I cheated on her with Kendra. She dropped me flat, her words still echoing in my ears: *You don't live here anymore. Pack all your stuff into your car and go. And please, don't come back. Ever!* Who could blame her? What the hell was I thinking?

To be completely honest, I guess I just became lost in a whole other world, enjoying all the attention from a really sexy girl, hanging out in a fantastic apartment in a glamorous city, arriving at rodeos in a car that probably cost more than some people's houses, plus somehow suddenly and miraculously being able to ride bulls better than I ever had before. I felt like a freaking rock star! So swept up in it all and just so damn full of myself. I feel like an idiot now, though. What I did has to be the absolute stupidest thing ever! I am overcome with depression, the kind that only occurs when you mess up big-time and know there is no one to blame but yourself.

Which brings us to right now. Reese wants me gone, so I am blowing off the school year and getting out of Dodge ... making my exodus. That's what she wants. Jay and I have decided to head out to Colorado, New Mexico, and Texas to rodeo. He says he's tired of school anyway and sees this as an opportunity to pour himself into riding bulls full time, maybe even make it to the National Finals. As for me, all I own is some clothes and my rodeo gear. My heart is heavy but I'm traveling light.

22

COWBOYS & INDIANS

Near the Arizona/New Mexico border lies the town of Gallup, New Mexico. The area boasts one of the largest American Indian populations in the entire country. Jay Yazzie's good friend, Sonny Begaye, lived on the Navajo Reservation there.

"Sonny and I go way back," Jay was telling Michael as they traversed the barren stretch of pavement slicing through the desert landscape. "We used to compete in Indian rodeos together. It was Sonny what got me into rodeo from the get-go."

A quick glance over at his passenger, Michael appeared interested, so Jay continued as he drove. "Me growing up Indian in an upscale urban community like Santa Monica, I always felt like the odd man out. Yeah, I know, pretty weird to be a Native American bull rider from a California beach town, right? No weirder than a cowboy from Chicago, I suppose," he said, slapping the steering wheel with a loud quick laugh before returning to a more pensive tone. "I was a troubled kid. Got into fights a lot. The kids at school would poke fun at me. Called me Cochise, stuff like that. Both boys *and* girls would do it. Even the freaking Black kids and Chicanos. I was low man on the totem pole."

Another glance to see whether his pun was appreciated. "I barely knew my dad, so did not have any strong male role model in my life. And he never instilled in me any semblance of Native American culture. But my mother understood what I was going through. A schoolteacher herself, she shipped me off to Catholic boys boarding school out in Chatsworth, a school mostly comprised of rich white kids, because she didn't think the public school could handle me. So, I ran track and played on the tennis team in high school just to try and fit in. But it never felt quite right."

He paused, reflecting, collecting his thoughts while Michael sat silently cogitating on the mental image of his cowboy friend wearing shorts and tennis whites.

Jay continued. "See, in those days, before the urban sprawl of Los Angeles consumed the San Fernando Valley, Chatsworth was a little country town surrounded by horse and cattle ranches. Passing by these ranches each day, I met another Indian a few years older named Sonny Begaye. Sonny was from a reservation in New Mexico, trying his hand at working in the white man's world. Had a job as head wrangler at one of the local horse ranches. To me, Sonny was like a dark-skinned oasis shimmering in this valley of wealthy palefaces."

Jay paused again, shifting his eyes from the road toward the passenger seat, making certain his metaphor sunk in. "Anyway, long story short, the following summer Sonny invited me to return with him to his home in New Mexico. I jumped at the chance. However, living with reservation Indians, I discovered that I really did not fit in that world either. I was too much of an L.A. city kid. But, while at the reservation, Sonny introduced me to the sport of rodeo. He taught me to rope and ride. But it was way more than that. He taught me to have pride in myself as a person, and to have indigenous pride in my heritage and my people."

Sonny Begaye – driving a brand-new Ford F-250 pickup truck towing a matching horse trailer with large letters stenciled across both sides that read WORLD CHAMPION INDIAN COWBOY – met them near the entrance to the Navajo Reservation, where the macadam quickly subsided to dirt and gravel. Introductions were made. He was remarkably handsome, standing at least six feet, straight as an arrow and moving with the gracefulness of a mountain lion. He greeted them with a warm smile and welcoming words, possessing that certain sort of charismatic nature that transcends cultural barriers and makes people feel instantly comfortable in their presence. It was easy to see why Jay had been drawn to him as a boy.

Sonny gave a tour of the reservation not seen, most assuredly, by too many non-Indians. Michael learned that the residents prefer to be called Diné, pronounced Di-Nay, rather than Navajo. "Diné is from our own language and means the people," Sonny explained. "The word Navajo comes from a Tewa-Puebloan word – nava hu – meaning place of large, planted fields." Michael was completely enthralled and, though he must have stood out as the whitest face, never felt the least bit uncomfortable so long as he was with Jay and Sonny.

Extreme poverty was prevalent throughout the reservation, it saddened and guilted Michael to bear witness to such undeserved fate that had befallen Native Americans. Sonny, his wife Haseya – a tiny bronze-skinned woman whose cherubic cheeks were spotted with tiny rubies of acne – and their toddler daughter named Sonlatsa seemed to be among the wealthiest inhabitants, and it was obvious they were widely respected throughout the tribe. While many on the reservation lived in traditional dwellings, called *hogans* – circular mud-like structures that reminded Michael of the geodesic domes at Drop City – Sonny, Haseya, and Sonlatsa resided in a modern double-wide manufactured home.

Jay and Michael stayed ten days on the reservation, turning down Sonny and Haseya's offer of a guest room, opting instead for the traditional Diné hogan.

"Amazing," Michael told Jay on the first night before the two drifted off to sleep, "here we are living in a hogan, just like Indians."

Jay retorted, "Speak for yourself, paleface. I was *born* an Indian." Then he chuckled.

Sonny owned a string of horses, some cattle, and had a small roping arena. Afternoons were often spent with Sonny and Jay teaching their non-Indian friend to rope calves and steers. Sonny was amazingly good, of course. Jay was pretty handy. And Michael tried his best.

He likened roping a calf to playing basketball, only in reverse: instead of throwing a round ball through a hoop, you threw a loop around the roundish head of a calf … all while astride a galloping horse. Michael may have become somewhat adept at riding rodeo bucking stock, but he had zero experience at roping. Jay laughed each time his friend missed a calf, the rope sailing off into the wind and the animal running free. Sonny, on the other hand, would simply smile and say, "Yah-ah-teh," which in Diné means it's all good.

Being an excellent coach, Sonny directed the boys toward team roping. A steer, somewhat larger than the calves, would be released from a chute, running into the arena, with Jay and Michael, as a team, chasing after it on horseback. One would rope the steer's head and the other throw a loop around the steer's hind legs. This is the way it's done when rounding up cattle for branding and traditional ranch cowboys must be able to competently complete the task. Jay preferred being the "header" – catching the fast-moving steer with a loop around the head, which would slow the animal down so his teammate could swoop in and rope the back legs. Michael was the "heeler" – though his roping skills remained marginal.

One evening, to repay Sonny and Haseya for their hospitality, Jay and Michael invited them to dinner at a restaurant in town. Michael was stunned to see a sign in one of the restaurant windows that read NO INDIANS ALLOWED. "I didn't know such blatant discrimination persisted in these modern times," he said, pointing out the sign to Sonny. "After all, this is the 1970s! Haven't we all experienced the marches for justice and racial equality?"

"I don't think Indians got much inclusion in those marches you speak of," Haseya offered sadly.

They ate elsewhere, but Michael asked Sonny if such a sign bothered him.

"Nope," he calmly explained with a shrug. "The white folks have their places, and we have ours. But we are going to get it all back one of these days." He then went on to explain the Indian philosophy that the white man would ultimately destroy himself and the Indian would justifiably regain custody of the earth. He concluded by leaning across the table, very close to his new white friend, and softly whispering, "*Hózhó Nahasdlii*."

Jay smiled, nodding. He translated. "It means, all will be beautiful once more."

23

ADDICTION

Sharing warm hugs and manly backslaps with Sonny, Jay and Michael left the Reservation, Haseya and Sonlatsa waving goodbye as they drove away, leaving the desert behind and traveling up steep mountain passes, heading north to compete at the *Sky Hi Stampede* near Kremmling, Colorado.

Arriving three hours before the start of the rodeo, they checked the draw sheets to see what bulls they were assigned to ride that afternoon. The bull drawn for Michael was named Charlie Brown. "Good grief!" Jay spouted, quoting the cartoon character of the same name, then doubling over with laughter at his own humor.

Spotting a small group of cowboys leaning against a fence overlooking the herd of bulls, they sauntered over to ask if anyone knew anything about this particular bull. The cowboys, chewing and spitting tobacco in careless cowboy fashion, pointed with a nod toward a hairy giant of a bull that was standing alone in the back corner, other bulls giving him room as if he owned the entire pen. The beast had horns as thick as a man's arm and twice as long.

Plowing a three-finger dip into a lid of Skoal and stuffing the minty tobacco behind his lower lip, one of the cowboys muttered, "Which one a you jaspers got that bull?"

Jay pointed a thumb at his buddy.

"Hmph, that Charlie Brown is one mean sum-bitch."

"He ain't almost never been ridden, neither," another cowboy added, spitting a long brown stream of tobacco juice downward toward the bucking stock.

"That ain't the half of it," a third cowboy added, shooting his own brown stream a full six inches further than where his compadre's spittle had landed, as if it were a cuspidor distance contest. "That bull is plumb crazy, likes to *eat* cowboys for lunch. He'll spin around, chase down a rider, and stick one of them long horns of his right into yer gut if he gets the chance."

This, clearly, was not encouraging news.

"Could all be bullshit," Jay whispered to his friend, just out of earshot from the others, seemingly unaware of the pun. "Let's ask the clowns, they're the ones really ramroddin' this outfit. They'll know the *real* story on your bull."

True enough. When it comes to the bull riding event, the clowns perform a valuable service. They act as bull fighters, distracting a raging bull away from a fallen cowboy. Rodeo clowns have saved the lives of countless bull riders at rodeos all over the country. To do so efficiently, the clowns study and learn the habits of the various bulls.

"That bull's pattern is for a big move outa the chute followed by some big high jumps, then he cracks back to the left in a tight spin. Almost nobody ever makes the dinger on him but if you do, you could win big," one of the clowns told them, but also confirmed that this bull was so mean there was no way they could save a rider if it was determined to get him. Jay was shaking his head from side to side, glad it was not his bull to ride.

The rodeo got underway. It was time for the saddle-bronc riding. A few chutes over from where Jay and Michael were watching the action, the gate opened and a wildly bucking horse jumped and kicked its way down the arena. Abruptly, the cowboy flew out of the saddle … but his right foot stayed hung-up in the stirrup. In a frenzied motion that instantly got everyone's attention, the rider, with his foot still stuck, was being jerked up and down like a ragdoll as the horse continued bucking across the arena. In the stands, a hush fell over the crowd. One could almost hear the helpless cowboy's skull crack as the horse kicked him mercilessly with both hooves in the head over and over again. The rider's foot finally dislodged from the stirrup, but only from the sheer force of the horse *kicking* him away, and he came tumbling down to rest in a twisted, crumpled heap on the dusty arena ground.

Watching all this, Jay mumbled under his breath, "He's dead. Gotta be. Ain't nobody could'a survived those blows to the head." An ambulance sped into the arena to cart off the motionless body that only moments ago was a dauntless young bronc rider. "Well, it's kinda good news for you, pard," Jay remarked to his friend. "Ain't never seen two riders die at the same rodeo. Looks like you're in the clear now."

There are six primary events that comprise a typical professional rodeo and they generally are presented in this order: bareback bronc riding, calf roping, cowgirl barrel racing (the only event in which females compete), steer wrestling, saddle bronc riding, and bull riding. Bull riding is always the closing event. The most dangerous saved for last.

Charlie Brown was of the Scottish Highlander breed. Neither Jay nor Michael had ever before seen such a bull. He was huge and hairy with a bushy, thick coat. So big he barely fit within the confines of the bucking chute, his nose touching the front slide gate, tail pressing against the back, and a rack atop his head that would shame a Texas Longhorn – protrusions so extensive that the bull had to turn his head sideways and at a strange angle just to fit. This position had his horns parallel to one side of his body, putting the rider at a distinct disadvantage. Each time Michael attempted to take a seat atop the animal, sliding up close to his rope for a good hand-hold, that horn would bang his knee like a cudgel, preventing him from beginning the ride in a secure position.

He was taking a good bit of time trying to get it right. Just outside the chutes, a few feet away, one clown was poised intently at the ready for the gate to open, while the other gamboled around the arena in a comedic Groucho Marx lope, administering jokes to keep the crowd entertained until the rider was ready. The moment drew near. Michael could feel the animal's muscles quiver, anxious for the chute gate to open, to unleash all the power and strength it possessed and rid itself of this interloper.

With a hurried nod the gate flew open, Charlie Brown blowing wild from the chute, erupting, bounding out into the arena, bucking high and hard. The rider focusing on avoiding those extremely long horns whooshing back and forth across his line of vision, but the gravitation pull accompanying each upward jump forcing him to lean forward, barely dodging the noxious spikes by mere fractions of inches. The clock ticking away, skyward surges, hard-landings with bone-jarring impact, twisting, turning, lunging, and kicking up dust that engulfed bull and rider like a tornado.

Three more strong leaps before starting a spin to the left, the rider feeling himself sliding into the well of the spin, sucked into a whirling vortex, right spur losing its grip. He tried not to think about the words heard earlier, *that bull likes to eat cowboys for lunch*! Only five seconds into the ride his face was buried in the arena dirt, the clowns distracting the animal away but not before it trampled the prone rider.

Scrambling on hands and knees, trying to put distance between himself and the thrashing bull, awkwardly gaining his feet and running for the safety of the fence but stumbling, unable to put weight on his left leg. Looking down, his boot was ripped, jeans torn, and blood was gushing from the leg. Clenching his jaw against the pain, one of the clowns helped him hobble to safety. "Ya didn't make it to the dinger but you was one helluva crowd pleaser," he heard him say.

Back behind the safety of chutes, a medic working the rodeo cleansed and bandaged the wound. "That'll hold ya for now, but it's just a poultice, you need to see a doctor straight away," he admonished.

Soon it was Jay's turn to ride. His bull was a Brahma, long-legged and built like a racehorse but with a hump on his neck and shoulders. "I'll be lookin' for eight when they pull that gate," he rhymed as he prepared to mount the animal. But Jay, too, hit the dust before the qualifying eight seconds had elapsed.

The rodeo ended and the two California bull riders left Colorado, heading to Odessa, Texas and Lovington, New Mexico to compete in two rodeos held concurrently. But the Sky Hi Stampede had a chilling effect, renewing their faith in consequence, especially for Jay Yazzie.

As they drove the winding road down the mountain, toward the flatlands of Texas, Jay gave an audible sigh. "Rodeo is a disease. An addiction," he said, conclusively.

"Yeah?" Michael replied, hunkering down on the passenger side of the truck's cab, pulling his cowboy hat down low to shut out daylight and closing his eyes, hoping a nap might ease the leg pain. "How so?"

Jay began to wax on rather philosophically, knowing he had a captive audience. "Take you, for example ..." he began.

"Okay, take me," Michael mocked.

"No, seriously," Jay continued. "I'm Indian. No offense, but you, my blond, blue eyed friend, look more like a poster boy for some beach party movie than you do the Marlboro Man. You are the epitome of the white man world where I had struggled for so long to fit in growing up. Yet you have escaped into *my* world, a world where cowboys and Indians are one and the same."

"What's your point?" Michael grumbled from under his hat, his leg was throbbing and he was in no mood for idle chit-chat.

"So, here you are at the Sky Hi rodeo and you draw a downright lethal bull. Everybody warns you that this bull is one bad-ass mother. To make matters worse, the same day, a bronc rider gets kicked in the head and killed. We both watched that rider die. After that, I really thought you might decline the ride. I would not have thought any less of you if you'da turned that bull out, refused to ride it. In fact, I *advised* you to turn the bull out. But you got on that goddammed killer bull anyway."

From the passenger seat, Michael stretched and yawned. "Cut to the chase, Kemosabe."

"Pardner, the way I look at it, guys like you have a lot going for them. You could return to the mainstream white world from which you came at any time, become doctors, lawyers, businessmen or whatever. With bull riding, it's not a question of whether ya might get hurt. That's a given. It's a question of just how bad yer gonna get hurt. And to climb on a bull with a reputation like that one and risk everything is either purely stupid, or it's an addiction beyond control. I know you're not stupid, so figure it must be the latter. That's when I decided that rodeo is an addiction, a disease."

Jay poked his passenger to see if he was still awake.

"I'm listening," Mike assured him.

"My point is that I, too, feel addicted to the rush of climbing on a ton of smokin' wild bovine. Nothin' like it, man. Nothin'! Like the sticker on my truck bumper says: I'M A LOVER, A FIGHTER, A WILD BULL RIDER! But, just between you and me, little buddy, this whole thing has caused me to re-think my own position on being a life-long rodeo cowboy. Might be an addiction I need to quit."

24

ROYALTY

And then the truck broke down. It could have been worse. It could have been out in the middle of nowhere, where the two-lane stretches endlessly toward the Tejas horizon with no help for miles. Luckily, it broke down just as they entered town, right in front of an oversized roadside billboard that read WELCOME TO ANDREWS, TEXAS – OIL CAPITAL OF THE WORLD, a stone throw from Odessa and just down the street from an auto repair shop.

With the truck laid up for a few days, they used the last of their collective funds to rent a car. The only one available in all of Andrews was a red Pontiac Firebird. A sporty little machine, especially compared to the truck. The girl who worked at the car rental place, named Patti, asked Jay if there was anything further she could do for him. He answered with a sly wink, "Well, do you know where a couple of California cowboys can grab a good meal and then latch onto some loose Texas cowgals?"

She laughed, recommending a local Andrews nightspot called Pepper's. "A total kicker joint," she said.

"Kicker joint?" Jay was not familiar with the reference.

"Shit-kicker. You two will fit right in."

Pepper's was packed with big hats, tight jeans, and scuffling boots as everybody shuffled around the dance floor, two-stepping to Texas Swing music. They were seated at the bar when Jay spotted Patti from the car rental place with a few of her girlfriends. She waved hello and walked over with one of her friends. "Hey y'all! I understand y'all are just a'lookin' for some loose women?" her friend teased. Her name was Debbie and Michael thought her lilting accent was as cute as she was.

"Which of you two fine young gentlemen is gonna dance with me?" Patti asked. Jay leapt to his feet and they two-stepped out onto the dance floor.

"Guess you're all mine, sugar," Debbie said, extending her hand for Michael to dance with her.

"I can't. Bum leg. Last time I danced was with a bull at a rodeo in Colorado."

"Ohh, I'll bet that hurts a lot, don't it?" she cooed, sliding onto the bar stool next to his. "Anything I can do to make it feel better?"

"I'm gonna pass on the Lovington rodeo," Jay said the following morning, waking up at Patti and Debbie's house. "Just gonna hang here with my new Texas sweetie. Besides, I wanna keep an eye on my truck. Make sure it gets fixed proper." Michael wondered if this had anything to do with Jay's rodeo addiction epiphany espoused earlier.

He drove alone to Lovington, New Mexico, less than two-hours away, arriving early enough to watch the rodeo parade. It seemed Lovington's entire population lined the streets to watch horses, chuck wagons, trick ropers, high school bands, girl scouts, all marching along the town's main street.

Michael intended to make his ride, then turn around and head back to Texas. His leg was tightly bandaged as he limped toward the chutes. The bull he drew was the exact opposite of the one in Colorado: it was smallish with no horns, red colored, but known to be an agile, powerfully quick animal that could be hard to ride.

Setting himself down on this feisty little bull, it snorted and reared up two times in the chute, as if to let the cowboy know it had no intention of making this easy. Though he'd taken some pain pills earlier his leg was still hurting as he locked his gloved riding hand extra tightly into a death grip on the bullrope, slid his body up close, tucked his chin to his chest, and nodded for the chute gate to open.

Lunging into the arena, the red bull energetically jumping and kicking like the healthy livestock athlete he was bred to be, making quick little turns, zigging and zagging with calculated tried-and-true maneuvers, doing his best to dislodge the human impediment from his back. His moves were fast but the rider felt completely in synch with him, somehow anticipating the animal's every move and shifting his own weight with that of the bull to stick like glue through every gyration executed. Flowing in a natural rhythm with the animal, tapping into his zone and feeling in control, to Michael the ride seemed almost to unfold in slow motion. The exact right bull and moment in time when everything just seemed to come together.

In the final seconds the bull went into a fast, tight spin to the right. A rider finding himself leaning too far left would get whipped into the stratosphere by centrifugal force, but this rider leaned with him, right into the spin, and felt so confident aboard this twisting toro that he was laughing and yelling "Yippee!" as his spurs kept moving in cadence to the jumps, racking up points with the judges.

"Let's hear it for this California cowboy!" came the announcer's excited voice. The ride drew hearty applause from the stands, and earned a score that placed Michael second in the standings; lining the pockets of his jeans with some desperately needed cash.

Exiting the arena, still limping, a river of adrenaline blocking most of the pain in his injured leg, he passed the Lea County Fair Queen out behind the livestock pens, an attractive young woman named Becky Sue. Her title was emblazoned on a sash across her torso and she wore a rhinestone tiara attached to her cowgirl hat. The local celebrity that she apparently was, Becky Sue had a retinue of people buzzing around her but waved to Michael like some smiling cheerleader, offering enthusiastic congratulations on a great ride.

"Thank you," he said. "Gee, I've never spoken to royalty before."

The cute little fair queen twittered, "Well before meeting *y'all*, I'd never spoken to anyone from California before."

"You lived around here your whole life?"

"Well, not yet, I reckon," she answered.

He smiled, acknowledging her witticism. They chatted for several minutes as he stowed his gear and prepared to head back to Texas. He had a bull to ride the next afternoon in Odessa.

"Oh, must you leave right away?" Becky Sue asked, sounding disappointed. "There's a big rodeo dance this evening. Please say you'll stay long enough to have a dance with me."

Elaborately sweeping the hat from his head and bowing deeply at the waist, like a knight to his queen, Michael replied, "How can I possibly refuse, M'Lady?"

The rodeo dance was held nearby at the VFW hall. When he arrived, Becky Sue was already in the process of leaving to attend to one of her fair queen duties but managed to stay long enough for the promised dance with Michael. One dance and she was gone. Well, that was hardly worth hanging around for, Michael thought. Standing alone now, surveying the noisy dance hall, he found himself casting admiring looks toward a girl who, in his opinion, was the prettiest one there.

Before long, this very same girl walked directly over to him and abruptly kicked him in the shin. Ouch! The same leg he'd injured in Colorado, causing the pain to flare up once more. Michael thought perhaps she had felt offended because he had been more or less staring at her, so he just limped quietly away.

She followed him, reached up and stole the hat from his head. This was becoming annoying. Retrieving his hat from her and turning again to leave, he heard her say to her friend, "He sure is a frigid one, ain't he?"

She approached again, this time her demeanor completely different, saying hello in an exaggeratedly timid little-girl voice ... before once more absconding with his hat, skipping off laughing. Not certain whether this might be some sort of flirtation, he walked over to again retrieve the hat. Handing it over, she said her name was Carol and asked if he wanted to go to a woodsie with her. He nodded, though not certain what a woodsie might be.

Within moments, they were in the rented red Firebird speeding down a dusty New Mexico Road. "Wow, such a fancy car. You must be one heck of a bull rider," she gushed with exaggerated appreciation.

Arriving at a remote spot out in the country, near a reservoir, they came upon a dozen pickup trucks parked in a circle and a crowd of folks, each with a drink in their hand, gathered around a bonfire. "See? A woodsie," she explained. Carol made the appropriate introductions, embarrassing Michael by bragging to all that this was "that California guy who made the great ride at the rodeo ... and he's with me!"

Sitting around the fire drinking beer, soon Carol announced her intent to go swimming in the reservoir. No one would join her. Michael declined, telling her he didn't have a change of clothes. She just thought that was the funniest thing. "Your clothes won't get wet, silly. Take 'em off and leave 'em on the ground."

"I don't think so," he said, pointing to his bandaged leg.

"Why, *everbody* knows this here reservoir is famous for its healing water," she informed him laughing. "Folks come from all over *'merica* to take a plunge. Even from all over the world, I *'spect.*"

The water was freezing cold, but they managed to keep each other warm. After a dip in the icy waters of the reservoir, Michael introduced Carol to "what we Californians call the *Horizontal Hula*." She thought that was a most amusing thing to call it, but already knew all the moves!

25

THE PARTY

Returning to California flat broke after traveling the southwestern rodeo circuit, the wandering bull riders went their separate ways. Jay wrangled a job working at the college veterinary clinic. Michael hired on at a ranch in Thousand Oaks, the very sort of *real* cowboy job he had always fantasized about as a boy. The nominal roping skills learned in New Mexico came in handy. Hours in the saddle herding cows, roping and rounding them up for ear notching and vaccinating was work he enjoyed – the more quotidian repairing of fences, digging post holes, blistering his hands swinging an ax or sledgehammer under a hot California sun, while still hobbling on an injured leg, much less so. Meager wages included a roof over his head – a tiny wood-paneled four-room bunkhouse nestled under the spreading branches of a two-hundred-year-old Encino oak tree that he shared with a fellow cowboy roughly his own age named Rick Braden. The two became fast friends.

Rick noticed his roommate coming out from a shower one evening after work and was alarmed: "Damn! That leg is all swelled up. You best have a doctor look at it. The sooner, the better!" The injury sustained at the rodeo in Colorado had taken a turn for the worst. Indeed, his calf and ankle were now swollen as thick as his thigh. He'd had no money or insurance to see a doctor and had decided to just tough it out. But medical attention now seemed urgent.

The doctor examined the swollen limb, dictating words as he probed to a nurse who was taking it all down. With his dictation completed, he straightened up, stroking his chin, staring off into space for several long moments, deep in thought. An excruciating silence through which a torrent of possibility noiselessly roared.

What the doctor then told Michael truly put the fear of God into him. "I'm not gonna pull any punches here, son. The leg is grossly infected and should have been properly treated long ago. Because you waited so long, there's a very real chance you might lose that limb." The notion of losing his leg was terrifying, how could he have been so stupid not to see a doctor sooner?

Frightening days in the hospital followed with his leg elevated and fluids being pumped into him, worrying whether he would ultimately leave with limbs intact, walking out on his own, or as a wheelchair-bound young man with his life inalterably changed. The pain that had disappeared for the most part some time ago, replaced by a numbness that fooled him into apathy, now returned in spades as his treatment progressed. Real pain! How was this a good thing? Nurses came and went. Was it his imagination, or did they leave his hospital room shaking their heads in dismay? The doctor, however, began to appear more optimistic with each passing day, assuring his patient that the returning pain was a positive sign.

When at last he was released from the hospital, it was with a mandate of several more weeks on crutches and no more cowboy work for a while … but he would keep his leg.

Occasionally the ranch was used by various Hollywood studios as a movie set. Whenever that happened ranch hands could earn extra money by camping outside all night, guarding the sets. Easy work that paid far more than their regular day jobs on the ranch, and perfect for a cowboy on the mend. Luckily, a Woody Allen movie was shooting at the ranch that would take weeks to film. By the time the movie folks finished, Michael's leg was mostly healed and the heft of newfound cash weighed heavy. "Let's throw a party!" Rick suggested. "No better way to spend it."

Word spread quickly about the party and nearly a hundred people showed up. Parked cars, trucks, and horse trailers scattered over an extensive swath of the property as people arrived.

Among the first of the arriving throngs was a flirty cowgirl named Sallie Ann Sawyer, flanked by two female friends who came looking for a good time. With SAS as her initials, everyone called her Sassy. She was known for being a rather well-navigated young woman with a particular penchant for rough stock riders, the type of girl commonly referred to by cowboys as a *buckle bunny*. Michael thought she was sexy as hell as she sauntered toward him and offered an inviting smile. A few drinks into the party found the two of them reclined on the bunkhouse sofa, brazenly kissing and fondling each other in a public display of licentiousness, both knowing where this inebriated behavior would soon be heading. That is, until Michael chanced a glance toward the opening front door of the house. Who he saw entering instantly sobered him.

It was Reese Walker. They had not seen each other in nearly six months, but in that single moment his world changed. She stood in the open doorway looking like a work of art in a frame, an aesthetic that took his breath away. She took a few short steps inside, appeared to be scanning the room but glancing over him without notice. Then, turning away, she walked back outside.

Michael leaped from the couch he had been sharing with Sassy and ran to the window to peer out. Reese was standing near the ancient oak tree … all alone. Girls don't usually come to things like this alone. They usually come with friends, or maybe a date. Surely she must have known that the party was being thrown by Rick and him. Could it be that is why she came alone? Perhaps hoping to reconnect with him? Michael dared to hope.

She began walking back toward the house, apparently to reenter. Michael dashed back to the couch, taking up his former position next to

Sassy. Reese headed for the kitchen where a small group had congregated, passing right by Michael and his date without so much as a glance. Though, she had to have seen them. He hoped seeing Sassy with him might cause Reese to betray some emotion, but she appeared completely unaffected.

He got up again, leaving Sassy on the couch alone. “Hey! Where do you think you’re goin’?” she warbled with an alcohol induced slur, grabbing at his belt to prevent his escape. He broke free, walking to the other side of the room. Leaning against a wall that offered direct vantage of Reese standing in the kitchen socializing with friends, he waited for her to walk his way. He waited a very long while, but Reese remained in the kitchen, laughing, talking, and seemingly having a good time. The urge to speak with her grew ever stronger.

It was well after midnight, the festivities beginning to wind down, the crowd thinning out, but Reese remained. Michael mustered all his courage, walking over to where she was still standing in the bunkhouse kitchen, and asked if they could talk. She looked him directly in the eyes with a challenging stare that nearly caused his knees to buckle. Then her look softened. Offering the most elegant of tiny nods, she silently began a deliberate walk toward the door leading outside, with Michael following close behind like a pleasantly surprised puppy.

Out in the cool night air, they walked without speaking until texture vanished from the party noise and it became but a dull murmur in the distance, moon and stars the only illumination. Always remaining a few steps ahead, he followed close, something telling him if he did not stay near to this woman she might suddenly vanish forever.

Suffering a long helpless pause, his mind searched for the right words. Words that might defrost a frozen heart, but he remained reluctant to pierce their silence. “I took a literature class once,” he managed to mumble at last, not at all certain where he was going with this. “But most of the books we had to read were pretty much on the boring side,” he added as an afterthought, shaking his head slightly, the last few syllables drifting away in the passing breeze.

She continued walking. He heard an apathetic sigh.

"There were a lotta words in those books, but I don't think even Mr. Webster has a word to describe what I'm feeling right now." His speech beginning to gain momentum, as if on a roll somehow with this literature track. "And if any of those books had a story with someone like you in it, well it would be worth reading to the very last word on the very final page." He stopped to catch a breath. "But I wouldn't want to reach that final page, though … because I'd want the story to continue."

He thought he saw her nod, but her back was to him and he could not be sure in the darkness.

"Actually, I don't want to *read* the story … I want to *write* the story! Co-author with *you*. A whole new chapter of our lives, one I could not imagine writing with anyone else."

Her head tipped back slightly, looking skyward at the stars as she continued with measured steps.

"Reese, you deserve so much better than someone who would treat you the way I did."

This time he was certain he saw her nod. Her walking slowed a bit.

"I can't change the past. I wish I could, I really do, but I can't. All I can do is promise to do better, to be a better person. If there is any way you would consider taking me back, even after all the incredibly dumb-awful things I have done, I will spend the rest of my life making it up to you. I have missed you so much. My greatest hope has always been that I'd get another chance to treat you right. Please, let tonight be that chance."

Abruptly she stopped her walking, turning to face him, studying his face in the moonlight as if to assess his sincerity. They stood there in the nocturnal countryside without speaking, just reading each other's faces. Then, leaning in and touching her lips to his, she kissed him.

26

JOURNAL

Funny thing, Reese is the reason I began rodeoing in the first place but, getting back together, she laid down the law: No more rodeo! Odd, coming from a gal who wears a trophy buckle the size of a car hubcap, but I did not argue. Whatever makes her happy, I'm there. Besides, nearly losing my leg, the mental image of hobbling around as an aging one-legged ex-bull rider was plenty of incentive to quit. And, let's face it, I was never going to be a world champion. Not even close.

So, I'm now working in the fast-food industry, recently promoted to assistant manager of Carl's Jr. – the one on Topanga Canyon Boulevard, across from Topanga Plaza mall. For sure not as glamorous as being a cowboy, but steady work. Truth be known, I pretty much hate it, but I've got to start making something of myself if I'm going to be a husband. Yes, that's right, *husband*. We are engaged. Reese still works at the bank and we've been saving our combined earnings to pay for a wedding. Traditionally it is the bride's parents who finance a wedding, I'm told. But her parents are unwilling to contribute in any way. In fact, they seem to be doing everything they can to break us up.

And the reason they oppose us getting married? Religious differences. Reese and I, as her parents so disdainfully put it, are not *equally yoked*. The Walkers are staunch Southern Baptists and don't much care for their daughter being involved with a *Catholic*. Reese's father claims Catholics are not even Christians. Crazy, huh? I'm discovering that there seems to be no position on which people are so immovable as their religious beliefs, and there is no more powerful ally one can claim to back them up than Jesus Christ, or God, or Allah, or whatever one prefers to call their Supreme Being.

Why does religion, or sometimes lack of religion, always become an issue anyway? Seems I've been down this road before. Apparently I didn't have enough Catholic guilt to share the view of high school sweetie Kimberly, that if we had sex God would impregnate her with a two-headed baby just to punish her; I wasn't Jewish enough to even *date* Erica Berg; I was *too* religious to be acceptable to Maggie's atheist mother; and now, because I was raised Catholic, I am not Christian enough for Reese's Baptist parents. How can so many people be so intolerant and dogmatic about something that is so completely unknowable to any living person?

Throughout history there have been countless relationships thwarted in the name of religion, I am sure. Not long ago I read a story that in the 1950s James Dean and an actress named Pier Angeli were in love, but her mother broke them up because Dean was *not* a Catholic. The mother arranged for Pier to marry singer Vic Damone, an Italian Catholic. Sixteen years after James Dean died in an infamous automobile crash, Pier Angeli committed suicide. Her suicide note stated that James Dean was the only man she ever truly loved, and she wanted to be with him again in the afterlife. The moral of the story? You should never let religion get in the way of true love!

So, I told Reese's parents the story of James Dean and Pier Angeli one evening when we all sat down to have a heart-to-heart talk. Her parents said they actually remembered when it happened. We then informed them that we intended to get married, with or without their blessing. Her mother finally conceded somewhat, telling us she would be able to accept "the inevitable" so long as we promised not to get married in a Catholic church and promise that we will not raise our future children as Catholics. Reese rolled her eyes, at which point her father chimed in, angrily emphasizing that he would rather see his daughter dead than standing in front of a Catholic priest getting married!

And he declared there will be absolutely no alcohol served at our wedding. I reminded him that Jesus turned water into wine at a wedding celebration. He just gave me an angry look and told me that true Christians knew it was non-alcoholic wine. The logic of why Jesus would create a non-alcoholic wine, simple grape juice, for people to celebrate with at a wedding, I find baffling. But it does not matter. Our marriage won't be affected by what building the ceremony is held in, whether there's wine, or who officiates. Love is love.

27

JOURNAL

I lost my job at Carl's Jr. The axe fell one evening after we had closed up for the night. The manager called me into his little office in the back, behind the cooking area. He sat me down, looked me in the eye and said: "Mike, after careful consideration, I have decided that you are just not cut out for the burger world." He handed me my final paycheck, I handed him my greasy apron, and that was that. Not cut out for the burger world? Seriously? I might've laughed were it not for the pain in my heart.

See, the week before, Reese and I had broken up. Most likely that is why I lost my job. Who could be expected to be happily flipping burgers when their heart is totally broken? Yes, that's right, Reese dumped me ... for the second time. Okay, I know I deserved being dumped the first time, but this go-round I thought I was doing everything right. It didn't matter. She's been living with her parents, who never accepted our religious differences (and pretty much despise me for being Catholic), and they've been putting so much stress on Reese that she finally caved.

We were sitting in my car outside the bank where she had just gotten off work. It was early evening but already dark and the drizzle that had lingered all day now turned to light rain drumming softly on the metal roof overhead. We kissed, we talked, we cried, we kissed some more. Her kisses were confusing – both welcoming and stand-offish, foreign and familiar. It was as if we both knew our story was finally coming to an end and simply wanted our lips to be touching when it did.

She confided all the turmoil with her parents had simply worn her down, made her feel as if something had just up and died inside her. Just then, I mean at that exact moment as if on cue, Carole King's song *It's Too Late* came on the radio. It was that hinge moment when we knew the end had arrived. Our swan song.

We held each other close, listening: *Something inside has died, and though we really tried to make it, it's just too late*. It was true, it did feel like something between us had died, we were not going to make it. When the song finished, we knew we were saying our final goodbyes.

It was only after I drove away that the sadness of it all began to really sink in. A feeling that my world had been torn asunder, and the sadness followed wherever I went for weeks, worsened by a series of further calamitous events. Right after getting fired, my car's engine blew up! So, suddenly I had no wheels. With no car to look for a new job, I quickly ran out of money. No longer able to pay the rent on my apartment, I got served an eviction notice. The world seemed to be collapsing upon me. No girl, no car, no money, no job, and on the verge of homelessness. My father often used to tell me that I was worthless, and all of this seemed to be proving him ultimately correct. A miscreant wastrel. Crap, I wasn't even good enough for the damn burger world!

Depression settled over me, smothering. Life became a daily crawl, actually more like swimming through mud, sinking into a downward spiraling, diminishing, darkening universe. It felt impossible to fight my way out of it. The present was unbearable, and the future didn't exist, offering little reason to go on. I became convinced that life was just not worth living.

Unable to sleep without the aid of pills, one night I swallowed the *entire* bottle of sleeping pills, washing them down with half a bottle of tequila. As my body became heavy with the weight of grogginess, I embraced the notion of escaping into an eternal slumber from which there would be no return. Those words played in my head, *from which there would be no return*. I spoke the words aloud, hearing them outside my head for the first time. With a jolt, the reality suddenly hit me that if I allowed sleep to come, I would never wake up. Never!

I found myself nervously reassessing my situation. A quote from Shakespeare flashed through my brain: *To be or not to be.* Wait! I wanted more options. I wanted to do both somehow: I wanted to live, to continue to *be*, if only the gloom of depression would go away and let me do so in peace.

With my head in the toilet, purging myself of the booze and pills, I desperately prayed for help from a higher power. It may sound insane to say I found Jesus in a toilet bowl, but that is exactly where I found him. At that precise moment I allowed Jesus to enter my life and, like a glorious sunrise after a dark and frigidly cold night, my world slowly warmed and brightened.

Already appropriately on my knees embracing the porcelain containing fouled toilet water, it may as well have been holy water for the euphoria washing over me. My life suddenly had new meaning. I now realize the most majestic choice we can make in life is to simply continue living. Why did I not see this before?

I have never been overly religious, but since that night I have developed some very personal attitudes towards God and Jesus Christ. Though, not necessarily in the context of the usual organized religions. More spiritual. To me, spiritualism is a personal relationship, whereas organized religion is more like crowd control.

The way I see it, Jesus taught us to love one another and forego material possessions to the extent practical. I think, perhaps, the closest I have ever come to living in the manner prescribed by Christ was when I was at Drop City. Crazy, huh? But everything at the commune was shared and ownership of material items limited to few possessions. Historically, the first Christians lived this way. Organized religion has lost sight of Christ's simplicity. This is likely why all the different factions, denominations, seem to conflict with one another.

All I truly know is that since accepting Jesus into my life, it is as if an enormous burden has been lifted. I feel lighter than air. A reborn child of God! All I had to do was open my heart and let His grace flow into me.

Just days later I noticed a job posting at the college. It was for a surgical orderly position at nearby Canoga Park Hospital. I had absolutely zero experience and wasn't even sure what duties an orderly performed, but with renewed hope I interviewed for the job and, in what should be considered nothing less than miraculous, I was hired. Basically, the job involved pushing a gurney around, picking up and delivering surgical patients from their hospital bed to the operating room, then to recovery room, and back.

Managing to *ambulate* (a word I learned from being an orderly) my dilapidated auto to the hospital parking lot, I worked by day and slept in the car at night. My boss, the head surgical nurse named Wilma, after discovering me sleeping in my car, made it her routine to tap on the car window each morning to wake me up. I'd shower in the doctor's lounge, pull on a suit of scrubs supplied by the hospital, and start my rounds with the gurney.

After a week or so of this arrangement, Wilma, a good Christian woman, took pity on me and offered room and board at her house, living with her family, in exchange for me driving her to and from work each day in her car (because I'd not yet earned enough money to fully repair my own vehicle). I immediately accepted, recognizing this as an act of charity because Wilma was perfectly able to drive herself.

Wilma has three sons. The oldest works construction and was able to get me hired at a construction project. Wilma encouraged my change of jobs, pointing out that it was the better career move. She knows how much I value her guidance.

My car is now fixed, I have my own place to live, and even managed to save a few bucks. Instead of earning a living flipping burgers or pushing a gurney, I am now learning a trade. Like Jesus and *His* earthly father Joseph, I'm becoming a carpenter. I grew up around construction, so it is not really that much of a stretch. I'm also experiencing renewed vigor toward school and am intent on finishing my college education. Hopefully soon I will have both a degree *and* a trade.

And if those are not blessings enough, I'm also back doing something I have always loved: making music. Looking back, it's funny how even when it seems like the whole world is against you, it still manages to spin you off in a direction that is not perceived as positive until later. And that's how music reentered my life.

It all began when my car was out of commission and I was forced to hitchhike to get around. A guy in a Dodge van picked me up in Laurel Canyon. He was older (maybe my parents' age) with longish wavy hair, salt and pepper beard, and a protruding mid-section. He said his name was Karl (with a K, he insisted) and for some reason we instantly hit it off. He asked where I was from and I told him originally from Downers Grove, the Chicago burbs. He said he knew the area well, that he'd also grown up in Chicago.

Anyway, one thing led to another, and he finally came to a stop at a wood-framed house that looked built into the side of a hill. "This is *mi casa*," he said. "You're welcome to come on in and continue our chat, if you like, before continuing your journey."

Exiting the car and walking up the front steps, he had a heavy limp. I noticed his right shoe was built up with a thick sole. He caught me staring, I guess, because he unabashedly volunteered an explanation. "Born with a club foot."

He had a guitar leaning against the wall. "You play?" I asked him.

"Not hardly," he replied. "It's there mostly for friends to pluck around on when they come over. Help yourself, if you like."

I picked it up and strummed through the dozen or so chords I knew. He threw me an encouraging look, so I sang a few bars of some song. He smiled kindly.

Before long a visitor arrived, a cheerful seeming guy around my own age. Karl introduced us. "Clyde," he said, "this is Michael. We just met today."

Clyde nodded my way. "Welcome to *The Compound*," he said, and right away I recognized Clyde was singer/songwriter Jackson Browne.

"Compound?" I wondered, aloud.

"Pshaw, Compound! Ineffable twaddle," Karl guffawed. "I owned a coffee shop/bookstore up in Portland in the late 50s that became a sort of meeting place for the Beat Generation. Moved to LA in the 60s and opened a bookstore near UCLA and, for whatever reason, it became some sort of damn hippie hangout. I tried to find refuge here in Laurel Canyon, but to no avail. So now they continue to arrive and mockingly, I imagine, call my home The Compound."

Clyde Jackson Browne smiled, shaking his head. "It's Karl. He just keeps attracting the wrong elements."

Karl rolled a joint and passed it around. I was still holding the guitar.

"You play?" Jackson Browne asked.

"Yes, he does," Karl answered for me. "Pleasant voice, too."

"Let's hear," Browne said.

Sheepishly I began strumming mindlessly with no clue what song to play for a famous singer. Somehow the chords of *Fire and Rain* randomly emerged. Jackson started to sing. After a few bars, I began to harmonize with him. *Thought I'd see yoooou one more time again*, we sang together before I finished with an exaggerated final strum. Karl, reclined in a comfortable-looking overstuffed chair, simply smiled.

"That was nice," Jackson Browne said to me. I set the guitar back down against the wall and he turned to face Karl's direction.

Apparently Karl, in addition to whatever other occupations he may have, was also a professional photographer because he produced, seemingly out of nowhere, several eight-by-ten, black-and-white snapshots that he had taken at some photoshoot and the two began discussing which ones Browne might consider for an album cover. I sat mesmerized just watching and listening.

Soon several other people arrived, I didn't catch all their names and did not recognize anyone famous, as I had Jackson Browne, but they all seemed to know one another, and I was beginning to understand why this place was called The Compound.

It was one of those huge WOW experiences: Meeting Jackson Browne, actually singing duet with him, sitting there listening to Karl and him casually interacting about album covers and music. It all truly impacted me. It was that very afternoon that my long-suppressed love for making music was resurrected.

I'd not performed in public since high school but decided to give it a go, and now have a semi-regular gig playing guitar and singing at a place called Patio Pizza in Simi Valley. I'm also an open mic regular at the Palomino Club on Thursday nights in North Hollywood, and at Doug Weston's Troubadour on Sunset Strip. Life is finally moving in such a positive direction. I've got school, a trade, and music. Thank you, Lord. I'll try not to mess it up.

28

JOURNAL

Today was definitely one of those "only in L.A." types of days. And I don't just mean the weather, which was sunny and around 75 degrees. I've been a carpenter for about a year now and today was working on a construction site up in Thousand Oaks, my old stomping grounds. The crew I'm on is framing a housing tract that butts right up to the periphery of the ranch where I formerly worked as a cowboy. Some might call that progress, but it kind of breaks my heart – knowing the ranch itself will likely soon suffer a similar fate.

Anyway, heading home to the Valley along 101 South, I decided to pull off the freeway at Kanan Road to grab a beer at the Quarter Horse Inn, another old stomping ground. I hadn't been there in a long, long time. So, for old time's sake I donned my cowboy hat, took a seat at the bar, and ordered a cold one and a burger.

The front door of the place was propped open to let in the breeze and I could see out to the gravel parking lot. I'd been sitting there a little while, nursing my beer, when I saw a Chevy El Camino truck pull onto the lot. El Camino is my dream vehicle: A half car, half truck hybrid. If I had the money, that is what I would be driving. This one was darn pretty and had two dirt bikes in the bed that were covered in mud. The driver got out, walked into the bar, stood near the entrance a moment, then headed over to where I was and sat down on the bar stool next to me. He wore mud-covered blue jeans, a sweaty tee-shirt, and lace up work boots. I figured he was a construction guy, like me.

"I really like your truck," I told him.

He said thanks, then sat looking up at the menu hanging on the wall, studying it. Finally, he turned to me and asked, "You a cowboy?"

I answered, "I've rodeoed a bit. Rode bucking horses and bulls."

With that, he began asking me all sorts of questions about rodeo life, what it's like to ride bucking stock, stuff like that. He seemed fascinated by it all, kept asking all sorts of questions and we talked for quite a while, during which we both consumed burgers and a couple of beers. Then he offered to pick up the tab. When I shook my head no, he said, "Listen it's my pleasure. I enjoyed talking to ya. I learned a lot about rodeo. Fact is, I'm looking at a script right now for a film about a rodeo hand and meeting up with you has been quite enlightening."

Script? Film? That's when it hit me. I have been sitting here this whole time with actor Steve McQueen!

"A movie?" I stammered, suddenly dumbfounded at the realization of who I'd been talking with.

He replied, "The part I'm reading is about a rodeo rider named Junior Bonner and you've given me some insight as to what he might be all about."

I let him buy the burger and beers, shook hands, and thanked him. We walked out to the parking lot together. "Nice bikes," I remarked, nodding toward the mud-splattered motorcycles standing up in the truck bed.

"Yep, they're a lotta fun," he answered. Then he got into the El Camino and drove away.

I walked over to my own truck, an older F-250 with a lumber rack that I'd recently purchased, shaking my head in disbelief, muttering to myself, "Just another ordinary day in L.A." Brushes with celebrities are part of life here in Southern California, I suppose. But damn! Steve McQueen?

PART FOUR

29

MARCIE

Michael did not really follow politics too closely, but nobody could miss the fact that the country was really being shaken up. President Nixon under investigation; Vice President Spiro Agnew resigned his office; and Agnew's replacement, the relatively unknown Gerald Ford, became the first VP in the nation's history to take office by being appointed rather than elected.

Also, there was a world-wide energy crisis going on: gasoline a scarcity, incredibly long lines at gas stations an everyday occurrence at the astronomical price of a dollar per gallon. President Nixon even signed a bill to reduce the speed limit on the nation's highways to 55 mph, rationalizing that driving slower uses less gas. Energy had become issue *numero uno.* Many people even claiming that the world would soon come to an end!

But, aside from the world possibly ending, Michael was feeling healthy, happy, and had a new love interest in his life: Marcie Baker. Initially he had found her so totally out of his league, both physically and in social status, that he never even considered asking her out. No way did he stand a chance with her. He was aware of the many suitors who had tried, all receiving polite but emphatic rejections, forests of men reduced to kindling, which begat the circulating rumor that Marcie was some sort of frigid ice princess.

Still, he decided to give it a shot. As a matter of fact, he gave it *three* shots: asking her three separate times for a date. Twice he fared no better than did the others – she said *no.* Where he found the perseverance to ask a third time is anyone's guess, but she finally said yes.

They went to a movie, *The Life and Times of Judge Roy Bean* starring Paul Newman, stopping for a burger and a milkshake afterward. The date was purely platonic but fun, and Marcie was surprisingly easy to talk with. As she was a young up-and-coming executive for RCA Records, they spent much of their date talking about the music business. Her knowledge of the industry fascinated him, and the list of talented artists she personally knew was very impressive. The real shocker for Michael, though, was when Marcie admitted she had heard *him* sing a few times.

"What? Where have you heard me sing?" he asked with astonishment.

"Oh, I get around. To be honest, I love your voice," she told him.

This was nice to know. "Really?"

"Why do you think I finally agreed to go out with you?" she teased. "I only go out with smart, talented guys."

"What about handsome?"

"Handsome is way overrated. Besides, you had two out of three going for you, isn't that enough?" she answered, laughing.

Driving her home in his truck, parking in front of her house, they sat chatting away as the minutes clicked by. Suddenly, for the first time all evening, they stumbled into a conversational lull – a slightly longer than comfortable bit of awkward silence, broken at last by his posing a question, apropos of nothing: "You ever gone on a date in a pickup truck before?"

She gave a sly smile, swiveling her eyes exaggeratedly in mock appreciation of the cab interior and the bench seat they both occupied, he behind the steering wheel, she on the opposite side. "Well no, I don't believe I ever have. Sure is roomy, though."

Her gaze returned toward him and held him with a look strikingly beautiful, enticing, all at once approachable. On impulse, he seized the moment to pull her close and kiss her. Any hesitation and he might not have had the nerve. To his delight, she immediately reciprocated, the two becoming lip-locked and groping each other in fits of passion that erupted seemingly out of nowhere; full tilt from platonic to concupiscent.

They continued making out in the cab of the truck like teenagers until five o'clock in the morning, still reclined supine on that spacious bench seat as the sun began rising to greet a new day. Finally, sitting upright and adjusting her clothes, she invited him into her house where she heated up SpaghettiOs from a can for them to eat. "Breakfast!" she declared. He never knew canned *anything* could taste so good.

Several dates later, Michael told her about the ice princess tag. She was already well aware of her off-putting reputation.

"Then why were you so, uh, *enthusiastic* with me and not with those other guys?"

A felicitous grin emerged. "Truth? I'm picky. But a girl just *knows* when the right guy comes along and, at some point during our very first date, I realized that you, Michael, were that guy. I know how corny it must sound, but I was waiting for my Prince Charming. And my prince is you."

To him it did not sound corny at all. He'd never been anyone's Prince Charming before. It was at that exact moment that Michael knew he was falling in love.

After more than a year of political turmoil dominating the news, President Nixon finally resigned from the office of the presidency. Marcie and Michael watched his resignation and the swearing-in of his replacement, Gerald Ford, on television, as did most of the country.

"No president has ever resigned before," Marcie commented. "It feels sort of strange somehow. I suppose it's a relief to have the whole sordid affair over with, though." Mere moments later, as if concurring, they heard the new president announce to America: "Our long national nightmare is over."

"We need to move in together," Marcie abruptly stated out of the blue. "The world is changing fast. Who knows what tomorrow may bring? I love you and I'm ready. Are you?"

Michael still found it amazing that this gorgeous young woman, who had guys standing in line vying for her affections, had chosen *him* to love. "Sure, let's go for it, Sugar Bear."

"Sugar Bear?"

"Yep, you're my Sugar Bear because you bring such sweetness to my otherwise bland life."

She gave him a look.

"Hey, if I am your Prince Charming, then you are gonna be my Sugar Bear, now and forever."

"Forever is a very long time," she replied.

They took an apartment together in Burbank, a nice one bedroom with a view, and life went from good to even better.

Marcie enjoyed listening to Michael play guitar and sing songs he had written, clapping enthusiastically afterward, saying, "You are definitely going to be a star one day, do you know that?"

"Sure, sure," Michael sarcastically humored her, "the next combo of Elvis and the Beatles."

But she was quite serious and became an ardent supporter of Michael's music, committing herself to enthusiastically touting his musical abilities to anyone who would listen. Working for a major record label, Marcie had connections and used them, never missing a beat at promoting the man she loved.

Invited to an industry party at the Beverly Hills home of actor/musician George Segal, Michael was her *plus one*. She raved to their host about Michael, whereupon the amiable Segal then pulled out a banjo and, in a room filled with music big-wigs, invited Michael to perform: "Sing boy, I'll be your orchestra!"

Through Marcie's efforts, Michael was soon an AFTRA union member, getting recording gigs doing vocal backgrounds on other artist's records and singing commercial jingles. Marcie would smile each time one came on the radio, certain she could discern her man's voice in the chorus. When he got a call back after an audition with The Johnny Mann Singers for a weekly television show called *Stand Up and Cheer*, Marcie cracked open a bottle of champagne, enthusiastically exclaiming, "Baby, we are on a roll!"

She arranged an audition with Alexander Cooperman, a well-known, highly regarded recruiter of musical talent, at his private office.

"Sing me the best song you've got," Cooperman told Michael.

"Okay. Here's a song I wrote called *One More Show*, it's about rodeos," Michael quietly prefaced, straddling a backless chair across from Cooperman and taking a moment to tune the guitar to his liking.

"Rodeos?" Cooperman asked with disinterest. "I'm from New York. What the hell do I know from rodeos?" He paused, a dour look on his face. "Okay fine, go ahead, let's hear it."

Long black highway stretchin' my way,
takes me where I want to go.
Oh, doesn't anybody really know how it feels to be free.
Got an Indian cowboy ridin' along,
I'm drivin' my truck and hummin' a song.
Just thinkin' about the bull that's a'waitin' for me.
This rodeo life is keepin' me free.
One more show, just one more show, then it's on to the next rodeo.

Cooperman held up his hand, signaling Michael to stop singing before the song was finished. "Not bad, but I'm not into cowboy songs. What else ya got?"

Without hesitation, Michael responded. "*Warm Regards*. This is one of my girlfriend's favorites that I've written. It's about a couple missing each other, anxious for summer to come so they will see each other again. She writes him a letter, but it turns out to be her last."

"Fine. Good. Let me hear your girl's favorite song."

She said I just can't wait for summer,
winter's almost through.
Springtime brings the sunshine anew.
But the waiting's such a bummer,
waiting to be again with you.
You know it sure gets lonely all alone here,
with ev-ev-everyone around.
And I just can't seem to find,
or write romantic lines,
so I'll just say what I think
but I don't know how it might sound.
I look at your picture and pretend you're here with me.
But I know you're not and it makes me more lonely.
So, I'm writing this letter all alone under the stars.
And then she signed it, Love and Warm Regards.

Michael noticed Mr. Cooperman tapping his foot and nodding his head. Taking this as a good sign, he continued singing.

But everything's in motion and life keeps moving on
and soon the things we love the most are gone.
And with the passing of the summer, I'm now sitting here alone,
under the stars, holding your last letter and warm regards.

"Okay. Better. Catchy tune. Nice hook. I like it. You sound a lot like John Denver, you know that? Unfortunately for you, the world's already got John Denver. But I like your song. What else you got?"

Michael played several more songs. When he finished, Alexander Cooperman sat staring blankly, looking almost catatonic. Michael wondered if he'd simply bored the poor man into a coma. Michael nervously waited for Cooperman to say something, to say anything; good, bad, or indifferent.

At last Mr. Cooperman sprang back to life and spoke. "I'm gonna send you over to Waxman at Capitol. He'll have you lay down some tracks at the studio. Demos. If you can produce something decent, I'll shop it around. See what we come up with."

Just weeks later, he walked into the iconic round, record-shaped Capitol Records building in Hollywood to record his very own compositions. Truly the opportunity of a lifetime, a most intimidating experience as well.

Escorted to a small studio inside the towering structure, Michael Perry sat in a booth and listened as studio musicians played the instrumental parts of his songs. These were all seasoned pros. The session drummer, a fellow named Hal Blaine, told stories of playing on several Elvis recordings. Frank Sinatra and Barbara Streisand, too. Michael was impressed beyond measure and blown away that he was in the presence of such talent.

Then he was told to sing the lead vocal part while the musical portion played in his ears through headphones. He did his best *not* to sound like John Denver. After that, he recorded the same lead vocal on top of the first, over-dubbing to give his voice more dimension. He and the studio background singers then added harmonies.

After each take, the newly recorded songs were played back on massive speakers so that everyone in the studio could listen. Several people passing by in the outer corridor also entered the studio and listened. One was popular recording artist Karen Carpenter, remarking that the songs sounded good. The studio engineer nodded toward Michael, indicating the importance of her comment.

It was a whirlwind recording session, double-booked studio time. In the end, they had recorded five songs in two days.

At the end of the second day, Michael was riding the elevator down to the lobby when the doors opened on another floor. In walked Linda Ronstadt. He recognized her instantly, offering a sheepish smile. She nodded absently toward him. Oh my gosh, he thought to himself, *Linda*

Ronstadt, what are the odds? Finding the courage to speak, he blurted, "I saw you perform at The Palomino Club. You were great."

"Thank you. I'm glad you enjoyed it," she answered politely without really looking at him.

"It was the same night I performed. Earlier. Open mic night," he added.

She gave him a brief inquisitive look. "So, you were my opening act then?" she joked.

"Well, one of them, I guess," he answered, self-consciously.

The elevator stopped at another floor. No one got in, the doors closed again.

"So, what are you doing here at Capitol? You have something going on?" she asked without looking his way, her gaze focused on the numbered floor designators, white numbers on a black panel.

A small cough escaped him, startled that she had graced him with a question in need of an answer. "I recorded some songs I wrote. Alexander Cooperman set it up."

"Alex?" She now turned full-face toward him. "Well, good for you. Maybe I'll give a listen."

And there it was: the perfect ending to a perfect studio experience.

Marcie became even more excited than Michael as he recounted the events of the past two days, throwing her arms around his neck, kissing him excitedly. "I knew it, I knew it, I knew it! I am so proud of you!"

To celebrate, they headed to nearby Smoke House Restaurant, a white tablecloth, dimly lit landmark located right near Burbank Studios that's been around since the 1940s. Gushing with old-Hollywood vibe, dark wood walls adorned with framed headshots of Hollywood celebrities, mostly from bygone eras, crowded nearly every inch of wall space. The couple stretched out into a red-leather U-shaped booth large enough to accommodate four or more patrons, ordered drinks, and perused the menu. Performing on a small stage nearby was the singing duo Captain & Tennille.

"They're amazing," Michael remarked. "But why is he called Captain anyway?"

"He used to play keyboards with the Beach Boys and, adding his own nautical theme I suppose, wore a captain hat. Probably the same one he's wearing right now. Beach Boy Mike Love started calling him Captain because of the hat, and it stuck."

"Wow, I loved the Beach Boys growing up. He played with them, huh?"

"I think they both did for a while," Marcie answered. "That might've been where they met."

"Amazing."

The duo took a break and Marcie waved them over. Introductions were made between Michael, Daryl Dragon, and Toni Tennille. Michael was only mildly surprised Marcie knew them since she seemed to know everyone in the music biz. Captain & Tennille currently had a hit song rising up the charts, their first, and Marcie applauded them over such success while managing a plug for her man. "Michael just recorded several demos over at Capitol, songs he wrote. You two should give a listen. Might find your next big hit there."

"Love to," Toni quickly responded.

"Ya never know," Daryl nodded.

30

SAIL AWAY SUGAR BEAR

It was a posh Hollywood restaurant where the RCA business dinner was being held. Members from the record company's current A-list music roster were seated at round tables in a private banquet room. Michael sat mostly silent, taking it all in, star-struck by the talent in the room. Nearby sat Waylon Jennings and his wife Jessi Colter, along with fellow country singer Bobby Bare. Somehow Marcie had worked her magic to get Michael and herself seated directly across from John Denver, perhaps the biggest star for the record company. She had long ago become accustomed, as part of her job, to conversing with musical celebrities, so with cheerful countenance remarked about the artist's new release, called *Annie's Song*. "It's so pretty," Marcie told Denver.

The artist smiled a thank you but, seated next to her husband, Annie Denver sarcastically responded, "Yes, John really poured his *whole* heart into writing it ... it took him all of ten minutes while riding a ski lift up the mountain!" This terse exchange seemed to add credence to what Marcie had heard through the grapevine, that the Denvers were having marital difficulties.

On the drive home after dinner, Marcie turned to Michael. "I don't care where he wrote it, *Annie's Song* is lovely." They drove on in silence for several minutes until she asked another of her out-of-the-blue questions. "Do you want to marry me?"

The question took Michael quite by surprise. "What brought that on? By the way, isn't it customary for the man to do the proposing?"

"I'm serious," she said. "If you love me, you should want to marry me."

"Is this because you think John and Annie might be having marital problems?"

"I don't know. Maybe. But mostly I feel like it's just the right time. I love you." Waving her left hand at him, pointing to her ring finger, she added, "I want a rock on my finger. Size five."

She had found her Prince Charming and did not want to take any chances of him slipping away, he supposed. Fair enough. He had found the girl of *his* dreams, his Sugar Bear, as well. "Listen, I cannot recall any time in my life when I was happier than I am right now. But, what's the rush?"

"Hey, you either want to get married or you don't," her terse response.

Two weeks later, a platinum ring, size five, with solitary marquis-cut diamond, the kind she always pointed out in the jewelry store windows, was on Marcie's left hand.

One of Marcie's acquaintances who kept a sailboat in Marina del Rey invited her out for an afternoon of sailing. She accepted, thinking Michael might enjoy a day out on the sea.

It was a thirty-five-foot vessel named *Lega-Sea*. "Wow, this is pretty cool … the idea of just letting the wind take you wherever you want to go," Michael told the skipper as they sliced through the waves of Santa Monica Bay. "I've never been sailing before but used to enjoy surfing a lot. Sailing feels like a natural extension of surfing – direct contact with the ocean, no engines, just the wind and waves."

"Ah, yes," the skipper responded. "But *sailing* takes the ocean experience even further by opening the door to travel and offshore adventure. The vast portion of this planet we occupy is covered by water. With just the wind for propulsion, there are few places a skilled sailor cannot go. Sailing is the very definition of true freedom."

Those words triggered something in Michael, resulting in such a display of immediate enthusiasm for the sport that the skipper invited him along on a forthcoming weekend cruise to Catalina Island, getting to spend four whole days on the boat; an invitation he eagerly accepted.

What a thrill it was crossing the ocean as they sailed toward the island, watching the distant land mass grow ever closer, lush hills eventually coming into view. Michael had never been to Catalina. Heck, he had never been at sea before. It may have been a mere weekend cocktail cruise for the skipper, but to Michael it was a transcendent experience that opened gates to a whole new world.

Returning to their apartment after his extended weekend on the ocean, Michael was met at the door by a very scantily clad Marcie who threw her arms around him. "Welcome home, sailor," she cooed in her most sultry voice. "Thought you might appreciate feasting your eyes on some smooth soft curves after being at sea with gnarly, smelly men all weekend."

He laughed and allowed himself to be led without protest to the bedroom. Only afterwards asking, "How would you feel about living on a boat?"

"Couldn't we just try a waterbed first?" she joked.

"Seriously. I suddenly have this fascination with living on a boat."

"A boat, or a yacht?" she asked.

Pulling the heavy Cambridge Unabridged Dictionary down from a shelf near the bed, then leafing through the pages, he read aloud. "Yacht: a boat with sails and sometimes an engine, used for either racing or traveling or for pleasure."

"It's your dream, not mine. But I don't care if it is a yacht or a rowboat ... just as long as we are together."

After that, any free time he had was spent at the Cal Yacht Club, crewing on *Lega-Sea* and any other boats in need of volunteer crew. Honing his sailing skills, he soon became a sought-after reliable sailor who skippers wanted on their yachts.

But he was not alone, there were other young men with an ardor for sailing and several friendships were forged. Aboard a racing sailboat owned and skippered by Roy Disney – nephew to Walt, the famous animator and founder of Disneyland – he met fellow crewmen Denton Todd and Noah Sark. Yacht racing became a frequent weekend activity. Afterwards, the three would talk enthusiastically for hours about their common dreams of having their own boats and crossing oceans.

Privately, however, Michael found himself worrying whether a tepid music career and forthcoming marriage might have him heading down a wrong path, one that did not lead to oceanic adventures.

Several months passed. One evening at dinner Michael made an announcement. "I'm leaving the music biz."

"Leaving?" Marcie rebutted with a sarcastic laugh. "You are only just barely arriving!"

"Precisely the point," he argued. "It has been months since I made any real money."

"Please, just hang in there, Michael," Marcie pleaded, sarcasm gone. "It will all come together. I know it will."

"I can't wait an eternity for the elusive *big break.* It's been over a year since I made those demo recordings at Capitol, and nothing has happened. And not making the final cut with the Johnny Mann Singers makes me realize this business is a total crap shoot. It's all just bullshit. Depending on someone else to *discover* me? To bestow some elusive big break? Bullshit! I hate all the ass-kissing and praying for some break that never seems to materialize. I need a more secure income. *Especially* if I am going to be a husband."

"So, what is it you plan to do then?" she asked, with just a hint of condescension.

"I've worked construction before. It pays good and I enjoy working outdoors."

"You're serious?" More than just a hint now.

"Absolutely. I was a carpenter when you met me, remember?"

Marcie, taking a deep, exaggerated breath, replied, "Honey, it is a sweet gesture. Truly it is. And I appreciate your concern about providing as a husband. But it's not necessary. You have talent. That's what attracted me to you in the first place. I completely believe in you. Just be patient, keep on writing songs and auditioning. I know you will make it. I don't care if the music gigs are sparse for a while. I am happy to support us for as long as it takes."

"What kind of a husband sits around letting his wife support him? It's just not right. My dad never let my mom support our family." Then, succumbing to the look of abject disappointment on her face, added, "Besides, I'm not giving up on music altogether, just supplementing it. I'm starting a new construction job next week. Let's just see how it goes, okay?"

Things began to shift in the months that followed. Arguments, while not truly heated, were frequent. It upset Marcie that he would often pass on auditions that could possibly lead to something big, just to earn a day's wages at a construction site.

"You don't want a music career anymore? What happened to *that* dream?" Marcie asked him one evening just before bed.

"Dreams don't pay the rent," he snapped.

She gave him a look, calling BS on that remark.

"Okay, sure. The dream is still there. Or at least somewhat. When it comes to music, sometimes it feels like you have taken over that dream. It's become something you want more than I do."

"That's unfair," she argued.

"I know. I'm sorry. Look, I love that you feel so confident about the music. But you *enjoy* hobnobbing with the movers and shakers, I don't. It's more than that, though. Since we got engaged, it feels like everything has changed. It feels like you have choreographed an entire life for us, and I'm just not sure I'm ready for all that entails. Even if I were to earn a decent living with music, you're all about settling down, owning a home in some upscale neighborhood, and even talk about having children as soon as we are married."

This time it was a look of incredulity, as if to ask what could possibly be wrong with all that?

He sighed. "Look, I'm sure these are perfectly normal goals to have. And I share those goals. I really do. But there are things I want to do first. Things that if you don't do them while you're young and unencumbered will be lost for eternity. A *maybe later* attitude often turns into a *too late* reality. That entire scenario of houses and babies can be obtained *after* we have lived out our adventures. What I'd rather do is use whatever money we have to buy a boat for us to live on, eventually sailing away to places most people only fantasize about. The boat would be our home, just knowing that we could sail away any time we choose would make us free."

Marcie sat silently listening. Her expression conveyed eloquently and with great economy several things, including weariness. She had heard variations of this speech before and had exhausted all her responses, tired of filling his sails with her wasted breath since the recurring theme always included being free and sailing away. This time, though, he ended with an ultimatum: "I remember you saying it doesn't matter if it's a rowboat or yacht, *as long as we're together*. I would really love for us to do this together, but either way I'm doing it."

Giving up on music and living on a boat became more than Marcie had bargained for. Michael was no longer the Prince Charming she had imagined. He was neither the struggling, dedicated musician she fantasized him to be, nor moving toward becoming the perfect loving husband she hoped he might one day become. So, without any further discussion, one morning a moving van pulled up and she moved all her things out. “You wanna be free? Knock yourself out! If you ever decide to grow up, let me know.”

“This is purely your decision, not mine,” Michael hotly responded, completely sucker-punched by such a turn of events and not particularly happy about it, but making no effort to stand in her way, even helping the movers load some of her things onto the truck.

But watching Marcie drive off in her car, following behind the moving van, he felt suddenly very alone. His Sugar Bear was gone, the apartment instantly feeling empty. Without her female touches that had made the apartment a home, the place seemed merely a barren, walled-in space devoid of warmth.

He spent that night on the oatmeal-colored leather sofa they had purchased together long ago, Marcie graciously leaving that and the stereo as the only remaining furnishings. No bed. Lying there, wallowing in vicissitude, feeling lost and wondering what to do next, a song came on the radio and just like that! – suddenly he saw the situation with a whole new perspective. *Someone Saved My Life Tonight, Sugar Bear* the singer sang. He could scarcely believe what he was hearing. Sugar Bear? *His* Sugar Bear? The song went on: *You nearly had me roped and tied, altar bound, hypnotized.* The lyrics were dead on! And just like in the song, she had decided to fly away – so, he should think of it as *sweet freedom*, and just say bye.

PART FIVE

31

MUDDLING TOWARD THE GOLDEN GATE

Dreams really do come true, Michael Perry thought to himself. There was blue sky overhead, the little twenty-seven-foot sloop he'd purchased pointing nicely toward the wind, a bit of spray over the bow. Setting sail from Marina del Rey, heading to San Francisco, crawling up the coast from port to port, a crew of three, himself and two sailing buddies: Denton Todd, preppie med-student, boy-next-door sort of handsomeness, tall, slender, a couple years older than Michael, loves sailing more than anything; and Noah Sark, chubby, long haired, bearded stoner with wide eyes and perpetual owlish look, living proof that hippies are still alive and well. All three embarking on their first serious ocean passage.

They dropped a hook at Santa Catalina Island the first night out and took the dinghy ashore to the town of Avalon, finding themselves at the raucous Marlin Club Bar. Tucked away on a side street two blocks from the beach, the three sat at the establishment's horseshoe-shaped bar made to resemble the prow of a ship, and ordered libations.

It was from this noisy bar in Avalon that he tried to call her, Michael lifting the phone, depositing the required coins into the slot, then hanging up before Marcie answered. No point in it. What would he even say if she answered? It had been seven months. She had done what she needed to do; he was doing what he needed to do.

A few nights later they were on a mooring in Santa Barbara Harbor, the boat gently rocking to-and-fro, folk songs and the pungent aroma of marijuana in the air, as the boys made music: Denton playing his harmonica, Michael on guitar, and Noah playing with the rolling machine, serving up fat joints.

"Here's a song I wrote a couple nights ago, when we were anchored at Catalina," Michael said, strumming a G chord. "Follow along on the harp, Denny. It's an easy chord structure." He began singing:

Sun goin' down on the horizon.
With its end the blackness of the night comes
with the moon and stars illuminating the sea.
I'm feelin' free,
because I'm sailing all alone in the night,
feeling you so close to me,
I long to hold you tight.
But by the light of day
you'll be so much farther away-ay.
What can I say? What can I do?
Don't look for me now, the choice was up to you.
And you decided to stay
so now I'm on my way
to who knows where?
I'm just sailing all alone in the night.
Feeling you so close to me, I long to hold you tight.
But by the light of day,
You'll be just that much farther away-ay.
Someday I may return, a thousand days hence.
But for now this is the only life that seems to make any sense.
And I know you won't be waiting forever.
That's why it's now or never
to be sailing all alone in the night,

feeling you so close to me, I long to hold you tight.
But by the light of day, you'll be so much farther away-ay
Yes, by the light of day, you'll be just that much farther away-ay.

"Good song, man!" Denton exclaimed, shaking spittle from his harmonica.

"Shit house mouse, that was a great tune, Michael!" Noah added with amplified enthusiasm, exhaling smoke from a jumbo hit he had been holding in his lungs.

"Thanks, guys," Michael said, "If I'm ever lucky enough to find myself in a studio again, I'd love to lay that one down with some strings, piano, percussion. That's the way I hear it in my head."

"Well, I thought it was great just the way it sounded right here on the boat tonight," Noah told him.

Departing Santa Barbara at dawn, sailing northward toward Point Conception, Michael leafing through the Sea Boating Almanac, read for the tenth time about where they were headed:

Point Conception, 118 miles NW of Pt. Fermin ... a bold headland 220 feet high that marks an abrupt change in the trend of the California coast. Point Conception has been called the "Cape Horn of the Pacific" because of heavy NW gales encountered off it during passage ... a marked change of climatic and meteorological conditions is experienced off the Point, the transition often being remarkably sudden and well defined ... causing heavy offshore gusts.

"Whoa! The Cape Horn of the Pacific," Michael uttered to himself, digesting those words, growing anxious. No one on board had any prior heavy weather boating experience, but that was partly why they were out here: to gain experience. If Point Conception proved true to form, they would soon be getting a serious dose of it.

By late afternoon seas were on the rise, as was the wind, with Denny at the helm. Noah remained topside, trying to deal with a sudden bout of seasickness. Michael was seated across from them when a large wave smashed into the cockpit soaking all three. "Get ready!" Denny shouted above the gushing roar. "We may all soon experience the unsettling reality of mal-de-mer."

It seemed an opportune time to don foul weather gear, so Michael went below. By the time he returned to the cockpit wearing *oilies*, the seas had already built to proportions such as he had never before seen, the little sailboat pitching and rolling violently, and Noah now retching miserably. The seas were confused and chaotic, with swells seeming to come from all directions.

Michael began creeping cautiously out onto the bowsprit to furl the jib sail, finding himself perched precariously out over the bow like some bare-breasted figurehead as the boat was plowing through enormous waves that kept coming, growing in size until they were as high as the spreaders twenty feet up on the mast. Another and another. Over and over. With each passing swell, the boat rising and then rocketing downward. At the bottom of a trough, Michael looked upward to see the next wave arriving, pulling the boat up its face until it was atop a rushing breaking peak, then sliding down the backside as the wave rumbled past.

A momentary breath of relief, then another mountain of water arrived, lifting the bow up, up, up to such a height that it seemed the boat was pivoting precariously on the transom – another foot and the entire boat would certainly topple over backwards. The wave suspending him out at the bow for a moment, dangling in mid-air clutching the bow pulpit for dear life, the entire boat shuddering, his eyes wide with horror as he looked downward at what appeared to be a thirty-foot drop. All at once the boat came free-falling down through the air with a final crash, water completely engulfing him as if being swallowed alive and whole, the bowsprit stabbing into the ocean like a dart thrust upon a watery dartboard. Prudently wearing a harness, body tethered to the boat, or most assuredly he would have been pitched overboard, headlong into the turbulent seas.

Making a return to the cockpit, force majeure winds were clocking at more than forty mph and seas getting impossibly heavier and rougher by the minute. Noah had long since abandoned any sense of dignity and was vomiting all over himself. Seeing and smelling it caused first pangs of nausea in both Denton and Michael, the latter quickly making for the port side rail, snapping the harness shackle to the lifeline and heaving his guts over the side.

Noah, now so violently ill he likely would have welcomed death, sought refuge below deck on the cabin floor, lying on his stomach near the galley, embracing a saucepan he had removed from the stove top, clinging onto it desperately with both hands, throwing up over and over into this receptacle. He would remain in this position for the rest of the night. Anyone going below would need to step over, and sometimes unavoidably step *on*, the prone Noah; hopefully avoiding contact with the vomit-filled pan.

With Denton steering the boat, Michael went below to get as much sleep as possible since they would be sailing around the Point all night and he would need to be well rested. It was a harrowing experience, thinking for sure he would be sick making his way about the undulating cabin, watching it bounce all around him, and smelling the vile stuff Noah had given up. Kicking off soaking rubber boots and jacket was like trying to undress aboard a rollercoaster. The cabin was spinning and lurching, making it feel like bed spins on a bad drunk. With vertiginous difficulty, he managed to make it to a bunk and tried to lie flat, desperately needing to take his mind off the putrid, violent world in which he was entombed, away from the spinning cabin, away from the stench of vomit.

Closing his eyes, he began to think about Marcie. Entering that never-never land somewhere between consciousness and unconsciousness, his mind began to fill with images of her. He could see her face, her eyes, and detect the smell of her hair, always so fresh and clean with a scent like coconuts. He could almost feel her touching him with a gentle caress. Her sweet voice soothingly cooing to him, "Miiiichael." First it came softly, as part of a fog-filled dream, then sharply: "Michael … Mike!" Jerked back to reality, it was Denny shouting his name from the cockpit.

My God, he wondered, how long have I been sleeping? Attempting to sit upright, he was immediately thrown out of bed by the boat's violent lurching, crashing into the galley table with an awful thud to his cheekbone.

Stumbling around in the dark, turbulent cabin, doing a sort of dance while trying to pull on his gear, he suddenly realized he was stepping on Noah who had, mercifully for him, passed out on the cabin sole. Sidestepping, trying to avoid the prone unconscious body, inadvertently placing his unshod foot into the saucepan which was now quite full of the retched stuff Noah had been spewing, it hit him that he was standing in puke. It all became too much for his senses to handle. Flying out the companionway, banging his head on the sliding hatch, and clambering out to the cockpit for air, then making haste to the starboard rail, he began throwing up violently.

Denton, shivering with cold, anxious to go below, implored, "Are you all right? Can you take the helm?" The wind whipping at his face, the ocean roaring like a freight train, Michael took the tiller as Denny made a dash below.

On deck alone in the middle of the night, not a sliver of moon nor a single star visible, it was difficult to see much of anything. Michael never imagined a night could be so utterly dark, the ocean so completely black. He could not even see the ocean on which he sailed, only hear its fury all around him.

The boat was pitching and ploughing through heavy seas, heeling over drastically, *burying the rail*, water pouring into the cockpit. Monstrous waves crashing, cockpit continuously filling with water nearly to the knees, salt spray heavy, burning his eyes to the point where nothing at all could be seen except the crimson light of the compass jumping wildly – the boat bouncing and leaping off course, not just a few degrees but forty degrees in a single leap.

Another enormous wave slammed into the hull with a deafening boom, the boat spinning a full 180 degrees, heading almost due east instead of the desired course of due west, then a moment later bouncing back to a westerly heading. "Just living the dream!" Michael shouted into the howling night.

With the first spark of dawn on the horizon, the wind subsided and the ocean surface became a flat gray. A thin thread of pale light played upon the formerly tempestuous waters. Several hours of gentle sailing followed before they entered Morro Bay, to be swept up in the five-knot current that flows down the channel. Zooming along in the fast-moving water, deftly maneuvering between rows of boats moored in the channel, they managed to pick up a mooring pendant and come to a stop.

Rowing the dinghy to shore proved a tough pull, going against that current. Upon reaching solid land, Noah immediately announced he'd had enough and was jumping ship. "Sorry guys. I know with the name I was born with I should be the best sailor in the whole freaking world, but I just can't go on." No one could blame him. He'd been fiercely seasick practically since the voyage began. Poor bastard.

On shore, the afternoon felt warm. Sea foam danced with splendor in the sun, beach sand scalloped by the breeze. Michael meandered along the edge of the water and sat on some rocks, watching families and couples frolicking on the sand. A mother and her young daughter wearing matching sundresses, discarded sandals in their hands, bounding unshod along the strand like graceful gazelles. There was also a fellow not much older than himself with a little tow-headed boy riding atop his shoulders, the boy gleefully shouting, "Take me in the water, Daddy!"

Watching all this created a tinge of envy, a feeling of strange aloneness, his mood turning unexpectedly heavy, questioning decisions he had made about not getting married. *What the hell is it I really want*? he wondered dolefully. He'd thought sailing out on the ocean was the answer he had been seeking, but watching this father and son touched his heart and suddenly raised doubts. He was leaving an awful lot behind to pursue a sailing life. By now he and Marcie would have been married and living comfortably in a nice house, perhaps planning a family of their own. The tide was going out. Suddenly everything felt like it was draining away.

Approaching quietly from behind, watching Michael taking in the view of the beach and sea, Denton placed his hand on Michael's shoulder, briefly startling him, and spoke more prophetically than he could have known. "This is the way we are meant to live, my friend. Not sublimating ourselves to a mold created by others. On a cruising sailboat you are the captain of your own life, and the *world* is your home."

Michael slowly smiled, his sailing reality coming back into focus, nodding obverse concurrence. Both he and Denton shared a common appreciation for the sea and similar aspirations of sailing across the Pacific to Hawaii one day.

Denny then added, "Cruising sailors are dreamers living out their dreams, and dreams are immortal."

Evening on the boat was cold but quiet, with gentle rocking on the mooring, the moon a distant egg in a nest of fog. Denton in the cabin reading a book. Michael softly strumming his guitar, silently humming a tune in his head.

"Play something," he heard Denton say.

More quiet chords, but humming aloud now. "I've got some lyrics that've been noodling around in my head. Wanna hear it?" he replied.

"For sure," his boatmate answered.

"Okay. Our next port of call is Half Moon Bay. So, I wrote a song about it. Goes like this." With closed eyes, he began to croon:

I see your face upon the sea, arising from the foam.
At night I hear you call to me, my darlin' please come home.
My darlin' please come home to me and say you're gonna stay.

Then I close my eyes again, and dream the night away.
Dream the night awaaay with thoughts of you.
Dream the night away with thoughts of Half Moon Bay.
Dream the night away with thoughts of you.
By the light of day we'll be at Half Moon Bay.
My ship she rocks a little more than gentle would describe.
And though she's been so good to me, there's an emptiness inside.
You see, my life is filled with sailing ships and castles in the sand.
Some say it's because I'm still a boy.
Some say it's because I'm a man.
But I can dream the night awaaay with thoughts of you.
Dream the night away with thoughts of Half Moon Bay.
Dream the night away with thoughts of you.
By the light of day we'll be at Half Moon Bay.

A final chord strum, then Michael opened his eyes. Denny was smiling at him.

"Christ, you just made that up tonight? It's friggin terrific. You amaze me, man. To be able to do stuff like that. It's a gift."

"Well, you've got movie star good looks, you're tall, and the brains to become a damn doctor. This is all I got," Michael replied.

They both laughed. Michael placed the guitar back in its case. The sloshing of water against the hull and creaking of the boat the only sounds as they called it a night.

Two days later, on a deep blue ocean and under a cloudless sky, the Bay area's famous and ubiquitous fog fortuitously absent, the little white sloop entered the waters of San Francisco Bay, sailing under the iconic Golden Gate Bridge with sails full and proud. Michael viewed crossing under this most recognized landmark of the West Coast as a kind of finish line for his first major passage, validation of a sort. He felt accomplished, more confident. Worldly somehow. Not quite yet an old salt, but already contemplating future passages across the Pacific.

The rare dream that is accomplished sets a person apart; the usual thwarted dream creates the bond of baleful kinship for most. So often he had been told by family – especially his father – and even friends, that it's just a fantasy, nobody really just sails off in pursuit of dreams. Well, guess again. Some do.

32

DISCO DUCK

The voice coming from the car radio announced: "A recent study has found *the* most average person in the United States of America is male, a member of the baby boom generation between the ages of twenty-one and twenty-six, with at least two years of college. And, drum roll please, *the* most common name for this most average American issss" ... there was a lengthy pause for dramatic effect ... "MICHAEL!"

"Oh fine," said Michael Perry, responding to the invisible person's voice coming through the speaker, "you have just described me! Just what I always wanted to be, the most average human being in America."

Near the corner of Corbin Avenue and Ventura Boulevard, in a part of the San Fernando Valley with the odd name of Tarzana, he turned into a parking lot with a sign that read DISCO PARKING ONLY and searched for a place to park his car. The lot was packed. After three spins around the lot, he noticed a car leaving and took that spot.

Tennessee Gin & Cotton Company seemed a rather odd name for the Valley's hottest disco. Hot or not, Michael pretty much hated discos; hated the music, hated the dancing, hated the whole scene. But they were all the rage for socializing and mingling with the opposite gender, so he felt compelled to frequent them.

The music inside TG&CC wasn't just loud, he could veritably *feel* the thumping bass – like some collective heartbeat coming from the patrons gyrating on the dance floor – pulsing up against the temples of his head.

The place had a so-happening-it-hurts ambience. A giant mirrored ball suspended from the ceiling spun round and round, reflecting flashing lights onto the crowded dance floor, bodies close in pulsing rhythms, shapes melting with shapes, nattily dressed couples spinning each other around. Males in Angel Flight suits, platform shoes making short men taller and tall men giants, all of them wearing gold chains around their necks; females in high heels, tight-fitting low-cut tops, tight denim, or short wispy skirts that twirled up as they spun around in dance.

He never fancied himself to be much of a ladies' man, and watching the suave cool guys who had the moves that caused women to gravitate to them made him wonder why he even bothered to come to places like this. So, he remained at the bar, his usual spot, swirling a Tequila Sunrise in his hand, seated on a bar stool, watching the synchronized flexuous bodies out on the dance floor. At the other end of the bar sat a girl. Alone. Blond. Fairly attractive. Full faced, almost cherubic. Around twenty-fiveish.

Bopping his head to the music, pretending to be watching the dancers while his eyes focused on her. A slash of lipstick across pouty red lips, long eyelashes, full rosy cheeks, heavy make-up, and wearing open-toed stilettos with Calvin Klein jeans that looked painted on. She sent a smile in his direction. Trying to be cool, he pretended not to notice. The smile quickly vanished, replaced by a look of failed flirtation, or perhaps just boredom.

With drink in hand, walking in her direction to stand immediately behind where she was seated, the scent of heavy perfume wafted his way. The song ended, she spun around on her barstool, facing him. The smile returned. "Hi," she said, a Harvey Wallbanger in her hand.

He couldn't hear her voice over the cacophony but read her lips. Stepping closer, leaning in and speaking directly into her ear, she tipped her head to accommodate what he might say.

"I'm Michael."

"I've seen you here before," she shouted back at him, though they were mere inches apart. "I'm Harper."

The music stopped ever so briefly, then started up again: Donna Summer singing, grunting, and moaning: *Ooooooo, Love to Love You Baby*!

"Oh my God, I love this song! Let's dance!" she shouted over the music, dismounting her bar stool, grabbing his hand and excitedly leading him onto the floor. Before he could protest, they were spinning, twirling, and dipping to the beat. Fifteen minutes of *Love to Love You Baby*, followed immediately by four more songs playing consecutively without any break, one flowing right into the other. The fortissimo then abruptly ending, they made their way back to her former spot at the bar, both out of breath and perspiring as if they had just emerged from a steam room.

"That's the longest dance I've ever had in my life!" he shouted to her.

"Me too," she shouted back, laughing while grabbing her purse hanging on the back of the bar stool, pulling out a pen and writing numbers on a drink napkin. Her phone number. Stuffing the napkin into his shirt pocket, she simply said, "I have to run. I'm already late. Call me." And she was gone.

Michael did call Harper. Twice, but no one answered. Yet, the following weekend at Tennessee Gin & Cotton Company, there she was. Her perfume preceded her, walking right up to him, taking his hand in hers as if no time had elapsed at all, saying, "Hi you! Wanna dance?"

"I'm still worn out from the last time we danced," he replied, joking.

She stood there for a very long measured moment with no expression as the music blared all around them. Then, filling the brief pause between songs, he heard her words: "Okay, so let's get outa here!"

Straight to her nearby apartment and into the bedroom. No formalities, no niceties, just groping, kissing, licking, fucking. Heavy breathing eventually returning to normal, she snuggled close to him afterwards, hoping to extend the intimacy they had just shared a bit longer. A vapid, fatuous intimacy perhaps, without guilt, without worry, and likely without a future, since now, in the afterglow of spent passion, a conversation of greater substance would surely follow, introducing themselves to each other for the first time without the cloak of percussive disco sounds and shouted single-sentence communication.

Perspiration glistened off her breasts. "Every time we're together you make me sweat," she joked.

"Me?" he replied, lightheartedly. "You're the one made me dance for a half hour straight last time ... and now ..."

"You're welcome," she interrupted with a chortle. "I like that you make me sweat. Burn some of this baby fat off."

"Baby fat?"

"I have a kid," she stated, unsentimentally. "An infant. I used to be much thinner."

He made no response.

"Does that turn you off?" she asked.

He stammered, "No, no. Uh, I don't think so. A kid, really? A baby?" He'd never had such pillow talk before, immediately after getting his brains fucked out. Maybe he *was* turned off a little.

"Her name is Elise."

"Where is she tonight?"

"At my ex's. Her father's place."

"You're divorced?"

"I was married to a cop. Less than two years. He's a complete asshole. Horrible temper. I just couldn't take it any longer. You don't really wanna hear all this, do you?"

"Maybe not," his honest reply. A divorced lady with a baby and some crazy-tempered cop ex-husband? She might be a pretty good lay, but this was probably more baggage than he was up for.

"Too much information too soon?" She asked. "I shouldn't have told you."

More stammering. "No, no. It's, uh, interesting. A baby. A cop husband. Anything else you wanna tell me?"

Two weeks later his telephone rang. "Hey, it's Harper."

"Oh yeah. Hi Harper." He'd not seen or called her in all that time. And now, here she was calling him. He wasn't even sure how she'd gotten his number. Must have given it to her in a weak moment, he decided.

"I was wondering if you would like to come over for dinner."

Silence. He felt awkward, not knowing how to respond.

With a sense of frivolity, neither feigned nor real, she added, "I make the best spaghetti and meatballs you've ever tasted. Really. You know, they say the way to a man's heart is through his stomach. I thought I might give that a try."

"How are you?" he asked. Still feeling awkward, the question sounding out of context.

"Great! No, good. I'm good. So, you wanna come over? Let me cook you dinner?"

"Okay. Sure. Why not?"

It really was the best homemade spaghetti and meatballs he had ever tasted, notwithstanding his own mother being Italian.

"The secret is that I make the sauce with wine and sugar," Harper told him.

Seated at the small dinette set in the cozy kitchen of Harper's one-bedroom apartment were Harper, Michael, and Harper's slightly younger sister. "This is my little sis, Daffy," she said, introducing them.

"Daffy?"

"My name's Daphne but everybody in my family has been calling me Daffy my whole life," the sister informed him. "It's because, when I was little, I couldn't pronounce my own name properly. I could only say Daffy, like Daffy Duck, and it stuck."

"I see," he nodded. "How about I call you Daphne, unless you start acting daffy?"

The girls both chuckled.

In a crib in the adjacent room, where he and his hostess had worked up a sweat in lusty coupling just weeks prior, was baby Elise. She was a beautiful little girl, as babies go, resting so peacefully on her tummy with tiny, closed eyes. But then, Michael knew almost nothing about what babies should or shouldn't look like.

"Hope you don't mind Daffy joining us," Harper said, adding with a quick wink, "She's my babysitter, in case we decide to go off and do something crazy later."

"No problem," Michael replied, though he was stumped by just what craziness she had in mind.

An empty bottle of Mateus with straw flowers protruding out the top was the table centerpiece. Near that was a freshly opened bottle of Chianti. "Can I pour you a glass?" Harper asked, noticing Michael eyeing the bottle.

"Sure," he said. "Why do Chianti bottles always have that straw skirt around the base of the bottle?"

"I've often wondered that very same thing," Harper answered. "I have no idea."

"I'm half Italian. You'd think I'd know," he joked.

"I'm Mormon. My whole family is Mormon. We're not supposed to know, because we're not supposed to drink wine," she joked back.

"Mormon? Isn't that like being a Quaker or something?"

"A Quaker? Like on the oatmeal box?" she asked, laughing.

"I don't know. I've never met a Mormon."

"Well, you have now. Though, I'm not a very good Mormon girl, I'm afraid. We are not supposed to drink or go to disco bars. Frankly, there is a whole bunch of stuff we are not supposed to do. But hey, I figure I'm only young once. I'll get religious when I'm thirty."

Small talk around the table made it apparent just how little Harper and Michael fundamentally knew about one another.

"Michael is a musician," Harper revealed to her sister, one of the few things she did know about him.

"More like a struggling musician these days," Michael corrected.

"Play in a band?" Daphne asked.

"Sometimes. On and off, different bands. I also work construction. I'm a carpenter."

"That explains how tan you are," Harper volunteered. "Outside working in the sun."

"Maybe. But I'm out on my boat a lot, too. Get plenty of sun out on the ocean."

"Oh? What kind of boat?" Harper asked. "Don't tell me, some sort of yacht or something."

"Not hardly. It's just a small sailboat. Twenty-seven feet."

"Uh oh. You're going to have a very sick girlfriend on your hands," Harper said, gesturing a vomiting motion with her hands to her face.

"Excuse me?" Michael responded, surprised by her referring to herself as his girlfriend.

"I'm sorry to admit, I don't really do well on boats. Especially on the ocean. Too much up and down. I get really seasick. I like solid, very dry land. I don't even like mud." She snorted at her own joke. "My ex and I spent our honeymoon on a cruise ship. I threw up every single day. It was definitely not fun."

Watching her speak, her words of little consequence to him, still grappling with the *girlfriend* reference, when Daphne interjected. "I've never been sailing. Gee, I'd love to go sometime."

A half moment later, little Elise began crying loudly from the other room and Daphne got up from the table to attend to her.

Ten days elapsed since that dinner. Michael thought of it amusingly as The Last Supper. In his mind, being divorced from a hot-tempered policeman and raising a baby was one thing but being prone to seasickness was clearly a deal breaker. And then the phone rang. He was more than a little surprised to hear Daphne's voice on the other end.

"I really enjoyed meeting you the other evening," she began, "you seem really nice. I was just kinda wondering if maybe you might consider letting me go sailing with you sometime. It sounds like such fun. Really.

I have always wanted to go out sailing on the ocean. Sort of a fantasy of mine."

"Well, the chance to fulfill a beautiful woman's fantasy is pretty hard to turn down," he replied, chuckling. "Is this okay with your sister?"

"She will be fine. I promise."

With breeze blowing her hair, and an expression brimming with enthusiasm even though she claimed never to have sailed before, Daphne looked to be someone totally in her element as they sailed out of Oxnard's Channel Islands Harbor where Michael currently slipped his boat, far less expensive than Marina del Rey. A couple years younger than Harper, with similar cherubic facial features, and flashing brown eyes that displayed a sense of perpetual inner merriment, she wore far less makeup than her sister and still managed to look just as attractive. More so, possessing an indefinable gamine charm with jeans, bare feet, denim blouse tied loosely at her waist exposing bare midriff, and puka shell necklace adorning her throat.

"This is wonderful!" she proclaimed through the wind, looking out at Anacapa Island ten miles in the distance off the port bow.

"Want to sail all the way to the island?" Michael asked.

"Oh my gosh, yes! Can we? An island, a real live island!"

In brisk wind with sails filled, the little boat was heeling on starboard tack, Daphne sitting on the low side, feet dangling over the side into the ocean water, squealing with joy like a little girl. Lifting her face into the wind, an earthy whiff of brine filled her lungs. Blue sky, brilliant sun, the ruggedly jagged island on the horizon, in this aquatic wonderland she was a perfectly placed part of the scenery and seemingly appreciating the wonder of it all immensely.

Skipper Michael, seated on the upper side of the heeling vessel, looking across and down toward her, was additionally appreciative of the undone topmost button on her denim blouse, glimpsing the exposed fleshy cleavage jiggling enticingly with every lurch of the boat through the waves.

Closing in on the leeward side of the island, the wind tempered until disappearing entirely. The sea became calm, flat, and so mirror-like they could see the boat reflected on the water. Sea lions splashed about alongside, some floating on their backs, waving a flipper as if to bid hello. Daphne was enamored with it all, like a child at Sea World.

The sailboat bobbed in place, making no weigh, the sails limp. Daphne, now reclining along the cockpit bench, her head in Michael's lap, looking upward, watching the boat's mast sway back and forth against the sky, dreamily remarked, "This is a truly perfect day."

Michael, leaning back against the cabin top, eyes closed, totally relaxed, scarcely managing to squeeze out a few syllables. "Mm hmm. It surely is."

"You know what would make it even more perfect?" she asked lazily.

"Cannot imagine."

"This," she whispered, raising her head off his lap to let her lips meet his. It was a gentle kiss from her that, with closed eyes, he did not see coming. Nor had it been anticipated, but immediately led to a more daring one from him, followed by a spontaneous eruption from them both of exploratory hands, and buttons coming undone. Jockeying for position, she shimmied beneath him, on her back, looking upward at the tall, rigid mast pole swaying back and forth against the blue sky as he entered her.

The sun was beginning to set, chill filling the air as they approached the harbor on return from the island. Daphne wrapped in a woolen blanket, the skipper held her close, his arm around her shoulders, other hand on the wooden tiller, steering the boat on a broad reach. Soon the vessel was snugly secured in her marina slip, surrounded within a forest of masts and riggings gleaming vermilion in the final sinking sun.

Daphne disappeared below into the tiny cabin while Michael went about dousing sails and tidying up topside. Peering down into the cabin, he spotted Daphne reclined in the V-berth. A flick of her head to the side beckoned him, indicating he should join her.

In the coziness of the warm cabin, it became a far more tender, gentle lovemaking than their earlier wild abandon in the lee of Anacapa Island. Afterward, discussing in ruminative rapport all that happened that day, until yielding to drowsiness and succumbing to sleep as the full darkness of night arrived.

A sunbeam entering through a tiny porthole awakened them. They dressed and exited the boat in relative silence. She wondered if things might feel different in the morning light. That he said so little while securing the boat and walking up the gangplank together, toward where their cars were parked, worried her. Thank goodness they had arrived in separate cars. If things were, indeed, different on this so-called morning after, at least an awkward hour's drive to the Valley together in the same car could be avoided. But her sister, who when Daphne expressed interest in him, said *Go for it, you don't need my permission, he's not mine*, would certainly gloat.

Perhaps a bit of levity is called for here, she thought to herself. Arriving at her vehicle, quickly spinning on her heels to face him, thrusting out her hand as if to formally shake hands, she deadpanned, "Well, thank you kind sir for the wonderful boat ride. I do hope you might invite me again sometime."

He smiled, pulling her close. They kissed for the first time that morning. "I think you can count on that," he told her. "To do otherwise would be just plain daffy."

33

JOURNAL

Been working in San Francisco the last couple of weeks. Frisco is a great city, but it feels good to be back in L.A. I've been with this construction company for quite a while now and they recently promoted me from carpenter to foreman. Probably more because I'm young, single, and willing to work out of town for extended periods than for any brilliance as a carpenter. No matter, it's a big step upward and I really like the job. A lot less physical work, but more responsibilities.

I thought my dad would be really proud of me about this promotion. Instead, he laughed. "Who in their right mind would make *you* a foreman?" Those were his exact words. Thanks Dad, I can always count on you for a real ego boost.

Flying into LAX, looking out the airplane's window, I could see the Channel Islands down below. I recognized Anacapa and Santa Cruz Islands easily enough, they look just like they do on nautical charts. God, how I wish I could just sail out over that far off horizon, past those islands which have become so familiar to me, in search of *new* islands, foreign latitudes ... maybe someday.

Yesterday, arriving home, I saw the light on my answering machine blinking as soon as I walked into my apartment. Five messages from Daphne. So, I gave her a call and we made plans to go sailing. Really glad I did, too. Because today has to go down on record as being one of the best days ever!

I picked Daph up early this morning and we went out on the boat. There was a certain magic going on today. We both felt it. The sun, the sea, being together again after weeks apart … it all came together to create magic. She seems to love being out with me on the ocean. When an occasional wave splashed onto the boat, she found it exciting, laughing with contagious delight.

As the day became warmer, Daphne removed her bikini top, cooing softly how nice it felt to have the breeze blow against her breasts. There were no other boats within miles of us and soon we were both naked as the day we were born and sailing along secure in each other's arms. The feeling exceeded erotic, bordering on spiritual. The two of us alone together on God's great ocean, the wind caressing our exposed flesh. We frolicked about the boat unclothed like two innocent children. Yet our frequent embraces feeding the arousal of adults.

After several hours sailing, we returned to the marina. Parking the boat in her slip, Daph and I *dove* immediately into one of the berths below and savagely made love, consummating the yearning that had been building between us all afternoon while sailing *au naturel*. We tore into each other with such greedy heat, I am surprised the fiberglass boat didn't melt! Any passersby might surely have wondered why the boat was bouncing so much in the slip. It was utterly fantastic! This woman, this boat, this day was as much as I could ever ask for. We stayed in each other's arms for a long while, enjoying the afterglow of perfect lovemaking as the boat gently rocked us to sleep.

Later, we got dressed and went ashore to the yacht club for some pizza, watching *Welcome Back Kotter* on TV as we ate. I'm not a member of the club, but nobody seems to care. I hang out there a lot. Afterwards, we strolled hand-in-hand back to the boat. The night still young, as are we!

It was a strikingly pleasant evening weatherwise, so we put up the sails and headed back out on the water. With a mere whisper of a breeze, just enough to keep the sails filled, the night air felt almost tropical. Incredibly romantic as we silently sailed down the channel, Daphne snug in my arms, the lights from the hotels and restaurants on shore illuminating the water like it was Christmas. The gentle sloshing of water against the hull was the only music we needed, so we kept the stereo turned off.

We cruised all around the marina before returning to our slip. Once there, we reclined on the boat's foredeck, looking up at the stars and all the sailboat masts silhouetted against the night sky. So beautiful, so serene. We lay there, nestled together, contemplating the moon overhead, talking for a very long while.

Much later, driving her home to the Valley, I looked over at Daphne in the passenger seat. She was asleep, still holding my hand in hers and looking like an angel. Her eyes were closed and she had the most peaceful, contented expression I have ever seen on anyone's face. My own expression may have mirrored hers; it has been a long while since I have felt so completely satisfied. It is 2:00 a.m. now. I just returned home and wanted to write it all down, so I will never forget.

34

THE CHANNEL ISLANDS

"When you sail you don't *battle* nature," he explained to her, "you become a *part* of nature. It's all about being self-sufficient out on the ocean in a perfectly organic way, not contributing to pollution, not burning fossil fuels ... just God's breath on the sails blowing you along. No manmade bullshit screwing up the environment, no motors, no pollutants ... just God and me, two buddies. I always feel so much closer to God while sailing His ocean than I ever did kneeling before an altar in some manmade church."

Being Mormon, the fact that Michael attributed everything to God was a welcome sign to Daphne. She loved listening to him talk about sailing and the ocean, the look in his eyes while concentrating on the wind and the waves. He was smart in a very sexy way. She savored watching him nimbly move about the boat with catlike balance, fussing with the sails, shirtless, tan, and fit.

He liked to sit on the high side of the boat, steering with his foot on the tiller, often directing his gaze away from the ocean to fix on her and give a boyish smile. She had never enjoyed being with anyone so much before, had never felt so comfortable with any man. It had been out of character for her to have engaged in sex so quickly with him, but she had no regrets. She knew, early on, she was *officially* in love for the first time in her life.

Today was the beginning of a weeklong cruise of the Channel Islands, the longest nonstop time they had ever spent together and the most miles she had ever sailed. Daphne had learned a good deal about sailing in the months they had known one another, and she liked to believe she had now become a valuable first mate.

It was around 4:00 a.m. There was a fair sea running, the waning night sky as clear as she had ever seen, with countless stars that were not merely overhead but stretched from horizon to horizon. Too nice to go below. She enjoyed staying topside under the stars with him steering the boat. He made her feel safe out at sea in the dark.

A few hours later, through the early morning mist, they spotted Santa Rosa Island, the second largest of the eight Channel Islands that stretch out for some forty-plus miles along the Southern California coast. It was a beautiful sight to behold, like a rare jewel rising up out of the empty ocean. They anchored just off a secluded beach, then landed the dinghy on the island.

Completely uninhabited, with wide white sandy beaches that seemed to stretch forever, this was truly a paradise. Sunny but brisk, they discarded their clothes to run naked down the beach, eagerly exploring a few of the many caves along the shore and daring to frolic with resident seals. Lying on the warm sand afterward, sunbathing in the buff felt free and relaxing.

"Can we just stay here forever?" she dreamily asked.

He smiled back at her. His smile was all she needed.

As twilight approached, the view from the boat looking back toward the beach somehow became even more beautiful. Colors on the island and the water took on a special hue at this time of early evening, making it seem as if they were part of an oil painted seascape.

The air temperature remaining comfortable, they ate dinner outside on the boat's foredeck. Michael softly strummed his guitar and sang a song about being a sailor on the lowland sea. A group of seals arrived, swimming and splashing, stirring up phosphorescence in the darkened water resembling *Walt Disney's Wonderful World of Color*. Daphne leaned closer to Michael, whispering into his ear, "Thank you."

"Thank you?" he asked.

"These are truly the most wonderful days of my life. Thank you for turning me on to this magical, fantastic world."

"Um, that would be God," he corrected. "He is the one who created all this. Thank him."

She smiled. "Okay then. But thank you for being you."

Daphne would have been happy staying at Santa Rosa Island longer, but there were other islands to explore. So, after two days they departed Santa Rosa Island and anchored at Pelican Bay on the north side of Santa Cruz Island. Reading aloud from the Nautical Almanac, she informed Michael that, *at twenty-two miles long, Santa Cruz Island is the largest of the Channel Island group – even larger than more well-known Santa Catalina Island, which ranks third largest.*

It was relatively cool when they had first dropped anchor, but the morning was rapidly warming up. "I'm going for a swim," she announced, stripping off her jeans and top and diving naked off the side of the boat. Treading water, her breasts barely visible beneath the surface, skeins of hair fanned out floating around her shoulders, she motioned for him to join her. He quickly followed suit, jumping feet-first into water he laughingly shouted was *scrotum-tighteningly cold!*

They spent the afternoon hiking and exploring Santa Cruz Island. "I'm sure we are not the first white people to set foot on this remote rock off the California coast, but it certainly feels like it," Michael surmised.

Indeed, the only worn pathways were those crudely roughed out by local sheep. The view as they reached the top of a very tall hill was breathtaking: 360 degrees of vast Pacific stretching out in all directions surrounding the island. Sitting on a rock, watching seagulls flying far below, it felt to Daphne as if they had truly reached the top of the world.

With sardonic humor, Michael began describing the possibility of developing a condominium project along the hillside to match those on the heavily populated mainland, pointing out perfect spots for a hotel and tourist resort. With a deprecatory nod he laughed at the foolishness of it all, while sadly acknowledging that much of the mainland must have once been this naturally beautiful, before developers raped the land to make their fortunes.

Evening on the boat was a bit chilly, so they huddled in the tiny cabin reading books by the light of a single alcohol lamp that hung by a hook on the cabin ceiling. For Daphne it felt deliciously primitive. This is what the Laura Ingalls Wilder characters must have felt like in *Little House on the Prairie*, she thought as she reclined against Michael's chest, the boat rocking as gently as a baby's cradle.

The brass chronometer on the bulkhead silently ticked midnight, that moment when tomorrow becomes today. "I could live like this forever," she whispered softly, barely disturbing the quiet. "Just you and me on this little boat." She turned her head to look at him. His eyes were closed; he had fallen asleep.

The next day they rowed the dinghy into a massive cavity in the island called the Painted Cave. The almanac declared it the largest sea cave in all of California: *The cave opening is more than eighty feet high with tunnels stretching more than a thousand feet into the island.*

The light from the tunnel entrance steadily diminished as they rowed deeper into the cave's interior. Deeper yet, all light became extinguished except for the fantastic colors glowing on the cave walls created by lichens, algae, and various rock types – indeed, it was a *Painted Cave.* Neither Daphne nor Michael had ever before experienced anything quite like it. The visual sensation of straining one's eyes to view the mottled illumination on the walls and ceiling, while listening to dozens of unseen seals leaping from rocky shelves into the dark water, splashing all around, was surreal.

Progressing still deeper into the cave, the resonating seal *songs* became almost deafening in the inky blackness. Daphne found it a bit spooky listening to all this wonderful noise in near total darkness, so dark that, although Michael was seated just inches from her in the dinghy, she could not really see him. The absence of light in the cave seemed to tweak her other senses, making them more alert. An intense fishy aroma permeated the cave.

"Of the five senses, stimulation of the olfactory nerves should not be discounted," she could hear Michael's voice in the blackness. "Scent is a larger part of life than we give credit."

Daphne did not find the extreme odor at all offensive. Somehow it even added to her enjoyment of the Painted Cave. There must have been hundreds of seals, fishes, pelicans, gulls, and other marine life making the cave their home, and she found it a fascinating experience being able to visit them in their natural environ.

Rowing back toward daylight, exiting the cave, Daphne shouted back, "Thanks guys for allowing us in. Hope *we* did not smell too bad to you!"

35

COW PALACE

Michael had been in San Francisco for several weeks running construction jobs. He loved being foreman and had been putting in long hours, only to collapse each night into a hotel bed. So, one Friday evening his boss, the project manager, suggested they have a little fun and take in the big rodeo at the Cow Palace.

"Ever seen a rodeo?" the boss asked, as they drove along the Bayshore Freeway.

"Um, yes. I've been to a few," Michael prevaricated, secretly smiling to himself. The boss had no way of knowing about his former rodeo career. He had entertained the boss on several occasions with colorful tales of sailing around Point Conception and cruising the Channel Islands, and imagined the boss viewed his young employee as an adventurous young man of the sea. Divulging a former rodeo life, on the heels of those sea stories, might come across as a bit too much adventurism to be believable, casting Michael as some self-aggrandizing fabulist who makes things up as he goes along. "Never been to the one at the Cow Palace, though," he added.

"Well, this is a big one. Should be quite a show," the boss said. "If you ask me, those cowboys are just plain crazy to ride those wild horses and bulls, but it's always exciting to watch."

"Funny thing," Michael began with hesitation, trying to decide if he really wanted to share this information with his boss, "I used to compete in rodeos." There, he had said it.

The boss drove on, without any response.

"It was in a previous life," Michael offered.

The boss laughed. "Jesus, you're not much more than a kid. How could you have a *previous life* already?"

"A bull rider to be precise," Michael added.

The boss clearly did not believe that for a minute, giving his passenger a skeptical sideways glance. "A bull rider, huh?" he mumbled.

"Mm hm," Michael confirmed. Then, as an offer of proof, added, "You know, I might be able to get us into the rodeo for free, because a lot of the rodeo folk know me."

Calling Michael's bluff, he sarcastically dared, "Okaaay, let's do that!"

It suddenly occurred to Michael that it had been years since he had spoken to anyone in the rodeo world. It might be a whole different crowd now. Maybe that offer to get them in for free was not such a good idea. Perhaps he just should have kept his big mouth shut!

Arriving at the Cow Palace, not far from the parking lot they spotted two cowgirls sitting on horseback who were obviously part of the rodeo. Michael walked up to them, not quite sure what to say, deciding to break the ice by name dropping. "Either of you happen to know a cowboy named Gary Leffew?" Leffew was a California cowboy who became World Champion Bull Rider several years prior. Anyone who is anyone would know that name.

"Yup, sure do. I know Gary ... and I know you too, Mike Perry," one of the cowgirls said, looking down from atop her horse. "You practically walked right past me without sayin' a word. You gettin' stuck-up these days?"

The boss's jaw dropped, utterly dumbfounded. Not only did this cowgirl know Mike's name but she was also a very attractive cowgirl to boot, an observation that was not at all lost on the boss man. Michael had not recognized her under the wide brimmed hat casting a shadow over her face, and her hair was now a different color, but she was someone from the old rodeo crowd: Debbie Hipple. Michael just stood there, grinning up at Debbie who was sitting tall and pretty in the saddle.

"You're not in the bull riding up here, are you?" she asked. "I haven't seen ya around in a long time."

With that, Michael turned and gave a long, lingering, ever-so-smug look in his boss's direction. The boss's face displayed absolute astonishment as the words *bull riding* sunk in.

"No," he replied, turning back to face Debbie. "I've retired from all that, don't ride bulls at all anymore. I'm up here for work and just thought I'd swing by the rodeo for old time's sake."

Debbie and Michael chatted for several more minutes, catching up on each other's lives. She had recently gotten married, he learned. "What about you?" she asked.

"Nope, I'm still single," he admitted.

She gave a tiny snort, saying, "Well, no fault in that. Sometimes I'm wishin' I was still single."

They both laughed.

"Well, if yer not entered, you and yer friend here might could use a couple tickets?"

Michael nodded and she handed him two free passes for admittance into the grandstands.

The boss man was duly impressed, it was obvious. As Debbie loped away on her horse, the boss, grinning ear to ear, raised his hand in the air, inviting a high-five. Slapping palms, he said, "Michael Perry, I don't think I will ever doubt you again!"

36

THE PLAN

Michael had not seen his friend Denton in over a year, not since they had sailed up the coast together. Now they were out for a day sail in Santa Monica Bay aboard Denny's new boat, a beautiful, blue-hulled thirty-one-foot ketch. "I'm all done with school and finally a real doctor," Denny told him. "This graceful lady is my first material dividend!"

It was great sailing with Denny again, the only guy he knew whose enthusiasm for sailing equaled his own. The only guy who seemed to completely understand the dream. On their prior voyage up the coast the two had spent countless hours discussing aspirations of cruising to far off islands. And so, as they sailed carelessly along on this splendidly typical California afternoon, they picked up the topic right where they had left off – with visions of coconut palms and tropical landfalls dancing in their heads.

Several hours slipped by, the late afternoon sun beginning to sink lower on the horizon, dipping behind Catalina, creating a halo-like glow encircling the island.

"It will be getting dark soon. Shall we turn around and head back to the harbor or keep on sailing past Catalina, onward to Hawaii?" Denton asked, facetiously.

"Onward to Hawaii!" Michael joked back with enthusiasm.

The two sat grinning at each other.

All at once, Denny's face lit up, almost like in a cartoon where a light bulb appears over the character's head when a brilliant idea strikes. "Damn!" he abruptly shouted. "Let's do it!"

"Do what? Sail to Hawaii?"

"Damn straight. Why not?"

"Now?"

"Get real. Of course not. But seriously, let's do it. I will have a couple months down time coming up before I begin my residency at Queen of Angels Hospital. It might be the longest stretch of free time I will ever have. This is the time to do it."

"You're serious," Michael said, incredulously.

"As a heart attack," Denton confirmed. "And I'm a doctor. I know just how serious that can be." There was unabashed excitement on his face as he went on. "Listen, we could both take some classes in celestial navigation, outfit the boat for long range cruising, whatever it takes. I am telling you, man, we can do this!"

"I don't know. It sounds great, but I pretty much always imagined sailing my very own boat to Hawaii someday, not just crewing. And, once I cross the pond, I won't wanna stop at Hawaii. I'll want to keep going, cruise the South Pacific."

Denton briefly looked crestfallen, as if his brilliant idea had just been proven implausible. Then his face lit up again with renewed alacrity. "You *will* be sailing your own boat and able to keep on sailing past Hawaii to anywhere you like."

"How's that gonna work?"

"You are going to sell your little twenty-seven-foot sloop and buy half interest in my boat! And you can keep on sailing to whatever exotic port you like. *Mi barco es tu barco*. We will sail to Hawaii together, then I will fly home, start my new job at the hospital, and use every vacation I get to fly out and meet up with you, to sail on to whatever the next destination may be."

Michael looked dubious. This only made Denton more animated as he worked on convincing him.

"Think about it," Denny went on. "I'm telling you, man, this is feasible. In fact, it is the *only* way it can work! The only way I will ever be able to do it. Once I begin practicing medicine at the hospital, I'll never be able to get months off at a time to do any long-term cruising. You will be realizing your goals doing the time-consuming stuff, the heavy lifting, maintaining the boat, sailing wherever you please. I will be realizing mine by arriving at whatever port we have the boat, and sailing together across more oceans. We both win!"

37

JOURNAL

I am going to do it! I am really going to do it … sail across the ocean in a small boat to a tropical isle! My friend Denny – make that Doctor Denny – and I plan to set sail for Hawaii! I have never been to Hawaii and the idea of arriving for the very first time by sailing across two thousand miles of ocean is just so incredible, I can barely get my mind around it. Our scheduled departure is still many months away and there's lots to do in preparation, like getting the boat ready for such a passage and learning bluewater navigation, for starters.

I already gave notice to the bosses at work that I would be leaving the company in a few months. Of course, they asked why. Telling them I'm sailing my boat to Hawaii and watching their jaws drop open was terrifically amusing. I realize what a great job I've got with a wonderful company, but a guy's got to know his priorities. Right? To quote the gospel according to Denton: *Money is over-rated. In the blink of an eye, our lives are gone. Don't be among those choosing to sacrifice their lives to mundane routine in pursuit of the almighty dollar.* Of course, this sage advice was dispensed by my friend who soon will be a wealthy doctor.

A week or so after that, the president of the company – Mr. Upshaw – called me into his office to discuss my decision to leave, even offering me a raise if I stayed. I remained adamant. In the end he said he understood, and even admired, what I was doing. He gave me his blessing and said to contact him when my voyage was completed.

He said he would make every effort to see that I'm rehired. That was amazingly nice of him.

So, my plan now is to work as many hours as I can and earn as much *dinero* as possible before leaving the company. I also plan to sell my truck and anything else I own because I won't be needing such stuff anymore. I am converting everything to cash, since it may be a long time before I will have any sort of income again.

Last night I drove over to Mom and Dad's house for dinner and to tell them my plans. Not sure why I thought that would turn out well. Nothing I've ever done has gotten my father's seal of approval. Just before setting sail for San Francisco last year, my father told me how *stupid* he thought that was. I can still hear his voice, chastising me on the eve of my departure: *Sailing is for rich lazy people with too much time on their hands! Normal people just don't do things like that. When are you going to grow up and join the real world?* Too bad he wasn't there when I battled fierce seas sailing around Point Conception, he would have seen just how *lazy* it wasn't!

It is as if his greatest joy has always been making me feel smaller than him. Still, last night at dinner I was excited to tell them about my plans for sailing to Hawaii. Dad just sat there, not even looking at me. Then, peppering his speech with barnyard expletives that deserve no repeating here, he launched into a completely unprovoked tirade about how people who do things like sailing across oceans have a few screws loose!

His face turned purple and the vein in his temple began visibly pulsating as he shouted at me across the dinner table. *Worthless bums and spoiled brats wasting their lives on frivolous nonsense!* Throwing his napkin down on the table and leaving the room, he added, *you should fit in just fine and dandy with all those good-for-nothings*!

The outrageousness of his words and attitude cut like a knife through the joy I had come over to share with them. But then, he has long seemed to me to be a man with little joy of his own for some reason. My father stands as a beacon of all that I do not wish to be. I don't want to look back when I am old, like in my forties or fifties, and regret not satisfying my youthful dreams. Perhaps I owe him for this.

Mom just called a few minutes ago, apologizing for Dad's behavior last night. Of course, *he* would never call to apologize. I thanked her for calling. "You know," she said before hanging up, "I still pray every night for Saint Michael to watch over you."

38

THE SNOWY GRAVESITE

Joe Perry both loved and hated California. He did not miss shoveling snow or those horrible Chicago winters, that's for sure. But he had lived in California now for several years and it still did not truly feel like home. The people in California were different. Everything was all about keeping up with the Joneses, and the California Joneses were damn hard to keep up with. Joe's next-door neighbor drove a goddam Rolls Royce. It was an old one but, still, how the hell do you keep up with that?

California people really annoyed him, a lot. Phonies. So many of the men were pseudo-intellectual, limp-wristed, unmanly cartoons. And California women, while he had to admit they were easy on the eyes, were all a bunch of phonies too. Total fakes. Though maybe that was just the very nature of all women everywhere. Women, in general, are misleading and fake: they wear makeup, dye their hair, glue on fake eyelashes, high heels give them fake height, undergarments reshape their figures. All of it fake!

And they don't just put on clothes to get dressed, like men do. No, women decorate themselves like goddam Christmas trees, adorned with dangling ornaments from ear lobes, wrists, ankles, you name it. They wear short skirts and low-cut tops designed to draw a man's attention to specific areas of a woman's anatomy, then take offense if the gaze lingers a millisecond too long.

So much talk lately about women's liberation, Women's Libbers they are called, claiming they don't want to be seen as sex objects. Total nonsense. No doubt in Joe's mind that women enjoy being desired sexually by men. Why else would they subject themselves to all the torturous methods of beauty, like tweezing eyebrows and walking around in uncomfortable heels? Total phonies.

So, while Joe did not miss the Midwestern winters, or even the muggy mosquito infested summers, he did miss the people. Somehow Midwestern people just seemed more genuine. Hardy folk, sturdy enough to withstand months of snow and muddy springtime thaw.

Most of all, though, he missed being a somebody: a big shot in town. Back in Illinois he was a well-known successful businessman, a home builder who had been offering the American dream of home ownership to hundreds of families over the years. He had a legacy. California had, thus far, quashed continuation of that legacy. Twice Joe had taken the state contractor license exam and twice he had failed. Failed! This outraged Joe, for he clearly knew more about construction than the egg-head morons who conjured up the exam questions. All that stood between Joe and California success was that goddam license!

It was a recent trip back to the homeland that caused Joe to fully realize how much he missed his former stature; the way people treated him with respect because of his business acumen, someone to be admired. A big fish in a small pond, perhaps. But in California he wasn't even a minnow in an ocean.

His estranged father's funeral was what had drawn him back. He had deliberated about going and almost did not attend, deciding only at the last moment to board a plane to Chicago in the dead of winter. There was no love lost between his father and him. The two had never been close when Joe was growing up. But the real disaffection came when Joe was in the army overseas.

In France and Germany, where many of his fellow soldiers partied and went wild when on leave, spending their military wages like water,

Joe had been living frugally, sending his pay back home to his father with instructions to bank the funds for him. Joe expected a nice pile of cash to be waiting upon his return to the states. But his father had spent nearly all of Joe's money, claiming times were hard and he needed the money to support the family. He wasn't even apologetic about it, just delivered the news as fact.

Joe never trusted the man again and had not spoken more than twenty words to his father in twenty years. Last time he saw the man he'd become a pathetic, fat, one-legged old geezer who had lost a leg due to diabetes yet continued to gorge himself on sugary foods. Likely, that's what ultimately killed him.

And now Joe found himself standing at the snowy gravesite, looking down as the casket was lowered into a frozen hole in the ground. It was damn cold weather, befitting the way he felt about his father. He shivered, the air like tiny needles biting into his exposed face. The barren trees nearby, like everything else in this wintry part of the country, looking as dead as any of the corpses buried in this cemetery. At least Joe would one day be buried someplace warm. His mourning family members would not need to shiver in the cold watching him being lowered.

He felt no emotion over the loss of his father. No sadness. Merely the circle of life. People are born, people die.

On the return flight to Los Angeles, Joe decided he was glad he had made the move to the West Coast after all. It was the right thing to do for both him and his family. California was the *Golden State*, land of opportunities. Sure, L.A. had its problems: the people were phonies and the air was polluted but, overall, it was a better place. More opportunities for his kids. Lots of money in L.A. A greater chance that his daughter Jaimie might someday marry some wealthy doctor or even a movie mogul. Joe smiled at the thought of his only daughter grown up and married to some rich guy, living in a mansion, all because Joe had moved his family to the land of plenty.

As for his son, he had never understood that kid, or any of his generation for that matter. So-called free spirits indulging in free love, spouting nonsense under the guise of free speech. An entitled generation who had grown up with everything handed to them, without truly earning anything. He worried about Mike. By the time Joe was his son's age he already had his own business, owned his own house, and had a wife and kid. Shit, that kid was now well into his twenties and still playing Popeye the Sailor. Lollygagging around boats. Joe could not understand that fascination at all; he hated boats. His one and only time crossing an ocean was in the Army on his way to war-torn Europe, an altogether horrible passage. And now, to Joe's utter exasperation, his son had stupidly given notice that he was quitting his job – the first really good job the kid ever had – to go off sailing. Was he insane?

Somehow, in this crazy upside-down California-land, a boy who didn't know shit from Shinola about construction had managed to finagle his way into a foreman position, and now he was walking away from it. Very likely Mike would never find a job that good again. Joe tried to talk some sense into his son, but to no avail. Twenty-six and still acting like a kid. Someday he'll be thirty and probably *still* a kid. Fifty! If Mike wasn't careful, life's opportunities were going to pass him by. He was going to wake up one day a destitute old man with nothing to show for it, too old to make anything of himself then.

39

READY FOR BLUE WATER

They christened the ketch *Makani Kai* – Hawaiian for sea breeze, since their maiden voyage would be trade wind breezes blowing them across the sea to beautiful Hawaii – and began outfitting her for an ocean crossing: beefing up the rigging, installing a self-steering wind vane, and a lengthy list of similar tasks. Denton was not yet making the big bucks associated with being a doctor, and Michael would soon be unemployed, so they tried to accomplish as much as possible with limited funds, buying many of the necessary items second hand. One of those items was a four-man inflatable life raft ... just in case the boat sank. The life raft came in a bag with a tag that warned not to inflate until needed.

"How do we know it even works if we can't inflate it to test it?" Michael wondered.

"Let's just hope we won't need it," was Denton's reply.

The sailors themselves needed some beefing up as well. Denton and Michael both enrolled in a correspondence course for celestial navigation, preparation for finding their way across 2,200 miles of open ocean in a tiny fiberglass boat that would likely take somewhere around twenty days. Hours were spent studying together, trying to learn navigation by the stars and planets using ancient tools of the navigational trade, like the sextant, and absorbing Bowditch. Completely different from *coastal* navigation, they quickly discovered this to be some very complex stuff: azimuth tables, sight reduction calculations, great circles, sidereal hour angles, equinoctial, and myriad other terms new to them. Neither had ever crossed an ocean before and it often felt a good bit like the blind leading the blind.

"So much math involved," Michael complained one evening after a long study session. "Never my best subject in school."

"I know," Denton nodded sympathetically. "But you'll get it. These are the most important fundamental skills any human being can learn: figuring out where you are by using the tools of our ancestors."

"I pretty much understand many of the principles involved, but it is beyond me how I am ever going to figure out my position at sea using what I've learned," Michael confessed.

"Not to worry," Denton agreed. "To be honest, I don't really understand a lot of this stuff either. But the more we use it, the more it will become second nature to both of us."

They stayed up well into late night hours planning the voyage, smoking doobies, listening to Lynyrd Skynyrd and Marshall Tucker blasting through giant speakers strategically placed on the floor. They also began discussing whether they might be better off with a crew of four, rather than just the two of them. "Turns at the helm and other shipboard tasks would sure be easier," Denton suggested. At some point, the idea of a crew that includes females was initiated and roundly applauded.

"Daphne has proven herself fairly proficient on a boat," Michael suggested. "I'm sure she would love to be a part of this."

"And there is a nurse I've been seeing. She doesn't really have any sailing experience, but I'll bet she might be up for this sort of adventure," Denton added.

"Looks like we have our crew!" They both slapped palms in the air.

40

HAWAII OR BUST

The ketch motored out of the slip and headed down the Marina del Rey channel to cheers and waves from numerous well-wishers, friends, family, and even a couple of photographers from the local newspapers. The send-off was far more elaborate than the non-existent one received on their previous voyage to San Francisco. Michael's mother and sister were among those who came to see them off. "Aloha! I love you, big bro!" Jaimie shouted. Conspicuously absent was his father.

Michael at the helm, Denton hoisting canvas, they switched off the engine and sailed out past the breakwater in the direction of the Hawaiian Islands – more than two thousand miles away across the sea. Looking back, they watched friends and family on the jetty continuing to wave farewells until morning mist and distance merged them all with the gray rocks upon which they stood.

Moving seaward, breaking from the gravitational pull of Los Angeles, the feeling was exhilarating! All four on board shared in it: Dr. Denny, Nurse Lisa, Daphne, and Michael – none of whom had ever crossed the Pacific before. Four bluewater virgins braving the wide-open ocean in a tiny sailboat!

Looking out at the vast gray watery universe that lay ahead, Denton proclaimed: "This voyage is an event that will imbue the rest of our lives with meaning." Then purposefully striding out onto the bowsprit, raising his arms skyward like a shaman, he shouted the words of Poet Laureate

John Masefield as loudly as he was able into the wind: "Hunger for a life beyond the limits of the land, where the wild ocean shouts upon the sand!"

By noon the wind increased to push *Makani Kai* along at seven knots. Joshua – the name with which they'd christened the new self-steering device, after the famous circumnavigator Joshua Slocum – was working perfectly, allowing all of them to move freely about the boat.

Daphne, sitting out on the bowsprit, was all smiles, bare feet dangling over the side, spray misting her face, dolphins dodging and weaving in the water below. Lisa and Denton, sitting atop the doghouse, were scanning the horizon for whales. It was the stuff of which dreams are made, a scene right out of a movie.

But it did not take long for their collective idealistic enthusiasm to get a dose of harsh reality. Seventy miles offshore, in the wake of San Nicolas Island – the outermost of California's Channel Islands – the sky clouded over, winds increased, and seas became large and deliberate. With the wind howling in their ears, Denton put the first reef in the mainsail as Daphne experienced her first bout of seasickness, her face a ghostlike waxen paleness, regurgitating over the lee rail.

Deep into the night, no one had quite yet obtained their full sea-legs. In the process of putting another reef in the mainsail and exchanging the working jib for a storm jib, Michael began to feel queasy. With the task of reducing sail completed – a rigorous undertaking in pitch black darkness while the boat is lurching like a bucking bronco – he, too, vomited over the side. They would spend the next thirty-six consecutive hours thrashing about, battling heavy seas, wind, and rain.

The light of dawn revealed a boundless gray seascape of marching waves assaulting the hull. Denton was now sick as well and would sleep the rest of the day, or as much as he was able.

Everyone on board was feeling horribly ill ... with the sole exception of happy-go-lucky Lisa. Nurse Lisa, the only non-sailor in the bunch, seemed to be handling the conditions just fine, remaining delightfully cheerful through it all.

Daphne, continuously vomiting until she had nothing left, was sickest of all. Plus, she was not able to face going down below into the cabin to use the toilet for any purpose, since the boat's motion is even more pronounced inside such a tight enclosure. Being inside the ship's head was like being in a single-person elevator with the doors closed, no ventilation, and the tiny room in which you are entombed begins bouncing not only up and down, but side to side as well.

So, whenever nature called, Daphne would do a balancing act topside, grabbing onto the shrouds which hold up the mast and hanging her backside over the rail to eliminate into the sea. Surely the most humiliating thing she had ever experienced in her life.

With Denton flat on his back in the cabin below, Michael's day consisted primarily of steering the boat and throwing up. While doing so, Lisa occasionally would pop her head out the hatch and, with a sarcastic guffaw, enthusiastically holler, "Hey! Are we all having fun, or what?"

By the third day, everyone had gained their sea-legs and the communal vomiting ceased. They all were becoming accustomed to living in harmony aboard thirty-one feet of floating fiberglass.

Lisa had even taken up farming on board, growing sprouts in some Tupperware containers so they would have fresh greens after the current victuals had been depleted. Michael was impressed; Lisa was always thinking ahead and never complained about anything. Though she did lodge one jocular expostulation at the skippers: "The *brochure* describing this *luxury cruise* promised lots of tropical sun and if I don't get some sun soon, I will demand a full refund!"

There had been no sun, but plenty of wind. Even with reduced canvas they were sailing more than one hundred miles per day. Too cloudy to get any good sextant fixes from the sun or stars for celestial navigation. Relying on *dead reckoning*, Denton guessed they would be picking up the trade winds any day now.

Squalls came and went, occasional hard rain battering the cabin top making for a deafening roar to those below. Michael enjoyed the rain. Alone at the helm at 4:00 a.m., soaked and cold after commanding the vessel through a night at sea, fresh rain felt refreshing on his face.

For Daphne, the pounding precipitation created a good deal of fear. Sliding the overhead hatch back a bit, cautiously emerging from the cabin, disheveled, looking like some little child's beat up toy doll, one that had been banged around and worn out, she joined Michael in the cockpit, nestling close to him for support against the up and down of the boat. Her head resting against his shoulder, she sat staring out at the nothingness. The rain lessened to a drizzle, accompanied by an odd watery petrichor.

"I think sailing a small boat across an ocean is like suffering from claustrophobia while surrounded by infinity," she said philosophically.

Michael offered a concurring nod.

She then confessed to him her growing trepidation that the frequent storms would capsize the boat out in the middle of nowhere and, with no one to rescue them, they would all drown. He pulled her close to calm her fears. To little avail, he suspected.

A week passed, then two. For the most part, the crew spent their days with hardly a trace of ennui, keeping busy about the boat, reading books, and observing the sea life around them.

Thousands of *velella* dotted the water, tiny jelly-like creatures that seemed to gain their locomotion by wiggling a small sail-like fin on their backs. Several washed aboard, giving the crew a close look at them, finding them harmless and able to be handled with bare hands. Denton suggested adding them to sauce and pouring over pasta but had no takers.

Also, one morning Lisa found a squid washed onto the foredeck and, using it for bait, began trolling for fish. Unfortunately, she only succeeded at entangling the fishing line with the taffrail log line.

Denton spent most days reading and playing music on his harmonica. Michael, who had never before visited Hawaii, was enjoying a book of Hawaiian stories by Jack London, preparing himself for arrival in paradise. Lisa was into a book Michael recommended to her, a true story about a teenage sailor who sailed around the world alone in a very small boat named *Dove*.

Daphne was able to keep busy during daylight hours, but each night when the sun went down she became nervous and fearful. Often, she would sit out in the cockpit all night long snuggling close to Michael.

With stars blanketing them, extending from horizon to horizon in every direction, Michael would point out the various constellations. "A canopy of eternity," he told her. "It looks as if someone has drawn with sparkling white chalk upon the unending blackboard sky."

"It really is a fantastic sight," Daphne agreed, nodding her head.

It seemed they were surrounded by stars, both overhead and upon the water as well. With Beethoven's Moonlight Sonata softly emanating from the tape deck and the little blue ketch slicing her way through inky black seas, they watched thousands of tiny phosphorescent particles shooting from the wake, looking like diamonds glowing against a velvet background, twinkling for but a moment before disappearing, only to be replaced by a thousand more with the next wave breaking against the hull.

"What a beautiful show put on by God especially for us," Daphne remarked. Her anxiety, like the shifting mood of a wind that scurries across the surface of the sea, often appeared to lessen with conversation.

"So, what were you like in high school?" Michael asked, a subject out of nowhere, trying to keep her engaged.

Daphne giggled. "Taft High School. I was a cheerleader."

He began teasing her, good-naturedly, about this. He thought he could see her cheeks flush with embarrassment, or perhaps it was merely the red glow from the binnacle reflecting on her face.

"What about you? You told me you were a band geek!" she retorted.

"Not a band geek. I played in a rock band. That is entirely different."

"Yes, but weren't you a drama dude, too? Musicals and plays?"

"Guilty as charged," he admitted, laughing. "You know, I once played the part of a sailor in our high school production of *The Blue, Blue Sea*. Who would have ever imagined that I would someday become a *real* sailor out on the open ocean, sailing to a tropical island with a beautiful cheerleader by my side?"

"Former cheerleader," she corrected.

They both laughed.

Then, more seriously, she confessed, "This sailing voyage is truly the stuff of dreams, but sometimes I just get so scared being out here hundreds of miles from the nearest land."

Drawing her tightly into his arms, he reassured her. "No worries, kiddo." Then, with an exaggerated British accent, sang, "Nothing to get hung about ..."

"Strawberry fields forever," she finished.

They laughed again, as if laughter was the cure.

Sailing onward into the night, however, neither they nor the others asleep below were aware that the drip, drip, drip of sea water slowly seeping through a tiny leak was threatening to sink their vessel to the bottom of the Pacific.

41

JOURNAL

Danger, Will Robinson, danger! At dawn I went below to wake up Denton for his turn at the helm. As soon as my foot connected with the cabin sole, I knew something was wrong. The floor was wet and squishy. Daphne, seeing the look on my face, was quickly on the verge of hysteria. Her shriek awakened Denny.

I got on my knees, lifting the floorboard to check the bilge. To my absolute horror, it was filled with water to the point of overflowing. I grabbed the hand pump and began pumping, counting aloud the number of pumps as I went.

In a heartbeat Denny was standing behind me with his hands on my shoulders, looking over my head and down at the bilge. One hundred twenty pumps with no noticeable diminution of water level. "Sweet Jesus!" he exclaimed. "We got us a fucking leak!"

Everyone scrambled around trying to discern the origin of the leak while I kept on pumping. Was it my imagination, or was the water perceptibly rising despite my efforts? The life raft that we had never tested sprang into my thoughts. There was no certainty it would inflate if needed. The normally unflappable Nurse Lisa was now wringing her hands and a look of sheer terror had taken over her features. Daphne was chanting, *Heavenly Father, please help us.*

Denny crawled into the cramped engine compartment with a flashlight and some wrenches. I could hear him banging around on things and cussing up a storm. He went about tightening everything he could get a wrench on, including the fitting around the propeller shaft.

Another couple hundred pumps and, at last, the water that had been flooding in finally appeared to be receding slightly. "Must've been the propeller shaft," he said when I informed him of my progress.

Some pretty tense moments experienced by all of us this morning, and God only knows how long it will be before the cabin floor dries. One cannot be too cautious on this great and unforgiving ocean.

I'm back out in the cockpit now, looking all around me, one wave after another, ad infinitum. Look in any direction and all one sees is sky and ocean. Sometimes it is such a jolt to realize that we are but the tiniest speck floating along in the middle of it all.

I tried the VHF several days ago with every station totally dead. Even an astronaut up in space has communication with a support staff on earth. We have none. We are as cut off from the civilized world as anyone could possibly be. Denny and I have even discussed, half joking/half in earnest, what should be done if one of us were to die out here. We are days, maybe even weeks, from having contact with the outside world. A body would decompose quickly. The only viable option would be to chuck the body overboard ... fish food! A gruesome thought.

Aside from this morning's scare, it has become a spectacular day. Embraced by the azure arms of a tropical sea, we've had twin headsails up and been *running* all day. This is what being locked into the Trades is all about! A glorious sensation, a mariner's mecca, sliding through curling waves with clear sky and a warm sun (finally).

I was able to get a good navigational fix at noon using the sextant. Denny says that the reason pirates are always depicted as having an eye patch is because after years and years at sea, staring at the sun for navigation ruins the eye they use to peer through the sextant. He was joking. At least, I think he was. Argh!

If I did my calculations properly, today's position means we have logged 1,692 miles thus far, putting us past the 3/4 mark, and getting closer to our rendezvous with paradise. Denny took a sun shot as well. But when he did the math, he came up with a slightly different position. So, who was correct? We flipped a coin. We call this technique "coin flip navigation."

Something else we did today? Making a big production out of writing notes and placing them into an empty wine bottle. We each wrote a personal message, followed by the request to whomever may find the notes to please contact us at the mainland addresses that we included. I put down my parent's address since I no longer have a mainland residence. With our messages to the world sealed securely in the bottle, we tossed it into the sea. I wonder, will the wine bottle go bobbing ceaselessly or one day wash up on some distant shore, our messages fading in the sun.

Evening has now set in. Picture this: coasting along, all sails drawing on a light breeze; calm, nearly flat seas; billions of stars above, shining more brightly than any landlubber could ever imagine; moon shadow trailing behind us in the water. Moving through eternal waves, gently rocked to-and-fro by the motion of the sea.

Barefoot and shirtless I sit in the cockpit with my shipmates. We are listening to Mozart's String Quintet Number 5 in D major on tape. This is the precise sort of night I have long dreamed about. Unless you're all about wealth, fame, or other such shallow pursuits, is there anything in all the world as purely enchanting as this? And, to top it all off, we are on our way to Hawaii.

42

JOURNAL

As we were chowing down our dinner last night, Daph and I both spotted a land mass at the exact same time, just as the sun was going down and the sky filled with an abundance of purples to color the sky. Then Denny and Lisa saw it too and all four of us began slapping palms and dancing around the boat. It was so damn exciting!

At first light, the islands of Maui and Molokai became clearly visible on the horizon. The sight and aroma of land began engulfing and stimulating our senses. Believe me, after nearly a month at sea with nothing but salt air, the scent of land nearly knocked me breathless – the tropical flora so awesome!

We sailed the length of Maui to reach the Pailolo Channel. Sailing down the channel was something else, the funnel effect between the two islands creating gale force winds! Oddly enough, these were among the roughest conditions we experienced the entire voyage, and right here close to land.

Rounding Maui, the entrance to Lahaina Harbor is a bit tricky if you are doing it for the first time, as we were. Requiring some careful maneuvering, we were able to spot the navigational markers and line them up. With Denny on the foredeck watching for markers, I sailed the boat into Lahaina Harbor.

My God! We have finally arrived! There are no words to adequately describe the elation which I know we are all feeling. Lahaina, Maui ... our first landfall in 21 days. And what a glorious landfall it is. Never having been to Hawaii before, I spent considerable time imagining what such paradise might look like as I sailed. And now, my first glimpse of paradise – Lahaina, a quaint little village dominated by the famous century-old Pioneer Inn, palm trees springing up along the sandy beach, and green mountains looming up in the distance – this is *exactly* how I had been picturing it. Right out of *Adventures in Paradise*! We made it!

YOUNG AND ALIVE

The reception they received at Maui was grander than any of them would have anticipated. Their arrival attracted a small number of tourists and other spectators, snapping photographs and asking all sorts of questions about the voyage. They felt like celebrities.

Tying up along a wooden quay, they began washing twenty-one days of salt and abuse from the boat, as well as washing down themselves – exuberantly singing and dancing around like lunatics, squirting each other with the dockside hose, relishing the cool clean sensation of *fresh* water on their skin for the first time since leaving California.

Daphne nearly lost her footing several times, not being used to terra firma. Regaining land legs took more than a few wobbly steps for Denton, Lisa and Michael as well. All of them looking quite the geriatric bunch, leaning on one another for support.

It was 3:00 local time when they arrived at Lahaina. By the time they cleared customs – although Hawaii is the 50th state, anyone arriving by private vessel must clear customs – and found a secure spot in the harbor to park the boat, it was nearly 7:00 p.m.

The first evening ashore was spent at the Lahaina Yacht Club, indulging in hot showers, enjoying a hearty meal, and gleefully accepting many rounds of congratulatory drinks, courtesy of LYC.

"I was down on the dock and watched you arrive," one of the club imbibers said to Michael, with a congratulatory clap on the back. "While most people's first impression of Hawaii is likely the inside of an airport followed by a taxi ride to some resort hotel, you arrived quite differently – sailing your boat right up to a dock extending from the shore of Maui, stepping off the boat, tying a dockline to a cleat, and taking your first steps upon the island. You, my friend, have experienced arriving in paradise as few others have."

Among newfound yacht club friends was a fellow named Kipp who owned a beautiful sailboat that he built himself. Being a carpenter, Michael was impressed by anyone able to build their own boat and told Kipp so.

"Impressed?" Kipp responded, with mock incredulity. "Anybody who I can impress deserves another round!"

And the drinks kept coming.

Several hours and rounds later, Michael and Daphne managed to stumble their way back to their floating home, while their boat mates continued frolicking in town. Michael was lying in the fo'c'sle, staring up through the open hatch at stars in the Hawaiian sky, Daphne nestled next to him. A warm tropical breeze wafting across their bodies, the boat was mercifully motionless, no more bouncing and lurching upon the open sea. His belly full and his head filled with tropical dreams, Michael whispered, "God, it is a wonderful feeling to be young and alive!"

"Mmm," Daphne murmured before drifting off to slumber, "it truly is."

44

ISLANDS AND STARS

After days exploring *The Valley Isle* of Maui, the second largest of the Hawaiian Islands, it was time to pull up anchor and set sail once again. The four began leisurely cruising *Makani Kai* to other Hawaiian locations, justifiably feeling far more like explorers than tourists.

First stop: the island of Lana'i where they spent several fun-filled days diving, discovering spectacular coral reefs and lava tubes. Swimming amongst thousands of amazingly colorful saltwater fish was something none of them had ever experienced before. The water so warm, comfortable, and clear they felt almost as at home as the fish.

From there, it was a twenty-two-mile sail to Kaunakakai on the island of Molokai. Almost entirely agricultural, tourists and outside visitors of any ilk were a rarity. Indeed, theirs was the only yacht in the harbor. The four *Haoles*, as Caucasians are referred to in Hawaii, were stared at with interested amusement by Molokai's rural inhabitants.

A pleasant reprieve from the limitations of a small boat at sea, each of them relished being able to hike for hours through the hills and forests of the island. Molokai's primary notoriety is the leper colony founded by the late Father Damien. For over a century, leprosy was a very real problem in these islands. Lepers were rounded up and isolated to this remote spot, as recently as the 1960s, and isolated from the rest of the Hawaiian population. A tropical Siberia.

From the Kalaupapa Peninsula, Denton, Lisa, Daphne and Michael walked down the steep cliff that leads to the leper colony. Daphne was shocked to learn that leprosy still exists and many lepers continue to inhabit this area. Nurse Lisa and Doctor Denny did their best to assure her that she need not worry about catching the disease though.

After weeks of exploring many of the less populated islands, it was time to head for Oahu. "Oahu," Denton explained, "is called the *Gathering Place*. It is where the city of Honolulu is located, where legendary Waikiki Beach and historic Pearl Harbor are located, and where eighty percent of the state's citizenry reside. Also, it's the most visited island by the *turistas*."

Setting sail for Oahu found them, once again, sailing through rather large seas with heavy winds in the Molokai Channel. It was a reminder of just how uncomfortable sailing in heavy weather can be. And it was this reminder that caused Daphne to reach a decision about something she had long been pondering.

She knew, at some point, Michael intended to continue with voyages to other archipelagoes, across wide expanses of ocean. That was his dream, but she knew now that it was not hers. This had been an amazing adventure so far, but she was done. The fear of more nights sailing in heavy seas paralyzed her. She had discussed her reservations many times with Michael but it was at this precise moment, with the boat once again lurching and salt spray stinging her eyes, that her final resolution was made. Denton and Lisa would be returning to their jobs in California soon, and she would be returning with them.

As the sun began to set, they sighted the Diamond Head crater on Oahu. A couple hours later they were tying up at a guest slip near the Hawaii Yacht Club in Ala Wai Marina, their crusty little blue ketch surrounded by shiny multi-million-dollar yachts from all over the world.

A few slips over from them was a spectacular eighty-plus-foot ketch named *Tatoosh* that absolutely dwarfed their own ketch. Classic lines, it was an older wooden boat, beautifully maintained. A solitary figure seated on her deck with a drink in his hand looked very familiar.

"Is that who I think it is?" Michael asked Denton.

Denton gave a long hard look in Tatoosh's direction. "Looks a lot like that actor from *Easy Rider*," Denton replied.

"Peter Fonda?" Lisa came rushing up excitedly from the galley below, Daphne close behind. But the lone sailor disappeared into Tatoosh's cabin before the ladies could see him.

"Seriously, Peter Fonda?" Daphne asked Denton.

Denton shrugged. Daphne looked to Michael for an answer.

"Dunno," he said. "Kinda looked like him though."

The next morning the girls were eager to begin exploring the tourist sights of Oahu, but Michael preferred to sleep in a bit longer. So, Denton and the girls walked over to a coffee shop located a few blocks away called Wailana's for breakfast. Michael would shower and join them soon.

A half-hour later, heading back to Makani Kai from the onshore showers, he found himself walking past *Tatoosh*. The same lone sailor was back out on deck, sipping coffee.

"Howdy," the sailor greeted, raising his mug high as Michael approached.

Holy shit! It *is* Peter Fonda, the little voice in Michael's head shouted silently. "Good morning," Michael managed to reply.

"I'm guessing from the looks of your boat that you folks did the transpac?" Peter Fonda inquired.

Michael just nodded, speechless. This was Peter Fonda!

"Where'd you sail from?" Fonda asked.

"California," Michael answered. "L.A., Marina del Rey."

"Me too. I mean that's where I sailed from too, a few years ago," the actor/sailor told him.

"We sailed to Lahaina first, then cruised around and ended up here," Michael said.

"Ah, Lahaina. That was my first landfall too, back when I made the crossing the first time. Jesus, don't you just love Lahaina? Fell in love with the place first time I set eyes on her. Lived there awhile, on this boat. Never wanted to leave. But eventually did. Miss those times."

"That's a lot of boat. She's beautiful," Michael noted, admiringly.

"Thanks. I don't really get to sail her much anymore. First time I've been on her in ages. Thinking maybe about selling her. I don't know. Maybe."

"Well, if you ever need crew, I'm available," Michael offered, mostly joking.

"I've got some boys that take care of her for me when I'm not here. Which is most of the time. They might let you tag along sometime if you're all that interested. Here, I'll give you their phone number. Give 'em a call, set something up." Handing Michael a slip of paper with the number written on it, he said, "Well, I need to make tracks. Flying back home in a couple hours. Nice talking with ya." Then he slipped below into the boat's cabin, once again disappearing.

Joining Denton and the girls at Wailana's, the first words Michael spoke were, "Boy, have I got a story to tell you!"

They rented a car and spent all week visiting the tourist sights of Oahu: Pearl Harbor, where the Japanese attack catapulted the U.S. into World War II; hiking Diamond Head; swimming with wild turtles – *honu* they are called in Hawaiian – on the famous North Shore; snorkeling in the natural marine sanctuary at Hanauma Bay; body surfing at Sandy Beach; shopping at International Market Place; and, of course, surfing at Waikiki Beach. The four of them were having an absolute ball, until melancholy began to set in toward week's end. Their romp together through paradise was reaching its finale.

As her final day in Hawaii drew near, nurse Lisa tried to remain her usual perky self but it was clear that she was in no hurry to leave this island paradise. She seemed to be savoring every lingering moment.

Denton was more upbeat. He knew he would be returning to do more voyages with Michael aboard the boat they owned together. The sooner he got back to work, the sooner he could venture out again upon the sea.

Michael and Daphne took a long walk along the sand of Waikiki Beach, holding hands, discussing a future that was about to end. "You know, you don't have to leave with Denny and Lisa, right? You know I want you to stay," he told her.

"Can I tell you something?" Daphne asked him.

"Of course."

"Returning to the mainland is not something I want to do," she conceded. "It is something I *have* to do. Just like sailing to far-away islands is something that you have to do. But I just cannot do it with you. It's not because I don't love you. I do. That's forever. You know that. I've never been so in love with anyone. If you said you wanted to stay here in Hawaii, live on the boat, spend the rest of our lives here together, I would do that in a New York minute. But crossing more oceans? It tears me up, because I really, really want to be with you ... but I just can't."

The following morning Denton, Lisa and Daphne would all be returning to the mainland. With a feeling of lament, Michael realized he would soon be all alone in paradise.

At Honolulu airport, there were final moments of intimacy. Denton and Michael sharing extremely warm handshakes and manly smacks on the back. Then Michael planted a gentle farewell peck on Nurse Lisa's cheek, to which she vigorously demanded, "Is that the best I get?"

Abruptly, Lisa grabbed him, enveloping him with a squeeze that made several vertebrae pop, before planting an extremely emotion-filled kiss on his lips. The force with which she delivered this final embrace, and the stunned look on Michael's face at being the recipient, caused everyone to laugh merrily, momentarily breaking the otherwise wistful mood.

For Daphne and Michael, their farewell began days ago and stretched right on to the moment she boarded her plane, each hoping right until that final moment that one of them might just say something that would change everything and keep them together.

Then they were gone, and Michael stood alone watching the plane take off. Several hours later he was sailing solo back to Maui.

45

HARBOR RAT

Anchored at Mala Wharf, just around the point from Lahaina a mile or so north, Michael Perry was seated in the bowsprit, feet dangling just a foot or two above the water, listening to KULA on the radio: Heart, singing *Barracuda*. Good station.

It was his day off. He'd been working all this past month with Kipp, an older yachtie he had met at Lahaina Yacht Club. Kipp was a one-man general contracting company and hired Michael to help with some finish carpentry on a new restaurant in Lahaina called Longhi's. Harder work and lower pay than being a foreman back in California but, living on the boat with no expenses, every penny earned could be saved.

"When I have saved enough money, I plan to set sail for Samoa," he had told Kipp.

"That's a mighty long sail," Kipp pointed out.

"When the time is right, my buddy from California will come here to Maui and we will do it together."

"Ah, youth," Kipp sighed. "I fully understand the *live for today and don't worry about tomorrow* mentality, but the future will indeed arrive one day and there may be a price to be paid for such wanderlust."

"You sound like my dad," Michael told him.

Kipp laughed, shaking his head, reluctantly admitting, "I probably do. But that doesn't make it any less true. Time is the only currency you spend without ever knowing your balance. Be sure to spend it wisely. Your generation thinks they will be young forever but one day you will wake up to discover you are *my* age."

The radio music switched from rock to the mellow sound of slack key guitar, the DJ announcing: "Here is local group Olomana performing their wonderful hit, *Ku'u Home O Kahalu'u*." The boat rocked gently in time with the music. It was so much nicer being anchored than tied up in a slip at a marina, so much quieter. Plus, it was free. The only downside was that every time he needed to go ashore, he had to jump in the dinghy and row. Depending on wind and sea conditions, this could at times be a tricky task.

Late afternoon he decided to row ashore to do a load of laundry, chuckling out loud upon realizing the tune he'd been absently humming to himself while rowing was *Michael Row the Boat Ashore*.

Beaching the dinghy, he hitched a ride into town for a hot shower at Lahaina Yacht Club and to pop coins into the clothes washing machines at the laundromat. Feeling all civilized and clean, he went on a shopping spree. He met a girl working in one of the tourist shops who was from California, the Valley. She had attended Pierce College. Small world. They talked for a while. He invited her over to the boat when she got off work.

"But how will I find you?" she asked.

"There is only me and one other boat out there. Just walk out onto the rocks and yell MIKE! I will hear you and row out to pick you up."

Deciding to splurge for a change on a good dinner, he chose the Blue Max Bar & Restaurant, a block away on Front Street. Located on an upper level, he traversed the steep flight of stairs, added his name to the long waiting list for a table, then sidled up to a seat at the bar to wait.

To occupy himself, he pulled out a notepad from his back pocket and asked the bartender if he could borrow a pen, then began writing the latest entry in his journal. Two stunningly beautiful young ladies sat down next to him at the bar. Real standouts, dressed to kill. Michael felt wholly inadequate sitting next to them with his grubby harbor rat appearance of cutoffs, tank top, Panama hat, and beard stubble. Good thing I just showered, he thought to himself, at least I don't stink. So, he was more than a little surprised when *they* initiated conversation.

"Are you writing a book?" one of them inquired, gesturing toward the notepad in front of him on the bar.

Maybe they were just slumming, he decided. "Um, well, yes, I am," he stammered, mentally excusing himself for such impromptu fabrication before deciding to qualify his fib. "Well, sort of anyway. I'm keeping a journal of my travels and experiences."

"Such as?" the other girl asked.

"I sailed over from the mainland and am living on my sailboat. Temporarily, that is. Until I decide to hoist anchor, let the wind fill my sails, and move on to wherever it takes me."

The one who asked the first question gave him a sincere-looking nod and smile. "Now, that truly sounds like the makings of an interesting book." She then informed him they were from San Francisco, had flown over to meet some friends in Honolulu who owned one of those multi-million-dollar yachts he'd been surrounded by when he was there, and just arrived at Maui earlier that very afternoon. Their friends would be joining them here for dinner soon.

Her name was Susan and she had a way about her that made every gesture seem flirtatious, reaching over to touch his arm in a more than friendly manner as she spoke … or maybe I have just been living alone on a small boat too long, Michael thought. The other girl, perhaps slightly older and with a British accent, was named Kiki. Both were impossibly good looking. Michael decided they had to be models or actresses.

The *maitre d'* called their name, not Michael's, even though he had arrived first, so the girls invited him to join them for dinner. Once seated, Michael made a grand production of presenting Susan with the tropical flower he plucked from the table centerpiece. With a girlish twitter she placed it behind her ear and wore it all evening.

They were chatting away, laughing, and having a terrific time when her "friends" walked in and joined them. Michael's jaw dropped. It was superstar Elton John, accompanied by a small entourage. Michael was dumbstruck. He'd been a big fan of Elton for years and found himself utterly speechless to be suddenly seated at the same table. Susan and Kiki noticed the stunned look on his face and thought it was quite funny. Elton noticed too, commenting: "Our guest looks rather like a deer caught on a dark night in a car's headlights."

Michael continued to just stare at the man. He couldn't help it.

"Helloooo," Elton was waving across the table at Michael who was still sitting with his mouth agape.

"Hi," Michael waved back timidly, causing Elton and everyone at the table to chuckle loudly.

This flamboyant entertainer, who often wore outlandish outfits on stage, dyed his hair the colors of the rainbow and performed zany stunts as part of his act, turned out to be a soft-spoken gentleman throughout dinner. He did not act the obnoxious part of a rock star in the least. Michael fought the impulse to mention his own music and get the star's input, deciding it wise not to go there.

When dinner was over, Elton John picked up the tab for everyone's food and drinks, politely excused himself, and left. One male member of the group remained behind, along with Susan and Kiki. It was suggested that they all go somewhere to dance. Michael was not dressed properly and, quite frankly, could not afford the inflated prices at the fancy dance clubs in town, so he declined. "I've gotta get back to the boat. Plus, I have laundry in the machines over at the laundromat." As soon as the words left his mouth, he realized how amazingly doltish that must have sounded.

Susan just laughed, taking his hand in hers, saying, "Well, I really enjoyed meeting you." Kiki gave him a goodbye peck on the cheek. And they left.

With a sack of clean clothes strung over his back and a hazy alcohol induced sense of bewilderment pertaining to the events of the evening, Michael began hiking back to Mala Wharf along the dark palm-studded coastal road – a slow rueful walk with time to think about what a wildly astonishing blunder he'd made. Two gorgeous ladies invite you dancing and you tell them you have to attend to your laundry? Stupid, stupid, stupid!

Throwing the clothing sack into the dinghy and starting to row out toward the sailboat, Michael heard his name being called off in the distance. He changed course and sculled in pursuit of whoever was calling for him. Amazingly, it was the girl he had met earlier that afternoon who worked at the shop in Lahaina. There she was, sitting on the rocks calling his name, perched like the famous little mermaid of Copenhagen.

"It's late," he called over to her. "How long have you been out here?"

"A little while," was her reply. "I told you I would come by."

Sure enough, she had. And now he was glad to find her waiting. She managed to jump into the dinghy without getting drenched and they rowed back to the boat. He stowed his laundry, then they sat around talking and drinking a bottle of wine that she had brought. Though he had consumed excessive quantities of alcohol earlier that evening, he welcomed the vino.

"So, how was your dinner in town?" she asked.

"You wouldn't believe me if I told you."

She spent the night aboard and he rowed her ashore the next morning. She offered to drive him over to her place and make breakfast, since he did not have any breakfast provisions on the boat, but all that alcohol consumption the previous night had now caught up with him. He had no stomach for breakfast.

He watched her drive away as he rowed back out to the boat, collapsing into the starboard bunk, not yet ready to face another day in paradise.

46

SAMOA

It is 2,600 miles from Hawaii to American Samoa, crossing both the Equator and International Dateline. In oceanic tradition, the two sailors celebrated crossing zero latitude by dousing themselves with seawater and praising the god Neptune. In the ship log, Denton noted: *The area of the equator is the only place on the planet where both the Big Dipper and Southern Cross can be seen. How amazing is that?*

But tying up at the Customs Dock and dealing with what seemed like an inordinate amount of bureaucracy had Denton arguing with the Samoan customs officials: "I'm an American citizen and this is *American* Samoa, so why are we getting such hassle?" They were at length granted permission to drop anchor in the harbor. Once they felt secure the anchor was properly dug in, they took the dinghy ashore.

The city of Pago Pago – pronounced Păngo Păngo – lies above the Bay of Pago Pago Harbor on the island of Tutuila, the largest of the islands that comprise American Samoa, and was simply the most beautiful place Michael and Denton had ever seen. The amenity of its lush verdure made Hawaii look like a dry wasteland by comparison, and they quickly found themselves enamored with the *fa 'a* – the Samoan ways.

They had only been onshore a short time, wandering aimlessly about the streets of Pago Pago, when they met two local girls, named Fono and Efi. Typical of Samoan people, they were quite tall. Nearly as tall as Denny, and he's well over six feet. Michael, substantially shorter, often joked that he and Denton resembled a seagoing Rocky and Bullwinkle. But the girls seemed equally interested in the tall sailor and his midget friend, inviting them to "shack up" and spend the night. "Eh, you wan shack up sailor mans?" the girls asked. The boys quickly discovered, however, that *shacking up* does not have quite the same connotation in Pago Pago that it does in the States.

The girls took the young men to their home and introduced them to their father, a towering Samoan man named Afasa. The entire family, or *aiga* in Samoan, welcomed them. Everyone sat on the floor of the *fale* – their palm-thatched open-structured home – talking and feasting; their hospitality, like Afasa's girth, genuinely enormous. Eagerly engaging their guests in conversation, the family clearly seemed less interested in the sailing adventures preceding Denton and Michael's arrival in Samoa and more keenly attentive to learning about life on the United States mainland, especially the everyday life of Denton the doctor.

After the sun went down, the family rolled bamboo mats onto the floor with pillows and stiff tapa cloth sheets on each for their guests to spend the night. There were no screens on any openings and the mosquitos feasted on the two young sailors, foreign blood quite a treat for the insects. A television stood in the corner of the room and Denny switched it on, silencing the volume so as not to disturb anyone, the bugs momentarily abandoning them, heading for the lighted screen.

In Pago Pago the residents may appear to not have much by American mainland standards, but they do get television supplied from the U.S. How odd it must seem to these Samoans, Denton thought, living so meagerly yet watching shows like *Charlie's Angels,* where scantily clad young women drive sports cars and wear expensive jewelry. Denton wondered what they must think of the way life in the States is portrayed on television. "No wonder they were so curious to learn about my daily life in California. It must all seem so privileged to them."

"That might explain why the customs officers felt like flexing their collective muscles at us when we arrived, two white guys on a yacht."

"Pretty small yacht, but I guess it's all in one's perception," Denton conceded.

With Denton onboard to look after the boat, Michael decided to treat himself to a little side trip to Apia in Western Samoa. He needed a break from the boat.

"Why Apia?" Denton asked.

"Apia is where the grave of Robert Louis Stevenson is located," Michael explained, pointing to a page in a magazine. "Says here that he is buried at the summit of Mount Vaea off a road dedicated in his honor called *Alo Loto Alofa*, which means *Road of the Loving Heart*. RLS was one of my favorite authors as a kid. He wrote *Treasure Island,* which just might be responsible for initially planting the seeds of all this island adventure I seek. I think it would be interesting to visit his final resting spot."

Western Samoa, an entirely different island nation from *American* Samoa, is located about one hundred miles from Pago Pago and air travel was the most expeditious way to get there. Michael inquired at South Pacific Island Airways, SPIA as it is commonly referred to, about the next flight to Western Samoa.

"Yes, there is a flight going to Apia," the ticket agent told him, seated behind a bamboo kiosk outdoors in the middle of a gravel lot not far from the airport runway.

"Oh good," Michael replied. "When does it leave?"

"As soon as we get eight passengers."

How many passengers do you have now?" Michael asked.

"Including you, makes two."

Three days later, Michael flew into Faleolo Airport at Apia in Western Samoa. He booked a room at the famous Aggie Gray's Hotel, famous in part because of its legacy as a bordello *servicing* American fighting forces stationed in the Pacific during World War II.

Legend has it that Bloody Mary, the fictional Tonkinese Madam of James Michener's book *Tales of the South Pacific*, was based upon the very real Aggie Gray of Western Samoa. Meeting Aggie Gray, Michael found it difficult to imagine this gray-haired, kindly grandmother as having such a sordid past ... but get her to talking and those twinkling old eyes and crafty wit bore a tangible similarity with her colorful fictional counterpart.

Modernly, Aggie's Hotel is widely known amongst voyaging yachtsmen as a place to come ashore, dry out, and enjoy creature comforts. True to form, he found several salty cruising sailors sitting around the bar at Aggie's, telling stories about surviving the perils of the sea and the exotic ports to which they'd voyaged. Though younger than most of these old salts, Michael soon found himself joining in, adding stories of his own to the general nautical braggadocio.

The swimming pool at Aggie's is unique in that it has a tall coconut palm springing right up out of the middle of the pool water, though Michael found himself more interested in observing three young bikini-clad women splashing in the pool. When one of them smiled at him, he waved, returning her smile. Emerging from the water, she walked over to where he was reclining upon a chaise longue and introduced herself as Linda. She looked very young, perhaps the daughter of one of the older yachtsmen he'd met at the bar. Conversing, Linda mentioned the year she had graduated high school – that dated her as three years *older* than Michael.

"Seriously? I would have taken you for a teenager," he admitted.

She tittered a honey-dripping Southern drawl, "Oh, you sure do know how to talk to a lady, don't you?"

All three were now out of the water, sitting close by. They were military nurses at a hospital back in the States, in Kentucky, and all three had that smooth Southern twang. They were renting a house for two weeks on the other side of the island and came over to Aggie's, Linda said, to meet some *real* sailors!

With that, Linda asked if she could take Michael's picture, saying she simply must have a picture of the handsome sailor she met in the South

Pacific to show her friends back home in Lexington. "Handsome? Me? Maybe you should put on your glasses and look again," Michael quipped. She laughed, but he was somewhat serious. Denny was the handsome sailor, not him. But Denny wasn't around just now, so why quibble?

Linda's friend volunteered to take the picture. They posed, Linda placing her arm around Michael, leaning close, cheek to cheek.

At some point, Linda invited him to come visit at their rented house. Michael had been living the life of a sea-going monk for so long her offer fell on very receptive ears, though it caused him to drift off for a moment in brief male mental fantasy ... *three sexy nurses and moi, alone at a tropical island beach house.* The fantasy interrupted when Linda shook him by the shoulders, returning him to reality, reiterating the invitation to which he had not yet responded ... adding that she would *really, really, really* like him to visit.

They spent that night together. Not Michael and all three nurses as he had fantasized, just he and Linda. Her friends sequestered in their respective bedrooms, Linda and Michael romped from the bamboo mat on the living room floor to the extra firm mattress in her bedroom. He soaked up the sexual encounter like a dry sponge after months of sea-going abstinence.

The next day, Linda invited him to stay the week with her. Watching her two girlfriends walk around the house wearing nothing but a towel and a smile was an offer he could not refuse, fantasy taking over his male brain again.

It was a smiling young man who days later, winging his way on SPIA back over the ocean toward Pago Pago, came to realize he very likely would never get to see the grave of his literary hero, Robert Louis Stevenson.

47

PRUDENT IN PARADISE

WELCOME TO THE SOUTH PACIFIC ISLAND KINGDOM OF TONGA, the sign in the harbor at Nuku'alofa on the island of Tongatapu read. In the 1700s, Captain James Cook sailed into this South Sea archipelago, unaware that the Tongans were planning an attempt to kill him and his crew, and ironically christened these the *Friendly Islands*. Now, going through immigration and customs formalities upon arrival in Tonga was very nearly a life and death event for Doctor Denton as well!

Thomas, a jovial, charismatic young fellow Californian hitchhiking his way around the South Pacific, had recently signed on to crew with Denton and Michael for the roughly five-hundred-mile sail from Samoa to Tonga. Somewhere in his prior travels, Thomas had been informed that bringing unlawful substances into that island kingdom was dealt with very harshly, including mandatory imprisonment. Thomas had two baggies of marijuana in his possession, so he decided to hide them. Having a penchant for pranksterism, he thought it would be fun to hide them in Denton's backpack, buried amongst the perfectly lawful substances contained therein, commingling with the pipe and tobacco Denton enjoyed smoking to while away the hours at sea, fancying it made him look more nautical.

A rather stern-looking Tongan inspections officer opened the backpack. After rummaging around inside the bag, he pulled out the pipe and five plastic baggies of leafy substance, two of which contained Thomas's marijuana.

The inspector selected one of the baggies, holding it up to the light, then cast an inquisitive look Denton's way. With justified demeanor of complete innocence, Denny unhesitatingly responded that it was pipe tobacco. The inspector opened the baggie and sniffed its contents. Apparently satisfied, he stuffed the five baggies back into the backpack and placed an *INSPECTED* tag on it. Luckily, the one baggie he sniffed did, in fact, contain only tobacco and he did not bother with the rest, apparently deciding no one could remain so calm if he were smuggling dope into the country. Indeed, had Denton known what Thomas had done, his composure would certainly have been compromised.

Shortly thereafter, reclaiming his stash, Thomas told Denton what he had done. Thomas thought it was highly amusing. Denton found nothing humorous at all about it and shuddered to think how close he had just come to spending time in a Tongan prison.

"You are a fucking idiot!" he screamed at Thomas. "I'm a fucking doctor. I would lose my license if I got convicted for drug smuggling. My life would be over!"

"Sorry, my bad. But that's why you love having me around," Thomas quipped, employing the affable charm that got him selected as crew in the first place.

"Fuck you! You're gone. Outta here! Get your shit off my boat and do not let me see your smirking face again."

Thomas looked to Michael for support.

"Don't look at me. Denny's right. What the hell were you thinking? There are plenty of other cruising boats here, you won't have any trouble getting on one. But you might wanna hurry. Once the word gets around about your shenanigans, nobody's gonna take you onboard."

That was the last time they saw Thomas.

They caught a taxi ride into the city of Nuku'alofa from a rotund, middle-aged American lady driver and her equally rotund Tongan husband. "*Malo e lelei*," she greeted them.

"*Palangi*," Denton heard the Tongan man grunt from the front passenger seat as the car bolted into gear.

From the rear seat, Denny gave a quizzical look. The driver, seeing the look in her cracked and broken rear view mirror, explained: "*Palangi*. It means foreigner. White person. Literally, it means cloud breakers, for the first Western sailors who came over the horizon centuries ago, breaking through the clouds with their ships."

Driving along unpaved roads, the taxi was a broken-down old car that jarred their insides at every bump. "Are there no paved roads in the entire country of Tonga?" Denton grumbled, still shaken and annoyed over the customs fiasco.

"Hey man, this ain't L.A.," Michael admonished, lightheartedly.

Indeed, the downtown roads here were gravel or dirt, with many deep potholes along the way. Not only that, but Nuku'alofa, the capitol city of this isolated island nation, was congested with slow moving traffic, prompting Denton to add, "Traffic kinda reminds me of L.A. though."

They both laughed. Even the large American lady chuckled upon hearing their comments. She then launched into an informative narration as she continued to maneuver through the congestion of equally dilapidated vehicles to her own.

"Tonga," she said, her enunciation tinged with a Tongan clip presumably from years of living in Polynesia, "is da only completely independent island kingdom in da South Pacific, a constitutional monarchy ruled by a king for whom the Tongans profess great fondness. There are approximately one hundred fifty islands, stretching from 15 to 23 degrees south of the equator, with a total population of almost one hundred thousand.

"Da people of Tonga pride themselves on their modesty. So much so that if a Tongan man walked in public shirtless, he would be arrested. And if a Tongan girl were to wear a bikini, even at the beach, *she* would be arrested. In fact, I advise that neither of you walk around without wearing shirts."

"Freakin' weird to have such puritanical laws for this extremely hot and humid island," Denton remarked. "It's so damn hot I feel like taking off my shirt right *now*."

The driver shook her finger at them. "Look out da window, see for yo-selves. Da women wear lots of clothes that cover the entirety of their bodies and carry parasols to shield themselves from da sun. Da men wear *lava lavas*, or *tupenu*, a tapa cloth garment resembling a skirt, and *ta'ovala*, a waistband of plaited grass matting. No Tongan is truly dressed without da *ta'ovala*. If they can wear all dat, fo sure you can keep shirt on.

"Tongans very religious, too. It is against da law to break da Sabbath in any way. It is a day for church and rest. No business. Not even taxi can operate on Sabbath."

The car swerved to avoid hitting two large swine that were traversing the middle of the road. The lady driver laughed, "In Tonga, pigs run free and people build fences to keep the pigs out, not in."

Arriving in the heart of the city, Denton paid the driver and thanked both her and her husband. "Sorry for my little outburst back there," he added.

"*Ma'u ha aho lelei*," replied the Tongan husband.

"What's that mean?" Michael asked the wife.

"Have a nice day," she said, then sped away.

They spent much of that first day seeing the sights and shopping in downtown Nuku'alofa. The American dollar is only worth about eighty-seven cents in Tonga, they were told. Even so, everything still seemed extremely inexpensive. So much so that normally frugal Doctor Denny went on a spending splurge, buying all sorts of souvenirs to take back home.

Browsing through the aisles of what appeared to be the largest shop in town, a store called Morris Hedstrom, Denton suddenly called out, "Mike, come here! You gotta see this."

Denton stood pointing to a poster on the wall at the rear of the shop, chuckling out loud. The poster, advertising some sort of contest, read: $2.00 RAFFLE B SUPPORT THE TONGA AMATEUR SPORTS ASSOCIATION SOUTH PACIFIC GAMES FUND B ENTER NOW! WIN YOUR OWN DREAM HOME OR $8,000 IN CASH!

"Wow," Michael whistled through his teeth, "an eight-thousand-dollar *dream home*. Shows what the cost of living is here in this island kingdom."

"I might just cash in my chips and retire here someday," Denton remarked. "By then I might even be able to afford to patch all the potholes and pave the roads around here."

Though Denton and Michael were *palangi*, making friends in Tonga, as they had discovered throughout Polynesia, was not at all difficult. And the friendships tended to grow exponentially, one friend quickly becoming many friends. A young Tongan man named Afah befriended them early on, inviting them to dinner the first day they had met.

Dinner was at the home of Afah's parents and the whole family turned out to meet and dine with the two *palangi* American sailors. Gathered around the table were Afah's parents, his older cousin Joe Siua, several of Joe's children, a Tongan friend of the family named Soakai Soane Mausia, plus Afah and Afah's wife, whose name sounded as if it included every letter in the alphabet and was unpronounceable to the Americans.

"Don't worry," she said, in perfect English. "My name in Tongan means beauty. You can just call me Beauty if that is easier."

The meal was a feast consisting of raw fish, octopus, papaya, pineapple, beef stew, breadfruit, and a deliciously fruity drink called *' otai*. "Thank you, everything was so delicious," Michael told Afah's mother as the dishes were being cleared by the women.

"*Ko ia*," she replied. "You are welcome."

"I must tell you," Denton added, "I don't eat near this good back home in America! No wonder Tongans are such large people." Everyone at the table laughed. Especially cousin Joe, a whopping jolly fellow, well over six feet and a couple hundred pounds, who guffawed all through dinner. Apparently, he thought everything was funny.

Joe proudly boasted that he has forty-two children! "Joe, how can that be?" Denton asked in astonishment. "There is no way you could be more than forty years old. How did you produce so many offspring?" Joe responded with a devious grin and by raising his eyebrows up and down in Groucho Marx fashion. Again, he and everyone at the table burst into laughter.

This prolific cousin of Afah's also happened to be the proud owner of Joe's Hotel, one of only a handful of lodgings in Nuku'alofa, and offered his new American friends a room free of charge for as long as they would like to stay.

"We appreciate that," Michael told him. "The generosity of Polynesian people never ceases to amaze me, but all our stuff is aboard the boat and we are quite comfortable there."

Afah leaned over to whisper in Denton's ear, "Good move. Your boat is probably more better. Joe's Hotel does not have any hot water. In fact, the water pressure at Joe's is little more than a trickle, even for cold water."

"Tell me more about your boat," Soakai said. "I love boats."

"Well, come down tomorrow and we will take you out for a sail," Michael offered.

Suddenly everyone at the table was interested in going for a sail. In the end, because the boat simply was not designed to accommodate that many people, it got narrowed down to just Soakai, Afah and Beauty. Beauty seemed especially excited about going sailing. "I know exactly where we can sail to," she said. "There is a spot on another island nearby where we can anchor and have a traditional Tongan feast on shore."

"You mean like a luau?" Michael asked.

"Exactly like a luau," Beauty answered. "Only better because it is Tongan!"

Twenty-seven years old, six foot three inches of rigid muscular frame, and a swart ruggedly handsome face accented by a thick flowing mustache, Soakai Soane Mausia turned out to be quite an excellent navigator. He knew all the reefs to avoid and, after a pleasant sail, directed them to a perfect spot for anchoring, only twenty feet offshore in the shade of looming coconut trees erupting skyward in tiers.

It was along this completely private pristine beach that they set up for the luau feast. Beauty, rolling up her pant legs and wading into the crystal-clear tidal flats, reached down into the water with bare hands and pulled up several fresh shellfish and a tiny octopus. Holding them proudly up in the air like trophies, she announced, "Appetizers!"

At Afah's direction, the two *palangi* got busy collecting dozens of fallen *niu* – dried out coconut husks scattered upon the ground to be used as charcoal for cooking. Soakai began digging a large hole, called an *umu*, that would serve as an oven. Afah would cook the main meal, *Lu Pulu*, consisting of several chickens that he captured roaming loose on the beach, gutted and wrapped in several layers of taro leaves, immersed in coconut milk, and slowly cooked over a fire of red-hot coconut husks placed in the *umu*. Yams, taro, pineapple, bananas, pawpaw, mango, coconut flesh, and tomatoes purchased prior in town supplemented the meat.

The beverage was coconut milk drunk directly out of coconuts picked off the trees all around. Afah and Soakai showed Michael how to climb the towering coconut trees, obtain the hard-shell fruit, and the best way to crack it open. It looked daunting, but soon Michael was scampering up and down trees like a native, making monkey noises all the while that put the Tongans in stitches!

The entire spread was placed upon a natural tablecloth of pandanus leaves on the ground. "What a wonderful way to consume a meal," Denton remarked. "If more people in America would eat sitting on the floor, they would have fewer back and hip problems."

"Spoken like a true doctor," Michael chided. "Not only is this fun and delicious, but educational as well. I mean, who knew I could learn to climb that high straight up a coconut tree?"

Afterwards, they decided to walk off their meal by hiking inland into the dense tropical forest. The trees were alive with literally millions of bats hanging upside down from the branches. The Americans found it rather creepy. "Must've made a wrong turn back there somewhere," Denny remarked. "When did we leave paradise and arrive at Transylvania?"

Michael laughed but their Tongan friends did not get the joke. "Tongans call them Flying Foxes and consider them sacred," Soakai told them.

They hiked until they came to a clearing containing dozens of dirt mounds with what looked to be empty beer bottles stuck into the dirt. Over one of the mounds was a sign that read: OFA-KI-LEVUKA.

"What is this place?" Michael asked.

"Tongan burial site," Soakai answered. "Tapu. We should go no further." At which point they turned around, retracing their path back toward the beach.

On the return sail, with Denton at the helm, Michael sat on the bowsprit watching the bow of the boat slicing gracefully through crystalline turquoise water as coconut palms along the shoreline seemed to be waving their farewells in the breeze. An ethereal dreamlike scenario, the atmosphere languorous and slow.

Denton was struck by the fantasy essence as well and remarked, "You know, one of my favorite television shows as a kid was *Adventures in Paradise,* starring Gardner McKay who, by the way, in addition to being a handsome actor was a real-life sailor. The show was loosely based on the stories of James Michener and focused around a young guy who sailed his schooner all over the South Pacific, each week finding new love and new adventure. Millions of boys like me, and probably plenty of grown men too, sat glued to TV screens watching this weekly fantasy unfold, dreaming of tropical ports and exotic island girls. And now, here I am doing it! It's simply amazing. How extremely fortunate to be out here on the water, with wonderful island friends, sailing in such tropical splendor. I'm a confirmed atheist, still I cannot help but say thank you God."

Perhaps as repayment for a splendid boat ride, Soakai wrangled an invitation for his new friends to attend a party at the fanciest establishment in all of Tonga: The International Dateline Hotel. Hosting the affair was the King of Tonga. His Highness King Taufa'ahau Tupou was a truly immense man, even by Tongan standards, weighing as much as three hundred pounds. They were told the king was an avid surfer, despite his enormity.

"Can you imagine the size of the surfboard needed for this guy?" Michael whispered quietly to Denton so neither Soakai nor the monarch would hear.

To which Denton replied, "King sized, for sure."

It was a large open room in which most attendees were seated cross-legged on the floor, except the king who was seated in a tremendous ornate chair, as Tongan dancers performed in the middle of the room. "Lakalaka," Soakai informed. "The dance celebrates life's beauty." Soon many in the room were joining in the dancing.

Several young Tongan ladies seated on the floor near the king drew Denton's attention. One had blondish hair, somewhat rare for Tongans, and kept smiling at him. Denton smiled back. Sipping a cool, clear, refreshing drink called kava, and emptying his cup with a final gulp, Denton asked, "Soakai, how do you say, may I have this dance in Tongan?"

"'E lava keu ma'u 'a e hulohula ko 'eni."

"Thanks." Denton stood up and was about to walk over and ask her to dance when Soakai grabbed his arm, stopping him.

"Whatta you doing?" Soakai sounded alarmed.

"Gonna ask that girl over there to dance," Denton told him.

"*Ikai*, she is related to the king. She is a Tongan princess. It is okay to just dance, but if she likes you and you kiss her, you gotta marry her."

"Marry her? I just wanna dance with her." Denton was sure Soakai was merely pulling his leg.

"Okay fine. But kiss-kiss and you gotta marry." He seemed serious. "*Tukufakaholo*, this is the Tongan way."

"They can't make me marry someone if I don't want to ... can they?"

"Prison in Tonga is not much fun," Soakai confirmed with a taunting smile.

That's all Denton needed to hear. He had narrowly avoided Tongan prison at the customs inspection with Thomas's marijuana. No point in tempting fate. Denton gave a final little wave to the princess. That was as close as he deemed prudent.

48

JOURNAL

It's the call that changed everything. Denny's call from the mainland came via the marine operator. The guy got married! Eloped! Says he's settling down, buying a house in Santa Monica, the whole nine yards. And he's just accepted some big promotion at work, assistant-head of pathology or some such thing. This was more than a hard tack to windward; this was a full-on gybe that would mean no more long periods away enjoying the good life cruising aboard *Makani Kai*. I'm happy for him, don't get me wrong, but it forces me to a major life crossroad. The boat is half his. I don't have the money to buy him out, and maybe wouldn't want to even if I could. I mean, we are a team.

So, I found myself back in Hawaii – anchored at Mala Wharf, Lahaina, Maui – trying to sort things out and get my shit together. I'd really hoped Kipp might have carpenter work for me, but he didn't. I managed to get gigs playing guitar and singing at the Pioneer Inn, at Kimo's, and Lahaina Lefty's that paid in food and a scant few dollars but, when those eventually dried up, found myself completely out of money.

Then, a few weeks ago, I went to a pay phone and called my old boss in California to ascertain whether a job might still be waiting with my name on it. I mean, Mr. Upshaw once said he would hire me back, but that was so long ago I wasn't even sure if he would remember who I am. Surprisingly, I was connected directly with Everett Upshaw himself, who accepted my *collect call* and actually sounded excited to be hearing from me, asking all sorts of questions about my sailing adventures and stuff. Best of all, he confirmed that I still had a job if I wanted it. He said the company had tons of work going on and asked how soon I might be expected back. I suggested that if he could wire me a small advance, I could be in California within the week.

So, reluctantly but out of necessity, the decision was made to return to California. I recalled something about Polynesian islands written by Herman Melville and hoped it would not prove true in my case: *For as the ocean surrounds the verdant land, so it does the soul of man. God keep thee there. Push not off from that isle, for thou might not ever return.* But push off I have.

Kipp agreed to keep an eye on the boat until Denny and I figure out what to do with her. It was early morning when he rowed me ashore in the dinghy. The waves were choppy and trying to beach the luggage-laden dinghy while keeping everything dry was no small task. I threw my stuff into a waiting taxi and was driven to a small airstrip where a six passenger Cessna twin engine flew me to Honolulu airport on Oahu.

I'm back on the mainland now, renting a nice furnished apartment in Marina del Rey, courtesy of Mr. Upshaw and his company fronting first and last month rents. My old sailing buddy Noah Sark lives in the same complex and helped me find these digs. I don't own a car but have use of a company truck to get around, so looks like all my needs are met. I cannot thank this company enough; they've helped so much.

Ya know, I have a memory from long ago of driving down the road in a different truck with my Indian cowboy friend, Jay Yazzie. I remember him telling me: "Mike, you're lucky. You could return to the mainstream white man's world from which you came at any time." Quite prophetic because return I have.

But adjusting to mainstream life is proving a little difficult. I cannot seem to shake the mellow aloha feeling acquired from sailing and living on tropical islands, and don't think I ever want to. Also, it may take a while before I get used to wearing shoes again.

PART SIX

49

JOURNAL

The company has me bouncing all over the place. One week I might be working in Sacramento, then the next week in Phoenix, or even Seattle. Don't get me wrong, I feel extremely lucky to have my old job back. The pay is very good and it feels nice to have money again. But there is not much time for anything else. My home base is an apartment near the beach but I'm not able to enjoy it much because working is all I do, and I'm gone a lot.

Which brings me to my buddy, Noah. He and his roommate Daniel were living upstairs in my building. Noah Sark and I go way back, he was crew on my boat when we sailed up the coast a few years ago. Daniel is a flight attendant and I sometimes catch a ride to or from the airport with him when I'm traveling for work. Both are great guys.

One night, though, at 2:00 in the morning, my phone rang. I thought, crap! There must be some emergency at work. But no, it was Noah. I was about to cuss him out for waking me up when I heard him sobbing on the other end. I figured for one guy to call another guy in the middle of the damn night and be crying, there must be something catastrophically serious going on.

"What's wrong?" I asked.

"Daniel is gone," Noah replied.

"Oh my God, he's dead?"

"No, no. He left me. We had a giant gross fight and he moved out. He said he never wants to see me again," Noah explained, still sobbing.

I wasn't getting it. "Well, that's a bummer. So, get another roommate," I groggily suggested.

"Get another roommate? I love him!"

Of course, I've always known Noah was gay. It's just not something that ever factored into our friendship, not something I ever gave much thought to and, while over the years we connected on so many other levels, such emotion coming from my friend, especially at such a wee hour, was confusing to me.

"I'm really sorry, Noah. But can we discuss this tomorrow in the daylight?"

The insensitivity of my question was met with silence on the other end. Suddenly, even in a half-asleep stupor, it hit me. "Okay, come on over. I'll make some coffee and we can talk."

Noah arrived a little stoned (as usual) but it was clear he was heartbroken. He and Daniel had been a couple for nearly a year and the sudden turn of events was emotionally devastating for Noah. Additionally, he explained, there was no way he could afford to keep their apartment without Daniel's monetary contribution.

"Don't worry," I told him. "You can crash here until you figure out your next move. I'm gone all the time. You'll have the place pretty much all to yourself."

So, I now have a roommate (at least temporarily). I'm glad to be able to help out a friend and it is actually kind of nice knowing somebody is taking care of the place when I'm working out of town.

50

JOURNAL

I've been spending most of my time working in Northern California these past several months. The company has promoted me from foreman to superintendent and I'm in charge of several Bay Area construction projects. A nice pay raise came with the promotion, so I'm pretty stoked.

Though work has kept me extremely busy, I managed to meet someone, a NorCal girl who has really captured my attention. Her name is Hillary Hartnel. She's district manager for a chain of clothing stores I'm building and came by one afternoon to check on construction progress. Extending her hand to introduce herself, we both felt an electric-like jolt when our hands coupled, causing us both to jump.

"Gosh, I'm sorry," I said, seeing her rubbing her hand.

"No, no, it's me. I'm wearing silk. Sometimes that happens. Static electricity," she replied, still rubbing her hand.

"Well, you didn't need to shock me to get my attention," I told her, with a nervous laugh, hoping she wasn't angry about it.

She looked up from her hand and smiled. "That was some *mondo* jolt."

Oh good, she wasn't angry. In fact, it turned out to be an energized conversation starter. Hillary, or Hilly as she sometimes prefers, is just a few years younger than me but still likes to sprinkle her conversation with adolescent expressions, like *neat-o*, *as if*, and *mondo*. Where most people might say something is terrific or huge, Hilly will say it's *mondo*. Initially, I found this a bit off-putting. Her father, she told me, is a tenured professor at Stanford University, so you would think she might have developed a more extensive vocabulary.

Anyway, I asked her out ... but Hillary told me she already had a date.

"Okay, well maybe some other time," I replied.

"No," she countered with only the shortest hesitation. "I'll go out with you. I can cancel my other plans."

Was it my hangdog look of disappointment that caused her mind to change? Or maybe it was that initial jolt that gave me the edge, who knows? But our date went great! So great that we spent every non-working hour together for the next several weeks. We just could not seem to get enough of each other.

However, my work in the Bay area was coming to an end. It was time to bid *adios* to Hilly and return to Southern California. We spent our final night together in grim acceptance that it would be our last.

The next morning, I got on a plane and headed for Los Angeles. The entire flight, I could not stop thinking about Hillary. She has the softest skin I have ever touched, and I longed to touch her once more. As soon as the plane landed at LAX, I did something I've never done before. Walking over to a ticket counter, I asked how soon is the next plane to San Francisco? There was one boarding in ten minutes. I got on it. No time to even claim my luggage.

I called Hillary upon landing. She was so excited that she dropped everything and immediately came to SFO to pick me up. "You returned!" she shouted gleefully. "I wished for it, and it came true!"

That night together was intense, Hillary's skin just as soft as I remembered, and I was glad I had returned. But one more night simply was not enough. So, the next day she played hooky from work and we drove out to the beach at Santa Cruz.

It was chilly and overcast, the beach virtually deserted, but walking hand-in-hand along the sand was the most splendid afternoon anyone could wish for. Gulls were pinwheeling in the gray sky and, in the far-off distance, we could faintly hear someone playing piano. Walking further toward the wharf, the music became more discernable. I recognized the piece as Rachmaninoff.

I turned toward the iconic boardwalk, craning my neck, looking upward at the massive colonnade with its old-world classic archways that date all the way back to 1907. Above each of the arches were large windows. One was wide open and I could see a man with a clean-shaven head seated at a baby grand piano. He was wearing dark sunglasses. Sunglasses indoors and on a day without sun, my initial presumption was that he was perhaps blind.

He continued playing beautifully, the perfect musical score for our romantic afternoon. As we got ever closer, I nodded toward him in recognition and appreciation. Turns out, not only was he fully sighted, he must also have been watching *us*, two lovers on the beach, because he casually returned my nod while continuing his rhapsody, making me feel as if the music was intended just for us. Hillary, holding my hand and looking out to sea, drew closer and put her head on my shoulder. I saw the piano man smile.

Later, we dined at a Chinese restaurant on the boardwalk. Hillary's fortune cookie read *Your present lover will never leave you.* She showed me her fortune with tears in her soft eyes and asked with hopeful expression, "Could this come true?"

This morning, Hilly drove me to the airport. She walked with me all the way to my plane. Much hugging and kissing ensued in a public display of passion that was uncontainable! It was then that Hillary said she loved me. She had tears rolling down her lovely cheeks. I should have responded in kind … but did not. With real reluctance, I got on the plane.

Taking my seat and watching Hillary through the airplane window, still standing in the terminal sadly waving goodbye, I was looking at someone I truly did not want to be leaving behind.

51

JOURNAL

Ronald Reagan, our former California governor, is now president-elect of the United States of America. I voted for Mr. Reagan, my first time ever voting in a presidential election. Not that my vote mattered. By the time I returned home from voting, the television announced that Reagan had already won the election. So overwhelming was his landslide victory that he did not even need votes from his home state to put him over the top.

I celebrated Reagan's victory alone in my apartment because my roomie Noah Sark moved out a few weeks ago. He landed a job at one of the studios, reading and analyzing screenplays. Even joined a union. Who knew there was a union for reading screenplays?

So, while my buddy's heart remains on the mend, he's in the chips again and can afford a place of his own. When I returned home from being out of town working, he was gone but left a really nice note thanking me for helping him get through a rough spot in his life: *I know there were some judgmental people with an unevolved sense of masculinity who gave you shit about us living together and I want you to know how much I appreciate what you did.* No problem, my friend. Happy you are back on a positive track.

Speaking of positive tracks, this morning I took the California Contractors exam. It might take a couple months to obtain the results. Once I get my license, I plan to venture out on my own, something I discussed at length with my bosses at work. They wholeheartedly support me. Mr.

Upshaw and a couple of the construction managers even wrote letters of recommendation to the State Contractors License Board. I owe these guys so much. I wonder how different my life would be had I not met them. Life and the events that prod us down our various paths continue to fascinate me.

I told my mother about taking the contractor test. I really did not want my dad to know, he's always so negative. But my mom blabbed and, sure enough, Dad told me not to get my hopes up, assuring that he's forgotten more than I will ever know about construction, and he was not able to pass the California test. I will just have to wait and see, I suppose.

52

ALOHA JOHN

The sign at the airport read MELE KALIKIMAKA. The winter slowdown in construction gave Michael the opportunity to fly to Hawaii and check on the boat. He and Denton had decided for the *Makani Kai* to be delivered back to California, and Michael was in the Islands to arrange for that transport. It felt good to be back in the Land of Aloha. He had missed it dearly – missed sailing, missed living on the boat, missed having a home that rocked with the motion of the ocean to lull him to sleep at night. A few days at Maui aboard *Makani Kai* was just what he needed. And relocating her to Oahu, sailing alone from Lahaina to Honolulu, an absolute joy. There was a professional captain in Honolulu who they hired to return the boat to California.

With the boat snug in a guest slip at Ala Wai Marina, he wandered off to enjoy dinner at The Chart House restaurant just a block away. There was a television mounted above the bar and whatever show was playing abruptly broke away for BREAKING NEWS! Being here in paradise once more, he cared little about news pertaining to the rest of the world – but this story immediately grabbed his attention, along with everyone else in the place: JOHN LENNON HAS BEEN SHOT AND KILLED IN NEW YORK CITY – murdered by a man from Honolulu!

There was an immediate and continued hush among the staff and patrons as the alarming story continued. When the station returned to normal programming, Michael put down his fork and left without finishing his meal.

He had a difficult time sleeping that night. At midnight he was still awake on the boat pondering the death of this generational icon. The following morning, he wandered foggily onto Waikiki Beach, collapsing on the sand in front of the Rainbow Tower at Hilton Hawaiian Village. He remained for over an hour, listening to local radio stations playing their tributes to John Lennon, grief filling him, tears streaming down his cheeks, his face moving in nervous twitches, chin quivering. A passerby asked Michael if he was okay, but he could not speak. He felt rather foolish, a grown man sitting on a public beach bawling like a baby. But he could not control his sorrow.

John Lennon was dead. No one should have their life taken so senselessly. He wept for Yoko Ono and for Lennon's young sons. He wept because Lennon was so intricately entwined with Michael's own formative years, that his passing seemed to symbolize the death of Michael's own youth; an entire generation's youth. He wept because, as the television newscaster had reported, there is no hope for any real gun legislation and more people will likely die as a result. He wept for future victims and the hopelessness of a society that cannot even pass a law to protect its citizens from themselves.

And so it was that John Lennon had been killed. Later that day there was a planned ten-minute vigil of silence to take place all over the world in his memory. Aloha John, Michael thought, I can only hope the aftermath of your passing will be that more people are finally encouraged to *Give peace a chance.*

53

THAT NEXT BIG STEP

It had been more than a year since their first date. Hillary sat holding hands with Michael across the table in the dimly lit Baja Cantina in Marina del Rey as mariachi singers serenaded patrons. She had flown down from Northern California to be with him, as she had done so many times before. But this time was special. Michael said there was something very important he wanted to discuss with her, that he was ready to take a *big step* in their relationship; that there was an *important question* he wanted to ask her. She loved him and was hopeful of what that next big step might be.

Gazing at him lovingly, radiant with anticipation of where this evening was leading, she waited, trying not to appear too anxious.

"I think we should be monogamous," he said at last.

"What? I thought we already were," she replied, trying hard not to look hurt.

"Oh. Wait. That did not come out the way I planned."

"It's okay," she reassured him. Then, trying to guide him in the right direction, "Wanna try again?"

She waited. Watching him sitting silently across from her, just staring down at his hands covering hers upon the table. Finally, he looked up and posed the question. She listened but sat unresponsive, staring into his eyes searchingly as if there might be more to this *important* question. So, he repeated it. "We love being together so much, why don't we move in together?"

Disappointment and joy competed for her emotions. She had assumed he was about to propose marriage. It was a perfectly reasonable assumption to make on an evening such as this, after dating for so long. When it sank in that he was *not* asking for her hand in marriage, she was instantly crestfallen. But it quickly passed, and she enthusiastically agreed to move in.

Perhaps move *in* was not the right word, for they would not be living in an apartment. Michael's boat had been delivered from Hawaii and they planned to move aboard. It did sound rather exciting, like a wonderful adventure: quit her job, move south, live together on a sailboat. She had never lived on a boat before. Prior to meeting Michael she had never even set foot on a boat, but enjoyed each time he took her out on the water, and she loved *her* sailor. The more she thought about it, the more it sounded like such a very romantic way to begin their life together.

54

DIAGNOSIS

Joe Perry shook his head in disbelief. It had to have been just a fluke that his son passed the contractor license test, while Joe had failed in his own attempts to do so. Twice! Or maybe that's what college had taught the kid, how to bullshit his way through written examinations. Christ, Joe knew more about construction than that kid would ever know. It seemed utterly preposterous that Joe could not get his license, but that Mike did.

To compound the matter, the boy was now talking about quitting his job to start a contracting business of his own. Jesus! What was that kid thinking? He had a great job with a solid company. For the first time the kid seemed to be going somewhere in life. A project superintendent, paid good money to simply stand around all day supervising subcontractors and tradesmen who knew their craft and what they were doing. Damn cushy position.

What in the world made him think he could run a company of his own? What the hell did he know about running a business? Joe knew, first-hand, about operating a business, making payroll, taking gambles, pouring his sweat into it. Joe knew how stressful one's own business could be. Mike had never experienced real stress in his entire charmed fucking life.

Besides, you cannot run a business while you're shacking up with a girlfriend aboard a goddam sailboat. You've got to have some actual skin in the game. For God's sake, this was insanity! Just because he was able to pass some written exam did not mean he was capable of running a business. Joe told his son as much. Tried to talk some sense into him. But would the kid listen? Joe knew better than to think his son would *ever* listen.

Joe was stewing about all this when Mary entered the room looking especially somber.

"We need to talk," she spoke softly, taking a seat on the sofa next to where her husband was reclined in an avocado green La-Z-Boy. "I've got bad news."

Crap, more whining and complaining about some bullshit thing. "Okay, spill it," he replied.

"Remember my appointment with the doctor I had a week or so ago?" she asked.

"Yeah, I guess," he said.

She began to cry. Christ, this was serious.

"The test came back. I've been diagnosed with cancer," she confided, her voice sounding choked.

Joe did not know how to respond.

"Breast cancer," Mary added.

"Does this mean you are going to die?"

"They caught it early enough. But it does mean that I will lose my breast," Mary answered, sobbing.

Joe pulled the recliner where he'd been sitting to its full upright position, so he was eye to eye with her, and stared at his wife. It was as if she suddenly had become some alien creature, not the woman he'd been married to all these years. This could not possibly be his spouse. No way could *his* Mary have cancer. No way could his extremely vain Mary lose a breast. The doctors might not think she was going to die but losing a breast would almost certainly kill her.

"Will you lose all your hair, too?" he asked.

"I don't know," she continued to sob, rising from the couch. "I really don't know."

He stood up and hugged her tightly with no further words.

55

DOUG'S HARBOR REEF

Autumnal weather had been so nice that Hillary and Michael decided to cruise over to Santa Catalina Island for a five day get-away and celebrate the Thanksgiving holiday. This time of year, the island not packed with tourists, they hoped to have the place mostly all to themselves. But Avalon, the only town on the island, turned out to be far more crowded than anticipated. Partly because a gigantic cruise ship on its way to Mexico was parked in the bay, unloading hundreds of passengers onto the streets of Avalon.

An afternoon of shopping the T-shirt shops in town and Michael decided he wanted to seek out a less crowded part of the island. Hillary preferred staying put. "I love Avalon. Besides, it took us more than six hours to sail over here and now you wanna leave already?" she protested.

"You know," Michael said, "there is an old song that goes *I found my love in Avalon Bay, I left my love there and sailed away.*"

"You better not ever leave me!" Hillary stood akimbo, hands on hips, her body language a clear statement. Wearing a pink polo shirt, argyle sweater draped over her shoulders, navy shorts, smooth tanned legs, top-siders on her feet – Michael thought she looked absolutely adorable.

"Then let's bug outta here and sail over to Two Harbors," Michael suggested.

Her expression showed dubious consideration.

"All right, how about we compromise?" he offered. "We'll spend the rest of the day here and head out first thing in the morning for Two Harbors."

"I've got my own old song to sing," Hillary snickered. "*Where you lead, I will follow.*"

"Good God, girl! You sing like Edith Bunker."

They both laughed.

The next morning they enjoyed a lazy sail toward the west end of the island. Arriving, they found no crowds and no problem picking up an excellent mooring close to shore at Isthmus Cove. Two Harbors was so named because there are two harbors: Isthmus Cove and Cat Harbor, separated by a half-mile narrow strip of flat land that is surrounded by steep hills. While Hillary may have preferred the shops and restaurants of Avalon, she had to admit this part of the island was beautifully serene, even with the only onshore amenities being one combination bar/restaurant and a tiny general store. It did appear a preferable spot to spend a nice quiet Thanksgiving holiday.

They enjoyed a long hike on the island, climbing the steep hills surrounding the Isthmus and encountering all sorts of interesting wildlife, including wild buffalo roaming the hiking trails. A mother buffalo and calf blocking the trail caused them to stop in their tracks for several minutes, waiting for the pair to pass.

"They are *mondo* enormous!" Hilly exclaimed. "I have never been so close to a buffalo. I had no idea they could be so big."

"Don't get too close," Michael warned. "These are not some zoo animals or domesticated pets. They are totally wild."

"As if! Why in the world are all these buffalo on this island, anyway? How did they even get here?" Hillary wanted to know.

"They used to film lots of movies here on Catalina back in the old days. Mostly Westerns. My understanding is that a dozen or so buffalo were shipped over here for a big scene in some silent movie they were making back in the 1920s. When the filming was completed, they just left the buffalo behind. Over the decades they proliferated and grew into small herds that now roam freely all over the island."

"Neat-o! So, these are the direct descendants of movie star buffalo," Hillary joked.

"I suppose you might say that," agreed Michael, laughing.

"I think I just did," her waggish response.

Doug's Harbor Reef bar and restaurant, the only eatery at this end of the island, provided a traditional Thanksgiving turkey feast for the couple, famished after a day of hiking. So much food that they were able to take doggie bags back to the boat with enough turkey and fixings for a second, and even third, meal. Between the turkey's tryptophan and being rocked gently by the motion of the boat, they collapsed into the cabin berth and slept like babies.

Rising early with the sun, the ocean was glassy calm. No wind, so they decided to motor a few miles further west to Emerald Bay where they anchored for the day. Hillary, sitting on the bow of the boat eating a sandwich made from Thanksgiving leftovers, looked over the side, straight down at the clear azure water.

"Oh my God! I can see straight down one hundred feet," she exclaimed. "It is so clear, like being in the Caribbean or something."

"I've never sailed in the Caribbean," Michael answered, "but I've been to a lot of tropical places and this water is as clear as any I have seen anywhere."

"Amazing! Look at all those fish swimming. Must be a squillion of them. That is so neat-o!"

"See the gold ones?" Michael was pointing to a dense school of golden colored fish just off the port bow. "Those are Garibaldi. I think they are the California state fish."

"California has a state fish? I had no idea," she replied.

"You have lived in California your entire life and don't know there is a state fish?" he chided.

"Never thought about it," she answered. "Though, now that I *am* thinking about it, I think we learned in school it was some sort of golden trout, or something. Garibaldi, huh?"

"Who knows? But I do know what the state fish of Hawaii is called. Do you know?"

"Not a clue," she answered.

"The Reef Triggerfish, in Hawaiian called *Humuhumunukunukuapua'a*."

"That just rolled off your tongue?" she asked, laughing. "Say it slower, so I can learn it."

"It's pronounced, hoomoohoomoonookoonookooaupooahah."

"Good thing we don't live in Hawaii. Easier to just say Garibaldi."

It was the dimming of the day, when late afternoon turned to evening. Neither of them felt like pulling up the anchor and returning to the Isthmus, so they spent the night anchored at Emerald Bay, snuggled in each other's arms, enamored with a waxing gibbous moon hanging in the cloudless sky and dome of stars overhead creating a chiaroscuro of bright and inky dark. Falling into a rhythm with the boat's rocking, they made love and drifted off in peaceful post-coitus slumber.

The next morning, however, dark loaves of clouds began rolling in and the seas turned choppy with white caps out on the horizon.

"Looks like a storm rolling in," Michael observed.

"Maybe we should head home," Hilly suggested.

"It's only Saturday. No rush. I say let's head back to Isthmus Cove and hope for nicer weather tomorrow to sail home in."

"*Oui, mon capitaine,*" Hillary responded, giving a French salute.

By mid-afternoon, as they motored back to Two Harbors, the sky was already dark and menacing, though the harbor water still remained relatively calm. They maneuvered the sailboat past several large yachts moored farther out, picking up their previous mooring closer to shore without any problems and prepared for what might be a stormy evening.

But the storm never arrived. Since it was too chilly to sit out on the boat's deck and there were no stars to look at, Michael suggested, "Wanna take the dinghy ashore and have a night cap at Doug's?"

"The Harbor Reef? Sure," Hillary agreed. "I really like that place."

The bar was not crowded, perhaps inclement weather keeping patrons away. There was a small party of four seated nearby, three men and a woman. They looked as if they had been imbibing awhile: laughing, talking loudly, several bottles of champagne chilling in ice buckets near their table.

Hillary was on her second glass of white wine when she suddenly leaned closer to Michael to excitedly whisper, "Oh my God! Do you see who that is over there?"

Michael began twisting to look over his shoulder when Hillary stopped him.

"Wait! Don't look just now. I'll tell you when. But I am pretty sure that is Robert Wagner over there."

"The actor? The one we watch on TV?"

"Yes! Hart to Hart. He has got to be the handsomest man I have ever seen. He looks even more handsome in person than he does on TV."

Michael began turning around again to look. Hillary started to stop him, then changed her mind, saying, "Okay, now. Look!"

Sure enough, it was the famous actor. He was with a somewhat odd-looking man and a beautiful dark-haired woman who looked vaguely familiar. A third man had his back to him.

"Maybe I should go over and ask for his autograph," Hillary suggested. "Oh, I really wish we had brought the camera. I would kill for a picture with that sexy Robert Wagner."

"That group at the table seems a tad raucous. I don't think you wanna go bothering him for an autograph. Celebrities don't like to be bothered on their off time. Besides, he sounds kinda drunk."

"They really do seem to be having a good time," Hillary remarked. "Oh, what I'd give to be at their table, hear what they are all laughing about."

At some point, Hillary and Michael decided to head back to their boat. The actor and his friends were still carrying on inside the bar. Their loud voices could be heard all the way outside as the two walked down to the dinghy dock. Michael started up the outboard and the voices were finally drowned out.

The wind was picking up, the waves in the harbor getting sloppy. Water splashed into the dinghy, drenching Hillary who was seated forward as they made their way back to the sailboat. "I'm sure glad we got a mooring close to shore," Hillary shouted over the noise of the wind and outboard. "I would hate to be riding in the dinghy all the way to one of those big yachts farther out there."

Back onboard, the sailboat was sloshing about side to side in the choppy seas, making sleep that night sporadic and restless. At some point, very late, they heard what sounded like the whirling of helicopters flying low that made sleeping near impossible. Michael looked out the portal windows on both sides but, seeing nothing but darkness and other boats rocking on their moorings, tried going back to sleep.

Still rocking the following morning, Michael slid back the cabin hatch, peering out for the first time. There was now a barricade of orange-colored police boats surrounding the harbor.

"What the hell is all this?" he wondered aloud.

Seeing Michael's head sticking up from the cabin, a police boat approached, hailing him.

"What's going on, officer?"

"Nothing to be concerned about," the officer replied. "Have you been on board all night?"

"Yes." What a foolish question, Michael thought.

"Anyone onboard with you?"

"Yes. My girlfriend."

"Did either of you hear anything out of the ordinary during the night?"

"Not really. Just what sounded like a low flying helicopter that woke me up."

"That *was* a helicopter," the policeman confirmed, stone faced.

"So, what's going on then?" Michael repeated. "We should head back to L.A. before the weather gets worse."

"I cannot really comment. But, if you are planning to sail back to the mainland, you'll have to wait a while. We are not allowing anyone to leave just yet," the officer said. "We will let you know when it's clear."

It was dark when Hillary and Michael finally poked the bow of the boat into their slip in Marina del Rey. Though the VHF radio had been all atwitter with squelching police transmissions, they had no idea what all that commotion had been about earlier at normally peaceful Two Harbors.

Michael was busily tying off the boat and hosing down the dirt and salt accumulation from their holiday cruise when Hillary shouted to him from inside the cabin. With shore power reconnected, she had turned on their little table TV and was watching the Sunday Evening News. "Oh my God! You have got to come see this!"

Leaping down the companionway steps and landing in a seat next to her, they listened to the news story unfolding.

... 51yearold actor Robert Wagner and Dennis Davern, the captain of Wagner's yacht Splendor, *sounded the alarm around 1:30 A.M. that Wagner's wife, actress Natalie Wood, had disappeared from the 60foot yacht the couple owned. Approximately six hours later, Wood's body, clad in only a flannel nightgown, red down jacket, and blue wool socks, was found floating face down in the Pacific about a mile away, 200 yards off Blue Cavern Point on Catalina Island. The 11foot inflatable dinghy belonging to* Splendor *had washed up on the rocks, its ignition key switched to off, the gearshift in neutral, and the oars up in a locked position. Wood grew up on the Silver Screen, winning over fans playing a little girl who questioned the existence of Santa Clause in Miracle on*

34th Street; to the teenage love interest of James Dean in Rebel Without a Cause, for which she earned an Academy Award nomination; Splendor in the Grass, opposite Warren Beatty; and so many other notable films, including, of course, as Maria in West Side Story, the musical/urban adaption of Shakespeare's Romeo and Juliet. The death of the 43yearold actress has stunned Hollywood.

"No, no, no!" Hillary began to cry. "That beautiful woman in the bar last night was Natalie Wood? My God, Michael, we were among the last people on earth to see her alive and we did not even know who she was."

Fellow actor Christopher Walken, 38, with whom Wood has been filming a sciencefiction thriller called Brainstorm, *was also onboard. The Wagners, accompanied by Walken and Davern, had sailed to Catalina Island's Isthmus Cove, an isolated spot located near the end of the island that caters to yachtsmen. They dined that evening at Doug's Harbor Reef, the only restaurant on the cove. Some of the restaurant staff thought the Wagner party was drinking rather heavily and remember worrying about their safety after the group departed.*

56

JOURNAL

It was with a heavy heart that we sold the *Makani Kai* and moved to dry land. I really hated to move off the boat. So many memories attached to her, it's downright heart-breaking. But, truth be known, I think Hillary will miss living aboard even more than I. It was our first home together.

The yacht broker sold our floating home to actor John Forsythe. He was the voice of Charlie in the *Charlie's Angels* television show and is the current star of a very popular TV show called *Dynasty*. Supposedly, Mr. Forsythe took one look at our boat and quipped: *This boat has character and seaworthiness all over it*, while whipping out his checkbook to buy it. Probably just chump change to him, but a virtual fortune to me.

Half the proceeds from the sale went to Denton, of course. My share I have mostly plowed into my new construction business. Shopping malls are popping up all over the country and I'm building the stores that go in them. With this infusion of cash and a lot of sweat from me, I am betting the business will really take off. As President Reagan says: *We are on the threshold of a new beginning, now we must stay the course*!

Hillary and I moved into a brand-new condo complex in Marina del Rey. It has tennis courts, swimming pools ... the whole nine yards. We are just renting since the units are selling for upwards of a half million dollars! Can you imagine? The new business is already beginning to turn a nice profit, but no way I can afford those prices.

Mom and Dad stopped by to visit, and they both seemed rather impressed by our new digs. "Oh my," Mom said, "tennis courts, swimming pool? You two are living like Lifestyles of the Rich and Famous!" Dad, in his usual fashion, downplayed it a bit, telling me that a fancy condo is just fine, but renting is for suckers, that I ought'a get serious and buy a *real* house. Maybe he's right. Maybe one day I will.

Just a few blocks from our new condo, over closer by the beach, I saw two guys a few days ago sitting on the street curb playing guitars and singing. One had a dark full beard and the other wore ripped jeans and a cowboy hat, their harmonies reminiscent of the Everly Brothers. I recognized the bearded guy from back in my own music days. We both played at local C&W venues, like the Palomino Club. He recognized me as well.

"You still in the biz?" the bearded singer asked.

"Different biz, now" I told him. "Construction biz."

"That's cool," he said, nodding approval. His hat-wearing friend, who had not yet said a word, gave me a disapproving look that said *traitor*.

"You live here in the marina?" I asked.

"In a way," he replied, sheepishly. "Lotta boats here in the marina. Currently my buddy & me are living on that boat right over there." He pointed his guitar toward a silver-colored 1962 Cadillac parked a few feet away.

"Seriously? You're living in a car?" My own haunting memory of when I'd been so destitute to live in my car emerged.

"Yeah, but it's a *big* car," he kidded. "Besides, it's only temporary. We got a pretty good gig lined up in a few weeks out Bakersfield way. Hey, hook us up to some juice and we got an old-fashioned rock-a-billy sound that will blow yer socks off. No lie. We're gonna cut some demos out there at Buck Owens' studio."

"Listen," I offered, "I live just down the street. You guys are welcome to come sleep on my couch till you head out to Bakersfield." They took me up on that offer, sleeping on the sofa several nights, a couple of which we three sat up till 1:00 in the morning jamming – playing guitars and singing.

But Hillary did not appreciate me offering refuge to strangers. "I cannot believe you're letting a couple street bums sleep here!" she shouted one evening from behind our closed bedroom door. "And on my brand-new sofa. Ugh!" I think they heard her because the next morning they were gone.

Anyway, to celebrate our first month in new digs, we ate at a nice restaurant followed by a movie at the Fox in Venice, a theater that plays older flix. It was the rodeo movie *Junior Bonner*, starring the late Steve McQueen. I told Hilly the story of my meeting McQueen years ago and how he pumped me for info about cowboys.

Hilly just smiled and said, "Of course you did. Nothing about you surprises me anymore."

57

EVERYTHING IN MODERATION

Riding the tsunami-like wave of shopping mall construction across the United States, Michael's business had projects underway all over California and now occupied an entire office building in Marina del Rey as headquarters for the company.

"Not bad for a guy who, back in high school, almost failed wood shop, huh?" Michael joked with Hillary when the office first opened.

"I'd say not bad is a *mondo* understatement. More like, damn great!" she retorted.

And they bought their first house, an hour away from the city, with a swimming pool and nearly an acre of yard. They also got a dog. Hillary had wanted a dog for a long time, but Michael could not justify having one until they owned a house with a yard. One day at the local pet shop he saw the cutest brown and white Springer Spaniel puppy and fell in love immediately. He brought it home to surprise Hillary. She named the dog Baxter.

Denton and Michael stayed in touch. "I always knew you were destined for success," Denton told Michael over lunch one afternoon at a restaurant adjacent to the Santa Monica Pier. "Just a hippie-sailing bum with an embarrassing knack for making money," he added with a wink.

"People call me doctor, but you've got street smarts. Why do you think we made such good boat partners? You were the yang to my yin … or perhaps vice versa, who knows?"

"This is the most productive, contented period of my life," Michael confided to his friend. "Wait, did I say content? No, no, no ... that's the wrong word. I'm happy, but not necessarily *content.* I'm anxious to keep moving upward and onward, making more money and expanding my business. I am anything but content, and I am thoroughly enjoying my discontentedness!"

Denton chuckled. "Not so bad becoming a card-carrying, home-owning member of the establishment, is it?" His pleated slacks and tweed jacket giving him a donnish look of authority on the subject.

"However," Michael interjected, raising an index finger for emphasis, "now that we have a house and a dog, and have become a sort of nuclear family, Hillary has begun the big push to get married ... to legitimize this whole arrangement."

"Well, do you love her?" Denton asked.

"Sure. I can honestly say that I love Hilly." He paused briefly. "But I can also say with equal honesty that I am *not* ready to marry her. She talks about marriage constantly, pointing out diamond rings every time we pass a damn jewelry store."

"Listen," Denton said, "marriage can be great. I like being married. Most of the time anyway. If you love someone you don't want them to slip away. But you've gotta trust your gut. If you don't think you are ready for marriage, then you probably aren't."

"Hillary threatens that at some point, if we aren't married, she will be outta here. That I will wake up one morning and she will be gone. So, I know a day of reckoning is inevitable. But I get your point, don't yield to pressure if my gut says the time is not right."

Walking out to their cars in the restaurant parking lot, Denton watched his friend unlock the door to a beautiful convertible sport car.

"Jesus! Business must be really is good," he said, offering an appreciative whistle.

"I bought my dream car!" Michael replied. "Brand-spanking-new Porsche 911 turbo-Carrera Cabriolet!"

"Whoa! Very cool. I'm not really much of a car guy but, man, that is fuckin' sweet."

"I spotted this ruby red beauty in the car dealer's window and went in, just to get a closer look. I've always liked the old bathtub Porsches, like the Speedster made famous by James Dean, and this new model looks like a modern version of those. It was the only one the dealer had, so I bought it right on the spot!

"When I drove it home to show Hillary, she walked outside, saw it parked in our driveway and said, 'Oh my God, what have you bought now?' She had a point. I mean, we've just recently purchased our big new home, more than four thousand square feet, way too much house for only the two of us. Then we had to furnish the entire place, since we were coming from a small condo and had never owned much more than a sofa and a bed before. And now a new Porsche. Think that's over the top?"

"Hey," Denton shrugged, "everything in moderation, I always say … including excess."

58

CANCER

She did not lose a single hair on her head. Mary had a choice, lumpectomy where only the affected part of the breast would be removed, or mastectomy where the entire breast would be removed. The doctor informed her that a full mastectomy offered increased odds the cancer would be completely eliminated. While a lumpectomy would allow her to retain much of her original breast tissue, radiation treatments would be necessary, and she would lose most of her hair. For Mary, the choice was clear. She hated to lose a part of her anatomy, but hated the idea of baldness even more. A year later, she was now cancer free and reconstructive surgery had restored a full womanly appearance.

She was whole … but her marriage with Joe decidedly was not. They had grown increasingly apart over the years. Though her marriage seemed to be failing, she had produced two wonderful children that were the world to Mary. She had kept news of her cancer from them. They had their own busy lives, and she did not want to burden them.

She was immensely proud of her kids. Jaimie had graduated from Gonzaga with a degree in music. She was exceptionally talented. Michael had a lovely girlfriend and was following in his father's construction footsteps. His contracting business was doing very well. She could now exhale, not worry quite so much about her kids. Fewer prayers to Saint Michael. She felt blessed. Though, now that they were grown and on their own, she sometimes felt extremely lonely.

59

SANTA BARBARA

Michael's construction company was flourishing, employing dozens of foremen, tradesmen, and subcontractors. Amazingly, among them was Joe Perry; something neither he nor Michael would ever have imagined in a million years. The company was building stores in shopping malls all over the state, tenant improvements that type of work was called. To Joe's great surprise, he enjoyed working for his son. He had been given free rein to run the jobs as he saw fit, without any sort of supervision or interference by his son. It was almost like being in business for himself.

And then came the offer. It seemed too good at the time for Joe to pass up. But the rift it would cause between father and son would become irreparable.

Joe was scheduled to begin a new project in Santa Barbara for Michael's company when a competing company offered Joe a job building a large store in another part of the state. Joe, figuring he could easily handle both projects and earn twice the money, clandestinely accepted the competitor's offer. His strategy was to let his son's project sit idle while he completed the competitor's project in record time, then return to Santa Barbara and work round the clock if necessary to get that one done on time as well. No one would be the wiser. It was a challenge, but Joe liked challenges. The trick would be to keep his son from discovering his plan.

Every few days Joe would phone in false progress reports to Michael on a project that had literally not yet begun, as he feverishly worked to complete the competitor's store. Michael deposited weekly payments into his father's bank account with no reason to doubt the validity of Joe's reports … until the day he received a telephone call from his client who was at the job site in Santa Barbara, showing up to check the progress, and discovering no work had yet begun.

"What the hell is going on?" the client demanded.

Michael had no answers. As far as he knew, the work had been progressing nicely, according to the reports received from his father.

Later the same day, Joe made his customary phone call to Michael at the office.

"Where are you?" Michael asked.

"Santa Barbara, of course," Joe answered. "Everything's going smoothly."

And Michael knew his father was lying. He had been paying his father for work not yet even started. On the phone, he confronted Joe: "The client is at the site in Santa Barbara right now. He says you are *not* there and that no work has even begun."

When Joe then confessed that he had been working for a competitor, Michael flew into a rage. "You're fired!"

"No, I can do this," Joe tried assuring him. "I can get both jobs done on time."

"Forget it! The client is upset because no work has begun. He is threatening to sue me! I am sending somebody else up there to do that project. You're fired!" the son repeated.

Michael felt betrayed. Outraged that his own father had lied and stolen from him. It was gut-wrenching. To make matters worse, in addition to the money he had already paid his father, he now had to pay a crew overtime wages to get the project completed in a timely manner, hoping to fend off a lawsuit from the upset client.

For his part, Joe was equally outraged to be fired by his own son. Who the hell did that kid think he was anyway? Getting way too big for his britches in Joe's opinion.

60

SOMETHING NOT QUITE RIGHT

The real estate market in California was sizzling hot and Michael decided to add a real estate brokerage to his construction and development company. He forged a deal with a small local real estate broker. As partners, the broker would run the sales aspects of the business and Michael the construction aspects.

But, on the home-front, Hillary was feeling bored. "I hang around this big house all day doing pretty much nothing." So, Michael encouraged her to get her real estate license and teamed her up with his new partner to learn the ropes. In hardly any time at all she was happily listing and selling houses, some for well over a million dollars.

"You know that listing I have right down the street? The *mondo* one on the corner?" she excitedly asked Michael one evening over dinner. "Well, I was holding an open house and there was this tall guy who walked in wearing tennis clothes. He was with a short Asian woman, also in tennis clothes."

"Not so unusual," Michael, enjoying her enthusiasm, replied. "There's a tennis club about a mile away."

"Yes, yes, I know. I'm just saying. Anyway, this tennis guy looked really familiar, but I could not quite place him. I had him sign my guest book. I always have a guest book so I can keep track of who attends my open houses. But the name he wrote, *A. Kilroy*, did not ring any bells."

"So, who was he?"

"I'm getting to that. So, I was giving him a tour of the house, watching him browse around, checking out the rooms, opening closet doors, looking out windows, just like anyone would do. At some point he said something that triggered my memory. *Oh my god! You're Batman!* I shouted this so loud that it startled him. His back had been toward me but now he spun around, and it was plain as day who he was. Don't know why I did not recognize him sooner. He smiled and said, 'Please, I prefer to be called Adam rather than Batman.'"

"It was Adam West?"

"Yes! But then I stupidly asked, Adam Kilroy? Because that's how he signed the guest book. He laughed and said, 'I just wrote that so you could say *Kilroy was here*.' I did not get the joke, so he explained: 'It's an old expression. Apparently before your time. People used to write *Kilroy was here*. Quite honestly, I have no idea why. It's just something people did.'

"I still didn't get it, maybe because I was just so excited to be talking with Batman. I told him that I grew up watching the show on TV and never missed an episode. He shrugged and said, 'I know. Everybody did. But I *have* had other roles, you know. I've not always exclusively been Batman.'

"Actually, I didn't know but nodded as if I did. Apparently unconvincingly because he then rattled off a list of his many prior and subsequent acting credits and told me about his years in Hollywood."

"Gee, that's cool that you got to meet your childhood TV hero," Michael replied when she paused to take a breath.

"I know. It was so neat-o! Right after he left, another prospective buyer who was exploring the house approached me and asked, 'Was that who I think it was?' I answered, Yup, that was the one and only Batman."

Hillary was a natural at selling real estate and was obviously enjoying her job and the interesting people she was meeting. But, as time went by, her stories were less frequent and enthusiasm seemed to wane. There was a vibe developing that seemed just a little bit off to Michael. Perhaps it was only his imagination, but he sensed a certain oddness between them recently. He couldn't quite put his finger on it, just something not quite right. Maybe we have both been working too hard, he pondered, not enough time spent simply enjoying each other. We need to get away. A couple weeks in Hawaii, just the two of us, might be the cure.

61

JOURNAL

Presently, I am relaxing out on the lanai of our suite at the Royal Kona Resort on the Big Island of Hawaii. The Kona Coast is perhaps my favorite place in the entire world. I'm listening to the Pacific surf pound only a few feet away against the black lava shore. Birds are singing, the breeze is gentle, the sky and water intensely blue. Hillary switched off the near-constant Hawaiian music that's been playing on the radio since our arrival, replacing it with *Manic Monday* by the Bangles. Happily, there will be no manic Mondays for us the next couple weeks. Work is on hold, no plans to even call the office. It's just the carefree vacation life for us.

Hilly is reclined fetchingly across from me right now, writing postcards and letters to friends back home. Presumably bragging about what a wonderful time we are having. I'm a very lucky guy to be here in this beautiful place with the woman I love.

She and I will be heading out in a few minutes for our morning run along the beach. Hillary has become quite a fitness nut. Besides jogging, she's been totally into aerobic dancing for the past many months and, I must admit, it has given her an absolute killer body ... to which I need to pay more attention. Aloha.

62

THE LETTER

Hillary had felt invisible for a long time. It was a deeply troubling undercurrent of despondency that gnawed at her. There was no one in whom she could confide, no one she might complain to. Most likely any confidant would surely think she had lost her mind, since her life appeared nearly perfect. A beautiful house in an exclusive neighborhood. Plenty of time to do whatever she pleased. A successful boyfriend. Expensive cars. Did she just feel under-appreciated? No, it was not that exactly. Just invisible. She could think of no word more precise to explain how she felt.

It was as if her life read like page after page of some droll novel in which she was an underdeveloped character; until getting her real estate license, then the next page brilliantly putting into context all that came before. Suddenly she was being noticed – by clients and peers – something she had not experienced in a very long time from anyone, including her workaholic boyfriend.

And there was this man, Michael's business partner, working beside her, praising her, noticing her. They began spending a great deal of time together, working, laughing, lunching, selling houses. She was once more visible. And she was aware of her visibility. Aware of him noticing her in special ways. That he was married with young children made it all seem safe somehow.

Then another of the novel's pages turned and the story became decidedly steamy. They were holding an open house together. Somehow, they found themselves in the master bedroom. They were touching. The front door to the house still unlocked, that anyone could enter at any moment making it feel all the more exciting. Touching led to kissing. It had been years since she had kissed, or been kissed by, another man. Fondling. It had been years since she had felt the touch of another man. They were on the bed. Passion came quickly.

From that page onward, there was no turning back. They met several times at houses and even in the office after hours. The greater the chance of discovery, the more exciting it seemed.

Hillary began to imagine she was in love with this man. How else could she keep having sex with him? Of course, she was not *really* in love. Deep down she was aware that he merely made her feel sexy, desired, important ... and visible.

And then she was in Hawaii with Michael, overlooking the grand vista of the Pacific. But she could not clear the other man from her thoughts. She tried, but he remained. Michael was sitting across from her, lazily basking in the sun, as she covertly drafted a letter to the man, letting him know how much she longed to be with him again. Anxious. Missing him. And she signed it *love*.

The letter arrived at his office on a day when his secretary – who normally opens the mail, placing it unread upon his desk – called in sick. So, it was the man's *wife* who came to the office to fill in on secretarial duties. Intrigued by the Hawaii postmark, the wife opened the letter from Hillary and read the contents. She became incensed, wielding the letter-opener like a dagger dangerously close to his private parts, she began yelling and screaming at her husband quite loudly, everyone in the office instantly learning of the affair.

Meanwhile, vacationing in the land of aloha, Hillary had no idea what had occurred back at the office. On the day she and Michael returned from the Islands, Hillary went merrily waltzing into the office only to discover that her secret was out. Horrified at being discovered, she raced off to find Michael, to confess the whole sordid ordeal before he heard it from someone other than her.

She found Michael at home in his study, talking business on the phone. She began pacing anxiously in the hallway, walking in absent circles, fingers fretting nervously with the hem of her skirt, waiting for him to finish his call. Rehearsing in her mind what she might say … but what could she say? What could she possibly say to diffuse such opprobrium? Perspiration accumulating on her upper lip, she was frightened, more so than ever before in her life. No idea how he might react. Scared that he would never forgive her. She wasn't sure she could even forgive herself.

Then, all at once, she noticed the quiet. Michael had quit talking and had hung up the phone. Fright climbed up into her throat with a bitter taste. Timorously she crept into his study.

"So, how did things go at the office?" he inquired breezily as she entered.

His innocence of the situation both touching and somehow pathetic, she stood in front of his desk and began to softly cry.

"Hilly, what's wrong?" he asked, starting to get up from his desk chair, genuinely concerned.

Without further hesitation, Hillary launched into a full tear-filled confession, explaining everything to the best of her ability. Michael, listening in disbelief, plopping heavily back down into his chair as if weighted by her words, sank into a cold torpor trying to process what she was telling him. Words sounding in trills too impossible to mentally conjugate into nouns and verbs, he heard without immediately comprehending. Impossible that the woman he had so completely trusted, whom he had loved for nearly six years, to whom he had remained faithful in all that time and had always looked upon as a life partner, could commit such betrayal.

He simply did not know how to respond. He didn't know what he felt more, angry or hurt. What he mostly felt, at that precise moment perhaps, was numb. With effort, he slowly stood, walking toward the door to leave.

"Please don't go," Hillary pleaded. "Please."

Unable to make it all the way out of the room, with a heavy sigh he collapsed into a wingback chair near the fireplace. Hillary went to him, kneeling on the floor in front of him. "Please say something. I am so, so sorry. You cannot imagine."

He sat silently, staring up at the blades of the ceiling fan slowly turning overhead.

"What can I do, Michael? Please. I'll do anything. Anything to fix this," she pleaded, whimpering.

More silence.

She moved her hands up his legs, caressing him. Burying her face in his lap.

"You need to leave," he finally spoke.

Still on her knees, she looked up at him in desperation.

"No, forget that. You stay. I'll leave."

Once more he stood up, causing her to reposition from kneeling to sitting on the floor, hugging her knees. She was sobbing loudly now. Then he shuffled out of the room.

Moments later, she could hear the garage door being opened. Three cars inside: a BMW, a Jeep, and a Porsche. The distinct whine of the Porsche starting up. She ran to the garage to stop him. The convertible top was down, key chain dangling from the ignition just to the left of the steering column. She leaned in, grabbing the keys, taking a step back as the engine instantly shut down.

He sat motionless, a fixed stare through the windshield at the blank garage wall in front of him, both hands in a death grip on the steering wheel. Seething. Finally, turning his head slowly to face her with a look so intense she involuntarily took a step back away from the car, he began speaking with measured voice and careful enunciation, pronouncing each word exactingly; his voice a quiet whisper at first, but escalating with each sentence. "This is what you do? You fuck this guy? Not just *any* guy, my fucking partner?"

He paused, then began again, shouting now. "Then, while I'm off in Hawaii stupidly thinking what a lucky guy I am to be there with you, you mail some sort of fucking love letter to this dirt-bag at the office? What kind of a person does something like that? And what kind of fucking partner is he? He's got a wife and kids, for Christ's sake!"

She took a step closer. "I'm sorry. It was me. It was all me," she pleaded in desperation. "I'm a terrible person. But I'm a person who loves you and will never, ever hurt you again. I promise."

Reaching out and snatching the keys back from her, re-starting the car and backing out of the garage, tires screeching on the concrete floor. And he was gone.

63

THE ARCTIC SEA

The Porsche roared up the coast of California, crossing the border into Oregon, then Washington, and kept going north. A place as different as possible from California was where Michael hoped to escape. In Vancouver, he parked the car and bought a last-minute ticket on a cruise ship bound for Alaska. He had no idea the enormity of such a massive vessel until actually boarding, like a floating upscale resort.

The air became perceptively colder as they cruised northward. He spent many hours in the ship's pub, alone; fitting surroundings for introspection, seated by a large window sipping hot toddies and watching the frosted landscape pass by.

It was a damp, drizzly day when the ship passengers disembarked for an onshore excursion at Juneau, the capital of Alaska. Only twenty-four miles of road, none that connect to anywhere outside the city, makes it the only state capital to be so isolated. Michael found the weather depressing and the isolation confining.

Next stop was the Alaskan town of Skagway. Here there were roads on which one could venture inland. Michael had already had enough of shipboard life. All that food, frivolity, and compelled comingling with fellow passengers not at all what he was seeking. Purchasing a used camper/van from a dealer in Skagway, he decided to go exploring.

Heading east in the camper/van, eventually connecting to the AlCan Highway – short for Alaskan-Canadian Highway – a mostly dirt/gravel road that he traversed for the next two and a half days into Canada's Yukon Territory. Often narrowing to a single lane with two-hundred-foot drops on either side, the road abruptly ended at a large body of water. Not sure how to get across, he camped there for the night, the serenity of moving water interrupted by howling wolves in the night and perceived movements of nearby unidentified critters. Early next morning, an old river barge came chugging up the waterway and ferried him to the other side.

Later that evening he arrived at Dawson City – Jack London territory – an authentic old mining town with streets of dirt, wooden boardwalks like an Old West town, and unembellished by any trappings of tourism.

Just outside the edge of town, he again set up camp, settling down for the night under a blanket of stars that erupted into the most spectacular night sky he had ever seen – Aurora Borealis. The Northern Lights set the sky ablaze with swirling purples, pinks, and deep green waves lasting but a few moments before disappearing, only to reappear several more times with equal brevity. He kept watching for more until sleep took him.

Dawn arrived, he packed up and drove on, continuing northward through the Yukon and re-entering the state of Alaska at a town named Tok. From there the road conditions improved, becoming two and four lane thoroughfares that took him to Fairbanks.

Fairbanks, Alaska, with a population of only ninety-eight thousand people, is the second largest city in the forty-ninth state. Such a population would place it amongst the smaller of California cities. But it wasn't small enough.

Michael chartered a small single-engine airplane and pilot to fly him from Fairbanks to Point Barrow, Alaska. He needed to be away from Hillary, the business, everything, and everyone. Barrow seemed about as far away as a person could get. Located at the most northern point on the North American continent, commonly referred to as the *Top of the World*, there are no roads connecting Point Barrow to anywhere else in the world. The only viable way in or out is by airplane.

Looking down from the plane at the frozen barren terrain stretching infinitely below, the landscape seemed to reflect his mood: sad, cold, dark, and enormously depressing. Frozen tundra – miles and miles devoid of trees or any other living plant. An Arctic desert stark and bereft of color where "Only Eskimos and a scattering of U.S. Military reside," the pilot informed.

Walking the frozen rocky beach of the Arctic Sea, along the Bering Straits where giant blue and white blocks of ice loomed menacingly, a prodigious whale bone arch abruptly rising perhaps twenty feet out of the snow stood tall – a monument erected by this isolated community to the still thriving whaling industry in the area.

Ice fog blinded him, and biting wind cut into his face like tiny knives. He lasted only minutes in such boister before taking shelter in the closest heated structure he could find, carefully climbing three ice-covered wooden steps of a tiny restaurant bearing a sign with the unlikely logo of a red chili pepper surrounded by flames: CRUZ'S MEXICAN GRILL – NORTHERNMOST MEXICAN RESTAURANT IN THE WORLD!

"Seriously?" he said aloud to himself. "All this way just to find a damn Mexican restaurant like in California?" But the interior warmth and aroma of food was most welcoming as he stepped inside to thaw.

Alone, losing himself in the bleak frozen world of Point Barrow, he fell into a sort of enervating mental hibernation. He would stay here as long as it took. *Midway upon the journey of life, I found myself within a forest dark, for the straightforward pathway had been lost.* Ancient words from some long-ago college course floating up from the recesses of his brain. Dante? A tidbit of trivial knowledge resurfacing at this precipitous moment seemingly right on target.

He also recalled another more contemporary but innocuous quote: *Trusting people is a dangerous way to live.* He had placed all his trust in Hillary, and she betrayed that trust. He wondered if he would ever be capable of such confident expectation from anyone again. She had been his North Star, now leaving him to wander life's abyss compass-less.

Seated at a window table looking out, like some detached figure in an Edward Hopper painting, the frozen landscape was bleak and blackened with grime. Then, at some point, fresh snow began to fall.

64

LIFE IS AN ONGOING PROJECT

She heard him arrive, the Porsche pulling into the garage, and she watched as he walked through the door into the house. It had been weeks. What would happen now? She fully expected that Michael would tell her it was over, that he wanted nothing to do with her after what she did.

To her amazement, that was not what happened. Days went by and they just went on about their business, living side by side in the big house. But nothing was as before. There was an ugly pallor that filled their lives. The tension was palpable. They did not converse, and the sparingly few words he would utter were never addressed directly to her. They were merely sharing space, breathing the same air, but that was all.

Hillary finally confronted him. "Please, can we talk?"

The question was met with an icy stare. "Fine. Let's talk," he answered.

"Where have you been all these weeks?"

"Alaska."

"No, really. Alaska?"

"Alaska. That's where I've been. Canada and Alaska. Now, how about you give me some answers?" He then began an inquisition about the details of her tryst with his business partner. Feeling she had already deceived him enough, she answered all his questions with forthright honesty. That proved to be a mistake. Once the questioning began, it never let up; each question requiring further explanation and detail. It was almost as if he were deriving some sick prurient pleasure from hearing about it.

Eventually she had enough of the non-stop interrogation. She simply stopped talking and stormed out of the room. He followed her, grabbing her by the shoulders, stopping her, spinning her around to face him. For a moment she thought he might strike her, but he didn't. He let go of her shoulders and stepped back.

"You are never going to let it go, are you?" she demanded. "No matter what I say or do now, nothing will be good enough. No amount of apologizing will convince you that I am sorry. And I *am* sorry, believe me. Especially that I hurt you so much. But it wasn't *all* my fault. For so long I have been pushed into the background of things."

"What the hell does that mean? What sort of things?" He was indignant.

"All you did was work, work, work and wheel and deal. Making money, that was your true passion, and it didn't feel like much was left over for me. So, when I finally found someone who genuinely paid attention to *me*, I couldn't help but enjoy it."

"I'm sorry," he found himself muttering, turning and walking away, entering his study, closing the door behind him.

"And what about marriage?" she shouted toward the closing door. "Was I expected to wait forever?"

The following morning he approached her, wanting to talk again. "Listen," he began, "I'm glad you told me exactly how you feel. How I made you feel. I just didn't know. I was too wrapped up in myself, I guess. I have become such an asshole. Not that I deserved what you did, but it has been a definite wake up call."

His words surprised her. They were conciliatory.

"Maybe sometimes the most important history one can learn from is their own." He paused a moment, reflecting back to a time when it was *he* who had cheated and begged to be forgiven. "You say I like to wheel and deal? Okay, then here is the deal. I am selling this house, the cars, everything. And closing my business."

"But," Hillary interrupted, "that's totally crazy. Please don't do that. I don't want to be the one driving you to do something so extreme."

"I'm the one who created this business and I'm the one who can shut it down! Between you and what my dad did up in Santa Barbara – lost me my biggest client and nearly got me sued – I just don't have the heart for the business any longer. Extreme? How about betrayal from the two people closest to me! How's that for extreme?

"Nothing in my current life really means much anymore. I've been looking at some photographs from my old sailing days. Barefoot, free, happy. Comparing those times to now, seems I lost sight of what really matters in life. Certainly not this fucking business. Certainly not fancy cars, fancy house. You with your Gucci handbags and me with this goddamned Rolex on my wrist that cost more than I used to make in a year. It's insane! Money should not be for buying *things*, it's for buying freedom. I'm done with conspicuous consumption. I'm really fucking done!

"I think maybe I was just trying to prove something to myself, or maybe to my father – look how successful I am, Dad. Can you finally be proud of me? I don't know. But I'm starting over. Divorcing myself from everything. Including California. I plan to make Hawaii my home. I have loved Hawaii ever since sailing there all those years ago and, damn it, now I am going back to stay!"

"What about me?" Hillary asked. "What about us? Is there still an us?"

"I don't know. You can come along or not, your choice. I am willing to give it a try. A new place, a new time? Life is an ongoing project. Who the fuck knows?"

PART SEVEN

65

JOURNAL

Christmas time in Hawaii has a holiday spirit all its own. The palm trees are all decorated and lit up and Santa arrives via surfboard at Waikiki Beach. Hilly and I have been living here on Oahu for almost a year. It's like being on perpetual vacation. Each morning I wake up and the biggest decision I make is which beach to surf at today.

Though, if I thought this pivot in life was going to be easy, I was mistaken. Moving here was initially fraught with mishaps. When we landed in Honolulu, Baxter – our doggie – was immediately removed from the plane and whisked away to the state quarantine area. This is where he would spend the next four months. Canine quarantine was awful, so sad to see him in that prison-like environment; no way around it, though. It's state law. Being without Baxter for that long would be difficult.

But, while Baxter had state-mandated lodging, we had trouble finding a place for *ourselves* to stay. On the day we arrived, all the better hotels were full. The only vacancy was at some older place off Kuhio Street that charged an arm and a leg for a barely habitable room overlooking the noisy street. Hillary found a cockroach in the bathroom, but there was nowhere else for us to go.

The second night here we both got food poisoning. The cramping, vomiting and diarrhea caused us to spend the next couple days in bed – and not in a fun way – at our crappy hotel room. Plus, we arrived during a record-breaking heat wave with extreme humidity. All these things only exacerbated the deep fissures still remaining between Hillary and me. This was not the life in paradise I had envisioned.

But I was determined, so as soon as we felt better, I went to the closest car dealership and bought a car – a little white convertible – and then started my search for a house to buy.

In Hawaii, I learned, title to real estate is seldom transferred in fee simple. Generally, the purchaser buys only the structure and the furnishings, not the land. The land is held in trust for native Hawaiians, as per state law going all the way back to the mid-1840s. It was startling for me that the high cost of housing here (even higher than California) does not even include ownership of the land. Took me a while to wrap my head around that.

On the upside, though, most houses here come furnished because it is so costly to ship furniture to and from the mainland, or even inter-island, that sellers often just leave the furnishings behind to be included in the sale. Also on the upside, since no ownership of land is being transferred, escrow time is short.

I managed to find a small house with a pool and ocean view and was anxious to get started on my new life as a resident of our nation's youngest state. The evening we closed escrow, Hilly and I dined at our favorite Mexican restaurant, Compadres. I sat looking out at Ala Moana Park and the ocean through the window from our table with a huge smile. Hawaii was now our new home.

Morning runs along the beach together helped to heal the wounds of the past and make us closer again. In fact, just a few weeks ago, Hillary and I ran the Honolulu Marathon! I'd been running farther and farther each day, getting up to around twelve miles. Hillary's been running right along with me. But the marathon was more than double that distance.

At sunrise, when Mayor Fasi fired off his starting pistol, there were more than ten thousand runners. Twenty-six miles later, I finished somewhere in the middle of the pack.

And for Hillary to have done it with me was a bonding experience that brought it all home for us as a couple. Only those who have completed a 26.2-mile marathon can know the exhilaration we felt crossing that finish line together.

Back at our house, after the race, Hillary and I stuffed our faces unabashedly with pizza, beer, and Pringles potato chips. Pizza tastes best when consumed without guilt. And, believe me, after running twenty-six miles we were completely guilt-free! We both felt a little stiff from such a run, but that was overshadowed by runner's euphoria.

We were relaxing in front of the television, and I was walking into the kitchen to get another beer, when I heard Hilly shout from the other room, "Oh my god! Come here quick!"

I hobbled back on tired marathon legs as fast as I could.

"Look!" she said, pointing at the TV. There on the screen were two guys, one with a dark beard, the other in ripped jeans and a cowboy hat. The announcer was introducing them as Grammy nominees for Best New Country Artists.

"Those are the street bums you didn't like sleeping on our couch back in Marina del Rey," I confirmed with a bit of smugness. "Goes to show, if you have a dream and believe in yourself, amazing things can happen."

Her comeback? "You'd think the one with the hat could afford jeans that don't have rips in the knees. I mean, he's on TV for gosh sake."

66

JOURNAL

Living here in Hawaii has offered exciting opportunities to pursue things I never would have had time for in my prior mainland life. *Bucket list* items as a kanaka friend refers to them: things to complete before you kick the bucket. I ran the Honolulu Marathon and competed in an Ironman contest. For a guy who never cared much about athletics growing up, finishing such endurance contests feels like a real accomplishment. Also, I've been studying karate at the Japan Center in Honolulu. In both mind and body, I feel I'm in the best shape of my entire life.

So yes, life is good here in the Islands. From our house we overlook Koko Head crater, Hawaii Kai golf course, and the ocean at Sandy Beach. But living in such a wonderland as Oahu, a person can still get the urge for a change. So, where to go to get away? Well, to one of the other nearby islands, of course.

Hilly and I recently took our dog Baxter and flew over to Maui for a few days. We took Baxter swimming in the famous Sacred Pools near Hana. Our indefatigable aquatic canine loved jumping from the rocks high above the pools and swimming under the cascading waterfalls.

There was a fellow there in the water who, watching Baxter's athletic antics, commented in a heavy British accent, "That's quite some dog you have there. A Springer Spaniel, isn't he? English like me." He laughed heartily at his own joke. Hilly and I laughed along and confirmed that he was correct about the breed, Hilly adding that Baxter often barks with a cockney accent.

He was a friendly enough Brit, with very long graying hair and beard that floated atop the water while his body remained submerged, looking like some sort of hairy crocodile with only his nose and eyes above water much of the time. In hindsight, it occurs to me that perhaps he kept his face submerged to keep from being recognized.

We learned shortly afterward that this woolly amphibious Brit was none other than former Beatle George Harrison! At the time, we had absolutely no idea that we were talking with one-fourth of the most famous rock band in history. To quote Hillary, this was "Mega mondo neat-o!"

Although George Harrison has always been known as "the quiet Beatle," he is certainly the only Beatle I ever had a conversation with.

As it turns out, we were told Mr. Harrison lives just a short distance from the Sacred Pools and swims there frequently. So Hilly, Baxter and I walked past the house where we were told he lived to get another glance at the famous rocker. It was a nice house, but certainly not a mansion or anything like one might expect from such a celebrity. The driveway was gated but I could see through the bars, and there he was out in front of his house just like a normal, regular, mere mortal person.

He looked in my direction and I waved. I think it was Baxter that he recognized, because he waved back. How cool is that? I could live to be a hundred years old and I'm sure I will never forget the day I swam with a Beatle on Maui. Add that to the bucket list!

67

PARADISE LOST

A sunny, breezy, typical day on the North Shore of Oahu. Michael was sitting on the wide sandy beach, idly watching Hillary and Baxter playing in the surf. The sun feeling warm on his body, boom box tuned to KCCN playing sweet Hawaiian slack key melodies, while marshmallow puffy white clouds floated above in the bluest blue sky. A living postcard from a place called paradise.

His love affair with these islands was born the moment he arrived via that little blue sailboat years prior. But he knew, in his heart of hearts, Hawaii was merely a temporary stop. A wonderfully beautiful, salubrious place where a person, a couple, can heal old wounds, sort things out, regroup, and get nurtured back to emotional health. *Living pono,* as the locals say – finding the right balance in relationships and life. It had been nearly two years now. He could feel the time to leave paradise drawing near. *Ka makani* – Hawaiian for the feeling is in the very air.

It was months earlier that a friend from the mainland came out to visit – Gerald Leoni, an attorney with the Los Angeles law firm Michael had used over the years in his business dealings. Michael always liked Gerry, both as a lawyer and a friend. He was charismatic, a Midwestern transplant, Italian-American, and only a couple years older than Michael. They had a lot in common.

Michael had never met anyone who loved their job as much as Gerry loved his. Leoni would talk of the courtroom as if it were the Roman Colosseum and he a brave gladiator going into battle, spinning his legal tales with enthusiastic intonations and all the animation stereotypical of his ethnic lineage. A complete workaholic, this trip to Hawaii was Leoni's first vacation from his law practice in years.

Sitting at poolside in the backyard of Michael's Oahu house, looking out at the Hawaiian hillside with the blue Pacific just beyond, Gerry remarked, "*Paisano*, you've truly got it made. Only in your thirties and you have already achieved the dream the rest of us work a lifetime to achieve: a carefree retired life in the Islands."

"Thanks," Michael responded, swirling ice in the drink he held in his hand. "But Gerry, you would not want this lifestyle. Too laid back. You live for the battle. I honestly cannot picture *you* ever giving up the glamorous career you have chosen and retiring to the tranquility of these islands."

"Nor you," the lawyer said, laughing. "You used to be a workaholic, too. But it looks like you have adapted just fine."

Michael smiled at hearing Gerry's description of his former self and the perceived adaptation. Truth be known, Michael missed the fast-paced business life he left behind and told Leoni as much. "There are times when I find myself bored with life in paradise. But what would I do back on the mainland? Construction? Real Estate? Been there, done that already."

"So, go to law school," Gerry suggested, casually swirling ice in his own drink before taking a sip.

"Yeah, right. I'm a bit long in the tooth to be a schoolboy again, don't you think?"

"Too old for law school? Sounds more like you are feeling too *young* for retirement," Gerry quipped.

"That's what I like about you, counselor. You always have a positive spin."

"Look," Gerry said, suddenly dead serious and using his most persuasive attorney voice, "law school would be a grind, I won't lie to you. But *paisan*, you are the best businessman I know. Seriously, you are. And I am the best lawyer you probably know. So go to law school, graduate, pass the bar, and we will team up to become unbeatable! I've been ready to leave the big firm and hang my own shingle for quite a while now. With you handling the business and me doing the lawyering, no way we could miss."

It was just idle chit-chat on a warm Hawaiian day, but Gerry's words lingered in Michael's mind long after his friend returned to the mainland.

On a whim, Michael took the Law School Admission Test in Honolulu and, to his utter astonishment, scored in the top two percent in the nation. He took this as a sign and, armed with such a score, began applying to law schools. Inexplicably, his application was denied at University of Hawaii but accepted by several schools in California, including one that offered an accelerated two-year program for those with top LSAT scores. Shaving off a year or more of school was appealing since he wasn't getting any younger.

Hillary, though not too crazy about the whole idea of returning to California – preferring to remain in the Islands where she and Michael had begun a happy new life together – made Stanford an option as well. Her father, a Stanford professor – not at the law school, but he had connections – offered to use his influence for Michael to gain admission.

So now Michael Perry sat quietly on the sand watching the mesmeric puissant rhythm of waves arriving on the beach, feeling the warmth of tropical breezes on his exposed flesh, and contemplating how different life would soon be. No longer residing on this lovely tropical rock in the middle of the Pacific, no longer a resident of the Aloha State. A student once again.

He looked out at the sea. California was somewhere out there in the far, far distance. Baxter was barking, tail wagging, snout covered with sand, Hillary laughing as she chased the dog in and out of the waves … and Michael just smiled.

PART EIGHT

68

ONE L

By December Michael was halfway through his first year of law school. "I survived the first half of One L hell!" he jubilantly announced to Hillary. Initially he'd been a reluctant student, concerned about returning to academia an old man in his thirties, and was relieved to discover several others his age, some even much older.

But relief was replaced by intimidation: on day-one discovering many classmates had already achieved high academic laurels – several with PhDs, and even MDs – scholars wanting to add Juris Doctorate to their resumes. One fellow student introduced himself as a former professor of genetics at Cornell University – to which Michael sheepishly responded that he used to own a construction company. Persevering had been difficult and humbling, achievable only by consecrating himself to a spartan study regimen.

"Had my doubts for a while, but so far I have survived."

"I never had any doubt," Hilly responded. "I wonder if your professors have figured out yet just how smart you are."

He rolled his eyes, though treasured her steadfast encouragement and support.

"Hey, I'm serious. My dad is a professor. I have been around brainy academic types my whole life. I know *mondo* smart when I see it."

They would be celebrating Christmas with Michael's family. While most families, one might assume, would be *proud* to have a law student son,

Michael felt certain that his would not. Not his father, anyway. Father and son had remained estranged the past several years, since the Santa Barbara incident, and he had kept his student status a secret. Though tempted to tell his mother, she would no doubt share that information with his dad.

"My dad most assuredly would not understand what the hell it is I am doing and I just wouldn't be able to deal with his likely reaction," he told Hillary on the drive to his parents' home in the San Fernando Valley. "He would belittle my situation. Probably tell me I'm too old to be a student. He might even start on a verbal rampage against lawyers in general, denigrating the entire profession as a bunch of worthless *sleazebags*." Being a law student, he told her, must remain a secret.

But Michael's father had an even bigger secret. One that he divulged the day after Christmas.

"Let's take a ride," he said to his son. They drove to a nearby tavern and sat side-by-side on stools at the bar. "I know we have not exactly been on speaking terms for quite a while, but I've got somethin' to tell you. I'm gonna have a sit-down with Jaimie, too. But you are the oldest, so I thought I should tell you first."

"What's this all about, Dad?" Michael asked.

"I'm leaving your mother," he said, as the bartender placed two glasses of beer in front of them. "It's been coming for a long time." Michael started to interrupt, but Joe held his hand up to stop him. "Before you go getting all high and mighty on me, just hear me out. For once in your life, try listening to your old man. Okay?"

Michael nodded.

"You're not gonna wanna hear this, but there's things you don't know about your mom and me. This might be hard to take, but things have never really been much good between us."

"Dad, I think that's been obvious for quite a while."

"Fact is, I would have left her years ago, but things kept getting in the way. Like her cancer. I couldn't very well leave her then, now could I?"

Without waiting for a response, he continued. "Truth is, Mike, *you* are the reason we even stayed together for *this* long."

"Me?" Michael was incredulous.

"Yeah. You and your sister. It was a matter of obligations. Just like in the military, a man has to live up to his obligations. When you were born, I made a promise to myself that I'd stick around till you were growed up. Then your sister came along, and I knew it would be even longer before I'd be going anywhere. But now both my kids are finally grown. The time has come."

"You don't love mom?" Michael asked.

"Yeah, I suppose I do. Been together a lotta years. That's gotta count for somethin'. But I met somebody a few years ago. I finally know what it feels like to really be in love."

"How did you meet this person?" Michael asked.

"She worked at my dentist's office. She's the gal who, you know, cleans my teeth?"

"A hygienist?"

"Right. Anyway, she was always so sweet and nice. So, one day I show up at the dentist office with no appointment, just to ask her to have lunch with me. She said, 'Sure!' We really hit it off. After that we began seeing each other pretty regular. It was like how you kids say it, I had found my *soul mate*."

"And you're leaving mom to be with this other woman?"

"I wish that was true, but no."

"Why not?"

"She's dead."

"Dead?"

"Yeah. She was married, too. Bad marriage, no kids though. She promised me she was gonna break it off, tell her hubby she wanted out. He's a pilot. Private pilot. Had a little Piper Cherokee. So, they was gonna fly up to Big Bear for the weekend. She promised she'd break the news to him then."

"So, what happened?"

"Plane crashed. Bad weather. Blizzard. Should not have been flying in that stuff. They both died."

"Jesus," Michael sighed.

"Saddest day of my life. And I couldn't even tell anybody about it. So, I buried myself in work. I worked and worked so I wouldn't dwell on it."

Michael wondered if that might have been the time period when he and his father had their falling out. Perhaps this was the reason, drowning his sorrow in work, thinking he could work two jobs at once, why he lied to his son about Santa Barbara. Had Michael known the true circumstances, perhaps he might have reacted differently.

"So, if she died, why leave mom now?"

"Listen," he said, staring down into his beer, watching bubbles rise from the bottom of the glass, "I'm not young anymore. Funny thing to hear myself say, because it just never crossed my mind that I could ever be anything but young. Seemed like there would always be plenty of time left. But this ... this was a goddam wake up call. She made me feel things I had not ever felt before. And her dying made me realize there's no more time to waste."

Oddly enough, the son had *never* thought of his father as young. The man had never regaled any stories of youthful adventure, nary a mention of boyhood friends, nothing.

"You gonna tell mom about all this?"

"No. She doesn't need to know all this crap. I'm just gonna tell her I want out and I'm leaving. She can keep the house and all that kinda stuff. I don't care. I've accumulated my own stuff. Stuff she doesn't even know about. Been stashing things away on the side for years, knowing this day would come. If she wants to file for divorce, I don't care. But I'd prefer not to have to deal with a bunch of dip-shit lawyers and all that legal shit. Only ones who come out smellin' good in a divorce are the fucking lawyers. We should just go our separate ways and let that be the end of it."

69

ONE ADVENTURE TOO MANY

As far back as she could remember, Hillary Hartnel had always wanted to meet *Mr. Right*, get married, have a baby, and live in a cute house in the suburbs. A simple, straight-forward life plan. Being, perhaps, a bit romantically naive, she had plenty of preconceived notions as to what Mr. Right would be like and what their life together should be. She had always been attracted to tall, dark-haired men, so that's the way she physically envisioned Mr. Right. Also, he would be a doctor – first choice – or a lawyer – close second. Michael was blond and not at all tall, he worked construction when they met, and then they lived on a sailboat. None of the criteria she had always imagined. Still, he was her life's greatest love.

But some things just cannot be compromised. When she arrived at the age of thirty, with still no commitment from Michael, Hillary decided it was time to change course. Thirty. You just cannot mess with that biological timeclock and the primal longing to have a baby. Time to move on.

With no recent employment history, other than selling real estate, and she was still smarting from how that ended, she felt fortunate to have landed a sales job at a major department store. She would be taking with her only necessities, and that included Baxter, her furry baby, for emotional support.

It was one of the most difficult decisions she ever had to make. She loved her life with Michael, but it became just one *adventure* too many. First it was living on a boat, then totally wrapped up in running a successful business, then uprooting their lives with a move to Hawaii, then abruptly back to California, and now more than two years with him completely immersed in studying the law. How long was she supposed to wait?

The irony was not lost on her, however, that she was leaving just as he was *ipso facto* about to become a lawyer: dream choice number two for Mr. Right's occupation. With all the courage she could summon, she gathered up Baxter and left.

70

TICK TOCK

Often he would think about her, just wanting to hear her voice again. It had been more than four months since Hillary left, the dimension of his life irretrievably altered. He missed her and wondered how she was doing. So, when the telephone rang earlier that evening, he was surprised to hear the familiar voice on the other end.

"How's school?" Hillary asked.

"Fine. I can finally see the proverbial light at the end of the tunnel."

"Oh good! Free at last!"

"Sort of. But after graduation there is still the whole bar exam thing. Not really a lawyer if I can't pass that. They say studying for the exam is even tougher than law school."

"Sounds perfectly dreadful," she said. "But it is a little hard to have sympathy for someone with a self-inflicted wound."

"I know, I know. How's Baxter? I miss him."

"He's good. I'm so glad to have him. He keeps me sane."

"And your new job at the department store?"

"Yea, it's pretty neat-o. I recently got promoted. I am now head of the handbag department."

A silent smile: he'd not heard the expression *neat-o* in a while.

"Congratulations Hilly," he said. "You've always been such a dynamo. I would not be surprised if one day you were head of the entire store."

There was a diffident chuckle at her end.

"I'm serious. You are an amazing person."

"Thank you," she replied.

"There's a song that makes me think of you every time I hear it on the radio," he said.

"Which song?"

He began to sing to her over the phone: *If I flew high like an eagle, it was only because you were the wind beneath my wings.*

"Oh my," her voice sounded of emotion. "That is the sweetest thing anyone has ever said, or sang, to me. I know that song. Do you really truly feel that way?"

"I do. You were right there with me, right from the start. You always believed in me. When I started my business. If I surfed a wave too big for my skills. No matter what I did, you were right there. When I ran a marathon, you were running right by my side. You were my moral support all through law school, too, even when I had my moments of doubt. You absolutely have always been the wind beneath my wings. If I never told you before, I want you to know that."

"Oh Michael. Thank you. We really did have something special, didn't we?" Her voice choked with emotion. "It was a magical, once-in-a-lifetime, ever-evolving medley we had together. I wouldn't trade it for anything."

He felt the same, the conversation lingering there before finally shifting to the real reason for her call.

"But I have happy news. Happy, happy news!" her voice suddenly excited. "I'm pregnant! About three-and-a-half months along."

Michael's brain did a quick involuntary calculation to determine if a three-and-a-half- month pregnancy could make *him* the father.

As if reading his mind, she said, "Don't worry. You're not the father."

"No?" Though worry was not really what he was feeling. More like a sudden inexplicable torsion of muzzy emotions.

"Nope. But we plan to get married soon. Probably next month."

Michael was completely stunned by Hillary's announcement but honored that she thought enough of him to call and share her joyful news.

And, though he was happy for her, he felt a profound sense of loss. Hillary had told him long ago that if he did not marry her, one day she would be gone. And that was exactly what happened. Aspirations toward marriage and fatherhood had long been an imperceptible current flowing through his life but other events seemed to always get in the way. For Hillary, the urgency of marriage and procreation was paramount, her perceived biological timeclock ticking loudly.

Stuck in the alternate universe of law school, all at once Michael was feeling his *own* timeclock, and the lingering imprisonment of higher learning, though graduation day was now not far off, made the ticking all the more pronounced. Tick tock!

The call ended. He found himself sitting in silent melancholy, alone on the sofa, law books scattered upon the floor around him. He had meant what he said to Hilly. She had, indeed, been the wind beneath his wings. He would forever remember her that way. But, thinking back, it seemed that perhaps he had always been defined by the women in his life; women who had inspired, guided, shaped, and changed the trajectory of his journey. And for that, he would always be immensely thankful.

PART NINE

71

TALK STORY

If Michael thought law school life had been difficult, working full time for a demanding law firm while studying for the bar exam kicked it all up a notch. It was at this firm where he first spotted Whitney Wilson, a first-year associate. Pretty, in a natural-no-makeup sort of way, mid-twenties, shoulder-length hair, darkly tanned, and a leggy 5'11" in heels and short skirt, it would have been difficult *not* to notice Whitney. With *Girl from Ipanema* coolness, she commanded attention from all the men in the office whenever she passed.

For whatever reason, she was enamored with all things Hawaiian and that's how they met. She saw the Hawaii license plates still on the white convertible Michael had shipped over when he moved back to the mainland, walked right up to him and started a conversation, asking all sorts of questions about living in Hawaii and why anyone in their right mind would choose to leave.

Michael explained he'd moved from Hawaii to attend law school and now he was studying for the bar exam.

"Oh, I just passed the bar this past year. I still have all my study materials. I can help you prepare for the exam," she offered.

Whitney lived in a little guest cottage just off the beach, located immediately behind a much larger home right on the sand. "The big house belongs to my uncle, he lets me stay here in the guest house for almost no rent."

"Sweet deal," Michael said.

"I know," she nodded. "But I really hope to one day move to the Islands. So, tell me. I realize you moved back to California for law school, but why not just attend University of Hawaii law school?"

"U of H said no, the California schools all said yes."

"Bummer. So, what was it that made you decide to leave life in paradise to become a lawyer in the first place?"

Michael then explained the whole story of how Gerry Leoni enticed him back to school. "What about you? Why did *you* decide to become a lawyer?" he asked her.

"Me? Oh, my dad is a judge. Lawyering is just in my blood."

She and Michael became instant friends and began keeping constant company. She helped him study for the bar exam, quizzing him with flash cards and explaining how to give the bar examiners exactly what they were looking for. She did not seem to mind helping him at all, as long as he also would *talk story* with her: telling stories about island life. "*Manawa mo 'olelo*," he told her. "It's Hawaiian. Means sharing stories."

Often, after several hours of studying, she would be sitting across from him, smiling, and whisper, "*Manawa mo 'olelo*." The books would close and he would share tales of sailing and islands well into the night.

Their platonic relationship slowly evolved into more of a romantic one. Although, he wasn't quite certain if *romantic* would truly be the correct word. It sometimes felt to him that lovemaking was merely her way of rewarding him for the island stories she seemed to enjoy so much.

He was sitting up in bed watching her across the room brushing her hair, bending her head to her knees, letting her hair fall forward toward the floor, then brushing upward from the nape of her neck. Throwing her head back and beginning to brush from the sides, she saw his reflection in the mirror.

"What are you grinning about?" she asked.

"Oh, I'm just trying to figure it out," he answered.

"Figure what out? Some question on the exam?"

"No. I am looking at you. You are so fucking beautiful. You're smart. You're a lawyer … and I'm not. At least not yet. You are years younger than me, yet at work you are my superior. You must be aware that any one of the male attorneys at the office would love to be with you. So, what the hell do you see in me? Christ, you're even taller than me! You are so far beyond me, I cannot figure it out."

She walked back, got into bed, lying beside him, quiescent. "Maybe together we form a necessary paradox. Or maybe it's because I see my future in the stories you tell, and that makes you the most interesting man I have ever met."

72

THE BAR

Michael was looking out the window at the endless expanse of Pacific Ocean and wishing he was out there on a boat, or surfing the waves, or simply relaxing on that beautiful beach, instead of where he was: seated at a long wooden table with stacks of books and papers splayed out in front of him. Bar review materials. Still, if one must be stuck indoors amongst the hunkered masses of students voraciously consuming words from the pages of law books, Pepperdine University Law Library, located high on a hill in Malibu overlooking the unending ocean, was certainly the least onerous place to be doing it. Though Whitney had helped him prepare all she could, the bar exam was now only days away and this was his final push to pump his brain with all the law necessary to pass.

As if the enticing window panorama was not enough distraction from studying, his eyes kept diverting toward a young woman seated at the far end of the table across from him. Amid stacks of books, treatises, documents, and stressed-out expressions on faces, hers shone like an insouciant beacon: flawless olive complexion, intelligent eyes, and the most perfect nose he had ever seen, with a slight upturn causing the lips to form a bow-like appearance. Her long chestnut brown hair was pulled back and worn in a French braid that nearly reached her waist while seated.

He whispered hello, which carried through the library silence to reach her across the table. She responded with a smile that revealed perfectly straight pearly white teeth. One thing led to another, and they made their way down to the school cafeteria where they could carry on a conversation without the need to speak in hushed library tones.

Her name was Lauren St. John. He thought that might just be the most beautiful name he had ever heard. She was not a law student, she told him, but intended to be one someday, visiting Pepperdine as a possible choice for pursuing her legal studies. "Beginning way back in high school I wanted to be a lawyer," Lauren told him. "I majored in Political Science in college, and since graduating I have been working as a law clerk at a small firm, just to get a bit of experience. Now I'm ready to take the big plunge: law school. I've been visiting several schools, trying to decide which to attend."

"So, you just happened to be here at this one today. Must be my lucky day that I am here as well."

"Yes, it must be fate," she chuckled with benign sarcasm.

He was enjoying their conversation and told her so. A nice break from cramming for the bar exam but he now had to get back to studying.

"Thank you. Me, too," she replied, starting to get up to leave. Then, leaning over and pulling a napkin from a dispenser on the cafeteria table and scribbling something on it, she handed it to him, adding with a smile, "Perhaps we can pick this up another time when you are not bogged down with studies."

It was not until after she left that he looked at what she had given him. It was her phone number. Area code 714. Damn! She's all the way down in Orange County.

The three-day bar exam was physically and mentally grueling, though more of an endurance contest than an intellectual challenge. The list of examinees who passed would not be published until three months after the exam, so there was no way anyone could know whether they passed until then, but the feeling of exhilaration when the proctor announced, *Time is up*! felt like a runner finishing a marathon.

"Here's to success," Whitney was saying to Michael later that evening as they clinked their margarita glasses to celebrate the end of the exam ordeal.

"I just hope I passed," Michael said.

"No doubt about it," she replied.

"Could not have done it without you, *ku'u ipo*," he said.

"*Ku'u ipo*, that means my sweetheart in Hawaiian. Am I your sweetheart, Michael?" she asked coyly.

"I suppose you are," he replied with a tone of acknowledgment.

"You are mine as well," she said. "But something even more, you are my inspiration. You have truly inspired me."

"How so?"

"All the wonderful stories you shared that I have enjoyed so much. I have decided to sit for the Hawaii bar exam. I don't suppose that I can convince you to do it with me?"

"Oh, sweetie, no. I just can't. I am done for good with anything that has to do with studying or taking exams. I'm *pau*."

Laughing, Whitney knew *pau* was Hawaiian for finished, done.

"Oh, I get that. I really do," she said. "I had hoped I might convince you, but I understand." She sat just staring at him for a long moment, as if trying to commit his face to memory in anticipation of never again seeing it. "I'm sad that our paths will no longer be the same," she told him. "But it is time to *hele* … to go and pursue my island dreams just as you did. I gave a two-week notice at work. My father wrote a letter to a lawyer friend on Oahu. There is a job waiting for me there. I'm moving to Hawaii."

Not at all what he wanted to hear but being a firm believer in a person pursuing their dreams, he attempted a smile of encouragement.

Looking past the smile, she saw a look of dejection take over his features.

"I will truly miss you," she said, emotion affecting her speech. Blinking back tears, she raised her glass to toast again. "*A hui hou. Aloha*, Michael."

"*Me ke aloha,*" he replied. "*Aloha wau iā'oe ku'u ipo*."

With liquid eyes and a soft nod, she smiled sadly. "I know. And I love you, too."

Weeks had passed since the big exam. He sat sorting through the now-defunct bar study materials, gleefully tossing most of it in the trash, hopeful he would not have any further need, his disposal abruptly halting upon finding a napkin on which was written a name and phone number. It was the one given to him by Lauren, the girl he'd met at the Pepperdine Law Library. The numerals read like code to finding a treasure. Wondering if she might still remember him, he dialed the number.

It was raining when Michael made the drive down to Orange County. They dined at the Velvet Turtle, seated at a cozy little table for two next to a window, the rain falling just inches away outside. Afterward they went for drinks at a bar called Magnolia Peach, Lauren choosing the places since he had no clue where to go in Orange County. The conversation was free flowing and easy. Lauren again shared her aspirations toward becoming a lawyer and was interested in hearing all about law school and the bar exam.

"I hear California is the most difficult bar exam in the nation," she said. "I intend to fully focus all my attention on studying the law so I will be prepared. I even broke up with my long-time boyfriend because I simply do not want any distractions for the next several years."

"Poor guy," Michael commented.

"Oh, he'll get over it. I made myself a promise: no distractions until I reach my goals."

"I get it. And I think that's admirable. You are obviously a woman who knows what she wants in life."

The music of Jimmy Buffet playing in the background at the bar, Michael segued: "I like Jimmy Buffett. He sings about the ocean and boats and life in the islands. He sings about my *former* life!"

"Oh yes, I really like his music too. You are so lucky to have had so many adventures sailing. I grew up in Iowa. No ocean, so it's something

I've really come to appreciate. In fact, I recently became a certified scuba diver."

"A Jimmy Buffet fan and you love the ocean. You are clearly a woman after my own heart."

Nursing drinks and talking for a long while, before they knew it, it was closing time.

"Looks like they are kicking us out," Michael observed.

Minutes later the two were sitting in his car parked in front of her apartment building, still engaged in a conversation that had begun hours ago.

Finally she said, "I would invite you in, but I have roommates. Kinda late if we were to wake them up."

"No problem. I understand," he agreed.

Leaning over from the driver's seat, he ever so softly touched his lips to hers. A gentle goodnight kiss.

She cocked her head to the side like a curious puppy, "Hmmm."

"Hmmm? What does that mean?" he asked her.

"Oh, just trying to rate that kiss on my internal kiss-o-meter."

"So, did it register sufficiently to pass?"

"I think I need another sample," she said.

73

JOURNAL

Buongiorno from Italy! I know, I know, I'm surprised to find myself here too. The result of an interesting turn of events, here's what happened:

It had been an extraordinarily hot couple days – record breaking hot – and the air-conditioning in the office had been out, so I arrived at work wearing shorts, flips, and aloha shirt. I figured who would care? I'd hole up in my little office with the door closed, doing my standard drudgery not-yet-a-lawyer work, and nobody would even take notice.

Ah, but somebody did take notice. One of the partners entered my work area and reprimanded me for not wearing proper office attire: dark suit, white shirt, red or blue tie ... and, for gosh sakes, proper shoes! I pointed out that the A/C was broken, it was god-awful hot, and I could work more efficiently dressed comfortably. He responded by ordering me to go home immediately and change. Normally I probably would have complied without complaint, but the whole thing somehow rubbed me the wrong way. Me, a grown man being sent home like some errant schoolboy.

So, I did go home ... but with no intention of ever returning. I suppose if Whitney had still been there she could have talked me off the ledge, convinced me not to quit, but she already made the move to Hawaii, so there I was – suddenly unemployed with nothing to do but sit around several more weeks waiting for the results of the bar exam.

Except, the very next day, I got a call from an old sailing friend and now, amazingly, here I am on a forty-two-foot yacht cruising along the stunningly beautiful Amalfi Coast of Italy. Lincoln Lee Edwards is his name. A great guy, closer to my parents' age than to mine, but with a youthful demeanor that makes him seem far younger than his years. We first met when I crewed for him more than a decade ago in Marina del Rey and we always managed to stay in touch.

A few years ago Lincoln decided to set off on a round-the-world sail and was looking for crew. He contacted me. First leg of his cruise was down to Mexico, followed by crossing through the Panama Canal, over to the San Blas Islands, and then up to Florida. Would I be interested? Absolutely! But I was stuck in law school at the time and had to decline. Another year or so went by and he contacted me again. Would I be interested in crewing on the leg from Florida to Bermuda? From there, crossing the Atlantic. Sounds amazing but sorry, still stuck.

Then his most recent call with another crewing invitation, this time in Italy. Perfect timing: "On my way!" I've never been to Italy before and to see it for the first time from the deck of a sailboat was an offer I couldn't pass up. So, rather than continuing to mope around unemployed waiting for exam results, I took what meager savings I'd earned as a lowly law clerk and spent it on a plane ticket to Naples, then took a ferry from Napoli to a little offshore island called Ischia, where I found the skipper living on his boat.

We spent a few days exploring the beautiful island of Ischia, then set sail for the nearby Isle of Capri and onward to the Amalfi Coast, where we are currently; exploring the arches near Fiordo di Furore, then on to Salerno – all places of equal splendor to any in the South Pacific I have visited. It's been years since I was last on the rolling deck of a sailboat but, as they say, it came back like riding a bicycle. I've been having the most wonderful time.

Lincoln has invited me to continue sailing around the Mediterranean with him – so tempting – but I told him *no can do*. I think I may have met the girl of my dreams and need to return before some far more handsome guy swoops in and steals her away. Besides, I placed a call to California and got the bar exam results. I am now officially a lawyer and in just a few days will be returning to California to start a new job. This time as partner in a law firm with my old friend Gerry Leoni.

74

JOURNAL

William Jefferson (Bill) Clinton was elected as the new president of the United States last Tuesday, ending twelve years of Republican rule. He will be the first of the Baby Boomers to hold that office, the torch being passed from one generation to the next. The following morning, adjusting to the idea of a new young Democrat president, life seemed rather strange, a little off center. People weren't quite sure if this was a good thing or not.

From the start, however, I rather liked this sunglass wearing, saxophone playing, hip guy that I'd seen on The Aresenio Hall Show and other late night TV gigs. I'm finding myself energized, like when Ronald Reagan was first elected a decade ago. I put Fleetwood Mac on the stereo and am happily singing along to our new president's theme: *Don't stop thinkin' about tomorrow ... Yesterday's gone!*

Yesterday is indeed gone and, for yours truly, the future is looking exceptionally bright. I am a newly minted lawyer, partner in a newly formed law firm ... and I'm in love. I don't think I have ever experienced such cosmic rhyme with any woman before. Lauren is amazing. She and I have been dating for the past several months. She had her choice of several different law schools but chose to attend one here locally so we wouldn't be apart. Just recently, we moved in together. Lawyer and law student happily cohabiting. I watch her studying so hard and remember the stress of being in law school. So far, it seems an easier job to be an actual lawyer than to be a law student.

75

WEDDED BLISS

Michael sat sipping coffee mixed with Equal artificial sweetener and Carnation nonfat, non-dairy liquid cream. A wholly unnatural morning blend, part of the wake-up regimen of a generation who not so long ago idealized only natural foods. He, like much of that generation it seemed, had changed a great deal – Boomers that went from drive-ins to love-ins, from free-love hippies to money-grubbing yuppies, and from anti-establishment to *being* the establishment. He watched as tiny flecks of undissolved creamer swirled around the rim of the cup.

Cultural tides aside, an enduring defining life juncture is that of marriage. Though he had perhaps been in love more than once during the course of his life, never before had he experienced such convergence of all the necessary pieces of the puzzle to form a lifetime commitment. Until now. The very thought of his current husbandly status brought a smile to his face.

Several months of he and Lauren dating, followed by a year living together, and in all that time they never discussed marriage. Not once had Lauren talked about getting engaged or wanting a ring. The idea was purely Michael's. He took her to dinner at their favorite Italian ristorante and halfway through the meal produced a tiny blue Tiffany box, pushing it along the white tablecloth toward where she sat across from him.

"What's this?" she asked, surprised to be getting a gift for no special occasion that she could think of.

"It's because I love you," he answered. "It's because you are the words to a song I've only been humming my entire life."

"Oh my, such romantic prose," she whispered, looking deeply into his eyes. Gingerly opening the box, her eyes now focused on the single sparkling diamond in a platinum setting.

"I've looked all my life for you, and now I've finally found you. Will you marry me?" she heard him say, as she placed her hand over her mouth in wonder and surprise. She had not been expecting this at all.

"Yes!" she answered, loud enough to be heard by the other dining patrons. Michael moved to her side of the table to sit beside her, slipping the ring onto her finger, and they kissed. On cue, but not planned, an accordion playing singer approached the table and began singing Italian love songs to the couple. Lauren started to cry, happy tears. Diners put down their forks and applauded.

It was a short engagement. "Why wait? I'm ready. Are you?" he asked.

"Absolutely," she agreed.

The wedding, held at the local yacht club, was presided over by the club chaplain, Reverend Metzenberg, a non-denominational ordained minister who also happened to be Jewish. Lauren's sister, Elizabeth, was maid of honor. Dr. Denton Todd was best man. Noah Sark and Gerry Leoni were among the attendees, as were family members from both sides … except Michael's father did not attend. Since his parents' divorce, he had vanished completely from the lives of Michael and his sister.

The bride arrived at the yacht club in grand style: by boat, on a picture-perfect day of azure water, bluest blue sky, and the hillside along the shore awash in a purple riot of flowers. It was the club commodore who escorted Lauren from the dock to the deck overlooking the harbor where the small group of invited guests watched her procession. As she had always dreamed of doing, Lauren wore her grandmother's wedding dress which was last worn in 1931. Michael watched Lauren approach down the aisle and held no doubt that his bride must be the most beautiful woman on the entire planet.

During their courtship he had often played guitar and sang songs to her, so it became Lauren's fondest wish for Michael to sing at their wedding as part of the ceremony. At first, he was reluctant because he had not sung in public for many years, but there was no way he could refuse his bride to be. He wrote a special song, sang it to her in front of the whole congregation, and meant every word he sang:

Our love is a warm love, like the earth to the sun.
Our love is radiant and glowing, stirring, yet mellowing,
separate yet one.
Our love is a story that's been told many times.
My love is your love and your love is mine.
I love you, I need you, I want you for all of my life.
These are the words I use to describe just what I'm feeling all
over the outside.
But on the inside, along with all of these,
there's a trust and a calm,
that makes my life awesome
as a gentle sea breeze.
And the willingness to please, makes your every whim my need.
Yes, our love is a story that's been told many times.
My love is your love and your love is mine.
Together forever, never to be undone, today we are one.

76

L.A. LAW

The law firm of Leoni, Perry & Associates was doing exceedingly well. After years with no real income living in Hawaii and during law school, Michael had blown through his savings to find himself virtually penniless upon graduation. Yet he and Gerry Leoni now occupied a warren of offices located on the eleventh floor of a high-rise building in the posh Wilshire Corridor of Beverly Hills, with several attorney associates, paralegals, and a couple legal secretaries in their employ. He sat looking out the window at the palm-studded boulevard below, busy with traffic, pondering how astonishing it was to find himself here. Marriage, law practice, law business, everything going so well that Michael found it almost frightening at times.

His partner, Gerry, had long ago discovered his love of the profession. "Best thing I ever did was become a lawyer!" he would often say. Leoni traversed his own long and winding road toward his métier. Growing up in Michigan, dropping out of college to marry his high school sweetheart, then becoming a Detroit policeman. It was an all-consuming, dangerous job and took a toll on his marriage. Divorce followed. He was offered a position with the FBI and relocated to the West Coast, but Leoni's greatest desire was to escape from everything to do with criminals and policing. So, he returned to school at night, finishing his degree, then on to law school.

His charismatic personality landed him a position at a medium-sized Los Angeles firm with a book of business that included large and small corporations. Leoni was assigned to represent the small to mid-size companies, whose owners and corporate officers appreciated the personalized attention he offered, which is where he met Michael.

Leoni had legal skills but wasn't good with money. Right from the start, he was impressed by Michael's business acumen and entrepreneurship. Their contrasting and complimentary talents inured to their mutual benefits as eventual law partners and the fledgling law firm flourished. But they recently experienced an odd event that, unbeknownst to either of them at the time, would soon forever change their firm.

It was late on a Friday, evening just setting in. Michael, returning from a mediation downtown, was surprised to find Leoni and several of the staff gathered around a television screen in the large conference room, long after office hours had passed.

"What gives?" he asked, walking into the room.

"Shhhh!" everyone in the room replied in unison.

They all were seated or standing around the conference table mesmerized by the events happening on the screen, watching a car chase being televised *live*. Police squad cars chasing a white Ford Bronco. Supposedly, inside the Bronco was football great *O.J. Simpson. The Juice*!

"What the hell is O.J. doing being pursued by police?" Michael asked.

"Gotta be some sort of stunt," someone in the room remarked.

But it was no stunt, as all of America soon found out. It was, indeed, the famous football-hero-turned-actor being driven down the freeway by his friend who claimed that O.J. had a gun to his head! O.J. was fleeing, the news announcer said, after being accused of the double homicide of his wife, Nicole, and a restaurant waiter by the name of Ron Goldman.

77

JOURNAL

For more than a year Gerry Leoni has spent most of his time doing *of counsel* work for the Simpson defense legal team. A lawyer in Johnnie Cochran's office, one of the lead defense attorneys in the O.J. Simpson murder trial, just happened to be a close drinking buddy of Gerry's, both of them avid baseball fans who met up regularly at a local sports bar and, knowing Leoni's background as a Detroit police officer and FBI agent, brought him into the case – the biggest damn criminal defense case of our lifetime!

Gerry quickly became one of a host of familiar lawyer faces seen on television each night giving commentary on the case, and it created a whole new avenue for him: criminal defense work. That wasn't really something I had any expertise or interest in pursuing, so Gerry has now spun off on his own. An amicable split of our firm, we remain friends and he has referred plenty of work since his departure.

So, I'm flying solo these days, managing the team all on my own. And that team has expanded. In order to better represent California business clients who also have operations in other states, I did something I never thought I'd do: sit for bar exams in Texas and New York, scoring high enough for admission to District of Colombia as well. The firm now has satellite offices in Houston, New York City and Washington, D.C. It's a brave new world!

Speaking of new worlds, or perhaps I should say *small* worlds, Hillary called my office the other day. It's been years since we last spoke. She said she had a legal matter to discuss with me and asked if we could meet. I told her to come to the office, but she asked if we could meet for dinner instead. So, we got together at a restaurant in the Valley. It was good to see her again. When you have lived with and loved a person for a big chunk of your life, a certain part of that never goes away.

We spent a good portion of the meal catching up on old times, and then she laid out her legal problem: she wants out of her marriage. Sadly, this comes after bringing a daughter into the world, the child she was pregnant with when last we spoke. I asked why she wanted out and she answered: *Because he's just too beige*. Seriously, those were her exact words. Translated from Hillary-speak, it means *he is too boring*. She followed up by complaining that after living with me all those years, she worries that almost any man will prove too boring. We both laughed, though she took pains to assure me she was not kidding.

She asked if I would represent her in her divorce. "Why me? I don't even do divorce work," I told her. She said I'm the person she trusts most in the entire world. That was totally flattering, and I thanked her, but declined representation, pointing out that having your ex-boyfriend as your divorce lawyer would surely cause needless conflict in an already difficult situation. Instead, I referred her to two other lawyers who specialize in divorce and would be far better suited to helping her.

Interestingly, I did not hear her use the word *neat-o* a single time.

78

THE SON I NEVER HAD

Turning seventy was a landmark birthday for Joe Perry. A party to celebrate this milestone was thrown for him by his *girlfriend*, Marie. Marie sent invitations to Joe's two adult children, Jaimie and Michael, who had neither seen nor communicated with their father in nearly a decade.

The children thought it quite odd to be receiving the invitation out of the blue, since their father had made no effort to see them prior to this event. Their initial inclination was to decline. But seventy was sounding damn old. How many more birthdays might there be for their father? Their beloved Nana passed away when she was in her late seventies. So, Michael agreed to attend. Irrespective of all that had transpired, he felt a familial obligation. After all, the man was his father. Jaimie, however, was living in Seattle now and had no intention of flying down for the birthday celebration. And, he told Lauren, this was something he should do on his own.

Michael had feelings of apprehension about seeing his dad again. Theirs had long been a strained relationship. He harbored no real grudge against the man but had been happier during the recent years of estrangement with his father out of sight and out of mind. And now, driving out to the California desert where his father resided, he had no idea what to expect.

The party destination turned out to be a trailer park in a brown and dusty little community called Banning. This was where Joe now lived.

Michael could not help but wonder how a once successful businessman ends up in a desert trailer park. No telling where life's path takes a person, he supposed.

Entering the park's clubhouse where the party was being held, Michael spotted a white-haired man across the room with his back to him, surrounded by three or four elderly partiers. A familiar burning sensation in the pit of his stomach, one not felt in years, suddenly lurched up toward his throat. Perhaps he should not have come. A woman near the white-haired man pointed in Michael's direction and the man began turning toward him. It was his father. It was showdown time, high noon at the OK Corral. Swallowing hard and hitching a shoulder, Michael walked toward his father but was completely unprepared for what happened next.

Coming face to face, Michael extended his hand to shake. Joe knocked it roughly aside … then wrapping both arms around his son in a fullon bear hug, embraced him, lifting him right off the floor. Joe's eyes were tear-filled, and the embrace lingered for a very long time. Joe was genuinely moved by the presence of his only son at the party.

Michael was speechless; never before had he been the recipient of such warm outpouring from this man. Once released from the bone-crushing caress, they each took a step back to survey one another. Though time charted through his face, the years had been kind to his father. He had a full mane of snowy white hair and, were it not for this lack of follicular color, there was negligible senescence; he had hardly aged a day. Except for one glaring difference – the man looked happy. More so than Michael could ever recall.

Joe spoke first, coming right out and saying how pleased he was to see his son. Hell, maybe age had mellowed the old man, Michael thought to himself. Let bygones be bygones. Michael told his dad it was nice to see him again, too.

An attractive woman in her sixties was standing directly behind Joe. Marie quickly introduced herself, thanking Michael for attending the party, saying it meant so very much to Joe. She appeared to be a warm and pleasant person. Michael found himself feeling glad that his father had this new woman in his life, and glad to see him finally looking happy. Seldom had he displayed any sense of joy while Michael was growing up, as if his father viewed his life as one long mundane task, his family responsibilities a lifelong burden. As soon as the last of his children were grown, he was gone, leaving their mother and virtually disappearing ... until now.

When the party ended, Joe was eager to show Michael around his home: a double-wide trailer containing some old furniture and every collection of nostalgic paraphernalia imaginable: garage sale relics from bygone eras.

"Sure is different from all the big fancy houses you built when I was growing up," Michael remarked.

"It's the best!" Joe responded with enthusiasm. "Houses are overrated. I love trailer life. I'm happy and free. Plus, Marie has her own double-wide just a few units over. Perfect arrangement to have with a woman: close enough so she's there when you want her, but just enough distance between us that I don't have to be with her all the time."

They sat in brown faux-leather chairs around a circular wooden table and chatted, or rather, Michael listened as his dad rambled, catching him up on the events of the last several years. Joe was now in law enforcement, working for the Riverside County Sheriff's Department, regaling Michael with stories of his physical apprehension of local thugs. Even at age seventy no young *punks* could get the better of him.

Getting up as he spoke and pulling several firearms from a gun cabinet, he boasted of his ability to target shoot with the best of them, even at his age. Sadly, though, now he was facing retirement from what he referred to as the best job he ever had. "Mandatory," he explained. "Suddenly I'm too old."

It was while in the military as a young man that Joe had first worked in law enforcement. "That's what I should have done when I got out of the service, joined the police force. Being a police officer is what I was meant to be. But we don't always get exactly what we want out of life, I'm afraid."

"Guess it's kinda like what Mick Jagger sang: you can't always get what you want, but sometimes you get what you need," Michael offered.

"Whoever this Jagger character is, sounds like he's got it about right," Joe agreed.

He continued talking, mostly about himself, for another twenty minutes, practically nonstop. Michael had never known his father to be so chatty or animated. Who was this man sitting across from him? At some point the one-sided conversation abruptly shifted from police work to reminiscing about his years working construction and all the fine buildings that were his creations. "Nice feeling to know they will live on, long after I'm gone. A man needs to leave something worthwhile behind, ya know?"

"A legacy," Michael suggested.

"Yes, that's a good word. A legacy," Joe concurred.

A small terrier entered the room and launched itself onto Joe's lap. "This is Brutus," Joe said, introducing the dog. "Brutus and I have been together quite a few years. He's like the son I never had."

The words stung Michael, causing him to physically flinch. *Like the son I never had.* A dog? The way the words readily rolled off his father's tongue, this was obviously a phrase he often used in describing his relationship to the animal. If Joe was aware of the cutting effect on the human son sitting across from him, he gave no indication of it.

"So, what about you? I hear you're a lawyer now, right?" Joe asked, finally shifting the subject from himself.

"Yes, Dad. I've been practicing law for quite a few years."

"Well," his father joked with a loud guffaw, "you know what they say, practice makes perfect!"

"And I'm a married man now, too," Michael said, offering a photo of Lauren for his father to see.

"Wow, she's a real looker. How did *you* manage to get such a hottie?"

"Miracles have been known to happen," Michael replied.

Driving home from the desert, it struck Michael that his father never asked what Lauren was like, how long they had been married, or even whether they had any children. His solitary reference to the daughterinlaw he had never met was only that she was "a looker" and "a hottie."

79

JOURNAL

The alarm clock went off this morning, September 11th, at precisely 5:55 a.m. as usual. I got up, sleepily trundled off to the kitchen to get coffee for Lauren and myself and returned to find her sitting up in bed watching TV. Peter Jennings of ABC News was speaking about an airliner that crashed into one of the towers at the World Trade Center in New York City. On the screen was a tall building with flames shooting from the upper floors. It seemed damned unlikely that what I was watching was just an accident. "Nobody on earth is that bad of a pilot," I said to Lauren.

Then Jennings incredulously announced that a second plane had just now crashed into the second tower of the same complex, and he now referred to it as an *attack*. I sat on the edge of the bed mesmerized, and then the TV showed the first tower crumbling to the ground as if demolition explosives had caused its collapse. A few minutes later, the second tower collapsed in the same manner. We could not believe what our eyes were seeing on the screen. This was just all too impossibly horrible.

Soon, we also learned that a third airplane had crashed into the Pentagon and this was now being called a coordinated attack upon America. This news was closely followed by the crashing of a fourth jet in Pennsylvania.

The entire nation was immediately put in shut down mode. Here in California, three thousand miles away from the attacks, Los Angeles on the television looked like a ghost town. I was scheduled to appear in court at the

Federal Courthouse at 10:00 a.m. Around 8:30, I began calling around to see if the courthouse would be closed but was unable to get through to anyone. All lines were busy. At 9:15, I contacted my secretary at her home to see if she knew. It was closed, she said. She somehow always knows about such things.

The rest of the day has felt like being in the Twilight Zone. Everything feels different than normal. People you don't know, people who you might not normally stop and converse with were talking to one another, conversing. Gardeners, businesspeople, police, parents, grandparents, people young and old from all walks of life mingling, all transiting through the same unspeakable episode. Politicians suddenly united, all on the same page. People who disliked the President, suddenly in full support of anything he said. For some reason, I felt an overwhelming need to display the American flag outside my house. Seems I am not alone. By noon most of my neighbors had done likewise. I don't recall ever before in my life experiencing such a strong feeling of solidarity as a nation. We all are sharing in the horrific events of this morning.

PART TEN

HOPE

A chilly winter's night. The grandfather clock in the hall was striking 2:00 a.m. and Lauren St. John-Perry was sitting pensively in front of a roaring fire, listening to Mozart's Symphony No. 40 in G Minor, one of her favorites. She was thinking about children. Wondering why, after years of marriage, they did not have any. Her marriage was otherwise perfect. She still felt as excitedly in love as when they first began dating. So often she would hear people talk about how couples must "work" at their marriage, but she had never felt like her marriage was something that must be worked at. Being happy together was just something that came naturally and effortlessly. Michael was the absolute love of her life, and she felt every bit as loved by him in return. He'd had a reasonably lengthy run at bachelorhood, and she certainly did not begrudge him that; glad any wild oats had been sowed and over with. He would often say it took a while to find the perfect woman ... and she was well worth the wait.

Since first getting married, Lauren and Michael intended to have kids. During all that time they had never used birth control or done anything to prevent pregnancy. But nothing happened. Then, last year they began *timing* their lovemaking to be the most productive toward creation of a baby. Still nothing. So, they consulted an infertility doctor who gave Lauren drugs that caused her to super-ovulate. But still no positive results.

Next, they tried artificial insemination. They desperately hoped this would result in a pregnancy, and the doctor seemed to think it would. But it didn't. So, they tried again. The doctor highly optimistic, saying all the conditions were perfectly in sync. Yet, nothing.

The highs and lows of all these procedures were taxing. Going from hopeful, to happy, to sad, disappointed, and depressed. But nothing could override the overwhelming desire to have a child. They would continue to try.

81

YOU STILL HAVE YOUR HEALTH

It was the annual trip to the California desert to visit his father, Michael's effort to keep alive the semblance of father/son relationship that had been resuscitated a couple years prior when his father turned seventy.

"You're kidding me, right?" Joe asked, shaking his head at the news his son just told him. "Do you have any idea how old you will be when that kid finally graduates high school?"

Michael sat, struggling for control at the way his father was responding to the announcement that he and Lauren were trying to have a baby. "Who's to say when the right time is to start a family?" he said at last.

"Who's to say? I am to say. Listen to me, you are too old. Hell, you're *both* too old. What is she now, almost forty? I didn't even know women that age could still have kids. You know your mother got pregnant with Jaimie when she was thirty. A fluke for a woman even that age."

"Dad, what the hell is it with you? Why can't you ever just be happy for me?"

Joe softened at the crestfallen look on his son's face.

"Mike, I *am* happy for you. I just don't think you are thinking this through. Listen, you have finally got the world by the ass. You are on top of your game right now. I mean, you and your wife live in a nice house, you both have your health, you being a lawyer seems to be working out pretty good. Having a screaming baby will change everything for you two. Believe me, it's a real fucking life changer."

"Sure, sure," Michael responded. "First of all, Lauren is a lawyer too. Not just me. Secondly, it probably seems like we have the perfect lifestyle, but it wasn't what we had envisioned when we first walked down the aisle to become husband and wife all those years ago. We both thought by now there would be a house filled with kids. Dad, we feel like we are a couple of emptynesters who never had the privilege of actually experiencing a full nest."

"Pshaw, you never seem to know when you have it good. Believe me, an empty nest is what most people your age are happy to have," he argued.

Michael just shrugged.

"Well, you'll do whatever you want. You always do. You have never listened to me in your entire life."

"Don't you wanna be a grandpa?"

"Your sister already made me one," he argued. "Still have not seen her kids. Lotta difference being a grandpa makes."

"Dad, I know she would love to have you go visit up in Seattle and meet your grandchild."

"I don't do well in all that dampness up there. That's why I live here in the desert. She should bring herself and her baby down here to visit her old dad, not the other way around."

"Well, Lauren and I are only a ninety-minute drive away. You will be able to see our child anytime you like."

"Listen, forget all this baby nonsense. Having kids ain't all it's cracked up to be. Take that bride of yours and travel the world. Enjoy yourselves. Do it while you still have your health. Health is everything. One of these days you're gonna find that out."

82

JOURNAL

Lauren is still not pregnant. How can this be? It seems we are a healthy, otherwise happy, loving couple with everything in the world going for us, except no apparent ability to do what most people probably take for granted: producing children! There are all sorts of modern, sophisticated medical techniques that could probably create life from a lump of coal, but none have worked for us.

We have done a total of six high-tech attempts, including *in vitro* fertilizations, over the last two years to get pregnant – even using two different infertility doctors – and have yet to achieve success. This has really been a blow to us. Lauren is taking it really hard and grows increasingly inconsolable. Suffering the emotional stress of all these procedures and failures, not to mention the many thousands of dollars we have spent in this pursuit, finds us wondering if we must resign ourselves to life without ever experiencing parenthood. Such notion saddens us both to an extent that is immeasurable.

It is two weeks until Christmas. A time of such joy for households with children, but there is no joy in our home. The holiday season only makes it more disheartening.

83

THE LIST

It was a magnificent room filled with enormous works of art, paintings by the great masters. The Salon Carre, Louvre Museum, Paris. Under a spectacularly ornate ceiling high above, four rather distinguished looking gentlemen, graying at the temples, one with a neatly trimmed white mustache that curled upwards at the ends in a way that seemed to form a whiskered smile – though not quite what Americans refer to as handlebar – stood huddled together.

Watching the four of them, mid-fifties, nattily attired, dark suits, one wearing an ascot, and all looking very European, Michael decided. He found observing the people at the museum even more interesting than the art, most of which he knew very little about.

The men were standing near a purplish banquette, looking up at paintings that hung on the wall behind, depicting graceful, almost erotic, subjects whose forms seemed to defy any sense of real human proportion. Presumably discussing the art, speaking French Michael could not understand, they appeared quite serious, pointing with sweeping gestures, stroking their chins in scholarly fashion, nodding their heads.

At the opposite end of the room, a young woman entered from the Grande Galerie. Attractively feminine, tall with infinite legs and perfect posture, her extremely short skirt sashaying rhythmically, heels softly echoing on the polished floor as she glided across the expanse of the salon without stopping to look at a single painting.

All four gentlemen ceased conversing, turning in unison their attention away from the art on the wall, preferring to watch this living work of art traverse the room. It was not necessary to understand French to recognize such universal male appreciation of the female form, making all four momentarily drop any sophisticated pretension.

Michael exited the room in search of his own living work of art.

Lauren was standing in front of the Venus de Milo, the famous marble sculpture of Aphrodite – Greek goddess of love and beauty. He took a few minutes to observe his wife from afar, appreciating her. Though they had been married for years, here in Paris he began to view her through different eyes, realizing anew what a treasure she is. It was as if they were newlyweds once more.

He was glad they had made this trip to Europe. After the lengthy and emotional rollercoaster ride of infertility treatments, trying every new procedure known to science with no luck, when he turned fifty and Lauren hit age forty, they finally gave up. Their marriage had produced no children. They decided to combat their immense disappointment over being childless by making a list of fantasy goals and setting about to accomplish everything on the list.

First, they purchased a little two-bedroom Laguna Beach bungalow with magnificent whitewater views of the California coastline, waves crashing onto the shore just outside their door. Then a slick twoseater German roadster that Michael had long been admiring.

Lauren pursued a serious interest in learning about wine, throwing herself into enology with all the resolution of studying for the bar exam, completing the Court of Master Sommeliers Introductory Course. To cap it off, one of Lauren's greatest fantasies was to tour the wine regions of Italy and France, and to spend time living in Paris, so that is what they did.

Life in the City of Lights proved to be excitingly romantic, living like Parisians; or at least American-quasi-Parisians. Drinking champagne at the top of the Eiffel Tower, sharing a kiss on the grassy knoll beneath; shopping along Champs Elysées, Boulevard Saint Germain, Montmartre;

a show at Moulin Rouge; dining at famous eateries such as Café Les Deux Maggots – classic Parisian outdoor seating where one can simply sit and watch the world go by while savoring its long history as a popular gathering place for writers, artists, and intellectuals – Café de Flor, and Le Procope – which has been in continuous operation since 1686 and is said to have once fed the likes of Balzac and Voltaire – as well as discovering scores of hidden bistros on less traveled avenues.

Using their small apartment just outside Paris as home base, they traveled throughout France and Italia – sometimes driving, sometimes flying, sometimes traveling by train. Rome, Venezia, Salerno, Amalfi, Pompeii – completely intoxicating with art, history, food, and overall culture that would take a lifetime to properly explore – but it was the wine regions that Lauren was most anxious to visit.

The awe-inspiring drive from Florence through Tuscan countryside was precisely the way Lauren had always envisioned Italy to be.

The first winery they visited, Fonterutoli, was founded in the 13th century. A stooped old Italian gent, who spoke no English, gave them a tour of the facility. They spent hours listening to this elder Italian explaining the vineyard's history, using elaborate gestures to illustrate the Italian words he spoke. Lauren was in heaven.

The days that followed were more of the same, exploring Italy's wine regions and tasting all the wonderful vino and foods. Whether walking through a medieval castle in the town of Montalcino or the beautiful ancient village of San Gimignano, Lauren soaked it all in.

When at last they felt they had absorbed all the Tuscan culture they could handle, it was time for a jaunt through the *French* countryside.

Monsieur Daniel Cathiard, the handsome owner of Chateau Smith Haut Lafite in Pessac Leognan, was wearing a double-breasted blue blazer with bright red pocket square perfectly protruding, his hair artfully tousled, looking every bit the French vintner right out of Central Casting as he gave Lauren and Michael a private tour. The three of them standing just outside his magnificent chateau when Michael remarked, "This is probably the most beautiful place I have ever seen."

"You are from California, no?" Monsieur Cathiard said in perfect English, but with a French accent so thick it took Michael a moment to decode his words.

Michael nodded.

"*Oui*, I have been there. Where in California is it you are from?" the Frenchman asked.

"Laguna Beach," Lauren answered.

The Frenchman's mouth dropped open. "No, no," he replied, waving his finger with enthusiasm. "I have been to Laguna Beach. My friends, it is *you* who live in the most beautiful place in all the world."

However, while appreciative of America, and California in particular it often seemed, many of the French wine makers they met were not so complimentary when it came to the competing product of American wine.

In France, it was explained, wine is an absolute passion, not just a business. The permanently stained purple fingers on the hands of many vineyard owners evidenced the hard work involved with harvest and in the barrel room with *pigéage*. The winemakers spoke of how the *Appellation d'Origine Contrôlée* regulations bound all the wineries in France to comply with strict irrigation requirements, harvest dates, the amount that could be harvested per hectare, and even the types of barrels they are allowed; rules that wine makers in the United States do not have to deal with.

In the U.S. you can plant any sort of grape in any region you choose, irrigate all you want, harvest as much as you please, and purchase expensive new oak barrels. No restrictions or rules. But in France, no amount of money will buy your way around having to follow the strict AOC regulations. So French winemakers are left with what nature deals them and must make the best of what they get year to year. This is why the French consider wine making to be an art, whereas in the States, they maintain, it is merely a business.

Living in Paris, touring the wine regions, meeting the wine makers, learning firsthand about wine, for Lauren the entire experience was an absolute dream come true.

As the plane prepared for landing at Los Angeles International Airport, Lauren and Michael sat holding hands, looking out the little port-hole window at the blue Pacific and rolling hills below. It was a crowded airplane. They endured the long 10 ½ hour flight with Michael sitting upright all night, Lauren's head in his lap as she tried to recline best she could and sleep much of the way.

The plane touched down at LAX and taxied to the gate.

"So," Lauren said, turning to her husband as the passengers began to disembark, "we have done everything on our list. What do we do now?"

"Start a new list, I guess," Michael answered with a laugh.

84

THE IMPOSSIBLE

Lauren sat quietly on the outside deck of their beach home watching the sun setting behind Santa Catalina Island, the sky turning brilliant orange, the outline of the island silhouetted in a golden halo. It was a sight she never tired of. Indeed, most evenings the couple could be found at this very spot, wine glasses in hand, watching the giant red ball descend into the sea.

Michael walked out to join her, carrying two glasses of red wine. Handing one of the glasses to her, "If this had gone on to Cuba it might be Castro enjoying it instead of us."

He was referring to a case of wine given to them as a gift by a most generous host at one of the wineries. When they checked the box of wine at Charles de Gaulle Airport, the handler placed the wrong baggage tag on the wine.

"Excuse me," Lauren addressed the man behind the counter in near flawless French – four years of high school French honed by this extended stay in France, "but that box seems to have an incorrect tag on it."

The handler quickly pulled the box from the conveyor belt just as it was about to disappear behind a wall. "*Oui,*" he replied, also in French. "You are most correct, Madame. My apologies. This tag says Cuba."

Lauren laughed, recalling the incident. "The Smith Haut Lafite," she said.

They clinked glasses. "Cheers."

"Sit down," Lauren said to her husband.

He sat on the deck chair next to her. "Something wrong?"

"No, no. Nothing wrong. I don't know quite how to say this …."

"So, just say it."

"You are not going to *effing* believe it."

He looked askance.

"No, really. You are not going to believe it," she repeated.

"Okay, now you've got me worried. What?"

"I think …," she began, then stopped, taking a tiny sip from her glass.

"You think what?"

"I think this may be my last glass of wine for a while."

"Huh? What do you mean?"

"Well, I have been feeling rather strange since we got back from Paris."

"Nothing unusual about that. Jet lag and all. It takes some people longer to adjust."

"No, it's not that. I mean … what I am trying to say is, I think I might be pregnant."

Michael sat staring at her for several long moments. "But that's not possible."

"I didn't think so," she replied. "But I took a home pregnancy test today. It turned out positive." She feigned a laugh and spoke with a tone of indifference, as if there was no way the test could be correct. Not after all the years they had tried so hard with no success. This was surely a false positive.

But Michael's features erupted into a smile so wide it looked as if his face would split in two. Leaping from his chair to hug his wife, Lauren instinctively recoiling as if preventing herself from being hugged to death, he gushed, "That is *absolutely incredibly incredible*!"

"I know, I know! It's just too amazing to be believed. That's why I'm not sure I truly do believe it. Unless Paris was even more of a romantic city than anyone thought," she laughed.

"Best thing we ever did, going to Paris!" he exclaimed.

Then, becoming more somber, she reevaluated. "I probably should not have said anything to you yet. Not until I see a doctor. Don't want to get your hopes up. I'm going in for a blood test tomorrow to find out for sure."

Lauren made the mid-afternoon cell-phone call to the doctor's office to get the results of her blood test from that morning. Michael stood close to her, trying to listen in, but nothing was discernable. The nurse on the phone at the other end related something unintelligible, to which Lauren replied, "What? What did you say?" The nurse repeated and Lauren's face lit up. "Wait! Here, tell my husband," handing the phone to Michael.

"Congratulations," he heard a voice say, "the blood test indicates a positive pregnancy."

They spent several moments just looking at one another, mouths agape.

The nurse interrupted the telephone silence. "Hello? Are you still there? You will need to make an appointment to come in for an ultrasound."

Michael handed the phone back to Lauren. She made an appointment to meet with the doctor, ended the call, and threw her arms around her husband. The happy couple began hugging and dancing around the room, unable to contain their joy.

A few weeks later the doctor did an ultrasound and pronounced them *definitely with child*. "A nice strong heartbeat," he announced.

Lauren was lying on the exam table, Michael standing beside her, holding her hand. They smiled lovingly at each other. This was their greatest wish come true.

"Wait!" the doctor added, excitedly, "Make that, *two* strong heartbeats!"

At that, Lauren burst into uncontrollable tears and Michael felt the need to grab a chair to keep from losing balance and toppling over.

"But, but, but that's impossible," Lauren stammered. "There are no twins in either of our families."

"Well, it looks like there soon will be," the doctor responded gleefully.

85

THE HARROWING DECISION

Michael had not felt this happy since he walked down the aisle with his bride more than a decade ago. Two beautiful new little lives were on their way, twins! Now, each time he heard a baby cry, any baby, anywhere, in a theater, grocery store, office, elevator, it sounded like sweet music to his ears. He could hardly wait to hear the healthy cries of his own two infants.

Already Lauren was feeling morning sickness that lasted all morning, all afternoon, and sometimes into the night, but the future daddy was ready to pick up the slack. He found himself literally *popping* out of bed around five o'clock every morning. For some unknown reason, he had more energy than he'd had in years. Often, by nine o'clock he had already run several miles along the beach, had breakfast, read the newspaper, fed Lauren, cleaned the kitchen, gotten dressed, and arrived at work with a spring in his step and whistling whatever the last tune was he'd heard on his drive.

It's an amazing feeling, Michael thought. For any guy looking to find the true fountain of youth, I would highly recommend having a baby after age fifty!

"I am thrilled to be having these babies. But how is it even possible to be having twins?" Lauren asked the doctor during one of her weekly check-ups. "I would think my most fertile years are behind me. Did all the infertility treatments somehow contribute?"

"It's true that women between the ages of sixteen and twenty-six are probably the most fertile," the doctor responded. "But, while they may have a greater chance of becoming pregnant initially, they do not have a greater probability of becoming pregnant with *twins*."

"I had no idea," Lauren muttered, mostly to herself.

"And," the doctor further explained, "while fertility drugs and family history are clearly known to boost a woman's chances of having twins, hormonal changes that come with age are another reason. Women over thirty-five have higher levels of a hormone called FSH, a follicle-stimulating hormone. Older women are, therefore, more likely to prepare more than one egg per menstrual cycle. Fraternal twins develop when two eggs are fertilized. So, if older women are more likely to produce more eggs per cycle, they are also more likely to have fraternal twins."

Mary Perry could not contain her joy upon hearing the news that she would soon become a grandmother. She loved being a grandmother to Jaimie's children but assumed her son and his wife were destined never to give her any grandbabies. It was a true miracle as far as Mary was concerned. A gift from God.

Joe, on the other hand, as his son and daughter-in-law sat across from him at the trailer park, was finding the idea of two middle-aged people disrupting their lives with a screaming infant to be somewhat absurd. And when they explained they were not just having *a baby*, that they were having two babies – twins – Joe laughed right out loud. He couldn't help himself.

Lauren mistook her father-in-law's laughter for joy, but that was not what it was. The laugh erupted out of a sense of astonishment and sympathy. Astonishment at the colossal change that his son was about to experience, turning his life upside down. Sympathy because Mike simply had no idea what he was getting himself into. It was difficult enough raising two offspring nearly a decade apart, as Joe and Mary had done with

Michael and Jaimie. But to have two babies, two crying infants at the same time, would be insurmountable. As inappropriate as the laugh may have been, it was the only display of emotion Joe could muster.

And then there were his words. "Well, this is what happens when you mess with nature and have doctors do all sorts of strange medical things to get pregnant. You hear about multiple births all the time as the result of such procedures. Hell, I remember seeing one lady on the news who had four babies all at once because of infertility treatments."

"Dad," Michael explained, with polite calmness. "We gave up long ago on infertility treatments. Lauren became pregnant the old-fashioned way … if you know what I mean."

Joe, realizing his words may have been spoken with a trace of asperity, softened his rhetoric. Leaning in close to his son, out of hearing range from his daughter-in-law who had excused herself to use the powder room, quietly whispered, "That's good, Mike. But is having twins at Lauren's age totally safe? I mean, even though we are all living in these modern times when so much is changing, still not too many women in their forties have babies, do they?"

Joe, intentionally or not, had planted the first seed of real worry into the minds of Lauren and Michael. At twelve weeks into the pregnancy, after a routine checkup, sitting in the private office of their doctor for follow-up consultation, they posed the question.

"I won't lie to you," the doctor responded. "The risk is certainly elevated after the woman hits a certain age. There is recent evidence that a man over fifty fathering a child may add to the risk as well. Nothing conclusive, but some indices it may be a risk factor. Compound the age risk factors with the fact that Lauren is carrying multiples, and the risk increases exponentially."

"What sort of risks?" Lauren asked.

"Numerous," the doctor replied. "Deformity. Brain dysfunction. And certainly, higher than normal risk that the pregnancy will never come to full term."

An uncomfortable silence fell, rippling out like a wake in deep water, feeling like it might drown them. As if finally coming up for air, Michael asked, "What can we do to reduce these risks?"

The doctor rose from the chair where he was seated behind his desk, walked over to his office door and softly closed it. Reclaiming his seat, he looked soberly at them, speaking through tented fingers that blocked his lips. "Listen," he began, sotto voce, "this is a Catholic hospital. So, what I'm about to tell you goes against policy, but I feel compelled to lay it out there."

Lauren gave Michael a worried look.

The doctor continued. "The biggest risk you face is that you are carrying multiples. Chances of a successful birth would likely become increased if there were a reduction."

"A reduction?" Michael asked, incredulously. "You mean, somehow terminate one of the babies?"

Lauren put her hand to her mouth, stifling what might have otherwise been an audible gasp.

"A reduction," the doctor repeated. "But yes, termination of one fetus in order to increase odds of survival for the remaining fetus and successful birth of a healthy baby."

"An abortion," Lauren summarized, tersely. "Aborting one of the babies."

"To be clear," the doctor resumed, "I am not advising such a procedure. I am not even suggesting such a procedure. I am merely addressing your question of how to reduce the risks."

The three sat in resumed silence for several minutes, the doctor still hiding behind tented fingers. "Listen," he began again, "I know you both have been trying to conceive for a long time. I know you both very much want to give birth to a happy, healthy child. To be brutally honest, you might never have this opportunity again. This is your shot. I feel it is my obligation to advise you of the risks and how to best achieve your ultimate goal."

"Would you be the one who performs the, uh, reduction?" Michael asked, unable to bring himself to say the word abortion.

"No. I would not. And this hospital would not be the facility. I can give you the name of a specialist if you are interested."

At fifteen weeks into the pregnancy, Lauren and Michael found themselves seated in the office of the specialist to whom they were referred. The office was located not in a hospital but on the ninth floor of a high-rise building in downtown L.A. The doctor was a middle-aged woman. On the credenza behind her desk stood a framed photo of a smiling teenage girl standing on a beach. The doctor noticed Lauren staring at the photo. "That's my daughter," she said.

"She's pretty," Lauren replied.

"Thank you. She is the greatest joy of my life. A treasure for whom I give thanks each and every day."

"I'm sure," Lauren acknowledged.

"But here is the secret behind that wonderful girl. A rather grim secret, but one that I should share with you. I was once faced with the very same situation you both find yourselves in right now. I was pregnant with twins. There were complications. It was a difficult pregnancy, and I had a very difficult decision to make. I chose reduction. I chose to terminate one fetus for the other to survive. It was the most difficult decision of my entire life. So, believe me, I empathize with the complexity and seriousness of what you both are going through. The most difficult choice you will likely ever have to make in your entire lives. I will not sit here and tell you how to choose. I can only tell you that, for me, it was the right decision. Every day I look at my daughter and I know it was the right thing to do."

"If we were to go forward with the reduction," Michael asked, "when would we have it done?"

"I could do it today if that's what you decide. Right now. I have a surgical room right across the hall. It is essentially a very simple procedure."

Lauren and Michael had been discussing, arguing, agonizing over this decision before even making the appointment with this doctor. Now they were here, potentially girded.

Wearing a gray hospital gown, Lauren was lying on her back on the exam table as the doctor performed an ultrasound. "There are still two heartbeats," the L.A. doctor confirmed.

"Which fetus would be the one terminated?" Michael asked.

The doctor answered, "The one closest to the birth canal."

Michael swallowed hard. He was standing next to his wife, holding her hand, much the same as when the very first ultrasound was performed by their doctor confirming Lauren was pregnant.

"Our primary doctor has not yet been able to determine the sex of the babies," Michael said. "Do you see any signs as to what they are? Can you tell?"

"Let's have a closer look," the L.A. doctor said, adjusting the pince-nez on her nose, then moving the wand around Lauren's tumescent belly while adjusting some knobs on the ultrasound machine. "Sometimes just a few days in fetus development can make a difference in determining such things." A moment later, "Yes, I am able to determine gender. Would you like to know?"

"Yes," Lauren replied.

"One is definitely female," the doctor said. Then, moving the wand to another part of the belly, added, "I'm pretty certain I can detect a slight protrusion on the other, likely indicating a penis."

"A boy and a girl," Lauren sighed, looking at her husband.

"Which is the one you would terminate?" Michael wanted to know.

"The female," came the answer from the doctor. "She's the closest."

Lauren, still lying on her back, looked up at her husband for consolation. Her hand in his, he could feel her pulse thrumming with fear and contrition. This new information was making it all the more stressful.

"I cannot decide. You decide," Lauren said to him, unable to make such a Sophie's Choice, squeezing his hand, closing her eyes tightly as if that might offer some escape.

With sudden abjure finality, Michael exclaimed, "Forget it! We're done! We never should have come here. Get off the table. We are going home. It's all or nothing. No reduction. I want both a son *and* a daughter to come into this world."

86

AN ENTIRELY DIFFERENT WORLD

All was quiet. In the babies' room, Lauren relaxed in a white wicker rocking chair, baby boy Travis Michael Perry asleep in his mother's arms while his twin sister, Morgan Marie, dozed in her basinet nearby. Both infants softly cooing and making faint little whimpers and gurgles. Sounds so sweet it melts the heart, Lauren thought to herself.

Looking about the room, decorated in blues, pinks, and yellows, teddy bears, toy sailboats, and bunnies, Lauren took it all in and smiled. I love being a mom, she pondered. I love my life. Every day seems so much richer now, it has more dimension.

The babies were now *almost* sleeping through the night. Almost, because usually one or the other would wake up crying at some Godawful hour while the other would sleep on through. Soon, Lauren hoped, they would both sleep completely through the night and she and Michael might finally get an undisturbed seven or eight hours of sleep.

They each had their own parental style of soothing the babies toward slumber. Each night Michael would place little Travis in his crib while hovering over him, softly singing: *Close your eyes, have no fear. The monster's gone and your daddy is here. My beautiful, beautiful, beautiful boy. Before you fall asleep let's say a little prayer, and we'll be out on the ocean, sailing away.*

With Morgan, he would rock her in his arms and croon *Angel Face, Angel Face, my sweetest, sweetest Angel Face.*

Sleep would come, but not for long. An hour later Lauren would return, hushing a crying baby lest they wake the other. She found just holding them close, gliding rhythmically to and fro in the rocking chair, while patting their tiny bottoms worked best. But often, she was reluctant to place them in their beds even after they had fallen asleep in her arms, unwilling to relinquish the closeness they shared.

Placing little Travis gently in his crib, Lauren tip-toed from the babies' room to the living room. There was the heavenly aroma of fresh baked bread. Vivaldi's Four Seasons was softly playing on the stereo, and Michael had opened a 2001 Chateau Souverain Cabernet, accompanied by focaccia fresh from the oven, topped with cheeses, fresh figs, balsamic vinegar, and pancetta. What a wonderful treat he had prepared while she had been putting the twins to bed. The babies were now asleep, the food and music very adult. It was like entering an entirely different world. Perfect balance.

He handed her a glass, they clinked. "To us," he toasted. "All four of us."

JOURNAL

This morning Lauren, the kids and I all went surfing at Doheny Beach, then rode our bikes back to Dana Point Harbor for a lovely afternoon sail on our boat. Right from the get-go I always knew I wanted my kids to grow up around beaches and boats so, after years of not owning a boat, once the kids came along I bought a 32′ sloop. We've been a sailing family since the kids were mere infants, and I mean that literally: Lauren and I would feed our babies their bottles in the galley of our sailboat and hold them in our laps as we ventured out on the ocean. By the time Morgan was four years old, she was already driving our inflatable dinghy with 6 hp outboard around the harbor.

Though I may have sailed thousands of nautical miles in my life, the only cruising I do these days is to take my family to Santa Catalina Island. The kids were around four years old the first time we sailed as a family to Catalina. The pure joy, wonderment, and exuberance I witnessed as they embarked upon the island made it crystal clear: this is the best sailing voyage of all.

Spending that first night on the boat ("camping on the boat" the kids called it), Morgan crawled into the berth with Lauren and me and proclaimed: "Daddy, I love this boat and this island sooo much. I think this has been the very best day of my life!" Now if that isn't the best endorsement for having a family boat, I don't know what is. Sailing to Catalina has become our annual summer vaccay the past couple years, and hopefully into future years as well.

Same with surfing. I'd not surfed much since my days living in Hawaii, but now I'm surfing again with my kids, *sharing the stoke* with them. Travis took to the sport right away ... at age five. We went out together to where some small waves were breaking and waited for just the right one. When the time was right, I pushed his board hard into the rising wave. He stood up on his very first try! He immediately wanted to go again, and again, and again! He'd say, "I want bigger waves, Dad! Let's paddle over by those guys," indicating the main take-off where the more advanced surfers were lined up. He was so amped I could barely keep up with him.

Not to be outdone, Morgan was not far behind in her enthusiasm. I pushed her into her first waves and in no time at all she was surfing right alongside her brother and me.

I swear it feels like I'm experiencing a re-do of youth through my children: They love boats, the beach, surfing, music ... all the things I love! Being with them, teaching them, watching them participate and learn, is such absolute joy. I sometimes hear people my age (and older) say things like, *Well, back in my day ....*

Heck, as far as I'm concerned, *these are my days*!

88

HISTORY REPEATS

Joe Perry had been in the hospital for weeks. He had fallen and hit his head. All alone, his housekeeper found him the following morning lying unconscious on the floor and called an ambulance. Complications incurred. Serious complications. Surgeons amputated his left leg due to poor circulation, generally caused by diabetes. He was also put on dialysis because his kidneys were not functioning properly.

"History repeats itself," Joe told Michael stoically when his son visited him at the hospital. "Your grandfather had diabetes. His leg was amputated, too. It's goddam scary, I tell ya."

"Like some sort of inherited karma," Michael muttered, recalling the frightful memory of nearly losing his own leg when he was trampled by a rodeo bull years ago.

"Your grandad was right about my age when he died. Lucky for me, I'm still around," Joe added.

"That's because you're too damned ornery to die," Michael teased.

"Maybe I should sue the hospital and these doctors. I could live out the rest of my days as a wealthy man. You're a lawyer, what do you think?"

"Hard to say," Michael answered with faux seriousness. "Since the amputation, you really don't have much of a leg to stand on."

Joe laughed heartily. In spite of it all, Joe remained uncharacteristically upbeat about his plight. Practically cheerful one might say. If Michael thought his father had seemed happy years ago at his seventieth birthday, the octogenarian Joe had become downright giddy. So very different from the man he had known growing up. And talkative.

During next the several days spent visiting the hospital, his father regaled him with stories of days gone by, tales the son had never before heard from this man who seldom revisited the past when Michael was growing up, who barely referenced any boyhood friends or events. The suddenly loquacious Joe was now eagerly divulging details of his youth, including the disdain he felt for his own father, the estranged grandfather Michael never really knew much about. Apparently seeing no correlation to his own parenting style, Joe characterized his father as mean, harsh, and with whom he had never felt a closeness.

But it was his military experiences and stories about his business successes that dominated. "Without a doubt," Joe proclaimed, "the two happiest periods of my younger life were my time in the army and my time in business." He enjoyed hearing his father's tales, though it did not escape the son's notice that his father's entire married life and years raising his children were never mentioned as part of his life's highlights.

Michael opened his laptop and placed it on the rolling tray stand at his father's bedside. Joe's grandchildren, six-year-olds Travis and Morgan, appeared on the screen.

"Hi Grandpa," the children greeted in unison.

Joe thought he was being shown a video of the kids.

"No, Dad. It's not video, it's Skype. The kids are live."

"What do you mean live?" He was confused.

"You're watching them live on the screen. Say something to them, Dad."

Joe raised a hand and waved at the screen. "Hello kids."

They waved back. "Hi Grandpa in the desert," for that is what they commonly called him. "We hope you're feeling better."

"They can see me?"

"Yes, Dad. They can see and hear you, just as you can see and hear them."

Joe was astonished. "Why, it's like Star Trek or something," he said. "I never thought I'd live to see the day."

Michael waited in the hospital room for his father to return from dialysis. It was a procedure that always left Joe feeling extremely weak. He was asleep when they wheeled him back. Michael read a book as he waited for his father to awaken. When he did, the two sat chatting as had become usual.

Finally, the son announced, "I gotta get home, Dad. It's been nearly a week. My wife and kids might forget what I look like if I stay away much longer."

"I understand," Joe responded weakly, beckoning his son closer. The elder man's breathing was heavy, forced, but the doctors had assured it was nothing out of the ordinary. "Gotta tell you something, Mike."

The son bent closer to his father, his ear inches from the man's dry wrinkled mouth.

"I want you to know, you done good, son. Had my doubts a few times, though," he said, his deeply creviced lips forming a tight smile. "I worried sometimes that you might never grow up. But truth is, I think I was jealous of your youth. And angry because it seemed like you were squandering it. I didn't understand and I'm sorry." Closing his eyes for a long moment, then looking up again at his son with obvious lassitude, adding, "I see now, we were both on the same road, just different paths. I'm so proud of the life you lived and the family you created."

Michael drove home that afternoon with a lump in his throat. These last days at the hospital were some of the finest times he had ever spent with his father. Why, oh why, did it have to come so late. He understood now that what may have appeared mean-spirited behavior from his father for much of Michael's life was merely a parent being scared for his child. Genuine fear that his son might not be on the right path. Doing his best to prod, albeit most often caviling and lacking tactfulness, toward what the father perceived to be the correct path. This was, perhaps, the only way he knew to show his love.

The 1960s and 70s were turbulent times to come of age and must have been quite confusing decades for parenting. As a father now himself, Michael had a new understanding of the motivations his own dad may have felt. For the son to have faulted his father for so many years was short-sighted. For the father to have, at last, acknowledged that there can be more than one correct path in life, and that he was proud of the one chosen by his son, was a milestone. This was all that Michael had ever really wanted: for his dad to be proud. And that was important because he loved his father.

The following week his sister flew down from Seattle to visit at the hospital. Only days later she called her brother. "You need to get back here. Dad's taken a turn for the worse."

89

THE TATTOO

Michael arrived to find his father in hospice. The hospice nurse greeted him warmly. "Oh, I am so glad you are here," she said, placing her arm over his shoulder. "He was waiting for you, waiting to pass until you were here."

Michael gave her a skeptical look.

Jaimie, emerging from a small room behind them, gave her brother a warm hug. "It's true," Jaimie confirmed, tears in her eyes. "The nurse is not just saying that. The last words he spoke before lapsing into a coma were, 'Is Mike here?'"

Michael entered the small room where his father was lying on his back, comatose, breathing with the assistance of a machine. This strong macho man from Michael's youth, this man who had always loomed so large in the eyes of his son, had been diminished to a near lifeless, shriveled fraction of his former self. His physical body shrunken like dehydrated fruit, looking almost like one of those Egyptian mummies discovered in the tombs near Cairo. The tattoo on Joe's forearm that he'd gotten as a young man in the military covering a large expanse of flesh from wrist to elbow, now faded and no larger than a golf ball. Whatever it had originally depicted no longer discernable.

Michael sat on a chair next to the moribund man and took his bony claw-like hand, holding it, tracing his fingertip along the thick network of veins. The pace of his father's grated breathing altered somewhat.

"You see?" the nurse remarked. "He knows you're here now."

She probably meant well, but Michael wished she would stop saying things like that. He was pretty sure that his comatose father had no clue as to who was in the room. It was just Jaimie, Michael, and the nurse. No other family members were present. Mary was not there. Why would she be? For her it had been a disheartening divorce and they'd not seen one another in decades.

"I will be right outside at my desk," the hospice nurse whispered, placing a gentle hand upon Michael's arm before leaving the room. "Let me know if you need anything."

Jaimie and Michael sat alone by their father's bedside watching him breath in and out ... waiting for him to pass. But he kept on breathing, in-out-in-out, hour after hour. Until he finally stopped breathing at 2:20 the following morning. No gasp, no moan, no gurgle. The breathing simply stopped.

Jaimie and Michael were tired. They had not slept all night, both displaying bruises of sleeplessness beneath their eyes.

"He's gone," Jaimie said.

Michael swallowed hard, tears in his eyes. "Hard to believe," he answered.

"I really wish I had not been here," Jaimie added. "The image of him, in my mind's eye, will forever be of a frail, dying man. I would much prefer to remember him as the strong, vibrant daddy I knew when I was a girl. This was simply awful. Please God, let me die in a car crash or some other instantaneous disaster. I do not want to go out the way he did. I do not want my family standing around my bedside waiting for me to die."

Michael nodded. "But you know what? Those final days spent with him when he was in the hospital? *That* is the way I want to remember him. That is the way I *will* remember him. That was when I finally got to truly know the man."

Joseph Perry received a full military funeral. In addition to his children and their spouses, a half-dozen or so mourners attended, mostly people who lived nearby and were his final friends. A flag draped casket contained his remains. Uniformed military men shot rifles into the air, the spent casings presented to Jaimie and Michael. The Stars and Stripes then removed from atop the casket, folded properly, and presented to them as well. It was a warm sunny afternoon when he was laid to rest beneath a flat stone marker indicating date of birth and death for Joseph M. Perry, TEC 5 US Army, World War II.

The following week was Thanksgiving, the Perry house filled with family for the festive holiday turkey dinner. Michael was seated at the head of the table with Lauren, Morgan and Travis nearby. Jaimie was there with her husband and children. They had flown down from Seattle for the funeral, staying to spend the holiday together. Grandma Mary sat at the opposite end of the table, looking fondly at her grown children, their spouses, and her grandchildren. Eighty-three years old, she looked healthy and vibrant.

They all joined hands around the table and bowed their heads. "I would like to give thanks for all of you at this table," Michael began. "You are all that matter most to me in this world. And I want to give thanks to my father. I am thankful that his hospitalization and suffering are over, that he has escaped the bonds of his infirmity and traveled to the other side. I am especially thankful to him for being the man he was."

"God bless Grandpa in the desert," six-year-old Travis chimed in.

There was a collective, "Amen."

THE END

EPILOGUE

JOURNAL

I'm recalling a great old Simon & Garfunkle song that goes: *How terribly strange to be seventy . . . Preserve your memories, they're all that's left you.* When I was very young and first heard those lyrics, it meant very little to me. Not so now.

It hardly seems possible, but I've hit the big seven-zero: Seventy. The same age my dad was when I attended his birthday party all those years ago thinking he likely did not have many more birthdays left. Seventy is just a number, some may say, but one surely auguring an entry toward elderness; an acknowledgement that time is catching up on a person. While I've been noticing more and more wrinkles, and have to concede that *numerically* seventy sounds ancient, I don't *feel* old at all. Then again, perhaps Dad didn't feel old either. I still recall the intensity of that strong bear hug he greeted me with, hardly the embrace of a feeble old man.

It's been years now since he passed, and I miss him. I'm enormously grateful that my father and I finally connected. I only wish it would have happened sooner. As a boy, *he* had a strained relationship with his own father – they did not speak for decades and *never* reconciled. This is a cycle I am determined to break with my own son and daughter. Nothing, absolutely nothing, is as important as my children knowing they can depend upon me and how much they are loved.

When this chapter of my life – that of being a dad, raising kids – comes to an end I will miss it enormously. Sadly, my dad never experienced the overwhelming joy of being a husband and a father – something greater than I ever could have imagined. I deeply regret not being a better son for him. I truly wish I had been. Perhaps it would have made a difference. Now that I have my own children, I find myself viewing my father quite differently and in a much more understanding way.

Still, his late-life revelations about time spent in the military and years in the construction business being the *best* of his life I find perplexing. It's a pretty sure bet that when my kids are grown and off on their own that I will look back on the years spent raising them as the absolute finest of my life.

And while my dad might not have enjoyed *my* teenage years, I am enjoying the hell out of Travis and Morgan as teens. Both kids grew up on the water with me taking them surfing and sailing, but had a lasting passion for neither. They went their own ways.

Travis loves music, sings in the high school choir, plays in a rock band, and has hair to his shoulders. I smile every time I look at him, remembering how my dad and I battled over the length of *my* hair at that age. His sport of choice is fencing. He also has an affinity for language and speaks both French and Japanese fairly fluently.

Morgan is the more athletic of the two. She's played varsity tennis since her freshman year, is the current captain of the girls' tennis team, and has a room filled with (mostly first place) horse show ribbons. Just like me, Morgan has her own horse she loves ... unlike me, she is a straight A student.

They are now roughly the same age I was when I began committing musings to paper, creating the journal entries that tell *my* story. Theirs is now their own wondrous story to write.

So, with the perspective of a septuagenarian, I've been reading that journal – decades of entries that began as a teenager, hundreds of hand-written pages, many salt-stained from ocean-going composition – reminiscing and gobsmacked by the speed at which it all flew by.

It feels like only yesterday and long ago at the same time. So many chapters to life and – though I'm loving *this* current chapter as husband and father – I know that, just like all the prior chapters, this one must end as well ... and I'm not sure how many might lie ahead.

The time allotted each of us in this game of life is short and perhaps I could have used mine more wisely. I've never been the *best* at anything. Never became world champion bull rider, never wrote a hit song, and certainly never accomplished any of the things that might make the world a better place. But I always ventured forward, perhaps stumbled forward might be more accurate, dipping my toe in the water and giving it a go.

While it just may be that destiny and chance are equally influential in how the world unfolds, I feel fortunate to have recorded a portion of the journey in contemporaneous writings, lest my aging memory forgets. And I am pleased to say a number of the people I have written about over the years in those journal entries remain among my friends.

Also, through the modern miracle of social media, I have happily reconnected with many others:

High school sweetheart, Kimberly, is a retired music teacher still living in the Midwest. At age thirty-two she married an electrical contractor. They have no children.

Maggie from the beach married a movie producer but is widowed and now owns an art gallery in Santa Barbara, California.

College roomie, Jarrod Berg, reunited with his former heartthrob, Harriet Schwartz, at their ten-year high school reunion. They married the following year. The couple has four grown children and live in New Jersey.

Erica Berg, Jarrod's little sis, is a real estate broker and part-time stand-up comedian in Las Vegas, Nevada. She and her partner of twenty-plus years were married in 2014, the year the state recognized same sex marriages.

College actress Ebony Yoder moved to California to pursue her acting career and had a reccurring role in a popular TV daytime soap opera in the 1980s, became an attorney practicing law with the ACLU in the 1990s, is married to a California state senator, and was a professor of law at Southwestern University in Los Angeles until retiring in 2020.

Hippie Vic from Drop City is a well-known author residing along California's Central Coast. Several of his published works include stories about the Sixties and communal living.

Indian cowboy Jay Yazzie gave up rodeo life not long after the Sky Hi Stampede rodeo and is now Dr. Yazzie, a veterinarian who owns an animal clinic with his wife, who is also a veterinarian. They live on a twenty-five-acre horse ranch in Oregon.

Cowgirl Reese Walker, a divorced mother of one adult son, became the first female deacon at her church, and is currently a GOP member of the Wyoming state legislature. Both of her parents are alive and well and reside nearby.

High school buddy Rob Mattis is a retired commercial airline pilot. Twice divorced, currently single, he recently moved to Orlando, Florida to live closer to his adult daughter.

Bryn Mawr grad Kendra Paul married her college sweetheart. They live in Greenwich, Connecticut and have a grown daughter who lives in England. I wasn't sure what to expect when I hesitatingly first contacted Kendra on social media, assuming she probably hated me, even after all these years, but her initial reply was a winking, smiling emoji wearing a cowboy hat.

World Champion Indian Cowboy Sonny Begaye passed away in 2009 at the age of 69, shot in the chest at close range by an intruder onto the Navajo Reservation. His obit called him a peaceful soul victimized by senseless violence. He had eight children and eighteen grandchildren.

Ranch cowboy roommate Rick Braden became a firefighter and died of lung cancer at age 40.

Head surgical nurse Wilma passed away in the 1990s. Her son is a successful building contractor in Ormond Beach, Florida.

Karl, of Laurel Canyon, took the iconic photograph depicting drums and a two-lane highway stretching off into the horizon that became the cover of singer Jackson Browne's album *Running On Empty*, reaching #3 on the album charts in 1978.

Record company exec, Marcie Baker, is married to a trumpet player in a well-known band. They have two grown children and live in Henderson, Nevada.

Singing star John Denver died on October 12, 1997, when his experimental amateur aircraft crashed into Monterey Bay on the California Coast. His music lives on.

Sailing buddy, Dr. Denton Todd, remains happily married and is the father of two grown children, a son and daughter. After retiring from medicine, he completed a two-year around the world circumnavigation with his son on their 44-foot sailboat.

Sailing buddy, Noah Sark, was a highly successful screenwriter in Malibu until his death in 2019 from injuries sustained in a car accident on Pacific Coast Highway. He is survived by his husband.

Disco-girl Harper, married to her third husband, is a great-grandmother living in Bakersfield, California. Her *baby* daughter, Elise, is a mother and grandmother in her own rite and lives in Ventura, California.

My transpacific sailing companion Daphne is married to an aero-space scientist, is the mother of five children, grandmother of two, and lives near Provo, Utah.

Nurse Lisa, of our transpacific sail to Hawaii, is a retired R.N. She never married and lives with her long-time boyfriend in a small Imperial Valley, California town where she runs a sanctuary for wild donkeys.

Maui contractor Kipp perished when a wildfire destroyed the entire town of Lahaina in 2023, including the Lahaina Yacht Club.

Construction boss Everett Upshaw lost his eyesight due to diabetes, subsequently created several non-profit organizations to benefit blind athletes, and continued to run his company, until passing away in 1993 of heart disease.

Hillary Hartnel became the western regional manager of a major department store chain before starting her own business and today owns a small chain of retail stores specializing in high-end handbags. She is married to her second husband, a doctor of dermatology. They live in Los Altos, California and her now-adult daughter lives in Milan, Italy, working in the fashion industry. Neat-o!

Gerald Leoni practiced criminal defense law and was a frequent Los Angeles television legal analyst until his death from a self-inflicted gunshot in 2003.

Whitney Wilson is a District Court Judge in Honolulu, Hawaii. She is married to a Professor of Hawaiian Studies at University of Hawaii, Manoa.

Jaimie Perry, my sister, holds a director position with a Fortune 500 company, is a mother of two adult sons, and grandmother of three. She and her husband live in Surprise, Arizona where she sings in her church choir.

Mary Perry, my mother, lived comfortably into her nineties at a retirement home in California's wine country, until becoming a victim of the covid pandemic in 2021. She is greatly missed.

Lauren St. John-Perry is a brilliant California trial lawyer who also happens to be an excellent wife, mother, the ultimate love of my life, and who, by the way, has not seemed to age a day since we first met.

AFTERWARD AND ACKNOWLEDGEMENTS

I never intended to write this book. Keeping a journal was merely a therapeutic outlet for a mixed-up teenager as I grew up wandering through an uncertain world. Fast forward to a dinner party I attended several years ago at a friend's home in Malibu. Seated next to me was a woman who introduced herself as a literary agent. I jokingly mentioned my journal to her and was stunned when she enthusiastically told me she would love to read it.

"It's hundreds of hand-written loose pages," I told her.

She laughed and told me to type it out, proofread it, and send it to her whenever it was ready.

It took the better part of a year getting that journal into shape to send off to her. She then kept the manuscript for a very long time – reading it, editing it. We had meetings about it and exchanged countless emails.

The original manuscript depicted all events exactly as they occurred in my contemporaneous entries and used the real names of people. "But the story lacks cohesiveness," she told me. "As well as creating too much liability referencing real people and their names. Besides, most true stories are not *absolute* truth, and unless you are a celebrity, memoirs don't sell." She suggested several story alterations and character name changes.

I was extremely reluctant to make the suggested changes. "It would become more of a novel rather than a true-life story," I complained.

"Exactly," she concurred. "A novel *based* on a true story. I'm glad you understand."

Many more months were spent adhering to her editing requirements. I don't know if it was my hesitation to fictionalize certain aspects of the story, or perhaps she simply decided to devote her time to more noteworthy authors and projects, because in the end nothing happened with the manuscript. It languished for years in my computer until I finally took another run at it, thanks to so many friends out there who have heard my stories over the years, read my magazine articles, and encouraged me to "write a book of all those adventures." Well, here ya go, hope it lives up to your expectations.

Also, let me say, I made no mention in the story's chronology of the 2020 Covid-19 pandemic and worldwide lockdown. The omission was intentional. We all had too recently emerged from those dark times, all with our own experiences, and I felt no need to have readers live it again through mine.

Special thanks to Ardath Goldstein-Weaver, Director North Carolina Arts Council and editorial board member of several national publications, for her valuable assistance and unending encouragement in the creation of this book. Without her, this book likely would have continued to languish in my computer, never to see the light of day.

Immeasurable gratitude to the late great commercial writing critic Karl Leopold Metzenberg for reading the journal in its original format, helping to find a home for the book, and constant assurances that it was an "… amazingly worthwhile project documenting a life of adventure."

Thanks also to Super Jim Suber for his commentary and editing skills. Especially for his sage advice pertaining to the urgency of getting this book *out there*: "You need to publish this book while there are still people alive that know who Linda Ronstadt and Jackson Browne are."

Also, thank you proofreader Sue Jorgenson for discovering and correcting all those little gremlins that snuck into the original manuscript.

Posthumous and heartfelt thankyous to the late Miss Barbara Barnes of Downers Grove, Illinois and the late Mrs. Charlotte Kilpatrick of Colorado (my real-life high school and college music/theater professors) for seeing something in me early on that I never saw myself and giving me a chance to shine. While many teenage boys had male coaches as mentors, mine were these two wonderfully gifted female teachers. They may have had only brief mentions in this book but were major influences in my life.

And, finally, thank you, thank you, thank you to all who read this book. I hope you enjoyed reading it as much as I did living it.

ABOUT THE AUTHOR

MICHAEL E. PETRIE is a surfer, ocean sailor, horseman, musician, and former rodeo cowboy turned attorney and award-winning writer. His work has appeared in numerous publications, and he is a frequent contributor to SAIL – World's Leading Sailing Magazine. He is the author of the psychological thrillers YOU'RE THE ONLY ONE I CAN TRUST and THIS GUY'S THE LIMIT, both of which were inspired by real-life experiences as a lawyer over a 30+ year career span. He lives with his wife, children, dogs, and horse in California. His music and videos of sailing adventures can be found on YouTube at Michael E Petrie. Also, follow him online at michaelepetrie.com and CalWriter.net.

www.ingramcontent.com/pod-product-compliance
Lightning Source LLC
Chambersburg PA
CBHW020245030826
48979CB00030B/2628/J

* 9 7 8 1 6 4 7 0 4 9 9 9 7 *